THE BEEKEEPER No.159

Coming soon from Titan Books

The Blacklist: The Dead Ring No. 166 (*March 2017*)

THE BLACKLIST™

THE BEEKEEPER No.159

STEVEN PIZIKS

TITAN BOOKS

The Blacklist: The Beekeeper No. 159
Print edition ISBN: 9781783298051
E-book edition ISBN: 9781783298105

Published by Titan Books
A division of Titan Publishing Group Ltd
144 Southwark Street, London SE1 0UP

First edition: November 2016
3 5 7 9 10 8 6 4 2

Did you enjoy this book? We love to hear from our readers.
Please email us at readerfeedback@titanemail.com or write to us at
Reader Feedback at the above address.

To receive advance information, news, competitions, and exclusive offers
online, please sign up for the Titan newsletter on our website:
www.titanbooks.com

THE BEEKEEPER No.159

CHAPTER ONE

The battered white van bounced and jostled over a rutted gravel road. Every jerk and jolt poked at Mala Rudenko's muscles until they ached. She set her teeth and shifted on the hard metal floor, trying one more time to find a comfortable position or a spot to sit that didn't involve jouncing. All she did was bump up against the other people crammed into the back of the van with her. The stuffy air was filled with the stench of body odor and fear. Mala could smell both on herself. Fear dried her mouth and tightened her stomach into a hard knot. The van had no windows, and the windshield was tinted, so Mala had no idea where she was. Her watch and phone had been taken from her, and she had already lost any idea of time. Her only clothes were a pair of shorts, sandals, and a thin T-shirt with GRRRRL scrawled across it.

Half the people in the van were chained to the walls, and they stared at the floor with deadened eyes. The ones who were not chained, those sitting on Mala's side of the van, grunted with annoyance whenever Mala shifted position and invaded the tiny scrap of territory they had carved out. They and Mala weren't chained because the driver knew none of them would try to escape. Mala huddled into herself, trying not to touch sweaty skin, trying not to bounce, trying not to be herself.

Did Father know where she was? Was anyone looking for her? The driver of the van, the man who had no name, had said almost gleefully that she would vanish and there would be no way to trace her. Mala swallowed. Was it true? Hell, she had no idea. Criminals would say anything, right?

At long last, the van came to a halt. The nameless driver and the guard riding shotgun—he actually carried a shotgun—got out and slammed the doors. The chained people continued to stare down at the floor. The unchained ones exchanged nervous glances. Mala held her breath. After a long moment, the back doors banged open, slamming bright sunlight into Mala's eyes. She flung up a hand to shield them.

"Out. Now," said Shotgun in a flat voice. "He's waiting."

The unchained people went first, groaning as cramped muscles straightened and wincing as stiff joints popped. Mala stayed in the center of the group. Her stomach growled and her legs wobbled a little, reminding her how long it had been since she had last eaten. They were a mixed bag of people, with an even division of genders, but they leaned toward young. A hot sun stared down, unrelenting, from a strip of clear blue sky above the road. Trees, thick and heavy, marched right up to the gravel. The undergrowth between the trunks was so thick, Mala couldn't see more than a few yards beyond the road's edge. Insects buzzed in the heavy, humid air. No houses, no telephone wires, no power lines, no cell phone towers, no sounds except an insect hum. No signs of people. Mala was seized with a desire to run, but she forced herself to stay right where she was. Where would she go? A bee buzzed past her face, and she restrained herself from swatting at it. No sense in getting stung and adding to her troubles.

Outside the van waited more than a dozen… people. Mala couldn't tell if they were men or women. They wore bulky jumpsuits made of some kind of green cloth, and oversized gas masks that made Mala's mind run inevitably to the bee that had just flown past. They carried long rifles, and wicked pistols were holstered at their waists.

One of the people, someone who didn't carry a rifle, pulled off his mask, revealing an older man, perhaps sixty years of age, with a startling shock of white hair and round coke-bottle glasses that magnified his brown eyes to an almost ludicrous degree.

"Sorry about our appearance," he said. "You arrived while we were making honey." He raised his voice. "Bring the rest off! Quickly, now! We can't stay here for long."

The driver, a nondescript man with a medium build, dull brown hair and an ordinary, forgettable face, produced a key to unchain the others, and the strange soldiers hauled them off the van. Several of them cried out as their cramped bodies were yanked into motion. One woman wet herself, and the sharp smell of urine tanged the air. Mala felt bad for her, but was glad it hadn't happened inside the van.

The white-haired man made a curt gesture, and one of the soldiers produced a duffel bag and handed it to the driver, who unzipped it. Mala caught a glimpse of a green pile of cash inside. The driver ran what looked like an oversized cell phone over the bag.

"Has there *ever* been a bug?" asked the white-haired man.

"Just part of the process," said the driver. He finished his inspection and tossed the duffel bag into the van.

The white-haired man shrugged this off and brought his attention back to the assembled passengers. His movements and his voice both crackled with energy, and Mala found herself compelled to stare at him, unable to look away.

"I'm Dr. Griffin," he said in a rich, powerful voice. "Forget your friends. Forget your families. They've already forgotten you. In time, you'll remember nothing but this place and these people, your new family. We will love you and cherish you and care for you—as long as you follow the rules."

"Honey," said a new voice. The little crowd moved aside, and an older woman came forward to take Dr. Griffin's arm. Her tone was soft. "You should tell them where they are. The poor things are scared."

"Of course, dear," said Dr. Griffin, still in his arresting voice, and turned back to the new arrivals. "You are in the Hive. Now come along. You too, dear."

They strolled arm in arm to the side of the road, where the bushes grew particularly thick beneath the trees. To Mala's surprise, two of the soldiers trotted ahead and pulled the undergrowth aside. A large clump of bushes swung outward, and it took Mala's startled mind a moment to work out that it was a gate, cleverly concealed to look like shrubbery. The soldiers gestured with their weapons. Mala and the other passengers nervously moved toward the path behind the gate.

One of the new arrivals, a dark-haired man who had

been chained, dashed for the trees. Dr. Griffin barked an order and a soldier aimed his rifle. Mala gasped and her heart jerked. The *crack* rang through the forest, but it was nothing compared to the young man's scream of pain. He went down at the tree line, clutching his left leg. Red blood spattered the green grass. Mala tried to look away but found she couldn't. Nausea sloshed in her stomach.

"Bring him," Dr. Griffin said in a deep, gentle tone.

Two soldiers, still in their gas masks, hauled the moaning man back to the main group and dropped him at Dr. Griffin's feet. Dr. Griffin put a gloved hand under his chin and lifted it, forcing the young man to meet his coke-bottle eyes.

"I know you haven't learned the rules yet," Dr. Griffin said soothingly, "but that's no excuse. You need to ask before you do something."

"I'm heading out now," said the driver brightly. Shotgun was already in the van's passenger seat. The driver jumped behind the wheel, and for a moment Mala was sure Dr. Griffin would order one of the soldiers to shoot him, too, but Dr. Griffin ignored him entirely. The van drove away, leaving a gray smell of exhaust.

"This event could be useful, honey," said the woman.

Dr. Griffin blinked at her, then nodded.

"Very good observation, Mrs. Griffin," he said. "Let me demonstrate. You." He pointed at one of the new arrivals, a woman in a red blouse. Like Mala, she hadn't been chained. "Come here."

Hesitantly, the woman obeyed. The young man, white-faced and clearly going into shock, struggled to get to his feet, but Dr. Griffin jabbed his wound with gloved fingers, and he howled in pain. Dr.

Griffin handed the woman a pistol.

"He will be punished," Dr. Griffin said. "Shoot him. In the head."

A murmur rippled through the group of newcomers, quickly stilled when the soldiers waved their weapons. Mala swallowed hard. Hell, was this for real?

"I... I... can't," the woman said.

"It's all right," Dr. Griffin said in his soothing voice. "I'm telling you to. You aren't responsible. No one will blame you. You are part of the group, and the group wants it done." He looked at the soldiers. "Don't we?"

"Do it," one of the soldiers said in a voice that came across as a buzzy whisper beneath the mask.

"Go ahead," murmured another.

"It's fine," said a third. "Shoot."

The others joined in, urging the woman to do as she was told. Their voices swirled like syrup in the heavy air, pushing and pressing with invisible hands. The woman held up the pistol, her own hands shaking. The crowd of soldiers chanted and murmured.

Mala didn't know what to do. She felt light-headed from the lack of food. The chanting, though it wasn't directed at her, gave her a floating sensation, like she was disconnected from her body. For a moment, every sense was heightened. Mala smelled the sweat of the man standing next to her, felt the melted-butter sun pouring across her shoulders, heard every rustle and buzz of each insect in the emerald leaves around her.

The woman brought the pistol around to aim at the terrified young man.

Mala stopped breathing.

The woman pulled the trigger.

The sound of the shot made the newcomers jump, but the soldiers didn't even flinch. A new wound flowered on the young man's upper arm, and he screamed again, a high, thin wail. Glassy-eyed and panting, the woman lowered the pistol. Dr. Griffin took it from her.

"Good, good," he told her. "You tried, and that was very good." Dr. Griffin removed his gloves and from one pocket produced a piece of chocolate, which he handed to the woman. She devoured it as tears ran down her face. With a smile, Dr. Griffin handed the pistol to Mala.

"Now you," he said.

CHAPTER TWO

Elizabeth Keen plopped into the coffee house chair and put her chin expectantly into her hand. "Well?"

The other seat's occupant, one Raymond Reddington, calmly set down the butter knife and reached for a small ceramic jar. From it he lifted a silver spoon and drizzled soft amber honey over his scone. Next to the scone plate sat a teapot and cup with saucer. Reddington's hat, a Giotto fedora, rested on the table a safe distance from the food. Behind them at the counter, the barista operated the noisy cappuccino machine with the sound of someone strangling an anaconda.

"You know, I'm usually more of a coffee person, but this tea is delicious, especially with the honey," Reddington observed.

"I wouldn't know," Keen said. "I like my black coffee."

"A deplorable habit reserved for factory workers and cab drivers named Steve." Reddington took a bite of scone with obvious relish. "Excellent! One of the few things the English got right. Astonishing how the topping comes from an insect's digestive tract. Did you know that some bees enslave other insects? One kind of bee creeps into another queen's hive, lays her eggs when no one is looking, and flies away. The larvae hatch and force the other bees to do their bidding. The honey you buy at the farmer's market might be made by slave bees."

At that moment, a barista deposited before Keen a cappuccino cup half as big as her head. She eyed it dubiously.

"I didn't order this," she said.

"Your friend," said the barista, and left.

Elizabeth Keen glared at Reddington across the table. Her dark hair and serious features gave her a good glare, and she knew it. Reddington, however, remained annoyingly immune, however much she used it on him, and she sometimes wondered why she bothered.

"You need to learn to live a little, Lizzie," he said in that maddeningly expansive voice of his. "Try new things. Steve the cab driver would be proud."

Keen, who had tried a thousand more new things than she cared to, all thanks to Reddington, continued the glare. Reddington sipped his tea. His round, close-shaved head and blunt features were schooled into a careful blandness that Keen found alternately fascinating and infuriating.

Sure, Keen knew a great many facts about Reddington. He had topped the FBI's most wanted list as head of one of the most powerful criminal networks in the world, and one day had walked into FBI headquarters and given himself up. For unknown reasons, Reddington had suddenly become happy to hand over information about the worst world-wrecking criminals on earth—but only to Special Agent Elizabeth Keen. Except Keen had never met him. She had, in fact, been on her way to her first day at work at the FBI, and had been more than a little startled to hear the Bureau's number one fugitive was demanding to speak with her—and *only* her—about something he called "the Blacklist."

Within weeks, Reddington had become the FBI's most secret confidential informant, while Keen had been sucked into a love-hate relationship with Reddington himself. A relationship that had destroyed her marriage, demolished her career, and nearly gotten her killed more times than she could count. His strange obsession with her safety—as he defined it—had wrecked her life. Yet, at the same time, he was a connection to her past, to her family, and she knew that, in his strange and twisted way, he cared deeply for her.

Oh yes, Keen knew a number of facts about Reddington, but even after several years of steady contact, she knew frustratingly little about the man beneath them. What drove him? What motivated him? Even now, after working with him all this time, she couldn't get a decent read on him. He sat in the hard, eat-your-scone-and-get-out coffee shop chair, his round features schooled into a flat mask she couldn't penetrate. His posture was relaxed but alert, a man who was aware of his surroundings but unconcerned by them. Nothing seemed to touch him or bother him—except Keen herself. Reddington showed an almost obsessive need to ensure her safety, strange when you considered her job. And whenever she threatened to walk away from their strange relationship, he inevitably did something dramatic to drag her back into it. This oddly made her feel a little better, like she had at least a measure of control.

"To go all the way back to my first question," Keen said, "I ask: well?"

"Well, what?"

"Why did you call me here? It sounded urgent, but all you want to talk about is vegan restaurants and slave bees."

"Ah." Reddington checked his watch and shot his cuffs while he was at it. "By this time tomorrow, we need to be in South Carolina. We're pursuing another member of the Blacklist."

Here Keen came quietly alert. Even though she had personally brought in literally dozens of international criminals, more than most FBI agents collared in an entire career, the thought that hundreds of others, bad to the toenails, still walked around free after torturing, killing, stealing and racketeering continued to outrage her. Any chance to bring down one of Reddington's Blacklisters made her ears prick up, her heart beat a little faster.

But all she said to Reddington was, "Who?"

"The Bodysnatcher." Reddington refreshed his tea. "He's making a handoff in a place that decided to nickname itself the Swamp State. Isn't that delightful? It makes you want to pack your bags and rush right down. I can't say that I've spent more than ten consecutive days there myself, but the Bodysnatcher feels no such compunctions."

Keen ignored the extra commentary. "What does this one do?"

"The Bodysnatcher makes people disappear for money," Keen said, tapping at a computer. "Lots of people. Lots of money."

The computer was in the center of the Post Office. Few people knew that the basement of a dull, warehouse-like structure in the middle of Washington DC housed a warren of offices, a crowd of FBI agents, and a large, circular meeting area, or war room. The building had once belonged to the real Post Office, so the agents who worked there told anyone with a lower security clearance that they worked at the Post Office, and the name stuck. A dozen computer monitors banked one wall of the war room, and a haphazard huddle of desks lay scattered about the floor. An electric hum crackled in the air—a case was in the making.

"Usually it's celebrities or criminals or other people who want to vanish permanently," Keen continued. "But, as you can imagine, the Bodysnatcher operates in ways that are bigger and more complicated than a new ID and social security number. Damn it, where is that missing persons file?"

"Here, let me," said Aram Mojtabai. Like everyone else at the Post Office, Aram was technically a Special Agent, but he had been hired for his computer savvy, not his field skills, and he almost never left the Post Office except to ride his bike home.

Peering over Aram's shoulder at one of the monitors was Donald Ressler. Keen gave an inward sigh. Lately she found herself going back and forth on Ressler. At one time, she had considered that there might be something between them. He was damned handsome, that was for sure—blond, blue eyes. But when circumstances had forced Keen into becoming a fugitive, Ressler had become her most dogged pursuer, which had put something of a strain on attraction. They'd had a couple-three "We're good, aren't we?" conversations since her return, but Keen still harbored a tinge of resentment toward him. On the other hand, Ressler had gone out of his way to be overly nice to her ever since, and there weren't a lot of people in her life who did that. So who knew?

"Maybe we should wait for Cooper," Keen said.

"He's on the phone in his office," Ressler told her. "Something big from the higher-ups. He said we should start without him."

"Is this the file?" Aram asked, and Keen looked.

"Thanks," she said. "According to Reddington, sometimes the Bodysnatcher's... people want to disappear and sometimes they don't, but they always vanish without a trace. Have you heard of Christian Heller?"

The photo of a red-haired, muscular man appeared on the screens.

"Oh yeah. The soccer guy who disappeared at sea," Ressler said. "Supposedly killed by his father-in-law, but never proved."

"Yes. Very difficult to find someone who disappears in the Pacific Ocean." Keen flicked the mouse. "What about Garrett Ivers?"

A slender man with brown hair and a scruffy beard popped onto the monitor.

"Everyone knows him," Aram said. "The reporter who was arrested in North Korea last year for taking unauthorized photos. The State Department shouted, but North Korea claims they never heard of him. No one believes it."

"Exactly," Keen said. "Heller vanished, with no way to look for him."

"The Bodysnatcher's work," Ressler said, grimly folding his arms.

"Who else is in that file?" Aram asked.

"Two Russian crime bosses, a poppy farmer from Pakistan, and an English politician who supported BP after the oil spill and needed to disappear fast," Keen said. "And those were just the ones Reddington knew about. They all wanted to disappear in ways that made it look accidental."

Ressler thought about that. "You said some of the Bodysnatcher's people *don't* want to disappear. What about them?"

"That's the other half of his business. Those people just vanish. On behalf of someone else. The Bodysnatcher has raised kidnapping to an art form. No sign of struggle, no clues, no leads, no witnesses. Most of the time, no one investigates because this class of clientele no one bothers about—homeless people, residents of mental hospitals, street kids."

"What's the Bodysnatcher's real name?"

"Even Reddington has no idea. The man keeps an obsessively low profile. It's one of the reasons no one has managed to catch him."

"Why does he grab victims who don't want to disappear?" Aram asked.

"The Bodysnatcher does a lot of work for clients who need a steady stream of people," Keen said. "He vets the victims, chooses those who both fit the type his client desires and are unlikely to be missed—or missed right away. His clients need labor for prostitution, domestic work, experimentation—"

"Experimentation?" Ressler interrupted. "The Bodysnatcher grabs people for *laboratories*?"

Keen nodded grimly. When you worked with Raymond Reddington, you learned more about the underworld than you cared to. "There are underground labs that, for a price, will circumvent a number of FDA regulations."

"Keen!" The voice belonged to Director Harold Cooper, who was smart-stepping it across a catwalk and toward the staircase that led down into the war room. His dark eyes missed nothing, and the staircase made his already impressive height even more imposing.

Following him toward the stairs was Cynthia Panabaker, an older, wiry woman with auburn hair and a sharp nose. Panabaker was the Post Office's third liaison with the Department of Justice. Keen had barely said ten words to her so far and had yet to form an opinion of the woman, though in Keen's experience, DoJ liaisons caused more problems than they solved. Panabaker said something to Cooper at the top of the catwalk stairs, then turned and went back into the office while Cooper descended the metal steps.

"You've briefed the others on this Bodysnatcher character?" he said in his husky baritone.

"Just finishing," she said.

"I've got something to add," he said. "Listen up, everyone!"

He tapped at the boards and on one of the screens, an animated wasp stung a cartoon face that wore a smug smile. The cartoon face made a surprised O and deflated like a balloon as the wasp flew away. YOU'VE BEEN STUNG! read the caption.

"What's that?" Keen asked.

Aram blinked up at the monitor. "Stingster."

"Stingster," Keen repeated.

"It's a revenge app," Aram added. "You download it, use it to mark embarrassing photos of an ex who did you wrong, and let it upload the photos to shame sites all over the Internet. It made the inventor rich. What was his name? Russalko... Ravinko..."

"Rudenko," Cooper said. "Pavel Rudenko."

"That's it!" Aram snapped his fingers. "Nowadays Rudenko has his fingers in lots of other pies, like airline travel, munitions for the army, even an actual pie company. All from this little app."

"I know that name," Ressler said. "He's huge."

You've been stung! blinked the caption again.

"What's this have to do with the Bodysnatcher?" Keen asked, puzzled.

Cooper said, "His daughter has been kidnapped."

A moment of silence passed at that. Finally, Keen said, "Who's the victim?"

Cooper clicked a mouse and a twenty-something woman with a round face and short brown hair flashed onto one of the screens. "Mala Rudenko. Pavel's daughter. Born and bred in America. She disappeared a few weeks ago. No traces, no ransom demand, no nothing."

"Weeks," Keen repeated, confused. "Wait a minute—this isn't a kidnapping. It's a missing person's case."

"Well—" said Aram.

Keen interrupted. "Why are we even involved?"

"Because of her father," Cooper said. "Pavel Rudenko is insanely wealthy, and he provides weapons and training for the military. When Mala didn't return his texts or calls, he became convinced someone snatched her up. Rudenko is friends with our new government liaison Cynthia Panabaker. So she—"

"Pressure," Keen finished. "Got it. We'll probably spend a big chunk of our budget to find her on a beach somewhere."

Behind them, Raymond Reddington cleared his throat. Keen and the others turned and blinked at him in surprise. Reddington rarely entered the Post Office. Too few exits, Keen suspected. His double-breasted Martin Greenfield suit fit him perfectly, all the way down to his Gucci crocodile shoes and gold horsebit buckles, and ever the gentleman, he carried his fedora in his hand.

"Reddington," Cooper said.

"Harold," Reddington replied with a nod. "How quickly can you gather a task force for a journey to South Carolina?"

"South Carolina?" Cooper echoed. "Do you know something, Reddington?"

"I know a great many things," Reddington said, "including the fact that by tomorrow, we'll all be in South Carolina. I suggest you pack insect repellent."

"I got Mala Rudenko's last known address," said a new voice, and Samar Navabi arrived with a brown folder. Her dark, curly hair was pulled back in its customary ponytail, and her brown eyes were serious. Her words were quick and crisp. "It was harder to track down than you might think. Hello, Reddington. Hey, Keen."

Keen nodded. As the only two female agents in the Post Office, it seemed to her that she and Navabi should be closer friends, but their relationship had never quite gelled. Navabi had an edge to her, was practical almost to the point of appearing detached. Keen had automatically profiled her as someone who had gone through some kind of private hell, and not just during her time at the Post Office. Hard choices had hardened Navabi, making her difficult to get close to—given what Keen had been through recently, she could respect that.

"Her father didn't have her address?" Keen said.

"They'd become estranged in the last couple of years," Navabi explained. "He says she withdrew from him, despite his efforts to keep in touch. All he had was a cell phone number. It's why her father became suspicious after weeks instead of days. He's had no trace of her."

"No trace," Keen echoed, then glanced at Reddington. "So Mala's disappearance is connected to the Bodysnatcher. And that's why we're all here."

"Perhaps I can speed things along," Reddington said. "The Bodysnatcher vets both his unwilling victims and his willing clients carefully. His unwilling victims are usually homeless, or live alone and have no friends or close family. When he has a willing client, he takes his time arranging for the victim to plausibly drop off the radar. He helps the client isolate him— or herself—from family and friends, sets up bank accounts so the client's bills continue to be paid, makes it look like the client has a new job or has even moved to another state. Then when the time comes to vanish, no one thinks twice. He's an artist, really. The fact that I have a lead at all is a small miracle."

"We need to investigate Mala's apartment before we go anywhere," Cooper said. "Could be clues there."

"There will be none," Reddington sighed. "And while I understand that the FBI is as bound by its rules as any other government organization, just be aware that the window of opportunity is closing. Call me when you're ready to leave for South Carolina. And don't forget the Deet."

He strolled away. Keen half expected him to demand that he follow her, but he didn't.

"The apartment," Cooper said, "and make it quick. I have the feeling you're going to South Carolina later."

CHAPTER THREE

Mala Rudenko's apartment was a fourth-story walkup so close to the Beltway that passing trucks made the windows rattle. Keen's lungs and shins were burning by the time she got to the top, but Ressler seemed unaffected by the climb, so she suppressed her urge to pant. The hallways were shabby and uncarpeted, in need of new paint and light fixtures, but at least the place didn't reek of urine, loud music, or shouts from other apartments. A lower-middle-class building gone to seed. So why was the daughter of a tech millionaire living here?

Rebellion, estrangement, privacy, Keen told herself. *Any number of things.*

Ressler had already called ahead to the super, a young man barely old enough to shave, let alone manage an apartment building, and he met them at the top floor.

"I haven't seen Mala in weeks," he said without being asked, "but I don't really pay attention. My place is in the basement, you know?"

"What about her rent?" Ressler asked.

"Paid through automatic deposit by her bank." He

started to unlock the door, but Ressler plucked the key from his fingers.

"We'll take care of it," he said. "You stand by the stairs. Just in case."

"Oh." He grimaced. "Right."

A tiny thrill of adrenaline sped Keen's heart. No way to know what might be in there until they opened the door. Dead body. Kidnapper. Maybe just a young woman who didn't answer her phone. The mystery tugged at her, tightened her veins. She and Ressler took up positions on either side of the door, and Ressler pounded the door with a cop's knock.

"Miss Rudenko?" he called. "Agent Donald Ressler with the FBI. Can you open the door?"

No response.

Ressler tried again with the same result. He slipped the key into the lock, twisted, and shoved the door open.

The duo boiled into the tiny apartment beyond. Keen rapidly took in details. Small living room and kitchenette combo, open door to single bedroom. Ikea furniture. Television. Cell phone plugged into wall. Thin layer of dust. No signs of people, living or dead.

Ressler took the bathroom. Keen hit the bedroom. More Ikea furniture. No closet. Clothes neatly hung on freestanding rack. Small luggage set beneath the clothing. Bed made. Dresser top tidy but dusty. Bathrobe on back of door. Window shut, view of brick wall. Keen swiftly checked under the bed, not expecting to find anything, and fulfilled expectations.

"Bedroom clear!" she shouted.

"Bathroom clear!" Ressler shouted back.

Keen went through the bedroom in more detail. Except for the dust, everything proved to be just as neat and tidy as her first impression. Nothing at all out of the ordinary, no signs of struggle, no signs of a hasty exist, no signs of packing. Keen sat on the bed a moment and scanned the room. Something bothered her, something—Ah! That was it. No signs of struggle or hasty exist, but no personal items, either. No photos, no posters, no trip souvenirs, no remembrances of past boyfriends. Just clothes and furniture. It could have been a room in a catalog.

She stuck her head in the bathroom, where Ressler was going through the tiny cabinet.

"I'm going to guess," she said. "No medications, no half-used makeup, nothing in the wastebasket."

He straightened. "How'd you know?"

"Bedroom's the same way. We probably won't find anything perishable in the kitchen, either."

Ressler went to check. "You nailed it," he called. "It's all canned soup and ramen in here. The fridge has nothing but salad dressing and soy sauce."

"There's nothing personal here to tell us anything about her—or to leave a clue. If the Bodysnatcher took her, he cleaned up well, just like Reddington said he would."

Ressler's phone buzzed. It was Aram, calling from the Post Office. He put it on speaker so they could both hear.

"I found Mala's financials," Aram said. "One bank account, two credit cards, automatic pay for her utility bills. At a quick glance, it looks like all her money is there. No unusual purchases."

"Where does she work?" Ressler asked.

"I'm not seeing any paycheck deposits," Aram said. "It looks like she lived—lives—off investments. But… this is weird." The sound of keys clacking came over the line. "You would think that she would invest in her father's companies. She hasn't. In fact, not one company in her portfolio is remotely connected to anything Pavel Rudenko owns."

"How were the stocks doing?" Ressler asked.

More clicking. "Not great. In fact, her dividends took a dive recently."

Keen thought a moment. "Did she sell off a large chunk of stock recently or anything?"

"Checking." Pause. "Yeah, she did. She has fewer shares now than before. That accounts for the reduction in dividends."

"And explains why she's living in a place like this," Ressler added.

"Here's something weird," Aram said. "It's showing she has a bad record with her utilities. Her power has been shut off three times in two different apartments. All three times, the reason cited was being behind in her bill, but when she protested, it turned out the power company had made a mistake, and they turned everything back on."

"Huh. Ask Cooper exactly how estranged Mala is from her father," Keen said.

"I'm here," came Cooper's voice. "I'll call him now."

Ressler took the cell phone from its table and unplugged it. The screen stubbornly refused to come to life, though the battery light showed a full charge.

"Her phone's been bricked," he said. "We won't get anything off it. Aram, can you get into her—"

"Ahead of you," he said. "I'm seeing no outgoing calls in the last two months."

"About the time her father stopped hearing from her," Keen observed. "Aram, are there any numbers *before* then that she called often? Ones that aren't family members?"

Yet more key clicking. "Yeah. A number for… give

me a sec... a woman named Iris Henning. Oh! She lives right around the corner from your current location."

"Best friend?" Keen said. "She might know something."

Cooper spoke up through the phone. "Keen, Navabi will meet you at the friend's place. Ressler, stay at the victim's and look for more clues while I call the father."

CHAPTER FOUR

Mala Rudenko lowered the pistol. The young man looked at her with pain-filled eyes beneath the canopy of trees. The surrounding soldiers were also staring at her, or they seemed to be, from inside their masks. Their whispers and chants swirled and hissed around her.

"We are the Hive."

"Do it."

"You want to."

"We want you to."

"We are the Hive."

"He doesn't like you, you know," said the white-haired Dr. Griffin. "He hates you. He hates all of us. He's one of *them*. The ones who don't understand us. The ones who want to kill us. Get rid of him. You have our permission."

"Squeeze the trigger."

"Pull it."

"He hates you."

"He hates us."

"Be one of us."

"We are the Hive."

"Mala," spoke up the older woman, "he's just like your father."

The words speared her with an icy nail. Mala felt her finger tightening on the trigger. It would be so easy. Dr. Griffin smiled and nodded. The barrel pointed straight at the young man's forehead. His eyes filled with pain and terror. Her finger tightened further.

"I... can't," she whispered, and moved the gun aside. A finger of disappointment slipped through her, and that surprised her.

The whispering chant faded. Mala swallowed, and the fear knot in her stomach tightened again. Dr. Griffin would be angry now and who knew what he would do to her.

Dr. Griffin exchanged a look with the older woman. She smiled and shook her head.

"That's all right, my dear," Dr. Griffin said. "It's your first day. My wife and I can't expect miracles."

He grabbed her hand and whipped the gun around. Mala had time to notice Dr. Griffin's hands were dry and soft, and wasn't that an odd thing to think about? His finger folded around hers, and the gun fired. It jerked in her hand and the *crack* pounded her ears and bones. A red flower opened up on the young man's forehead and a scarlet spray exited from the back. He went down without another sound. The sharp smell of cordite hung in the air.

Mala couldn't react, couldn't think. She had just killed a man. She had ridden with this man all the way from Washington, felt his sweat against her skin. Some of it was probably still on her. Now his corpse lay at her feet. Blood flowed from his wounds, creating a scarlet flood for the ants on the ground below when a moment ago, he had been alive. His death was her doing. Her ribs turned to iron bands and the ground tilted a little beneath her, and only Dr. Griffin's grip on her arm and hand kept her steady.

"Well done," said Mrs. Griffin, the older woman.

"Indeed," Dr. Griffin said as if Mala had just poured him a perfect cup of tea. "And next time you'll do even better. But no chocolate for you. Do you understand why?"

His tone was mild, but his hand remained tight around hers, and his eyes bored into her skull.

"Yes," she whispered.

"Wonderful! This way, then."

Dr. and Mrs. Griffin went first. The soldiers herded the group down the wide path behind the camouflaged gate. It wound through the shady green trees and would have been a perfectly pleasant summer walk if not for the fact that Mala had become a killer. She couldn't comprehend it. She didn't *want* to comprehend it. It was too big, too awful. She couldn't have done such a thing.

"Dr. Griffin wanted me to do it," she whispered to herself. "He made me do it. The soldiers made me do it. It wasn't me."

And it wasn't. She glanced around at the Griffins and the soldiers. They had wanted her to do it, too. The young man had tried to run, even though the soldiers and Dr. Griffin had said not to. It wasn't her fault, no it wasn't. It was the group's decision, and she was part of the group.

The group came around a bend to a clearing that rose upward to a low mountain. Partway up, an outcrop of rock jutted out from the slope. They crossed the clearing in hot sunshine and Mala realized that the outcrop was the mouth of a cave, one large enough to drive a semi into. A soft plinking sound reached her, maddeningly familiar. A wave of hunger swept over her and she swayed dizzily, but the soldiers urged her forward. She wondered what would happen if she just refused. Mala remembered the young man—*crack*, blood, ants—and kept moving.

"Inside now," Dr. Griffin said, and the force of his personality pushed them ahead.

When they entered, the sunlight cut out as if someone had shut off a faucet. Cool air washed over Mala and she felt marginally better. The cave had a floor of packed earth and the entrance had been carefully smoothed. The plinking sounds were louder now. The group shuffled farther down the tunnel. Mala realized they were going deeper under the hill. The plinking increased in volume with every step.

Abruptly the tunnel burst into a great cavern the size of a cathedral. Mala stared about in awe. The pale stone walls rose high up, and a wooden scaffolding created a complicated series of ramps, balconies, and staircases that ran in a hundred directions. Electric bulbs brought in light bright as the sun. But the true masterpiece was the walls.

The walls were carved in intricate geometric designs—triangles that formed larger triangles that formed yet larger triangles. Ocean waves so lifelike they seemed to bob up and down. Dizzying series of hexagrams. And in the center of the back wall was a great tree, fully twelve feet tall.

All over the catwalks and staircases were people armed with hammers and chisels, their faces guarded with plastic masks. They chip, chip, chipped at the limestone walls, striking mallet to blade with a thousand little plinking sounds every minute. They worked with the intense concentration of people on a mission, of people with a *purpose*. Mala swallowed. This was a true group.

"Welcome," boomed Dr. Griffin, "to your new home. Welcome to the Hive."

CHAPTER FIVE

Iris Henning's place was also on the fourth floor. As they started up the stairs, Keen wondered what the hell it was about these women that required them to take the highest apartment possible.

"Why can't these places keep an elevator?" Navabi puffed behind her in accidental agreement.

They reached the apartment. This time Keen knocked and got no answer. She and Navabi traded looks. Keen knocked again, then on a whim tried the doorknob. Unlocked. Keen nodded, and Navabi shoved the door open. She rushed inside, pistol out.

At first glance, the small apartment beyond was empty, but the sweet and horrid smell washed over them in a terrible wave. Keen pushed back her gag reflex.

"You getting that?" she asked.

"Yep," Navabi agreed. "Rancid."

Grimly they pulled gloves from their pockets and went through the apartment. This time, Keen took the bathroom. She switched on the light. The smell was considerably stronger here, and Keen was forced to choose between personal safety and violating a potential crime scene with vomit. The sanctity of the crime scene won. She holstered her pistol and put a handkerchief over her nose to ease the smell. Her urge to vomit lessened, and thank god. When she pulled aside the shower curtain, she found herself looking down at Iris Henning.

The body was partially immersed in water, bloated and black. Hair splayed out in an awful cloud. Her skin was soft as rotten fruit. A thin drizzle ran from the faucet. The water in the tub had turned a cloudy gray, and Keen's entire skin shied away from it. The urge to throw up came roaring back, and she took deep breaths through her mouth to hold off. Even through the handkerchief, Keen's nose and stomach were turned inside-out by the stench, and she swallowed hard to avoid throwing up. This had been a thinking, living person, and now she was a pile of rotten flesh and split skin in fetid water. Keen staggered away and all but bumped into Navabi.

"Bedroom's clear," Navabi reported. "Bathroom's not?"

"In no way," Keen replied. "We need a forensic team. Don't go in there."

Navabi went in there.

When she came back out, her expression was undisturbed, but her face was pale. "I hate that kind," was all she said, and Keen didn't know if Navabi meant the body or the killer or both. Keen activated her phone and made the call.

"Normally I'd want to have a look to see if we could tell how she died," Keen said when she was done, "but I think I'll leave this one to the professionals."

"No argument," Navabi agreed, sinking onto the couch. "We'll have to process the whole bathroom once forensics gets here. But in the meantime—why kill Iris? Is it related to Mala's disappearance?"

"Could be," Keen mused. "Reddington didn't mention that the Bodysnatcher killed, but that doesn't mean he wouldn't. In fact, now that I think about it, killing Iris makes a great deal of sense. Reddington said he—the Bodysnatcher—was meticulous about covering his tracks. Iris knew something, and the Bodysnatcher killed her to ensure her silence."

"What would she know?"

"Maybe Iris saw the Bodysnatcher kidnapping Mala," Keen mused aloud. "Maybe Iris was even there when it happened."

"So why dump her body back here?"

"To leave Mala's place pristine," Keen said.

Navabi nodded. "Meanwhile, the water in the bathtub will wipe out a lot of clues—fibers, foreign hairs, DNA traces. Forensics will strain the tub, but did you see that the faucet was on? A lot of trace will be washed down the safety drain."

"Meticulous," Keen said, opening a window to help clear out the smell. It helped only a little. "So who hired the Bodysnatcher to take Mala and why?"

"Her father?" Navabi hazarded. "They're estranged. Stingster guy is wealthy and powerful. Maybe he wanted her back. It's like a man to want to control his daughter."

"Not all men—" Keen objected.

"A great many," Navabi countered. "Men always want control. The men in my family tried to control me. Reddington tries to control you."

Keen found herself starting to protest that he didn't, then stopped herself. Reddington was continually meddling in her life, trying to control her. He rarely did it directly, opting instead to convince her that what he wanted her to do was right, and more often than not, she found herself agreeing with him. And why the hell was that? Reddington had been in her life for so long now, it felt like he had been there forever. Ever since Sam Scott, her adopted father, had died, Reddington had slipped gently into the role he had once occupied; the world's strangest adviser and protector, and for reasons he had still not fully explained.

"Anyway," Keen said, "we should explore the possibility that Mala's own father hired the Bodysnatcher. But that opens the question—"

Keen's phone buzzed. Annoyed, she checked it. Dembe, on a burner phone, though she knew who was really calling. Reddington himself used cell and satellite phones sparingly, preferring instead to make other people call for him. She answered.

"He's downstairs," Dembe said without preamble. "He wants to see you."

"When we're done here," she said, thinking about the control again.

There was a moment's hushed conversation over the line.

"He says it can't wait. He has more information about the Bodysnatcher and Mala Rudenko."

"What? Why didn't he mention this earlier?"

Another consultation, and Dembe came back on the line.

"Timing."

Navabi gave Keen a sideways look as she clicked off.

"Don't say it," Keen sighed.

"But we're going downstairs, aren't we?"

"I am," Keen said. "Someone has to stay up here to keep the crime scene secure and brief the forensics team."

"So it's not just men who want control," Navabi said.

Keen ignored this and trotted down the stairs to the street, where Dembe opened the back door to Reddington's town car. To her surprise, Donald Ressler was in the front seat. Every fold of his suit was perfectly pressed and the knot in his tie was first-date straight.

"What are you doing here?" she demanded as she climbed in.

"Cooper sent me," Ressler said. "You and I are joining the advance team."

"I've had Dembe pack you an overnight bag," Reddington said, gesturing to the floor. "South Carolina awaits."

"You need to come clean with what you know," Keen said sharply. "I can't go in here blind and—"

"Of course, of course." Reddington twirled the fedora in his lap, then set it on one knee. "I've discovered the Bodysnatcher will be leaving with Miss Rudenko from the splendid hamlet of Roebuck, South Carolina in…" he checked his watch "…three hours and twenty minutes. He will travel south on Highway 215, which is locally known by the far more picturesque Stone Station Road. We have just enough time to set a trap for him and rescue the wealthy technology heiress."

"That's convenient," Keen said.

"Isn't it?" Reddington agreed mildly.

"Why don't we just grab the Bodysnatcher from wherever he is in Roebuck?"

"Because although I can tell you when he will be taking the hapless Miss Rudenko away from Roebuck, I'm afraid I can't tell you exactly where in Roebuck he's holding her. Hence the reason timing is so crucial. Director Cooper was kind enough to send a small task force to meet us at Roebuck, though we'll be able to travel in something more comfortable. Think of it as a perk."

"Of what?" Ressler said.

"Of knowing me. By the way, I love that tie, Donald. Isaia is you."

The "something more comfortable" was Reddington's private jet. Keen had ridden in it a number of times, but still couldn't quite get used to the luxury. In her experience, flying was cattle lines at the airport and fighting over arm rests with small children. It definitely was not leather captain chairs, plush carpet, mahogany-paneled walls, and a wet bar. Reddington offered her and Ressler drinks from the latter, and both of them declined. Keen tried to pump Reddington for more information and utterly failed.

"It'll be easier to tell everyone all at once," was all he'd say.

So instead Keen spent the rest of her time on the phone with Cooper and consulting with Ressler. Cooper had already sent a small tactical team ahead to meet them in Roebuck.

"Our best bet is a mock stop," Navabi said over the speaker. "You and Ressler fake a breakdown that covers two lanes. We've done it before."

"The team waits inside the stalled out vehicle, and when the Bodysnatcher pulls over, we grab him," Keen finished. "Works."

"Simple, straightforward, little to go wrong." Cooper said from the phone. "Do it."

"No FBI identification on the agents, please," Reddington said. "It needs to appear that everyone works for me."

"If you must," Cooper agreed. "I'll tell the field office."

"Anything at Iris Henning's murder scene we should know about?" Keen asked.

"Nothing," Navabi said. "Whoever killed Iris covered his tracks well. Forensics is trying to get something from the bath water, but we aren't hopeful."

"Why wasn't the door locked?" Keen asked.

"Forensics didn't find scratches on the lock to show it was picked, and you saw yourself the door wasn't damaged," Navabi said.

"So Iris let the killer in," Ressler said.

"Or he had a key," Keen added. "Who would have a key?"

"Landlord, super, a neighbor." Keen could almost see Navabi ticking off on her fingers. "Family members."

"I hate to intrude on FBI business," Reddington said.

"That has to be the biggest lie I've heard you tell," Keen said in a mock scold, "and that's saying something."

Reddington ignored this. "The murder you're investigating is unimportant. A distraction from the real case."

"It's important to Iris and her family," Cooper said.

"The local gendarmes can tidy up these matters. We already know who the killer is and why he did it."

"We know the Bodysnatcher probably killed Iris to keep her quiet about Mala's kidnapping," Keen said.

A small look of surprise crossed Reddington's face, giving Keen no small amount of satisfaction.

"I'm glad you settled that. There's no reason to continue the investigation, then."

"If the Bodysnatcher is as careful as you claim," Cooper said from the phone, "this may be one of the few times he left an actual clue to his identity or his motives. We don't want to miss it."

"Crossing t's and dotting i's," Reddington said. "If you must, Mr. Cooper. Just remember that this is not an investigation. It's a fishing expedition, and we're out to catch a whale."

They arrived at a small airport in South Carolina and Dembe drove them in a sleek black sedan to the little town of Roebuck. Keen got an impression of 1940s cracker box houses interspersed with trailer parks and pre-fab houses trying to look upscale before they got to what passed for a town center near a grain elevator and a gas station.

"Nothing says home like a bedroom community," Reddington said sagely. "Do you see that house over there?" He pointed at a white home with red trim. Thin pillars held up the roof over an antebellum-style verandah. The front yard was immaculately mowed and planted with a rainbow riot of flowers. A green metal sign announced something in gold print, but the print was too small for Keen to read as they drove past.

"That," Reddington continued, "is a bit of Roebuck history they're desperately trying to forget. The Gorey family has owned that house since the 1700s, and did they keep slaves! When the bit of nastiness we now call the Civil War developed, a member of the Gorey family shot and killed a young soldier. Before the war, the Goreys claimed the soldier was a Yankee. After the war, the Goreys claimed he was a Rebel."

"So the story depends on which side is winning," Keen said as the house vanished into the distance.

"Doesn't it always? You know, legend also says Mamie Gorey was afraid the family silverware would be stolen and melted down during the war by those dreadful Yankees—with some justification, I might add—so she gathered up all the silver, a pile of gold coins they'd earned from selling a coffle of slaves, and her collection of emerald jewelry and gave it all to her husband Jacob and son Robert. She told them to take it to the woods far away and bury it where no one would find it, until the war ended and they could get it all back."

"Uh oh," Keen said. "Which one of them didn't come back?"

"Oh, they both came back," Reddington said, "but neither one of them survived the war. And what with one thing and another, neither of them got around to telling anyone else where everything was buried. Each of them figured the other would always know." Reddington shook his head. "Neither thought both would meet the Grim Reaper."

"What happened to Mamie?" Keen asked.

"You know, I have no idea," Reddington replied. "The Gorey family still lives in that house—it's on the National Registry—so ultimately everything must have come out all right for her, but I'm sure she ate a great many carrots first." He shot his cuffs and checked his watch. "We have half an hour before the Bodysnatcher leaves his lair. If we aren't on that stretch of road in time, he'll vanish into the wilds of Appalachia."

Keen set the timer on her cell phone for thirty minutes so she wouldn't lose track.

A minivan with tinted windows was waiting for them at the grain elevator. The van had six agents inside it, all in flak jackets, all strangers to Keen. They must have been from the South Carolina field office. None of them wore visible badges or FBI insignia. They had been told this was a covert operation and that the FBI's involvement was to be kept quiet. This was the only way Reddington would allow himself to be involved—the criminal world had no idea Reddington was in bed with the FBI, though Keen rather doubted Reddington would put it that way.

Ressler grabbed a shotgun and told the driver about the fake breakdown plan while Keen scootched into one of the bench-style passenger seats. The agents occupying it gave grudging ground, and Keen noticed with an internal sigh that she was the only woman in the van. Suddenly she very much wanted Navabi there, but she was two states away.

"Let's head out!" Ressler said.

Keen let him run the show, even though it was her and Navabi's plan. Not because she wanted to defer to him. She needed to think. Something else was happening here, something big, but she couldn't see what it was.

Keen's cell phone read twenty-one minutes.

The van rushed down the road. The agents made small talk and cracked dumb jokes like agents always did when they were nervous.

"I'm Rob Gillford," said the agent next to her. His holster pushed into Keen's side, and it was on his right. Almost absently she noted this meant he must be left-handed.

"Liz Keen," she said.

"Who is this guy we're going after?" he said. "We didn't get much of a briefing. They even ordered us to leave our IDs and badges behind. Some kind of bigwig thing, but they didn't say what."

"I don't know much either," Keen said, semi-truthfully. "We got a tip that he's a big-name kidnapper, and he has a high-level victim."

Gillford sighed. "Yeah, that's all we got, too. We're all mushrooms, I guess."

"Mushrooms?" Keen said with raised eyebrows.

"Kept in the dark and fed sh—uh, manure."

Keen laughed, warming to his tone. "I've heard worse swear words than that, Agent Gillford. Believe me."

"Trying to break the habit," Gillford said ruefully. "My little girl is learning to talk."

Little girl. Keen pushed unwanted thoughts and memories firmly away, but with limited success. "I can see where this is going."

"Yeah. The other day my computer crashed in the middle of a World of Warcraft quest, and I forgot she was in the room. Second after I finished swearing, I hear this little voice repeating a stream of bombs."

"Oh crap!" Keen said.

"That's definitely not what she said. My wife heard, and let me have it. So I'm off swearing for the next, oh, eighteen years." He laughed. "You got kids?"

Keen was expecting this. She had long ago decided what she would say when someone asked her this. Still, the question stung with unexpected sharpness. She hid behind her ready answer.

"No. One day. What's your daughter's name?"

"Bethany."

Keen nodded and let him talk about play dates and potty training, but her main attention was on the upcoming fight with the Bodysnatcher. And likely with Reddington. In her experience, Reddington never handed the FBI a Blacklister for free. He always stood to gain something from their capture—or death. Sometimes it was mere money—and here she could hear Reddington's voice saying, *I have expenses. My tailor doesn't work for free.* Sometimes it was revenge. Sometimes it was to get someone out of the way so one of Reddington's schemes could move forward. In other words, Reddington wasn't herding them toward the Bodysnatcher out of the goodness of his heart or out of a sense of justice. He wanted something. But what? What would a professional kidnapper who kept an obsessively low profile have to offer Reddington? She didn't know, and it was frustrating. Reddington, of course, wouldn't say.

Twelve minutes on the cell phone.

"The other day—it was so cute—Bethany wanted to tuck *me* into bed for a nap," Gillford was saying. "I about melted."

As far as Keen knew, Reddington never lied to her. Exactly. Quite. But he often dodged questions or outright refused to answer. He doled out information at his own pace to suit his own purposes—or to help Keen. Sometimes his reasoning about what qualified as "help" was a little twisty, though, and even though he had always defended her in the past, she couldn't bring herself to fully trust him. He knew more about her than he was telling.

Keen realized she was stroking the Y-shaped scar at the base of her right hand. The spot had been burned when she was young, and after it healed she had developed the habit of stroking the shiny skin for comfort when she was nervous or unhappy, the same way a child might stroke a blanket. She always traced it the same way, starting at the base of the Y, running up the left side, around the top of the upstroke, down into the valley of the Y, back out again, and down the right side. It tickled just a little, and always made her feel better. Keen had tried a number of times to break herself of the habit, but had lately decided it was harmless, so why not? It wasn't like she was smoking cigars or drinking bacon milkshakes. Except why was she doing it now?

Six minutes on the cell phone.

A silence from Gillford, and Keen realized with a start that he had asked her a question. She tried to backtrack and found she had no idea what he had said.

"Sorry," she said. "I spaced for a minute there. Nerves, you know?"

"I hear that." Gillford touched his revolver with his left hand, confirming Keen's earlier suspicions.

Nerves. She *was* nervous, and it made her stroke the scar. Keen did a quick run-down. A mission always made her nervous. They were about to apprehend a dangerous criminal, one who had a hostage. Who wouldn't be nervous?

But it was more than that. Something inside her was warning her that this whole mission was already going wrong.

Up the Y, down the valley, up the other side, and down again. Hmm.

"We almost there?" Gillford asked.

Keen held up her phone so Gillford and the other agents could see.

Three minutes.

They all tensed. Keen leaned forward in her seat. They were cutting it close.

The van reached an empty stretch of road that ribboned through forested foothills. Reddington's rented car was hanging back about half a mile.

Ressler checked the GPS. "This is it. Our guy better be right about this."

"Is he ever wrong?" Keen countered.

"Who do you mean?" Gillford asked. "Your informant?"

"Yep," Keen said tightly.

One minute.

The driver twirled the wheel. The van spun sideways and blocked the road. Keen touched Gillford's shoulder with a tight smile, then jumped out with Ressler, shut the doors, and popped the hood.

Hot yellow sunshine melted over them and made the pavement shimmer with heat. Sweat burst out on Keen's forehead. Ressler whipped off the yellow Isaia tie Reddington had admired, stuffed it into his pocket, and unbuttoned the top of his shirt, playing the part of the slightly rumpled husband on a long car trip. He leaned into the engine. Keen got the spare tire and the jack out of the back and tossed them onto the berm, where they'd be "accidentally" in the way of anyone who tried to drive around them, then stood back and pretended to talk on her cell phone. It annoyed her that Ressler was looking at the engine instead of her, but her skill as a profiler reminded her that most people still expected the husband to fiddle with the car while the wife called for help, and they didn't want to make their target suspicious. A quicky undercover mission wasn't the time to strike a blow for gender equality.

Reddington's car backed into a track that ran into the woods and hid there like a cop hungry to hand out tickets. He got to sit in AC comfort with a martini while they stood out here in the awful sun. How did it always happen this way? She wiped sweat from her face with her sleeve.

Another van—white, its windows also tinted—slid into view. Keen's heart quickened. She deliberately didn't exchange a look with Ressler, whose backside was poking out from under the hood. He must be even more miserable than she was, with the heat of the engine gently roasting him.

The other van drew closer. When it was maybe fifty yards away, Keen nodded, as if someone on her cell were saying something important, and looked up, apparently seeing the van for the first time. She put her phone away and waved both arms at it, putting a look of relief on her face.

The van lurched over to the gravelly berm. For a bad moment, Keen thought the driver would try to drive over the junk she had strewn across the gravel and get away. Then the van stopped. Keen plastered on a smile and forced herself not to reach for her weapon. Ressler came around the hood, looking fake surprised.

"Honey!" Keen sang out. "Maybe these people can help us." But she did not trot over to the driver's side of the van. Instead, she stood directly in front of the van, her chest tight as a drum. Mala Rudenko was in that van, alone and scared and sure she was going to die. Keen wouldn't let that happen.

We're here, Mala, she thought. *Just hold on a few more seconds.*

The van sat silent at the side of the road. Keen waved again.

"Can you help?" she asked loudly. "My cell is running out of power."

Still no response. Keen went over possibilities in her head. She could wait. She could signal the team and they could pour out of their own van. She could—

The white van's door opened with a little squeak. Keen held her breath, but stayed where she was. Her skin prickled, and she wanted a Kevlar vest in the worst possible way.

"Hey, sweetie." Ressler trotted up, wiping his hands on a handkerchief. "Are these people able to call someone?"

"I don't know who it is yet, darling," she said through clenched teeth.

A figure stepped down from the van and came around the door. He was tallish and thin and wore a brown suit, nattily tailored. And he carried a hat that he clapped on his balding head. Keen blinked at this. Wispy tufts of gray hair poked out from underneath the hat, and the sun gleamed off a gold watch on his wrist. The man seemed to be in his late sixties, but still straight of back and joint. Keen suppressed a gape. *This* was the Bodysnatcher? He couldn't win a wrestling match with a bag of cats, let alone kidnap a healthy adult.

"You seem to be in a bit of trouble," the man said in an English accent. "Could I be of assistance?"

The minivan doors burst open. FBI agents exploded onto the road. In seconds, the man was surrounded by helmeted officers pointing pistols and rifles at his chest. Gillford held his pistol in a lefty grip. The man's eyes widened slowly, as if he didn't quite understand what he was seeing. His hands came up, shaking with either palsy or fear.

"You can have my van," he said in a frightened squeak. "Just don't shoot. I have grandchildren."

"Who are you?" Ressler demanded from behind his own pistol.

"I'm… that is…" he stammered.

"Good heavens, gentlemen, put your weapons down." Reddington came around the FBI minivan. "This isn't the Bodysnatcher."

The guns didn't move, and the man continued to look bewildered.

"Who is he?" Keen asked.

"This," Reddington said, "is Stuart Ivy."

CHAPTER SIX

•

"That doesn't exactly answer the question," Keen said. She edged around to the open driver's side door and peered in. At first glance, the van seemed to be empty. Anyone inside would have to be hidden in a secret compartment. No sign of Mala Rudenko. Keen downgraded the van from *probable threat* to *unlikely threat*.

"Raymond Reddington!" Stuart Ivy said in his rolling accent. His hands were still up, but they had stopped shaking. "It's about time you arrived. Though I wasn't expecting so many rifles pointed at my head."

"Stand down," Ressler said, and the agents obeyed.

Reddington, meanwhile, gave the close-mouthed smile Keen recognized as the one he used when he greeted friends—and underworld contacts. He held out his arms. "Stuart!"

"Red!" Stuart brought his hands down and embraced Reddington. "Really! We need to do more than just talk on the phone."

"I don't like phones—" Reddington began.

"—You never know who's listening," Stuart finished with a close-mouthed smile of his own, and both men laughed expansively.

Utterly baffled now, Keen came around the front of the van.

"Who is Stuart Ivy?"

"Ah." Reddington backed away from the man. "I'm being dreadfully rude. Stuart Ivy, may I present my associates Elizabeth Keen and Donald Ressler." He pointedly didn't introduce the other FBI agents, leaving Stuart to assume they were anonymous mercenaries or bodyguards.

"We don't really have time to talk," Stuart said. "Might I suggest we hustle along, as you Americans like to say?"

"Where's the Bodysnatcher?" Ressler asked.

"Still on his planned path." Stuart checked his watch. "But I'm afraid your plan to catch him has changed a little."

"What is going on?" Keen snapped.

"I am here solely to confirm a number of Mr. Reddington's suspicions," Stuart said. "The Bodysnatcher's actual van is somewhat farther down the road. If we hurry, we can catch him up."

"Though you don't want to catch him," Reddington added. "You want to follow him."

"We're going to need more than that," Ressler growled.

"The Bodysnatcher is a minnow on our little fishing expedition, Donald. I believe I already told you we were hunting a whale. Someone much higher on the list. I wasn't entirely certain, but my good friend Stuart has just now confirmed everything, so we're good to continue with the next stage."

"Mr. Ivy was your source of information for the Bodysnatcher, wasn't he?" Keen said.

"We really should move along," Reddington said.

"Not only will we lose the Bodysnatcher entirely, we're still blocking the road."

"How are we going to find him if he isn't even in sight?" Ressler said.

"I assume your team is conversant with radio tracking," Stuart said.

"Yes," Keen said warily.

"An associate of mine placed a device on the Bodysnatcher's van. This will follow it." Stuart patted his pockets, came up with a tobacco tin, a folded travel toothbrush, and a safety pin before finding what looked like a smart phone. "That's it! Give this to your driver and you'll have the Bodysnatcher in no time!"

"I'll take it," Keen said.

The device showed a flashing red dot and map coordinates that Keen had to unscramble in her head.

"He's a couple miles away."

"Let's ride in my car," Reddington said. "The other van will be too crowded."

"What should we do about this van?" Gillford cocked a thumb at it. His left thumb.

"That?" Stuart frowned. "Just something I picked up. We can leave it."

Moments later, they were driving down the road again. Dembe and Ressler rode up front while Keen, Reddington, and Stuart Ivy sat in the rear. Reddington told Dembe to blast the AC on arctic, which Keen at first appreciated, but it quickly chilled the sweat on her scalp into a damp ice pack. Gillford was back in the FBI van, of course.

Keen phoned Aram.

"Can you follow a GPS tracker if I give you the frequency?" she asked.

He snorted. "Give me something hard. I mean,

something difficult. I wouldn't want something hard. I mean, I would, but not a—"

"I know what you mean," Keen interrupted, and read the frequency numbers from Stuart's device.

There was a slight pause. "That's not a GPS signal. Your tracker is using a weak frequency that I can't follow up here. It's more like a walkie-talkie."

"Huh." Keen relayed this to the others.

"Well, of course," Stuart said. "A GPS signal can be tracked by outsiders. I wouldn't carry such a thing on my person!"

"Great," Keen sighed. Then, to Aram: "Can you track my phone, then?"

"I already am. You're on the highway, heading south. Don't…" The signal crackled in her ear. "…lose you."

Keen plugged her free ear with a finger. "Repeat that? You're breaking up."

"I said, don't worry—we won't lose you."

The map function on Ivy's phone showed a flashing red dot about two miles south of them. She reported this to Dembe and Ressler. Dembe sped up.

"First things first," Keen said. "Who are you, Mr. Ivy?"

"Please call me Stuart," he said. "I've known Red for a long, long time." He glanced at Reddington with an expression that would, under most circumstances, pass for fondness. Keen, however, caught something else underlying. A tension. Even, dislike? She narrowed her eyes. This bore watching.

"The first thing is actually what's going on with the Bodysnatcher," Ressler interrupted from the front. "And with Mala Rudenko."

"The Bodysnatcher is unwitting bait, Donald," Stuart said. "Miss Rudenko is not in his van at the moment because he delivered her to the whale we are hunting some weeks ago. Right now, the Bodysnatcher is making another delivery to that whale, and we are following with our little harpoons."

"And who is this whale?" Keen asked.

Reddington tapped the fedora on his lap. "Dr. Benjamin Griffin. Also known as the Beekeeper."

"Really?" Ressler said dryly. "We're going to sting the Beekeeper and take his honey? Have tea and scones?"

"Very droll, sir," Stuart said. "But the Beekeeper is dangerous, quite dangerous indeed. The bees he keeps are actually people. He… keeps them. The Bodysnatcher brings him people, and he incorporates them into his hive. They work for him. They obey him. And they love him. Indeed, they do."

Keen shuddered and touched her scar. "How does he manage that?"

"The good doctor was quite the renowned psychologist and pharmacologist in his day," Reddington said. "He worked with the military for years, trying to perfect techniques to quash individual thought and create a sort of groupthink, as it were. But his work with drugs and chemicals proved too controversial for even our boys and girls in uniform. They ended his relationship with them, quite emphatically, as I recall. Angry but undaunted, he went underground. Quite literally."

"Wait." Keen tapped at her phone, then made a face. She barely had one bar. The mountains must be interfering. At last she got an internet connection. "Is it this guy?"

She showed them a picture of a gray-haired man, clean-shaven, thick glasses. Both Reddington and Stuart peered at it.

"That is he," said Stuart. "Though that photo seems

to be at least twenty years old."

"Wow." Keen put the phone back in her pocket. "Benjamin Griffin. We learned about him in Behavioral Sciences. He had created an entire army within the army—a bunch of soldiers who obeyed *him* instead of their commanding officers. They gave him classified information, secret documents, even access to research facilities that no civilian knows existed. It was a masterpiece of group thought and crowd manipulation—and a horror. When he was found out, his army fought to the death for him. It was a little civil war at the base. Worst of it was that it was friend against friend. Griffin escaped and no one knows what happened to him. The army rounded up the guys he'd brainwashed, but it took an entire team of therapists to undo everything he did. It was horrible."

"Which is why it's incumbent that we catch him now," Reddington agreed. "The problem has always been that the Beekeeper keeps himself well hidden. But Stuart here got a rare lead on him through the Bodysnatcher. We follow the Bodysnatcher, we find the Beekeeper."

Keen took her phone out again and checked it.

"Poor signal out here—"

"The mountains," Ressler agreed.

"—but the tracker says the Bodysnatcher's van is still about two miles ahead of us." She double-checked the map coordinates, then checked the map on her phone. This was a pain in the ass. "He seems to be heading into the Sumter National Forest."

"That would make sense," Ressler said. "Big chunk of federal land. Isolated. Heavily wooded in the Appalachians. Easy to hide in there. Could you speed up some more, Dembe?"

Dembe glanced over his shoulder at Reddington, who nodded, and the car picked up speed. The van behind stayed with them. Keen kept her eyes on the little red dot. Now they were gaining.

A silence fell inside the car, an oddly uncomfortable one. Keen shifted in her seat. Ressler stared out the window, and Dembe kept his eyes on the road.

After a moment, Keen found herself saying, "How do you know Reddington, Stuart?"

"I don't believe we have time—" Reddington said.

"Now that's a story," Stuart interrupted. "Red stayed with my wife Vivian and me for… quite some time when he was a young man, even younger than you are, my dear. It was almost like we were a family, in some ways."

Keen did some math in her head.

"That was not long after you… left the Naval Academy, then?"

Reddington turned his head sideways in that gesture she found both familiar and infuriating. He used it whenever he wanted to change the subject.

"Stuart and I have quite a history. Did I mention his wife Vivian is a descendant of the Gorey family?"

"The ones with the house and the slaves and the silver?" Keen said, surprised.

"The very same." Reddington chuckled. "After the war, a branch of the Goreys went back to England. Stuart and Vivian spent years looking for that buried treasure. Nothing but torn trousers and broken cuticles to show for it."

Stuart blushed lightly. "Don't let's go into that, Red. You owe me, you know. Vivian and I taught you a great deal. Without us, you wouldn't be where you are today."

"Is that so?" Keen interjected, leaning a little closer.

It was rare to hear anything about Reddington's past, especially where it didn't involve Keen herself. "What was your interest?"

Here Stuart's eyes took on a faraway look.

"Purely selfish. Viv and I never had children, and it was nice having a young person about to pass on our accumulated wisdom."

"Wisdom? Is that what you call it?" Reddington raised an eyebrow. "God knows where I would be now if I had followed your *wisdom*." There was a moment of uncomfortable silence, then Reddington's voice softened as he said, "If nothing else your aphorisms could certainly use some improvement."

"I took them from the greatest," Stuart protested. "Never give a fool a break."

"Sucker," Ressler said. "It's sucker."

"Vulgar," Stuart said. "Also, you draw more flies with honey than motor oil."

"Vinegar," Reddington corrected almost absently.

"Does that make it any less true?" Stuart responded. He ticked off his fingers. "Never let emotions cloud a deal. Don't let your concern for someone else endanger your safety. That kept you alive more than once."

Keen blinked. "Really? You taught Reddington that?"

"Vivian learned it to her great dismay," Reddington said.

Keen was multi-tasking, keeping an ear on the conversation and checking the tracker at the same time. The latter had frozen due to a lack of signal. But even as she watched, it found a signal again and updated. The Bodysnatcher was a mile ahead of them. Traffic on the road was light, at least, so they'd have no trouble spotting him. Stuart's comment, however, brought her head up.

"What happened to Vivian?" she asked.

"I know a few embarrassing stories about your Mr. Reddington, too," Stuart said, ignoring the question.

Keen let it pass. "Tell, then!"

"Stuart—" Reddington said.

Stuart leaned back in his seat. "I remember when Red was a young man and he had his eye on a young lady who lived a few houses up the road."

"Stuart, don't you dare," Reddington warned, but there was more than banter beneath his words.

Keen looked at both men sharply. Her trained eye picked out a stiffness in their posture, an overly succinct pronunciation of their words. It pointed to a definite tension growing between them.

"No way. You have to go on," Ressler urged, oblivious.

Stuart's eyes flicked toward Reddington.

"Well, somehow he managed to get the girl's phone number, and he decided to write a poem about how he felt about her."

"You wrote adolescent love poetry?" Ressler said in utter delight.

"It wasn't adolescent," Reddington sniffed. "It was a Petrarchan sonnet, and I would match mine against anything the old Italian bastard wrote. Stuart certainly wouldn't appreciate it. His poetry all begins *There once was a man from Nantucket*."

"Whatever, man," Ressler said from the front seat. "You wrote a love poem."

"You might try it sometime, Donald. Women respond to men who show them actual emotion."

"Red did more than write a sonnet," Stuart said. "He rang the girl up and proceeded to read it to her. He had just finished the final couplet when the voice on the other end said, 'I think you meant this for my daughter, love.'"

Keen burst out laughing. "No! You read a love poem to your girlfriend's *mother*?"

"In my defense," Reddington said, "they sounded exactly alike on the phone."

Stuart was patting back a laugh. "We've never let him forget it, Vivian and I. Or, we didn't."

"What did happen to Vivian, then?" Keen repeated.

Before anyone could answer, Keen's phone buzzed. It was Aram.

"Where the heck are you going?" he demanded.

"What do you mean?" she asked.

"I was away from the keyboard for a second because I had all this coffee from that new place Navabi found up on North Avenue? She's gotten me addicted to their salted caramel lattes, but then I have to run to the bathroom every—"

"Aram," Keen interrupted.

"Oh, right." Aram coughed. "Anyway, when I got back, I saw you guys have really booked it south of your previous location. What did you do—get into a race car?"

"I don't know what you mean." Keen glanced out the window at serene trees and foothills. "We're going at a normal speed. The Bodysnatcher's van is—"

"You're something like ten miles farther south of your previous location," Aram cut in. "Not far from Fort Daymon, in fact."

"I've never heard of Fort Daymon."

"Military base. Army. Seriously—don't... geography of... country?"

"Aram, we're nowhere near any military base." Pause. "Aram?"

"Hello? Hello? Keen, I... can't—"

The signal cut out. Keen made a face.

"What's going on?" Ressler asked.

"Aram thinks we're near some military base. Fort Demon or something."

"Daymon," Ressler corrected. "Geez, that's miles away from here. He's way off."

"We seem to have reached the forest," Stuart said blithely.

A left turn with a large wooden sign meant to be reminiscent of a log cabin proclaimed they could enter the Sumter National Forest. Dembe took the turning and Ressler pulled out his phone.

"Better send an update back home," he said, then frowned. "I'm not getting a signal."

Keen checked her own phone again. No bars. The tracker's signal still worked, however, and it reported the Bodysnatcher's van a short distance ahead of them in the park. She relayed this to the group.

"The mountains interfere with cell phones," Reddington said.

"But not a walkie-talkie signal," Keen said. "That seems weird."

Reddington's car and the FBI van glided into the park. A ranger in a brown uniform stood guard. This was going to get sticky. Normally any FBI agent could flash a badge and get in, but no one was carrying ID. Not only that, Keen hadn't had a chance to resolve whether or not Stuart knew about Reddington's relationship with the FBI. She was operating on the assumption that he thought she and Ressler worked for Reddington. Before she could consider the problem further, Reddington rolled his window down and showed a card to the ranger on duty. He waved them by with a smile.

"I'm a member in good standing of the park

society," Reddington explained. "Free admission is one of the perks."

Dembe guided the car along a twisting road. The speed limit was fifteen miles per hour, but the moment they got out of sight of the ranger station, he sped past that. A mile into the park, Keen checked her phone again—still no signal. The red dot was on the move.

"There's a road ahead on the right," Keen said. "Take it."

"How big is this place?" Ressler asked.

"Just over five hundred eighty square miles," Stuart said. "A third the size of your state of Connecticut. Between the mountains and forests and caves, a number of people become lost in here every year."

"Fantastic," Keen growled. They were now several miles into the park and they hadn't encountered a single other vehicle. Nothing but thick forest and slanted mountainside. Keen, born and raised a city girl, had no idea where she was or how to find her way without checking her phone.

"Hurry up," Ressler said to Dembe.

"We will not lose him," Dembe replied. "In fact... there!"

He pointed ahead of them. A white van was just turning down a gravel side road. Keen wondered who the Bodysnatcher had locked inside it. They must be terrified, sure they were alone and about to die.

We're coming, she thought. *We're almost there. Hang on!*

But who was this Beekeeper? Keen thought about a man who had a mass of people stuffed into a house or a basement somewhere, people who had been tortured and brainwashed into loving him and obeying him. Like any decent psychologist, she knew quite a lot about both cults and Stockholm syndrome, ways in which ordinary people could be persuaded to think in abnormal ways. With a combination of isolation, poor food, sleep deprivation, and other conditioning methods, a charismatic leader could persuade nearly anyone into following him—and it was always a him. Keen had never heard of a cult led by a woman, unless you counted Clementine Barnebet, who had allegedly persuaded a dozen people to commit ax murder on her behalf, but that had been over a hundred years ago and evidence of her group being a cult was spotty.

Benjamin Griffin, the Beekeeper, would be another animal entirely. He wasn't interested in killing. He brainwashed people into becoming his pets. Keen's insides churned at the thought. Even after years of studying the underside of the human psyche at the FBI Academy and more years of pursuing it in the field with the Post Office, she couldn't get past how horrific people could be. She had caught criminals who dissolved victims into soup, who had tortured and killed members of their own family, who had mutilated women and smiled all the while, but she didn't fully understand their reasoning. Sure, she knew the theory—most of the time it was a need for control mixed up with bone-chilling childhood trauma and abuse—and she had learned how to think like these terrible people, but she still didn't have a perfect instinct, one that let her get fully into the head of a killer or his victim.

A part of her was glad about that.

The Bodysnatcher's van was less than fifty yards ahead of them now, and the road had deteriorated into a dirt track. Keen leant forward, halfway into Ressler's seat. Abruptly, the black van swerved and spun to face them. Keen's heart jumped, and she automatically reached for her holster. Dembe hit the brakes, jolting Keen off-balance. Behind them, the white van crunched to a halt on the gravel.

A swarm of people burst from the woods and surrounded the white FBI van. They wore strange gas masks that hid their faces and gave them an insectoid look. Rifles and revolvers shone sleek and deadly in their hands.

"Down!" shouted Keen.

The swarm opened fire on the van. The crack of bullets and smash of glass filled the air. Rows of holes opened up in the metal. Its doors were flung open and FBI agents poured out. The first one was Gillford. He raised his weapon to fire, then dropped, caught by the swarm's bullets. The pistol fell from his left hand. Keen's breath caught in her throat.

"No," she whispered.

One of the swarm also fell—and then another agent.

Dembe wrenched the wheel around and hit the gas. The car spun sideways on the road so the passenger side was facing the besieged FBI van. Keen's gaze was riveted on Gillford. He wasn't moving, and the horrible hole in the side of his head told her everything she needed to know. She thought about Bethany. Who would teach her to swear now?

"Damn it!" Ressler said.

The spell broke.

"Ressler!" Keen shouted. "We have to get these guys to safety!"

Dembe was already moving. Since he had turned the car, it now formed a rudimentary shield between him and the FBI van. The Bodysnatcher's black van was behind him, but at the moment, it sat quiet and ignored—a lesser threat. Dembe reached into the back and with impressive strength, yanked the startled Reddington bodily over the front seat into the driver's compartment before Reddington could even react. Then Dembe shoved open his own door and spilled out, his Glock in his hand. Fortunately, the swarm was concentrating its fire on the van. The smell of cordite hung in the air. Gillford's body lay motionless on the road.

"Oh dear, oh dear, oh dear," Stuart moaned.

"Go!" Dembe snapped at Reddington. "To the trees! You too, Elizabeth! I will cover!"

Reddington didn't hesitate. He dove past Dembe and ran toward the tree line. One of the swarm noticed and aimed at him. Dembe fired first, and the swarmer dropped. Then Dembe vanished into the trees after Reddington. Seconds later, he fired from cover.

"I'm taking Stuart," Keen shouted to Ressler.

Ressler scrambled across the car and out the driver's door as well, keeping low. Bullets split the air, and Keen's skull prickled. Any moment one would crack her head in half. The other agents were fighting back, but guns at close quarters when you were caught by surprise were terrifyingly ineffective. Blood flowed from a hundred wounds, and the screams of wounded men filled Keen's ears.

Ressler took aim with his pistol. It looked puny.

"Go!" he shouted.

Keen was already moving. She shoved her door open and dragged Stuart out.

"Stay low!" she said.

"I know how to exit a gunfight," he snapped, and with surprising agility scuttled toward the tree line. Keen followed, leaving Gillford behind, hating herself for it, having no other choice.

When she reached the trees, wood cracked and a warm line of blood scored her cheek. Keen dropped to her stomach and crawled into the undergrowth. After a moment, she realized Stuart Ivy was nowhere to be seen. Damn it, damn it, damn it! Where was he? And where was Reddington? The bushes were thick and they blocked her view. The gunfire and screams continued. Another bullet smacked into a tree less than a foot above her.

Sweat ran down Keen's back. A big part of her wanted to rush to the aid of her fellow agents, but another part of her pointed out that she was outnumbered, outgunned, and outmaneuvered. She needed to keep moving, find Reddington, find Stuart Ivy. Her jaw clenched.

Keen crawled deeper into the brush, then cautiously raised herself up a little higher so she could run in a crouch. She took a moment to fumble for her cell phone, but it had no signal. Of course.

The shooting stopped. Keen halted, confused. Where was she? Greenery surrounded her on all sides, and the escape had disoriented her. The canopy obscured the sun, so she couldn't even use that as a reference point. Mouth dry, she circled around to her left a little, hoping to flank the group at the road, but she didn't dare move faster for fear of drawing attention to her presence.

"Elizabeth!"

The harsh whisper snapped her head around. Dembe was peering around a large tree and gesturing at her. She duck-walked over to him, adrenaline touching every vein and muscle. Behind the tree was Reddington, looking as angry as she ever saw him.

"Are you all right, Lizzie?" he asked, calling her by the nickname she allowed no one but Reddington to use.

"I'm not hurt," she said.

"What's this, then?" He put out a finger and didn't quite touch her cheek. She had forgotten about the cut, but now that he had brought it to her attention, she felt the sting.

"It's nothing," she said. "Where's Stuart?"

"I have no idea," Reddington said. "I was hoping he was with you. Have you seen Donald?"

She tightened her jaw again. Ressler had covered her and Stuart while they ran for the trees. She had left him behind. It had been the right thing to do, absolutely by the FBI's extensive book, but that didn't stop the sharp pang of guilt and wave of worry. She thought of him sprawled on the ground beside Gillford, his sightless blue eyes staring up at the equally blue sky, scarlet blood pouring out of his chest. No. He wasn't dead. He couldn't be dead.

"I don't know what happened to him," she admitted.

"And the Bodysnatcher?" Dembe said.

"I didn't even see him," Keen replied, peering around the tree. "Are we worried about him?"

"Not overly," Reddington said. "Neither of us can get a cell phone signal out here. I don't suppose...?"

"No," Keen said.

"It's either the mountains or the Beekeeper, or both," Reddington said.

"Take this." Dembe handed Keen a pistol. "It's my extra."

A motor coughed to life in the distance, followed by a second. Voices shouted, doors slammed. The motors faded away. Reddington and Dembe exchanged looks.

"I will go see," Dembe said.

"I'll come with you," Keen said, but was halted by Reddington's firm grip on her elbow.

"You need to stay here with me, Lizzie." His voice was calm but firm, a father speaking to a daughter.

"It's my job, Reddington," she said, torn between exasperation at him and worry for Ressler. Hell, she was even a little worried about Stuart Ivy, and she had only just met him.

"And my job is to keep you safe," Reddington countered. "There's nothing you can add to Dembe's woodcraft anyway. See? He's already gone and you won't catch up with him."

He was, too. Keen sighed heavily and bit back a sharp retort. Instead, she said, "You know I work with the FBI, and danger is part of the career description. When you try to shield me, it looks like I can't do my job."

Reddington looked truly surprised. "When have I ever been concerned with what anything looks like?"

"An interesting question from someone who makes a living deceiving other people," Keen couldn't help saying.

Reddington turned his hat in his hand. Jesus, he still had his *hat*.

"Lizzie, you've examined human psychology carefully, and I'm in genuine awe of your skill. I'm sure that all your training and instincts tell you that human beings are never completely consistent. No matter how many claims they make to the contrary, inconsistencies eventually show themselves. The politician who defends family values visits prostitutes. The man who keeps a spotless home drives a car filled with trash. The police officer who tickets others breaks the speed limit on his way home from work."

"Are we really having this conversation right after a gun fight?" Keen asked.

Reddington ignored her. "But I'll tell you that human beings are marvelously consistent. Underneath, at the base, they always—*always*—act the same. Their surface behaviors may change, but underneath, we all stay the same. Even I. When I look at you, I can't see the FBI. I see the daughter of my best friend in her Hello, Kitty pajamas and I see a promise I made. So I do what I need to keep you safe. I'm perfectly consistent that way."

Keen shook her head. He made sense, sure, but…

"You're also stalling me so I won't go after Dembe."

"See? Consistent," he said, shaking a finger. "And here's Dembe back again."

Dembe emerged from the bushes, not bothering to hide his movements, which told Keen a great deal all by itself.

"Is he dead?" she blurted. "Ressler?"

Dembe spread his hands.

"I do not believe so. All the cars are gone. So are the bodies. I had a look at the tracks, and I saw no blood near the place where Mr. Ressler was standing. If he was shot, he shed no blood."

Keen's knees weakened a little, and she let herself lean against the tree.

"What else?"

"I did not find Mr. Ivy anywhere. I believe he was captured. The other agents were killed and their bodies dragged into the van."

A heavy wave of grief came over Keen, and she closed her eyes beneath it. She hadn't known Gillford long, but it had been long enough. Now she wished she had paid more attention during their conversation.

"I'm sorry, Bethany," she whispered, and she wasn't sure whether she was talking to Gillford's daughter or to her own memories of loss.

"We need to keep moving," Reddington said. "The Beekeeper will be looking for us." He reached into his jacket pocket. "He and his people will be watching us, probably expecting us to follow the road and try to locate a cell signal, and they know this area."

"We can't leave Ressler and Stuart Ivy with the Beekeeper," Keen said.

"Hold on," Reddington said and he produced from his pocket a folded piece of paper the size of a mailing envelope. It took Keen a moment to understand what it was. As if they were in a French café instead of a forest surrounded by an army of armed madmen, Reddington unfolded the paper to the size of a poster, studied it, and turned to check his orientation against the road far behind them.

"A *map*?" Keen peered over his shoulder.

"The current generation is too dependent on technology, Lizzie." He looked at the map again, then uphill at the low mountain ahead of them. "This way."

He strode off into the woods.

CHAPTER SEVEN

"The Hive guys went that way," Keen protested, following Reddington. He made for a strange figure, tromping through the woods in his still-impeccable suit and alligator shoes.

"That's why we're going this way," Reddington said. "Would you say this is north?"

"A little more to the left," Dembe replied. He plucked the map from Reddington's hands. "Allow me, my friend."

"Thank you, Dembe. Must we climb?"

"A little." Dembe traced a route with a finger. "But not as much as you might think."

"Where are we going?" Keen demanded.

"Somewhere safe so we can work out the next step," Reddington said. "Coming, Lizzie?"

Keen checked her phone again. No signal. Of course. All her instincts screamed at her to run back, to go after Stuart Ivy and Ressler, but she was outnumbered and outgunned. Reddington was right. Besides, if they reached higher ground, they might eventually get a signal and be able to call Cooper. He would be worried by now anyway—he hadn't gotten an update in over an hour.

The trio tramped through the hills and woods. Undergrowth scratched and tore at Keen's skin and clothes. It came to her that Dembe was following a faint trail, probably one created by animals. That was smart of him—on a trail there would be fewer traces if someone from the Hive decided to track them. She tried to avoid snagging her clothes on bushes. The close, humid air prickled around her neck and scalp, and she was sweating heavily.

"There." Dembe pointed. Halfway up the slope perhaps forty yards ahead of them was a large, tumbledown wood cabin with an old-fashioned stone foundation that said Civil War era to Keen. It was partly built into the side of the hill and half hidden by trees and undergrowth. Vines crawled across the walls and what remained of the roof. Keen doubted she would have noticed it if not for Dembe's pointing finger.

"There what?" Keen said.

"We can regroup," Reddington said. "Come along."

Dembe led them around one side of the cabin to a rickety-looking door. The place smelled of moss and old leaves, and the trees leaned in protectively. A surreal feeling stole over Keen, as if she were in a fairy tale. It wouldn't have been out of place for an old woman in a long black dress to cackle at them from one of the second-story windows. Keen shuddered despite herself. Dembe pushed the door open to reveal a small entry area, reached around inside the jamb, and touched something. There was a harsh screech and a shuttered metal door rushed upward. Keen jumped. The shutter door had been painted to blend in with the back wall of the entrance.

Reddington gestured. "After you, Lizzie."

Keen cautiously crossed the threshold. The interior

was bright and airy, though stuffy and warm. Rustic wood paneling, exposed beams, high ceilings, comfortable raw-wood furniture, stone fireplace, marble kitchen, shiny steel refrigerator.

"What—?" Keen sputtered. "Where—? How—?"

Reddington tossed his fedora on the long dining room table.

"I'm appalled at your low opinion of me, Lizzie. When have I ever entered a place where I had no safe house?"

"In a federal park?" she squawked.

"The house actually belongs to a dear friend in the Russian mafia," Reddington said. "He comes to the country only infrequently, but when he does, he likes to keep a low profile."

"Does the Beekeeper know about this place?" Keen demanded.

"We wouldn't be having this conversation if he did. What are you looking for?" he asked.

Keen was searching the cupboards and tabletops. She opened doors and checked under the end tables. "The phone," she said. "I need to call Cooper. Now."

"A landline in this day and age?" Reddington dropped onto a couch.

She made a face at him. "Fine. We have no cell phones and no landlines. Logic says we should start walking until we get a signal, call the Post Office, and get a task force in here right away. God only knows what the Beekeeper is doing to Ressler and your friend."

"No." Reddington shook his head. "The Beekeeper and his Hive will be watching the roads and the trails out of here for us, and they know the area. They will find us, and quickly, if we try to leave."

"What about the park rangers?"

"A number of them are working for the Beekeeper."

"Which," Keen said slowly, "is how the Hive knew we were coming. The one who checked your card at the gate recognized you."

"Indeed."

Keen checked her phone again, hoping against hope. No signal. "I don't understand why I'm not getting a thing. Don't the parks have cell towers?"

"The Beekeeper at work," Reddington said. "I believe he and his Hive have gained control of a large portion of this park. It is likely they have a signal disruptor that interferes with cell phones and GPS."

"GPS?" Keen repeated. "So Aram doesn't know where we are?"

"I doubt it very much," Reddington said. He seemed perfectly calm, as if they weren't trapped in the middle of a trackless wilderness. "Aram and Director Cooper have no doubt decided we are somewhere in this park, but as Stuart pointed out, the place is a third the size of Connecticut, with fewer street signs, and very difficult to search. The Beekeeper chose his hiding place well. Dembe, would you be so kind as to check the solar generator? We'll need baths tonight, I'm sure. And turn on the air conditioning."

Dembe nodded and left.

Keen perched on the edge of an armchair. "What's your connection to the Beekeeper, Reddington?"

"My connection?"

"It's clear you don't care one way or the other about the Bodysnatcher. You want the FBI to take out the Beekeeper." Keen warmed to her subject. "The Bodysnatcher was nothing but a starting point, just like you said. You arranged for Stuart Ivy to find the Bodysnatcher and confirm that he was taking people to the Beekeeper. Once you knew that for certain, you had us switch targets. Why? What's the Beekeeper to you? And what's Stuart's role in this?"

"Stuart's role?"

"He's more than just a contact. You've known him for a long time. There's something about his wife that you two won't talk about. I need to know, Reddington. Our lives might depend on it."

Reddington cocked his head. "The Beekeeper has used the Bodysnatcher for years to bring people into his Hive. He's holding dozens, perhaps hundreds, of people prisoner. He brainwashes them into obedience and raises them like children. His army is growing bigger and bigger, and he's become a threat. Isn't this something the FBI wants to stop?"

"You always have an angle, Reddington," Keen countered. "Some personal reason to go after a Blacklister. You treat the FBI like your personal set of attack dogs, and believe me, it gets tiring."

"I don't think we're in much of a position to argue about it, Lizzie. It's unlikely the Beekeeper will find us here, but we can't stay holed up forever."

Keen changed tactics. "What's the deal with Stuart Ivy?"

"The deal?"

"The two of you have a long-time connection, that much is clear. When did you meet him?"

Reddington paused for a long moment. There was a *whoosh*, and cool air drifted through the room. Dembe had found the air conditioning.

"Stuart is a dear friend," Reddington said at last. "I honestly don't remember what year we met, but it hardly matters. I was green around the edges, and Stuart was… well, he was Stuart. A gentleman. Genteel. Gentle. And his wife Vivian was the sweetest lady who ever packed a .32. But then Vivian died, and it all fell apart. Stuart fell apart."

"How did she die?" Keen asked.

Reddington rose and headed for the gleaming bar.

"You know, I believe my Russian friend always keeps his liquor cabinet stocked with the ingredients for the best Black Russians in the world. You can take the man out of Moscow…" He clinked around behind the bar and came up with coffee liqueur and vodka. "Here we are! Care for one? Best fermented potatoes and coffee beans money can steal."

"None for me." Keen sighed. "We need to figure out what to do next. We can't run, and we can't hide here forever, and we can't leave Ressler and Stuart in the Beekeeper's hands, either. He might be torturing or killing them right now."

"Doubtful." Reddington dropped ice into a shaker with a set of silver tongs. Clearly whatever generator Dembe was checking on worked a treat, even with no one around. "The Beekeeper is a master at psychological conditioning, Lizzie. His preference is not to kill, but to assimilate."

"Assimilate," Keen echoed.

"Of course." Reddington poured dark liqueur into the shaker, and Keen caught the rich coffee smell. "He only killed the agents because he assumed they had come to kill his own people. Once that threat ended, he took prisoners. After a few weeks of his treatments, they'll beg to do whatever he wants."

"Ressler's a strong guy, and not stupid," Keen objected.

Reddington unscrewed a bottle of top shelf vodka.

"Donald has a sharp mind and he's a fine agent. But the boy takes to rules like a baby to his bottle. Starve him, drug him, hypnotize him, give him a new set of rules, and he'll turn his considerable brain power to any cause you like. He won't be able to help himself. And Stuart—"

"What about Stuart?"

"Stuart is looking for something, I fear." Reddington poured in a measure of vodka, thought a moment, and poured in a drop more. "He's alone in the world. He doesn't have anyone to hold onto. Prime material for the Hive, even if he is of the older generation."

"Then we need to act," Keen said.

Reddington shook the shaker amid a rattle of ice as Dembe re-entered the room.

"The generator is working fine," Dembe said. "We have enough power and hot water for quite some time."

"Thank you, Dembe." Reddington poured the drink and ice into a glass. "What about ammunition and weapons? We can—"

"I know what to do," Keen interrupted.

Both men turned to look at her.

"You do?" Reddington said.

"I'm a profiler," Keen said. "I've studied Dr. Griffin and people like him, and I know how they work. I know their methods and their tricks. I can be a double agent within the Hive."

"No," Reddington said flatly.

"My training and experience put me on equal footing with the Beekeeper," Keen continued as if he hadn't spoken. "Now that I know what's going on, I'm in the perfect position to let myself get captured, find Ressler and Stuart, and take down the Hive from within."

"No," Reddington repeated.

"They won't be able to hurt me. I know what they're doing and how to prevent them from harming me.

Even better, I know how to fool them into thinking I'm the perfect little bee."

"No."

"The clock is ticking, Reddington," Keen said. "You'll have to do better than *no*."

"I won't send you into danger like that," Reddington said.

"This is my *job*, Reddington," Keen snapped. "These people are in danger, and I can save them. That's what I *do*. It gets dangerous sometimes. You need to live with that."

"Lizzie, I can't control what you do with your career, but right now, this isn't about that. If it makes you feel any better, I would say the same thing about Dembe going in. You aren't doing it, and that's final."

Keen set her jaw. "All right. What's the alternative? We're sitting here in the dark."

"I will go and scout," Dembe said. "We need more information. If I'm lucky, I might find a car to steal."

"A much cleaner idea." Reddington sipped his drink, then looked at it. "Perfect. You know, Stuart taught me how to make these."

Keen rose. "I'll go with you, Dembe. It'll be dark soon, so we should leave now."

"Lizzie—" Reddington began.

"I can't just sit here," Keen said. "I don't know much about woodcraft anyway, so I'll hang back and run for help if Dembe needs it. If he gets captured, someone needs to know about it."

"I don't—" Reddington tried again.

"What does your military training tell you about scouting?" Keen said to Dembe.

"Go in pairs," he said promptly.

"There you are," Keen said. "Two against one."

* * *

"Where are my people, Aram?" Director Cooper glared over Aram's shoulder at the computer banks. Aram tried to ignore this. He hated it when people leaned into the computers—it felt like someone was reaching into his pockets or grabbing his bike. However, Cooper was the boss and could do as he liked.

Aram flicked over to a GPS map. "Keen's phone last showed up here." He pointed. "They were heading toward Fort Daymon. Some of the other agents had phones, too. Ressler, for one. Their phones showed the same location."

"The Bodysnatcher was taking Mala to a military base?" Navabi said, coming toward them. She was sipping from a takeout coffee cup, and Aram smelled the rich caramel. "That seems strange. The last place he'd want to take a kidnapping victim is the army."

"Why aren't we getting a phone signal?" Cooper said.

"I don't know," Aram admitted. "There's plenty of cell phone coverage in that area, and GPS is strong, too. Unless..."

"Unless what?" Cooper asked tersely.

The light dawned over Aram's face and the realization broke. "We're being spoofed. Holy cow—I never thought I'd see it on this scale, but it's the only thing that makes sense."

Already his fingers were darting across the keys. The screens shuddered and flickered as he typed faster.

"Please explain," Cooper said.

"In English," Navabi added.

"Okay, look." Aram pointed at the map of South Carolina again. "Here's where Keen and the others were before I left my keyboard for a minute. When I got back, they'd jumped south so they were near the army base. I was asking Keen about it when she cut out. It's classic spoofing."

"And spoofing is…?" Cooper prompted.

"When someone broadcasts a fake GPS signal that's made to look like a real one. The fake signal carries a message that says you're somewhere else and makes a GPS receiver such as a cell phone show you the wrong location. When I look at Keen's location, I'm reading data uploaded from her phone, not from the satellites themselves, so if her phone thinks it's in the wrong place, I do too." Aram's mouth was dry. He grabbed his own latte and sipped salty liquid caramel. "One kind of spoofing is called a 'carry-off attack.' It broadcasts a fake signal that synchronizes with the real one, then gradually increases its power until the fake signal overpowers the real one and slowly makes your phone or whatever show you as being in the wrong place."

"Like that captured drone in Iran," Navabi said.

Aram looked at her. "Yeah. 2011. No one knows for sure how the Iranians managed to capture a Lockheed drone, but one of the main theories is that they spoofed the drone into thinking home was northeastern Iran, so it flew right to them."

"And you think Keen's phone was somehow spoofed in this way," Cooper said.

"I'd bet a lot of money on it," Aram said. "I don't think she, Ressler, and Reddington and the rest of that team are anywhere near Fort Daymon."

"So where are they, then?"

Aram was forced to spread his hands. "I have no idea."

Cooper stared at him. "Are you telling me," he said

slowly, "that we've lost an entire team of FBI agents?"

"That… seems to be the case," Aram admitted. He couldn't look Cooper in the face. This was his fault, somehow. He shouldn't have gone to the bathroom. He should have been at his station. He would have noticed something, gotten some kind of clue that let him figure out where Keen and the others were. Guilt, the most familiar of all his emotions, settled over him like a heavy coat.

A moment of silence followed. Then Cooper said, "Get creative. Satellite scans, surveillance cameras, anything you can think of. I'll send ground teams to check their last known location."

"Harold," Cynthia Panabaker was standing on the catwalk above the bullpen, her expression tight. "Pavel Rudenko is on the phone. He wants a word."

Cooper pinched the bridge of his nose as he turned away.

"Find them, Aram. Find them *now*."

"Yes, sir," Aram said to his boss's retreating back. Navabi met his eyes, and nodded. Together, they picked up their latte cups and dropped them into the trash.

"What does Mr. Rudenko want, Cynthia?" Cooper asked, dropping into his chair while Panabaker leaned against the desk.

"The usual reassurances, I imagine," she said wryly. "But walk carefully—he supplies weapons to the people who make all our bosses happy."

"The chain of command," Cooper sighed, and punched the speaker phone. "Mr. Rudenko. How can I help you?"

"Hey, Harry!" said a voice with a strong Brooklyn

accent. Cooper winced. No one had called him Harry since fourth grade, but he didn't think it politic to correct Rudenko. "You got an update on my daughter? I love her like a… daughter, you know? We taxpayers expect great things from the Freakin' Bureau of Investigation, am I right?"

"Our agents are pursuing every possible lead to find your daughter, sir," Cooper replied carefully. "She's our top priority."

"But you got squat," Rudenko shot back. "What the hell kind of operation you running, Cooper? General Park at the Pentagon, he's expecting a big shipment from me soon, but I'm thinking I'm gonna be too broken up about all this to handle it, and things'll be delayed, you know? I'll have to tell him that it's because of you folks, since that's the truth. And when it comes time for your budget allocations—"

"I get it, Mr. Rudenko," Cooper said quickly.

Panabaker held up a piece of paper on which she had scrawled *Give him something*.

Cooper grimaced. "We have a strong lead. Our agents are in South Carolina now following it up."

"Where in South Carolina?"

"Cell phone operations aren't very good down there because of the mountains," Cooper replied, "but they were in the vicinity of Roebuck. We're also dispatching a team to the area near Fort Daymon."

"Fort Daymon? Hey, I've got lots of friends in that place. Let me send some of my guys in to help you. They're good—well-trained, great arms. All legal, thank you NRA. They'll work with—"

"That's all right, Mr. Rudenko," Cooper interrupted, meeting Panabaker's horrified expression. "We've got it covered. It's best if you just stay by your phone in case someone calls you."

"You sure? My Team Green Alpha is the best in the—"

"Thank you, Mr. Rudenko," Cooper said firmly, "but no. We'll be in touch." And he hung up.

"Just what we need." Panabaker shuddered. "A crackpot with an army running around South Carolina."

The woods were quiet except for aggressive birdsong and the rustling of small animals in the undergrowth.

"Stay back ten or fifteen steps. Be ready to run," Dembe said. His Glock was out and the safety was off. Keen didn't bother drawing the weapon Dembe had given her. It would be worthless in any situation where she might need it. The Hive outnumbered her several dozen to one. She didn't know why Dembe was bothering.

They skittered down the hillside, keeping to trees and bushes. Keen stayed several paces behind Dembe as instructed, nervously trying to watch in all directions. Her FBI training at Quantico had included a unit on outdoor maneuvers, but that had been a long time ago, and all her field work since those days had been in cities and inside buildings. She knew all about checking behind doors, in cupboards, and in closets, how to look for trouble under beds, behind shower curtains, and in crawl spaces. But the outdoors, especially the woodsy outdoors, offered too damn much cover in all directions, and it felt like someone or something might leap out at any moment. Her gut clenched up and she tried to force herself to relax. A tense agent made mistakes.

Ignore trees that are too thin to hide a man, she told herself. *Look through the bushes. Don't move in a straight line. Remember your starting point. Note landmarks. Don't forget to look up.*

Dembe reached the bottom of the hill. Keen crouched near a tree. Dembe paused, checked, motioned for her to follow him. Keen obeyed. They continued on in this fashion, with Dembe pausing to look for danger and Keen crouching until he motioned for her to keep going. Cicadas buzzed in the trees and mosquitos whined in Keen's ears. Sweat dripped down the back of her neck and her clothes itched against her skin.

After fifteen or twenty minutes of careful progress, they ascended another hill and found themselves looking down a partially cleared slope on the other side. Partway down, an outcrop of rock stuck out, and Keen worked out that it was actually the entrance to a cave. Only a few trees lent shade, and the grass was well trampled. Dozens of people dressed in camouflage, many wearing the odd goggle-like masks, strode in and out of the cave. Keen's breath caught. It was like looking at a hornet's nest. Dembe took a small set of binoculars from his pocket.

"Where did you get those?" Keen whispered.

"The house." Dembe scanned the area, taking care not to let the lenses reflect anything toward the compound.

Keen let him concentrate, then said, "Can you see Ressler down there? Or Stuart?"

"No. But look." He handed her the binoculars and directed her gaze. The cave entrance leaped into giant size. Dembe had her pan to the right, and she sucked in another breath. Camouflage netting hid a number of lumpy objects. One of the masked people obligingly pulled part of the netting aside, revealing a machine gun nest and several crates of what Keen assumed were ammunition.

"The Beekeeper's army contacts are paying off," she murmured.

"Indeed. If we bring the FBI in here, there will be a bloodbath." Dembe pointed farther uphill. "Do you see that?"

A clump of waist-high boxes caught her eye. They looked a little like dressers for clothes, complete with drawers, and there were thirty or forty of them in all. It took Keen a moment to recognize them.

"Beehives," she gasped. "The Beekeeper has actual beehives!"

"Yes," Dembe said, "but that is not what I was pointing out. Go a little more uphill."

She finally saw what he was talking about. With narrowed eyes, she refocused the binoculars. A man was pointing some kind of remote control device at the sky. Above him hovered a four-propeller helicopter drone. No, two of them. No, a dozen of them. The man made adjustments on the controller, and the drones dipped and swayed together. They swooped about the sky like starlings changing direction in unison.

"They play with remote control helicopters," she said. "Is this some kind of boys and their toys thing?"

"I can't say."

More motion caught her eye. Keen brought the binoculars around to check it. A masked figure crawled out of the ground some distance uphill from the cave entrance, followed by a second.

"They have a back door," she reported, handing the binoculars to Dembe so he could look.

"Probably more than one," Dembe agreed.

"Something to watch." Keen thought a moment. "Let's circle around and see if we can get a look from the back. Maybe find one of those back exits. We could use it as a surprise attack when the rest of the task force gets here."

"*If* they get here," Dembe said.

"I'm always optimistic." Keen scrambled to her feet and started out, then halted when a heavy hand landed on her shoulder.

"I go first," Dembe said. "Stay low."

They circled around the ridge until they were looking down at the back of the enclave or compound or whatever it was. The sunlight poured down over them both, hot even though it was getting on to early evening. Thirst tugged at Keen, and she wanted more than anything to take a cool shower and collapse onto a couch in an overly air-conditioned room with a bowl of ice cream. Instead, she used Dembe's binoculars to scan the light woods for more back exits.

"There," she said, pointing. "And there and there."

"You have sharp eyes," Dembe said.

"They must have dug them." Keen handed the binoculars back. "It's too convenient for all of them to be here by accident."

"No doubt," Dembe said. "We—get down!"

They were already on their stomachs in a clump of scratchy bushes, but Keen obligingly brought her head down. About thirty yards downslope, a trio of Hive workers with rifles were tromping along a thin trail. They would pass below their hiding place in a few seconds. She pressed her lips together.

"Give me your pistol," she whispered to Dembe. "Quick!"

Startled, he did so. "What's the matter?"

"When you get back to the cabin," she said, "apologize to Reddington for me."

"Apologize?" Dembe stared at her. "I do not understand."

Keen ejected the cartridge from Dembe's Glock and

tossed it a few yards away so he wouldn't be able to recover it quickly, dropped the pistol, and bolted from their hiding place. She half ran, half tumbled down the hill, nearly spilling into the armed Hive workers. She pretended to trip and went to hands and knees directly in front of them.

"Oh crap!" she said.

Three rifles snapped up to aim at her.

"Don't move!" one of them said.

Keen froze. "Don't shoot! Please!"

They hauled her upright, expressions hidden behind their eerie masks. Keen carefully kept her gaze away from Dembe's hiding place. One of the men searched her, found her own pistol, and took it.

"Who else is with you?" he demanded.

"No one," she said meekly. "I've been wandering around since you all shot the others. I ran and ran and got lost. Are you going to kill me?"

"We're taking you to Dr. Griffin," he said. "Welcome to the Hive."

They led her away. Keen could almost feel Dembe's eyes boring into her back.

CHAPTER EIGHT

The first thing that struck Keen was the noise. The sound of dozens of hammers and chisels pinging away at stone, the sound of pickaxes and shovels striking rock, the sound of shovels chuffing at earth. Ahead of Keen yawned the enormous, cool cavern lined with catwalks and ladders, and at the back was a great two-story tree picked out in stone and bas relief on the banks of a stone river, its roots curled around a great boulder. Other designs swirled across the cavern walls—ocean waves, interlaced hexagons, a sunrise, a triangle made of triangles made of triangles. The place was incredible, a network of beauty and activity hidden away beneath the ground. Stone dust hung in the air. Men and women in dust masks and goggles swarmed around the room, rushed in and out of side tunnels in a constant stream of work. She counted at least fifty people in this room alone. She swallowed, suddenly feeling very small and alone. Maybe her plan to ditch Dembe and get herself captured by the Beekeeper's people hadn't been such a good idea after all.

Hold it together, she told herself. *You can out-psych*

this guy. Do it for Ressler. And Stuart Ivy. And all these poor people.

The smell of cooking food permeated the damp air, making Keen's stomach growl and reminding her of how thirsty she was. One of her guards pulled off his mask, revealing the face of a perfectly ordinary man several years younger than Keen herself. He was armed with a taser, a pistol, a rifle, and pepper spray. She wondered how long the young man had been living here and if the Bodysnatcher had brought him. Was this place, a place filled with stone chips and weapons, everything he had ever known?

The young man snagged another passing masked Hiver—a drone, Keen supposed they should be called—and said something. The drone nodded and rushed away. His own rifle bumped against his shoulder as he ran.

"What is this place?" Keen asked, making her voice shake. It didn't take much. "Where are my friends? The ones you took from the van?"

"Dr. Griffin will explain that," the young man said.

"Could I have some water?" Keen asked. "I haven't had anything to drink since… since the van happened."

A huge man nearly seven feet tall reached for the canteen at his belt, but the young man stopped him.

"No, Pug."

"But she's thirsty," said Pug in a thick voice.

"No. Only if Dr. Griffin says it's okay. Got it?"

Pug nodded and put the canteen away.

"Who is Dr. Griffin?" Keen said. "Is he in charge? Will we see him?"

"You are seeing him now." A white-haired man wearing coke-bottle glasses strode up. He wore a khaki shirt and trousers.

"Hello, Dr. Griffin," said Pug. "It is nice to see you."

"And I'm glad to see you, Pug. Your manners are improving. You should be proud." He turned to Keen. "And you are…?"

"Elizabeth Keen."

"Welcome to my Hive, Elizabeth," Dr. Griffin said. He had a rich, sonorous voice, and his presence pushed at the cavern walls, filled the space like water filled a pool. "Be glad you arrived. You'll never leave. You needn't worry about Mr. Reddington or your obligations to him. You'll stay here forever."

"You will like it here," Pug said.

Keen blinked, then abruptly realized that the Beekeeper thought that she and the others worked for Reddington, he didn't know they were FBI agents. Ressler must have kept up the fiction and Stuart Ivy had either gone along with it or still didn't know the truth himself. Since no one had FBI badges on them, the Hive would have no way to know the truth. Yet.

"Mr. Reddington won't like what you've done," she said. "He's mad. He'll come after you."

"I'm counting on it," Griffin said. "And I'm counting on you and your friends telling me all about him and his organization. Come along, now. Orderly, please."

He led Keen with the guards past the working drones and down a side cavern. Electric light in wall sconces flooded the tunnels and caves, keeping the place well lit, and the floor was mostly packed sand. The smells of food were driving Keen to distraction now, and her mouth was dry as a raisin. She tried to watch Dr. Griffin for clues about his personality and his thinking, but it was difficult when she was light-headed from a lack of food and water. Still, she forced herself to think. Griffin walked with a straight, confident air; a man who genuinely expected obedience from those around him. He had an active man's build, but was putting on weight, which told Keen he was letting himself slow down. No doubt he believed it when people told him he looked good. There was a definite strut in his walk, and his eyes flicked toward Keen now and again. He was showing off the caverns and wanted to see if she was impressed. A vain man who needed his ego stroked. She filed that thought away.

And still, he had an air of power about him. The presence she had noted before. He was a stone in a river. Water flowed around him, moved because he was there. It wouldn't occur to him that anyone would *want* to disobey him, and most people would indeed do as they were told.

"Where is Mr. Reddington?" Dr. Griffin asked casually. "It isn't safe for him to be out in these woods at night. Bears and wolves and coyotes wander everywhere."

"Bears and coyotes are scary," Pug said.

"I have no idea," Keen said. "We got separated after the fight. Why did… why did you kill everyone?"

"Too many of you to keep," Dr. Griffin said.

"I don't understand."

"Mr. Reddington had clearly uncovered our location, and at an awkward moment, too. We couldn't afford to let you go, but we also don't have the resources to assimilate all your compatriots. We had to cull a few, as it were. But that's all right. They're being buried as we speak, and everything is nearly finished."

"Culling is okay as long as the Beekeeper tells you to," Pug said in a happy voice that sent a chill down Keen's back. She thought about little Bethany, who would never hear her father swear again, and had to force her hands to remain still, and not lunge for the Beekeeper's soft neck.

"Here we are," Dr. Griffin said.

They had arrived in another large room, though whether it was artificial or natural, Keen couldn't tell. It was unrelieved stone, undecorated and harshly lit by wall lights. Sand gritted on the floor. Lining the walls were a series of human-sized cages that reminded Keen of dog kennels. Her heart leaped. Inside two of them were Donald Ressler and Stuart Ivy.

"Keen!" Ressler grasped the bars of his pen. "Jesus! Are you all right? Where's—?"

"I don't want to talk about it," she interrupted pointedly. "They haven't hurt me."

"I'm glad to see you, my dear," Stuart said from his own pen. "But not under these circumstances."

Standing next to the cages was an utterly nondescript man in dark gray sweats. He had a bland face, colorless hair, gray eyes, and an average build. Keen couldn't put a finger on his age. It could have been anywhere from thirty to fifty. He was the kind of man you met at a party and completely forgot about the moment you started talking to someone else. A bell rang in Keen's head.

"You're the Bodysnatcher," she said.

The man didn't answer. Instead, he turned to Dr. Griffin.

"You do owe me for the last batch," he said in a soft voice. "I brought Reddington into the park, as promised, putting myself at considerable risk."

"I don't *have* Reddington," Dr. Griffin pointed out. "I wanted him in my Hive. Imagine the possibilities! Now I don't have him."

The Bodysnatcher shrugged. "You didn't ask me to snatch Reddington, just to get him here. I did. I'll be on my way now, and if you need more people, let me know through the usual channels."

"Of course, of course."

Dr. Griffin gestured at Pug, who grabbed the Bodysnatcher by the arms. He yelled in surprise as Pug lifted him bodily and tossed him into one of the open pens. Another guard slammed the door shut. The lock clicked.

"What the hell are you doing?" the Bodysnatcher demanded.

"You are going to stay with us," Pug said. "It will be fun."

"We're at a delicate phase in the operation," Dr. Griffin said mildly. "The final phase. No one leaves. Welcome to the Hive. You, too, Elizabeth."

Hard hands shoved her into a pen of her own. Keen went to hands and knees within the bars, and her own lock clicked behind her.

"You son of a bitch," Ressler snarled.

Dr. Griffin strolled over to Ressler's pen, and peered at him, his expression as serene as a stone Buddha's.

"You think you'll be difficult. You think it'll take a long time to bring you around to the way of the Hive. But I see you, Donald Ressler. Inside you is a little boy who fears chaos, a little boy who sucked his thumb in terror when his mother left him alone to run to the corner store for milk, a little boy who always told the substitute teacher what the classroom rules were, a little boy who performed every humiliating task his fraternity brothers set for him during hazing season because it was in the rules. Here, Donald, we keep absolute order. There are no exceptions and no gray areas. You'll fit right in, my son. Right in."

Ressler spat a series of words at him that startled

even Keen. The Beekeeper seemed unfazed.

"We need to teach you, Donald," was all he said. "You need to learn the rules. In an orderly way."

"Orderly," echoed Pug.

The Beekeeper nodded to the drones. From the wall one of them took a Y-shaped device designed to trap a person against a wall, a man-catcher. The other drone whipped Ressler's cage open and with lightning speed, the first then caught Ressler under the arms in the rubbery prongs of the Y and slammed him against the stone wall at the back of his pen. Pug giggled.

"What are you doing?" Keen grasped the bars of her own cage, her heart pounding.

The Beekeeper drew a taser from his belt.

"Rule Number Two: *Drones speak with respect*, Donald. Drones who disobey are stung. We keep order here."

"Back off. Don't!" Ressler fought against the man-catcher, but he had no leverage. The Beekeeper calmly pressed the taser against his flailing arm. There was a *snap*.

"Ressler!" Keen cried.

Ressler convulsed, his face a mask of pain. He went limp. The drone holding the man-catcher withdrew it, and Ressler dropped to the ground. The Beekeeper, his face a picture of calm, kicked him in the stomach. Ressler grunted but his muscles didn't respond.

"You will address me as 'Dr. Griffin' or as 'Beekeeper,'" the Beekeeper said. "And you will follow our rules. Do you understand?"

Ressler pushed himself up to hands and knees. Like all agents, Keen had been hit with a taser as part of her FBI training, and she knew exactly how he felt—a burning pain at the spot where the taser hit, an awful jolt of electricity, loss of muscle control even though you were wide awake, weakness afterward. If the user cranked the power high enough, it could knock you out, or even kill.

"*Do you understand, drone?*" the Beekeeper repeated.

Ressler remained silent.

Keen silently willed him to answer. She knew what was coming.

The Beekeeper moved as if to taser Ressler again, then backed out of the cage. "Very well," he said. "The old man, then. Go ahead, Pug."

"What?" Stuart said.

Pug didn't bother with the man-catcher. He hauled Stuart out of his cage and brought him to the Beekeeper.

"I broke no rules!" Stuart protested. "We can talk about this, sir. I am perfectly—"

"A slight against one member of the Hive is a slight against all," Dr. Griffin said. "And to punish one member of the Hive is to punish all. Your pain will become his pain."

"But—"

"Wait!" Ressler said, and pushed himself upright again. "I'm sorry. Sir. I… didn't mean disrespect. I apologize. I understand the rules."

Dr. Griffin gave him a beatific smile that made Keen's skin crawl.

"Very good, new drone. That's very good. Here you go. Some nectar."

From a nearby cooler on the floor, he produced a bottle of soda and set it in Ressler's cage. Cold water droplets and bits of crushed ice glistened on the bottle's rounded contours. Keen's gaze was riveted, and her thirst burned. The thought of the cold, quenching nectar washing down her throat was almost unbearable.

"Oooo," said Pug. "Nectar! What do you say now?"

"Thank you?" Ressler said. He cracked open the

bottle and drank. His troubled expression became one of relief.

Keen recognized what was happening. The group leader created distress, blamed it on the new member to create feelings of guilt, then offered both a solution to the distress and a physical reward when the member applied the solution. The sugar and caffeine in the soda would give Ressler a temporary kick that would make him feel good for a short time, and Ressler would associate following the rules with the sugar high from the soda. Classic conditioning. But the sugar rush would wear off soon, and bring a crash afterward, allowing the Beekeeper to create more distress and offer more solutions. All this Keen saw in an instant, but she couldn't say anything without revealing who she was and why she was here.

"Good drone," the Beekeeper said. Then he touched the taser to Stuart's arm as Pug let go. Stuart gave a cry of pain and dropped to the floor. Keen gave a cry of her own. The guards dragged the moaning, gasping Stuart back into his pen.

"Did you feel his pain, Donald?" Dr. Griffin said. "I'm sure you won't make a mistake again. Soon you'll be ready to join us in full. In the morning, we begin."

"It won't hurt long," Pug said with a reassuring nod. "And you'll feel better. Really! It'll be okay."

"Come along, Pug," said Dr. Griffin.

"Okay, Beekeeper."

When he and the guards had left, Keen turned to Stuart. She couldn't reach him through the narrow gaps in the bars, but she could see him. He was an old man. What if the taser had stopped his heart?

"Stuart!" she whispered. "Are you all right? Stuart!"

Stuart slowly sat up on the stone floor. He blinked

blearily. "That was not an experience I care to repeat."

Ressler set the empty soda bottle with its cap in the corner of his cell. Keen knew he didn't want to throw it away in case it became useful somehow. He might find a way to carve a tool out of the plastic, or even fill the bottle with his own urine to make it heavy and therefore useful as a weapon.

"What happened to you?" he said to Keen. Stuart's cell was between them, so they talked past the older man's head. "The last I saw, you made it to the woods. Did you get hold of… anyone?"

"No cell signals anywhere," Keen said. "Reddington and I found a place to hide, but I got caught. What happened to you two?"

"They stopped shooting and grabbed me," Ressler said. "A group of them flanked Reddington's car, and that was the end of it. I thought they'd kill me, but they just hauled me in here. I still don't know why."

"They want us to join, of course," Stuart said calmly. "Don't you see? They always need people. If we stay long enough, we'll be members of the Beekeeper's Hive."

"The hell with that," said the Bodysnatcher from his own cell. Keen jumped a little. She had all but forgotten he was there. "The Beekeeper was one of my best clients. Now this? I'm not joining anything, and screw his Hive. I'm getting out of here."

The thirst continued to burn at the back of Keen's throat, but her investigative instincts took over anyway.

"I'm Elizabeth Keen. This is Donald Ressler and Stuart Ivy. What's your name?"

"BS," he said dryly.

"Reddington called you the Bodysnatcher," Ressler said. "Is that who you are?"

The man shrugged. "Some people call me that."

"Did you take a woman named Mala Rudenko?" Keen asked.

The Bodysnatcher looked at her.

"I don't talk about clients, either to confirm or deny."

"Look," Ressler said reasonably, "we need to work together if we want to get out of this."

"Sure, sure." The Bodysnatcher paced his cell. "That doesn't mean we're going to be best friends and make s'mores, okay? I just want to get as far away from here as possible."

"Hmm," Stuart said.

"What do we do?" Ressler said.

"I'm thirsty," Keen said. "And starving."

"As am I," Stuart put in. "We all are. Except for him. Ressler."

"Me?" Ressler looked taken aback.

"He gave *you* an extra favor. A bottle of pop," the Bodysnatcher said.

Pop. Not *soda.* That was Great Lakes dialect. Keen filed that away.

"He likes you," Stuart continued. "He *favors* you, the pretty boy. The chosen one."

Ressler flushed a little. "Now look—"

"Don't do that," Keen interrupted. "That's what the Beekeeper wants. He's going to use rewards and treats, and give them out unevenly. It's prison psychology. We get mad at the person who gets the extra food instead of getting mad at the person who's giving out the pain and the rewards. Don't fall for it."

"It's hard when you're half dehydrated," Stuart growled.

"Just follow along with what he says and look for an opening," Ressler said. "They'll make a mistake eventually. Our biggest weapon is that they want us alive.

And we have people who will come looking for us."

"In this place?" the Bodysnatcher scoffed. "No one finds anything in this place. People vanish all the time. How do you think the Beekeeper has managed to keep his location a secret for so long?"

"Where do they get the food from?" Keen countered. "They have to get that soda from somewhere."

"Don't know, don't care." The Bodysnatcher slumped down in his cell. "Wake me up when room service gets here with morning coffee."

Keen exchanged looks with Ressler. He shrugged. She took a quick inventory of her cell. It wasn't much bigger than a closet. Close-set steel bars made up the front and sides, and the stone of the cave created the back wall. A camp toilet squatted in the corner, and Keen cringed at the thought of using it, especially in front of Ressler. On the floor was a thin foam camp mattress topped with a flimsy blanket. Already her earlier sweatiness had turned into a chill—the cave was probably in the fifties—and she was glad of her suit jacket and high-necked blouse. Nothing else in the cell—no sink, no tap, no water supply, no window. God, she was thirsty. The Beekeeper was deliberately keeping her that way.

Keen sat cross-legged on the mattress to think. She couldn't plan aloud with Ressler, not with the others in earshot. And it was damned hard to form coherent thoughts with her tongue as heavy and dry as sand.

Cult leaders like the Beekeeper were narcissists. They thrived on the worship and control of their followers. Flattery, utter obedience, and total belief in everything they said—even the stuff that made no sense—paved the fastest paths to their hearts. Many of them were also motivated by sexual demands and used their followers as harems. Keen shivered, hoping it wouldn't come to that. Most of them didn't believe the twaddle they flung at the faithful, but a scary handful actually did. These were the most dangerous—they would choose belief over self-preservation. David Koresh and Jim Jones had been true believers. Both had died and taken most of their followers along with them. It would be easier if the Beekeeper was motivated by greed, power, or both.

A drone, unmasked, entered the room. "Lights out."

The little cavern was plunged into blackness so absolute, Keen couldn't see her own fingers when she waggled them in front of her eyes.

"Keen?" Ressler said from the dark.

"Yeah?"

"We're going to get out of here."

She heard the nervousness in his voice. "Listen to me, Ressler. You, too, Stuart. And Bodysnatcher guy, whatever your name is. No matter what they tell you to do, do it. Go along. Don't give Griffin an excuse. Got it?"

"Yes, understood," Stuart said. "It's cold in here. It's hard to believe it's a hot summer night up there."

"Fold your mattress in half for better insulation and curl up on it," Ressler said. "We have friends who'll come for us."

"John," said the Bodysnatcher suddenly.

"What?" Keen said.

"Call me John," replied the Bodysnatcher.

"Is that your real name?" Keen said.

"It's either that or the Bodysnatcher."

"Let's sleep, please," Stuart put in. "I have the feeling we'll have precious little of it."

Working in the absolute darkness, Keen folded her mattress in half as Ressler advised and curled up under her blanket, trying not to think about her itchy skin or her dry throat or the chill that was settling over her. Maybe Reddington had been right. Maybe this hadn't been the best course of action.

Lights blasted into eyes and snapped her awake. A terrible noise crashed through the cell.

"Wake up!" said a drone. He was banging on the bars with a billy club. "Up!"

Keen found herself on her feet with her heart in her throat and no memory of actually standing up. She had gone from dead asleep to warp speed with no transition between, but now the alarm was wearing off and fatigue settled back over her. Her mind felt stiff and foggy. How long had she been asleep? There was no way to tell without her watch or a view of the sky. She felt disoriented and off-balance. Her mouth was so dry, her tongue had become a pile of sawdust.

Her eyes adjusted to the glare. Ressler and the others were on their feet as well, though Stuart was moving more stiffly. The thin mattress and the stone floor weren't kind to arthritic joints.

A young woman held a styrofoam tray by a sideways slot in the bars. On the tray were a jelly sandwich, an apple, a sealed plastic glass of orange juice, and a tiny styrofoam bowl with what proved to be honey in the bottom. It was the orange juice that held Keen's attention.

"You may eat," said the woman. She was dressed as a drone, too, but didn't wear a mask. Her belt bristled with a pistol, a taser, and extra clips of ammo. "But first you must say the blessing."

"Blessing?" Keen croaked.

"Blessings on the Beekeeper, blessings on the Hive," the girl singsonged. "We are one with the Beekeeper, one with the Hive."

Keen was still half asleep, but enough of her was awake to want to rebel. What kind of whack job...? However, her parched body demanded that orange juice, held tantalizingly just out of reach.

They're empty words, she told herself. *This is why you're here.*

Keen tried to repeat the words, but had forgotten half of them, and her stiff tongue barely obeyed her anyway. The woman prompted her until she got it right.

"...one with the Hive," Keen said at last.

The woman passed the tray through. Keen snatched it from her and ripped open the orange juice. It was one of those stingy cup-sized deals that cheap companies set out at conferences. Keen could have emptied it in a gulp. But she forced herself to drink slowly. The sugar in the orange juice coursed through her veins and perked her up even as the liquid washed some of the dryness from her throat. Once that was done, she was able to pay better attention to the woman.

And then she realized: she was looking at Mala Rudenko.

CHAPTER NINE

"Mala," said Keen gently.

The woman looked startled. "How do you know my name?"

"Your father is looking for you," Keen said quietly. "He's worried about you."

Other drones, including Pug, were delivering similar trays to Stuart, Ressler, and the Bodysnatcher—or John, she supposed. Each delivery required the prisoner to recite the same blessing. Stuart said it quickly. Ressler and John did so with obvious reluctance.

"No!" Pug was saying to Ressler. "You have to say it like you mean it! Now try again. I know you can do it, okay?"

Keen whispered, "We'll get you out of here. Help us any way you can."

Mala looked away. "No one gets out of here. No one escapes the Hive. You'll see that."

"How so?" Keen murmured. "I mean, Dr. Griffin isn't all-powerful."

"Don't talk like that!" Mala hissed. "It's a sin, and they'll hurt you. Just do as the Beekeeper says, and everything will be fine."

Keen pursed her lips under a wave of pity and heartbreak. Poor Mala had gone missing weeks ago, and during that entire time, she'd been in the clutches of the Beekeeper. She had become a full-blown member of the Hive, a drone who would drink a whole barrel of special Kool-Aid if they told her. What had the Beekeeper done to her? The pity turned to outrage. It wasn't just Mala—it was all the drones. The Beekeeper was snatching them away from their homes and raising them like animals to be his slaves, body and soul.

"It'll be fine, yeah," Keen said. "You're right. I'm sorry."

Mala glanced around, as if afraid one of the others might hear. "And Pavel Rudenko isn't my father. He never was."

"How do you mean?" Keen was wolfing down the sandwich now. It was strawberry jelly on white bread—pure carbs and no protein. The apple and the honey were the same. All of it was designed to give Keen a sugar high that would crash in an hour or so, leaving her weak and shaky and wanting more food, a fact the Beekeeper would certainly exploit. He knew his stuff.

"The Beekeeper is my father," Mala said earnestly. "The Hive is my family. We'll be your family, too."

Keen nodded, hiding her interior dismay. The Beekeeper's brainwashing had gone deep. Keen checked for crumbs on the tray. Her plan was to join the Hive, but observe carefully and find a weakness to exploit. The Beekeeper wasn't perfect, and neither was the Hive. Play along, pretend to get sucked in, then bring the Hive down from inside. Just like the bees who invaded a foreign hive.

"I don't know what kind of family treats you like this," Keen said as if more bewildered than angry.

"The shocks and the cages. Isn't that over-the-top?"

"Only if you disobey," Mala said. "It's bliss if you just obey. Everyone knows that. Desire creates conflict, but obedience erases desire. Obey the Hive, and you have no desire, no conflict. It's bliss."

"Huh." Keen crunched the apple down, taking care to suck out every bit of moisture as she went. "I'll have to think about that."

"What's happening now?" Ressler was finishing his own tray of food. He looked rumpled from sleep.

"Put these on," said Pug. "Give us your clothes. You'll match us now!"

Each of the newcomers were passed a folded pile of cloth through the bars. Keen shook hers open. It was a drab green jumpsuit, same as the ones the other drones wore, though these had no belts for weapons. Outdoors, they would blend well into the woods. Keen retreated to the rear of her cell and turned her back to change.

"No underwear!" another drone barked. "We're all the same underneath!"

Until you meet skin, thought Keen sourly. She refused to look toward Ressler—or Stuart—and managed the change as fast as she could, feeling the eyes of the drones on her all the while. Were the men just as bothered, she wondered?

Once everyone was done, the drones opened the cages and handcuffed each of the prisoners with their hands in front.

"If you try to run, the Beekeeper says we have to kill you," Pug said matter-of-factly as the cold cuffs clicked on Keen's wrists. "There are lots and lots of Hive people down here, and they will catch you. I would be too scared to run away."

"There's no need for these." Stuart held up his bound hands. "I certainly won't hare off. These old bones of mine wouldn't make it far anyway."

"We always follow the rules," Mala said. "Come on."

"Where are we going?" John the Bodysnatcher demanded.

"The Circle," said Pug happily. "You will join us!"

The drones hauled them down one tunnel, and then another. There was a whole warren down here. They ended up in a small room lined with poured concrete and lit with harsh white light. Keen blinked at the brightness. A circle of plastic folding chairs sat in the center, along with a cooler. Keen had been expecting something rather less prosaic—a stone altar or diagrams painted in red on the floor. This looked straight out of WalMart. Ritual work for a trailer park.

Her gaze went to the cooler, wondering if food or water might be in it. Thirst still burned through her, and the food had done little to fill her stomach. She knew very well that deprivation of food, water, and sleep were all tools of indoctrination into large groups. The military, in fact, pioneered several methods, and the Beekeeper, Keen remembered, had spent extensive time training soldiers in the army. Knowing this didn't change her desire for water or sleep one bit.

"Come to order now. Sit," came a commanding voice and the Beekeeper himself entered the room, looking well-fed and comfortable, easy in his power. Even his white hair was neatly combed. He adjusted his coke-bottle glasses and gestured at the chairs. Cautiously, everyone took seats. The drones, including Mala and Pug, stood in a ring outside the chairs, guarding. Dr. Griffin took up the chair closest to the cooler. The taser still hung from his belt. The other drones each carried multiple weapons.

"There's no need to fear," Dr. Griffin said in that calm, measured voice. "You are one of us. One of my family. One of my Hive."

"What if we don't want to be?" John growled. "You and I had a deal. We—"

"You want to be one of us," the Beekeeper interjected, "even if you don't know it yet. We start all of our sessions with a salute. It goes like this." He patted his chest over his heart with his right hand twice. "We are the Hive!"

All the drones around the circle patted their own chests and said in unison, "*We are the Hive!*"

"Now you." The Beekeeper removed a box of snack crackers and a plastic bottle of honey from the cooler. "Everyone together now. 'We are the Hive.'"

Ressler folded his arms around the handcuffs. The Bodysnatcher didn't move.

Keen glanced at the tasers each drone carried. It was clear what would happen if she disobeyed, and in any case, she wanted to convince the Beekeeper that she was joining the Hive, get them to trust her so she could find out what they were up to and take them down from inside. Therefore, she should go along with the salute.

No, she thought almost instantly. Dr. Griffin wouldn't believe a conversion if it came too quickly. With another unhappy glance at the tasers, she pursed her lips and remained silent, though her heart beat fast in painful anticipation.

Stuart felt no such compunctions. He patted his chest and said, "We are the Hive."

"Excellent, Stuart!" The Beekeeper squeezed a dollop of honey onto the cracker and held it above Stuart's nose. "Open."

Uncertainly, Stuart opened his mouth and Dr. Griffin dropped the honeyed cracker inside, like a trainer rewarding a dog. Stuart crunched. Keen's mouth watered despite herself.

"What do you say?" Dr. Griffin prompted.

"Thank you, Beekeeper," Stuart said, spraying crumbs.

The Beekeeper beamed his praise, then turned to the others. "The rest of you failed your first order."

Before Keen could react further, a taser tapped her back and electricity jolted through her. It was as bad as she remembered from her training. Her muscles convulsed and burned, and she went limp.

"I am sorry," Pug said behind her. "But you broke a rule. Are you okay?"

John and Ressler both shouted out as they got taser jolts of their own. John fell out of his chair, and two drones hauled him back into it.

Anger and pain in equal measures flared in Keen, but she couldn't do much about either. Her muscles took several seconds to respond, and awful pain followed. Finally she was upright in the chair again.

"Just follow the rules," Mala told her quietly. "You don't need to think. Just do."

The other drones were murmuring to John and Ressler. Keen forced herself upright as Dr. Griffin took out more honey and crackers.

"Once more," he said. "We are the Hive!"

All the members of the outer circle repeated the salute. So did Stuart. Then John.

Keen sat on her anger and decided she could get away with obeying now. She tapped her chest. "We are the Hive," she said.

Ressler remained stubbornly silent.

"Very good!" Dr. Griffin clapped his hands like an elementary school teacher and held a honeyed cracker over Keen's nose. She felt like a puppy being offered a treat, but she was so hungry, she found she didn't care. "Open."

"Hooray!" Pug said.

She crunched the sweet, salty treat down, savoring it. John and Stuart got one each, and Keen couldn't help but notice that this was Stuart's second one.

It's your own fault, she thought. *You could have had one the first time.* She clamped down on that line of thinking. It was what the Beekeeper wanted.

"Donald," the Beekeeper said, "you still need to learn."

"Screw you," Ressler said, and screamed when the taser hit him again.

"Twice, please," the Beekeeper said. "Once for disobeying, and once for disrespect."

"No swearing," Pug agreed.

Keen looked away when Ressler screamed the third time. Her face was hot, and she wanted to hit the drones, attack the Beekeeper. But she sat still.

"Now, Donald," the Beekeeper said again when Ressler had recovered, "once again. We are the Hive."

Everyone in the circle except Ressler repeated the salute.

A spark snapped from the taser in the hand of the drone behind Ressler, and this time Keen said, "Please! Just say it, Ressler. For me."

Ressler looked at her, his blue eyes hard. She pleaded with him silently. A drop of sweat slid down Ressler's cheek. The circle held its breath.

At last, Ressler nodded. He slapped his chest with his cuffed hand. "We are the Hive," he said.

"Delightful!" the Beekeeper shouted, reminding

Keen for a horrible moment of Reddington. The Beekeeper dropped a honey cracker into Ressler's mouth, then took from the cooler a half-sized bottle of cola. "And this is for you, Elizabeth, my star pupil, for helping Donald see the way."

He placed the cool bottle in Keen's hands. Everyone was watching in undisguised envy. Keen could almost feel the liquid pouring down her parched throat, especially after the salt from the cracker. The Beekeeper nodded encouragingly.

"Please, sir," she said, "may I give it to Stuart? He needs it more."

The Beekeeper clapped his hands again. "You've just uncovered Rule Number One, Elizabeth."

"The needs of the Hive outweigh the needs of its members," intoned the people in the circle, including Pug.

"But in this case," the Beekeeper continued, "your need outweighs Stuart's. So drink up."

"Oh." Keen kept her voice meek. "Thank you, Dr. Griffin."

She drained the bottle. It was the best soda of her life. Ressler gave her a look of... jealousy? She couldn't blame him. The cool soda washed her throat clean and made her extremities tingle. The Beekeeper's beaming face surmounted it all, and Keen made herself look elsewhere. She didn't want to connect that image with the delights of the soda.

"Now we're going to play a game," Dr. Griffin said. "It's called Judge."

"May I watch?" An older woman—gray hair pulled into a bun, gray eyes, crow's feet—entered the room. She wore a modestly cut gray dress, and Keen wondered why she was the only person who wasn't wearing a green jumpsuit.

"Hi, Mrs. Griffin!" Pug almost shouted. "I am glad to see you!"

"Honey," Dr. Griffin said reproachfully, "we're at a delicate moment. I'd much rather that you—"

"But I enjoy this part so much," she whined. "Please?"

"She should stay," Pug said in a quiet voice.

Dr. Griffin reached up and took her hand from his chair. "I can't say no to you. Just stay out of the way, then."

"Of course," she said. "We are the Hive."

"We are the Hive," said everyone in the room automatically, including Keen.

Mrs. Griffin edged to the wall and leaned against it, folding her bony arms against a non-existent chest. What kind of life did the wife of a cult leader live? Keen didn't want to think about it.

"As I was saying," the Beekeeper said, drawing Keen's attention again, "the game we're playing is called Judge. It helps us remember that without the group, we are all unhappy, low-born insects, but together we are strong. The rules are simple. One person sits in the center of our security circle and confesses to the group any sins he or she has committed or thought of. The rest of us shout the Hive's opinion of those sins. Mala will go first to demonstrate."

Mala took the chair in the center of the circle. Her face was tight, and Keen noticed how her body was tense. Mala might be familiar with the game, but that didn't mean she liked it.

The young woman took a breath and said, "I thought about my father today and wondered what he was doing."

Mrs. Griffin and all the drones in the outer circle

pointed at her. In one voice, they shouted, *"Filth!"*

Keen jumped. Stuart flinched. Mala bent her head. Pug nodded.

"Everyone together," the Beekeeper prompted. "Sins cannot be expiated without the will of the group."

"But it's not a sin to think of your family," John objected.

The drone behind John stung him with the taser. John jerked in his chair and went limp, then recovered with a groan.

"Order. It is a sin to think of your life outside this group," the Beekeeper admonished. "And John—you have something to confess when your turn comes. Now, everyone?"

The new members, including John and Ressler, pointed at Mala and, without much conviction, said, "Filth."

"Stronger!" the Beekeeper ordered. "Louder! Feel the hatred toward her sin!"

They exchanged glances, then obeyed. "Filth!"

"Again! As loud as you can."

"Filth!"

The shout reverberated against Keen's bones like primal drums.

"Continue, Mala," said Dr. Griffin.

"I wanted more food after the last meal," Mala said. *"Filth!"*

Keen's head felt floaty, like a bit of flotsam in a wave pool. The abrupt sugar rush and the shout swept her away.

"I... wanted time by myself," Mala said. *"Filth!"*

"Very good," the Beekeeper said. "You are forgiven, Mala. Come out of the circle."

Mala looked shaken, but exited with dignity. Her

eyes met Keen's as she moved, and she gave a small nod, though Keen didn't know what it meant. Still, Keen nodded back. An ally was an ally.

The Beekeeper gave Mala an entire package of cheese sandwich crackers. Mala tore into them. The smell of cheese spread—protein—filled the air, and Keen stared with open desire at that package. Licking her fingers, Mala returned to her place behind Keen.

"Donald, you next," said the Beekeeper.

Ressler glared at Dr. Griffin. "I don't—"

"Just do it, Ressler," Keen put in quickly. "Please."

The drone behind him raised the taser. Ressler cut himself off and took the central chair, his handcuffed hands in his lap. His blond hair was a mess, and his eyes were rimmed red.

"Three sins," said Dr. Griffin. "You'll feel better once you confess, Donald."

"I don't know what a sin is," Ressler said, not quite growling.

"Anything that keeps you apart from the group," Dr. Griffin explained in his even voice. "Deeds or thoughts about food you aren't allowed to have, sexual desires, forbidden behaviors and thoughts leading to the same."

"What behaviors are forbidden?" Ressler asked.

Keen recognized his tactic. He was stalling, trying to buy time. Standard FBI procedure. But in here, those rules didn't work. No one knew where they were. Except Reddington. And anyway, Keen reminded herself, she *wanted* to be here. She wanted to find a way to bring this smug bastard down.

"Anything that goes against the direct orders of the Hive is forbidden," Dr. Griffin said.

"And direct orders come from… you?" Ressler said.

"Now you know!" crowed Pug.

"I often speak for the Hive," said Dr. Griffin. "Its voice is my voice. Confess, Donald. What sins are you hiding?"

Ressler chewed on his lip. "I... wanted some of Keen's soda."

Everyone, including Keen, pointed and shouted.

"*Filth!*"

"I felt tired and didn't want to come here to this circle," Ressler hazarded.

"*Filth!*"

"I want to go home," Ressler finished.

"*Filth!*"

"Nicely done, Donald," said the Beekeeper. "Quite orderly. Don't you feel better now?"

"Sure," Ressler said tightly.

"Uh oh," said Pug.

Calmly, and without apparent rancor, the Beekeeper stood up and slugged Ressler across the jaw.

Keen jerked upright and almost scrambled to his defense, handcuffs or no. Only the movement of Mala's taser out of the corner of her eye held her in her chair.

"What the hell?" Ressler snarled.

"You lied," the Beekeeper boomed, standing over him. His powerful presence pressed Ressler into the floor. Tension tightened the room. "You didn't feel better. Never, ever lie to us, Donald. We'll know. Ask for the Hive's forgiveness."

Ressler glared up at him. He remained silent for a moment.

Keen held her breath.

Ressler said, "Will you forgive me for lying?"

The Beekeeper beamed and the tension was broken. "Of course, Donald. All you need do is ask." And he gave Ressler a packet of cheese-spread crackers and a cup of apple juice.

Ressler clearly tried to hold back, but he ripped through them like a child at snack time anyway.

"Stuart?" the Beekeeper said.

Stuart gravely took his place in the center chair, as if he were attending a group therapy session. In a twisted way, Keen supposed, he was.

Stuart didn't hesitate. "I was angry at the people who shot my friends," he said.

"Filth!"

"I wanted more food and drink."

"Filth!"

Keen found herself shouting louder than before.

"I wanted a shower. Still do."

"Filth!"

"Excellent!" The Beekeeper clapped the old man on the shoulder. "Do you feel better?"

"Actually, I do," Stuart said, looking surprised. "Who knew?"

"Now *that* was the truth."

The Beekeeper gave Stuart crackers and soda, which Stuart took back to his chair with dignity.

"Elizabeth?" the Beekeeper said.

Slowly, with reluctance she didn't have to feign, Keen took the center chair.

"I... wanted more food and drink," she began. That seemed safe.

"Filth!"

Keen wasn't prepared for her own reaction. She had been sure she was ready for the assembled group to yell at her. It would just be empty noise. But the shouted word punched through her with unexpected power. For a split second she was back in high school, wanting to be part of the popular girl group that sat at the center table in the cafeteria, but the pop girls laughed her aside, and she slunk to a table in the corner instead. Keen hadn't thought about that incident in years, had thought she was long over it, but the disapprobation of the crowd brought it crashing back to her, and she felt ready to slink off to her corner again. Her shoulders slumped. Forcing her thoughts to change direction, she tried to reassert herself. She was an adult, and had done nothing wrong. These people had murdered a dozen agents, including Agent Gillford, and kidnapped her. Why would she care what they thought? She started to straighten herself—

—and remembered why she was here. Ressler might be here to fight. Keen was here to infiltrate. She allowed her shoulders to slump back down, the picture of unhappy timidity. She cast about for something to confess, something that would help her cause. Her eye lighted on Mala and an idea came.

"I envied Mala her beauty," she said. "I wanted to look like her."

Mala looked startled, and she missed the *Filth!* admonition. She cocked her head, and smiled a little at Keen, who shrugged.

"And your third sin?" the Beekeeper prompted.

Keen opened her mouth and, to her horror, realized she was going to say something about her daughter. Give that up to the Beekeeper? Never. Not even to ingratiate herself. Her fingers found the Y-shaped scar on her left hand and she traced its outline—up one side, in and out of the valley, down the other side. Her will strengthened a little. Her words changed before she could say them.

"I wanted to take Stuart's crackers," she said.

"*Filth!*" the group shouted.

The stress was over. Keen accepted the packet of crackers and the juice from Dr. Griffin and took her original seat with shaky legs.

"Doesn't that feel better?" said Dr. Griffin.

And Keen had to admit she *did* feel better, in a weird way. It was no doubt caused by a small endorphin rush when the stress was lifted. However, this allowed her to nod truthfully, and the Beekeeper accepted the gesture gravely.

"You're becoming part of the group," he said. "I'm proud of you."

"Yay!" said Pug.

Keen tore into the food and gulped the juice without comment. John the Bodysnatcher was up next, but Keen barely listened to his confession and shouted "*Filth!*" by rote. She was sleepy now, and wondered what time it was. The disorientation made her feel unnerved and restless, off-balance.

"Nicely done, all of you," the Beekeeper said. "You're well on your way to becoming full members of the Hive. We'll protect you from our enemies, the ones who want to hurt us, who want to stop us, who want to bring us down. Remember, you—we—are strong together. No one can stand against us. Follow the Hive, and you will have strength beyond your imagination. Together, we will take this country back to its rightful place. We are love! We are life! We are the Hive!"

Everyone in the room tapped their chests twice and repeated, "We are the Hive!"

Ressler did it a little late, but he did it.

"Now it's time for work," the Beekeeper said. "That's Rule Number Three: *Work keeps the hands busy and the soul happy.* The drones will show you. Off you go!"

Mala and the rest of the outer circle prodded Keen

and the others to their feet. They shuffled out of the room, leaving the Beekeeper and his wife behind.

"Where are we going now?" Keen asked Mala, who was walking beside her down the tunnel.

"A side chamber," she said. "They always need work. If you do well, you can be promoted to working in the main chamber, under the Great Tree."

"I love the Great Tree," Pug said. "It's so beautiful."

"The Great Tree?" Keen echoed, confused.

"The stone one, carved into the side of the cave," Mala said. "You must have seen it when you came in. Dr. Griffin found it in this cave. It was carved long ago by the Great Elders. They spoke to him, and told him this was a sacred place. They gave him the wisdom to start the Hive, and we have been here ever since."

"I would like to examine this Great Tree in more detail," Stuart spoke up. "It sounds like a transformative experience."

"It is," Mala agreed, "but that privilege must be earned."

"What's transformative mean?" asked Pug.

"Quiet now," said another drone. "The Great Elders judge us by our actions, not our words."

"Yes," said Mala, ducking her head.

"Sorry," added Pug.

"What time is it?" Ressler asked.

In answer, his accompanying drone jabbed him in the ribs with a taser. Ressler grunted and went down. Keen suppressed an urge to reach down to help him and instead schooled her expression into one of disinterest. The drones pulled the others up short to wait until Ressler recovered enough to drag himself to his feet. He stumbled against a drone for a moment, and the drone had to help him upright.

"What the he—what was that for?" Ressler demanded.

"Rule Number Four," barked the drone. "There is no time."

"No time," John repeated. "That sounds... enlightened."

Ressler tightened his jaw, but said nothing more. The masked drones led them the rest of the way down the tunnel to a small room that was definitely a work in progress. The walls were rough-hewn stone, the floor was uneven, and only a single bulb on an exposed cord provided light. Pickaxes, hammers, chisels, and other tools littered the ground.

"Put these on," a drone commanded, handing each of them a goggle-eyed mask. Keen realized it was meant to protect her eyes and lungs from dust. "Start chipping. Enlarge the room."

Keen picked up a pickaxe and swung it against the wall. The shock clanged through her hands and wrists.

"Not like that!" said the drone. "Together. I'll make the rhythm. Orderly, now. One, two, three, go!"

The group chipped at the room in unison while the drone chanted and the others stood guard with their tasers.

Keen swung her pickaxe like a good little drone.

Pug beamed. "You got it!"

CHAPTER TEN

Time passed in a fog for Keen. She couldn't tell how much time, couldn't even guess at hours or days. She never saw sunlight or a clock, and the Hive interrupted her sleep patterns so badly, she couldn't keep track of anything through the haze of fatigue. She suspected they weren't letting her have more than three or four hours of rest at a time. And food was a continual problem. Whatever they gave her, she snatched up and gulped down. The food was high in carbs, and protein was in rare supply, so she was always a little hungry, a little light-headed. The initial rush of sugar always made her feel a little better, even grateful, and she fought against the feeling, recognizing it for the manipulation it was. But it was difficult when she was so damned *tired* all the time.

The mind-numbing labor forced her to work in unison with Ressler, Stuart, and John, endlessly chipping out the room. It was an eerie sensation, working to the rhythm chanted by the masked drone with Ressler and the others in masks that made them look like goggle-eyed insects.

And every day—if she defined a "day" as the time between sleep cycles—she endured the Circle sessions with the Beekeeper. The litany of "sins" began to sound the same.

"I wanted to talk to my mother."

"*Filth!*"

"Last night, I had a dream about sex."

"*Filth!*"

"I snarled at one of my fellow drones."

"*Filth!*"

"Yay!" said Pug.

During these sessions, Keen always angled to sit near Dr. Griffin so she could get a better idea of the man than she already had, learn to read what was behind his words, but this was proving difficult. The fatigue and hunger were taking their toll, as was the constant fear of punishment. She'd been tased five or six times for sins and mistakes, and the thought of breaking one of the Beekeeper's rules was already making her flinch—which, she knew, was exactly what he wanted. Often Mrs. Griffin watched the sessions, always wearing the same gray dress, though she never reacted with more than a nod or a tiny smile. The one time Dr. Griffin addressed her directly, she only shook her head and backed away.

Keen did her best to show she was defecting away from Reddington and to the Hive. She answered questions about past sins, even though a number of them were awkward or embarrassing and she saw Ressler flush deeply. She did the nasty chipping work until blisters rose on her hands and her arms were covered with scratches and bruises from flying bits of rock. She pretended to be hesitant, then caved in and said what the Beekeeper wanted to hear. And yet, she sensed he hadn't quite warmed to her, though neither did he seem to suspect she was anything but another captive drone on the way to full brainwashing.

Mala, however, was another story. More than once, she smiled at Keen while slipping what passed for breakfast through her cage bars. At one point when they were on a break between work and circle time, Keen found herself alone with Mala some distance from the others. She glanced about, then decided to take a chance.

"This place is incredible," Keen said in a low voice, "and Dr. Griffin is a smart man, don't you think?"

"Oh, he is." Mala nodded. "We are the Hive."

Keen tapped her chest. "We are the Hive. Look, I know it's kind of frowned on to ask this kind of stuff, but just between us women—do the men here, you know, *do* stuff to you?"

"You mean like rape?" Mala said, shocked. "Dr. Griffin would never allow that. It's why he asks all those questions about sex. We have to control our impulses for the good of the group. If we aren't a good group, *they* will destroy everything we've worked for here."

"Right, yeah," Keen said. "That's a relief. I was really worried, you know?"

Mala touched her shoulder. "You can set that aside."

"You're a good friend." Keen paused. Now that they'd established a sort of intimacy, she could continue. "You mind if I ask how the Bodysnatcher got you here?"

"How?" Mala asked, puzzled.

"Yeah. How he grabbed you up without anyone noticing."

Mala stared at her in increasing bewilderment. "He didn't grab me up."

"He didn't?" Now it was Keen's turn to be confused. "Then—"

"I hired him to bring me here." Mala gave Keen a beatific smile.

"You—" Keen stopped herself, though her mind was whirling. Mala *wanted* to be here. "Why?"

"Most of us want to be here," Mala continued. "Only a few are transplants."

"Transplants?"

"People who are… selected. Pug, for example. He played college football, I think, but the Beekeeper selected him and had the Bodysnatcher bring him in because the Hive needed his strength. It took a lot of work to make him see things the right way, but the Beekeeper is really smart. He's always working to make the Hive strong."

Keen's jaw dropped and goosebumps crawled over her skin in cold prickles.

"Did the Beekeeper make Pug… the way he is?"

"He was majoring in English or social studies or something unimportant, but here, he's making a real contribution," Mala said. "I know it's a little hard for you to understand right now, but Dr. Griffin—the Beekeeper—is a great, great man. You can *see* his inner light. He protects us from *them*, the ones who suck away our souls like hornets stealing honey from a hive."

"Right," said Keen. "No, I get it. I'm… still learning. I want to learn more."

Mala took her hands. Keen still wore handcuffs.

"I'm glad, Elizabeth. Here there's no need to worry, no need to think about the outside world. Dr. Griffin protects us all. You'll be ready to help us in the main chamber and make honey and—"

"I saw the beehives up there." Keen pointed to the roof. She had learned not to say *outside* some time ago. "Is that what you mean by making honey?"

"Oh! No, no." Mala giggled a little. "That's just Dr. Griffin's hobby. It's how he started. Those apiaries—that's what they're called—are generations old, and he's nurtured them for decades. Just like us."

"And you—we—make honey, too?"

"Well…" Mala glanced around conspiratorially. "I shouldn't, but… you're coming along, right? You're entering the Hive, right?"

"We are the Hive," Keen said, tapping her chest.

"We are the Hive," Mala agreed. "The others are busy. Put your mask on and come on."

Keen obeyed, heart pounding now. Mala led her down other tunnels, and Keen tried to keep track of where she was. The warren was incredibly complex. Some of the caves were obviously natural, others had been dug from the stone—incredible, what slave labor could accomplish—and still others were natural caverns that had been enlarged. They passed a barrack lined with beds and lockers, a huge kitchen, a game room or lounge, and even what looked like a research lab filled with electronic equipment on one side and jugs of chemicals on the other.

A group of drones, unmasked, came toward them down the wide tunnel. Keen's breath caught in her throat and she tensed, but Mala continued walking, unconcerned. Air rattled in Keen's stuffy mask, and she pulled her sleeves down farther to hide the handcuffs. They would recognize her. They would drop her to the floor with painful tases, and then Dr. Griffin would punish her. Already her skin prickled with the anticipation of pain. Then Keen's fingers found the Y shape of the scar. Her heart slowed, and she straightened. *Walk with confidence*, she told herself. *If you look like you have something to hide, they'll suspect you.*

The drones passed by, chattering as they went, without giving Keen or Mala a second glance. When they were a few steps down the hall, Keen let out a long breath into her mask and her knees wobbled a little with relief. They hadn't recognized her. She—

"Hey!" One of the drones turned. All the others stopped. Keen's stomach twisted and fear sweat trickled down her back. Her mouth dried up.

"Are you taking the replacement shift in the kitchen?" the drone asked.

"Not us," Mala said. "They're coming along later."

Two of the drones looked at each other, then shrugged.

"We are the Hive." Keen tapped her chest.

"We are the Hive," everyone in the tunnel repeated. The drones turned and went on their way.

When the others were out of sight, Mala and Keen both collapsed against the wall. Mala was giggling like a child.

"That was great!" she said. "You totally fooled them!"

Keen smiled grimly inside her mask. So Mala wasn't entirely a Hive drone. There was a spark of rebel still in there somewhere. Not only that, Keen and Mala were sharing a moment, and it was something Keen could use. Her ability to get at Dr. Griffin seemed to be limited, but Mala was something else. The poor woman was clearly deluded, and the only way to help her was to destroy the Hive and get her out of here. For that, she and Keen had to become good friends.

"Is this a sin to confess later?" Keen said, pushing the bond between them.

"You're awful!" Mala said. "I don't think we should. Should we? Won't Dr. Griffin know?"

"I think we should keep quiet about it," Keen said. "That won't be a lie, technically."

"Okay." Mala seemed less sure of herself now, and Keen wondered if she had gone too far. "Let's go."

The tunnel opened into a cave that was only a little smaller than the big one out front. To Keen's surprise, it had machinery in it—a forklift, a robot arm, more laboratory equipment, and a bank of computers that lined one wall in a manner eerily reminiscent of the Post Office. A pile of what Keen guessed were packing crates covered with canvas drop cloths sat against the opposite wall, and a large doorway at the back, one big enough to admit a good-sized truck, was screened off with camouflage netting. Keen caught a glimpse of moonlight through the weave. It was night outside, then. Her brain tried to reorient itself around this new information. How many days and nights had she been down here? She had no idea.

"Is anyone in here?" she whispered.

"Not at this time of… not right now," Mala said. She strode to the pile of packing crates, which rested on pallets for the forklift. "This is where we make honey."

"I don't understand." Keen kept her voice low inside the mask, even though the great cavern was patently empty. The place seemed to swallow sound, and the grand space felt more like a church than a storeroom.

"See?" Mala pulled aside part of a canvas covering. Keen's fingers went cold. On the crate was stenciled a green circle. Within the green, three red circles orbited a fourth. Underneath were the words CAUTION: SARIN.

"Making honey," Mala said.

Keen swallowed hard. "You're making sarin gas? Like they used in Syria?"

"Like the methamphetamine," Mala said.

For sale, Keen thought. *Got a nice little weapons factory, don't you, Dr. Griffin? Meth and weaponized gas for sale. ISIS must love you.*

"What are all the guns for?" Keen asked. "All the weapons outside?"

"Dr. Griffin won't let outsiders hurt us," Mala said. "*They* are coming for us any day now, but we're ready."

"Who's *they*?" Keen said, keeping her voice low.

"Outsiders. The government and its allies," Mala said, equally hushed. "They're looking for us. They know how powerful the Hive is. We have groups all over the country, and when we rise up, we'll own the country at last. You're lucky you got in when you did."

"All over the country?" Keen's head was spinning. "You mean there are enclaves like this one in other places?"

"Well, yeah." Mala twitched the cover back into place. "Houston and New York and inside the Pentagon. And the International Space Station."

"The Space Station?" Keen was starting to feel like an echo.

"Dr. Griffin has been running it from the start," Mala said. "It's why we have all this communications equipment. We need it—he needs it—to contact the station. He keeps the cameras off us and when the time comes, he'll zap our enemies with the station's laser beams."

Oh.

The world righted itself and Keen was on firmer ground. The hallmark of a cult leader—create an *us vs. them* mentality, inflate the sense of the group's power, make outrageous promises that can't ever be proven. An awful idea came to Keen, and she asked the next question carefully.

"Are we hiding here because the… end of the world is coming?"

Mala blinked at her for a heart-squeezing moment. Doomsday cults were the most dangerous. They *wanted* to die, were taught to commit suicide, either by their own hands or by running into a hail of police bullets. Dismantling them was nearly impossible without all the members dying in some way. They also killed people who didn't want to die.

"Don't be silly," Mala scoffed. "Why would the world be ending?"

"Oh, good," Keen said, then took a little breath. *I hate to do this to you, Mala.* "I don't want to die, you know? Like your friend Iris."

Long pause. Keen could see the news break over Mala's face. Disbelief, followed by pain, followed by more disbelief.

"Iris is dead?" she gasped.

"I thought you knew," Keen said. "The FBI found her in her bathtub. She was… I'm sorry… someone had killed her. They think it was to keep her quiet about something. Was it about you? You being kidnapped?"

"Oh god." Mala put her hands to her mouth. Tears welled in her eyes. "Oh, Jesus. I didn't know. The Bodysnatcher promised no one would get hurt. That I'd just disappear."

"He must have figured Iris knew something," Keen said. "Did you say anything to her?"

"It's my fault!" Mala pulled at her hair. "I told Iris I was leaving, but I swore her to secrecy."

Keen tried to hug her, but her hands were still cuffed in front of her. Mala leaned against her and sobbed. Keen could smell sweat in Mala's hair.

"The Bodysnatcher must have found out," Keen

said, pushing the point home and hating herself for it. "Maybe he got hold of your texts or something."

"Oh god," Mala repeated. "No one was supposed to die. She was my best friend. The Beekeeper is—" She halted.

Keen waited a heartbeat. "Is what?"

"Nothing." Mala stood upright and swiped at her cheeks. "It's nothing. We are the Hive."

"We are the Hive." But Keen saw the seed of doubt.

"What are you doing in here?" said Dr. Griffin.

Keen jumped. Mala squeaked. The Beekeeper was standing in the entrance to the tunnel with three drones behind him. One of them was Pug. The Beekeeper's arms were folded and his face was a thunderstorm.

"You aren't supposed to be here," Pug said with a dark frown.

"I think it's time you were both re-educated," Dr. Griffin said. "Extensively."

Mala paled and looked ready to faint. Although Keen's heart was pounding hard enough to shake the front of her jumpsuit, she stepped forward.

"Don't blame her, Beekeeper. It was me."

"Was it?" The Beekeeper leveled a hard glare at her.

Keen lifted her chin. "I went off exploring and found this room. Mala came after me. She was just about to bring me down to you."

The Beekeeper turned his hard glare on Mala. "Is this true, child? Don't lie, now. I'll know."

"I… I…" Mala swallowed.

Keen silently urged her to lie. After sitting through several of the Beekeeper's circle sessions, Keen had come to the conclusion that his power to detect lies wasn't omniscient. He was just a good guesser. But Keen couldn't say that for sure.

"Mala?" the Beekeeper said.

"It's… true," Mala said. "I hate to rat out a fellow drone, but I followed her here. I stopped her before she damaged anything. I think she was just curious, Beekeeper."

"Please don't do anything awful," Keen begged. "I just wanted to see something besides the chipping cave and the cages. I'm so sorry."

The Beekeeper's face was hard. "Bring her back to the cages," he ordered the drones. "Mala, you should have caught this earlier and will have extra work duties in the coming days."

"Yes, sir," Mala whispered.

The drones hauled Keen to the cage room, where Ressler, Stuart, and John were already locked in.

"Where have you been?" John asked. His bland face was pale, and lines were beginning to show.

"Out and about," Keen replied shortly.

Once her door was shut, the Beekeeper entered.

Stuart grasped the bars on his own cage. "We are the Hive, sir," he said.

"We are the Hive," the Beekeeper said absently. "Elizabeth, I was most disappointed in you today. You were coming along splendidly, and then… this."

"I said I was sorry," Keen said. "I want to learn, I do. I just… got bored. It's a sin, I know. Please forgive me."

"Forgiveness must be earned," the Beekeeper said, and Keen wondered if that was a rule, too. "During the next session, I think, we'll take stronger measures. Meanwhile, Stuart, these are for you."

Pug opened Stuart's cage and swapped out his thin foam mattress for a real one, thick and soft. He also gave him an extra blanket.

"You will like these," Pug told him.

"Thank you, Beekeeper," Stuart said, surprised.

"Your sessions are going well," the Beekeeper said. "Tomorrow your work shift will be in the Great Room." And he left.

"What did you do, Keen?" Ressler asked. He was pale and shaky, too. The imprisonment was showing on him.

"I'll tell you later," Keen said.

"I hate this place," Ressler muttered.

"Really?" Stuart tested out his mattress. "I'm quite coming to like it."

"Was that sarcasm?" Ressler growled. "Because I'm not in the mood for—"

"Not at all, dear boy." Stuart lay back with his hands behind his head as if he were in a fine hotel. A soft note entered his voice. "There's less to think about here."

"What do you mean?" Keen said.

"My—our—needs are taken care of," Stuart said. "No money worries, no rent, no bills. And when I'm working, I'm not thinking about…" He trailed off.

"Your wife—Vivian?" Keen hazarded.

Stuart's silence spoke for him.

"How did she die?" Keen asked in her psychologist voice.

A sigh from Stuart's cage. "Not now. Not yet."

"I want the hell out of here," John said. "And I can confess to that in that stupid circle tomorrow, and the next day, and the next."

"Tonight," Ressler said. "We're escaping tonight."

A pang went through Keen. Ressler wasn't an experienced woodsman, and it didn't seem likely he'd slip past the Hive's watchful eyes. Not only that, but escaping would blow Keen's opportunity to bring down the Hive from within. On the off-chance

Ressler managed to get away and alert the FBI to their exact location, the FBI would lay siege to the place, resulting in a standoff every bit as bad as Waco. Worse, actually—the Hive had sarin gas and wasn't afraid to use it. Keen thought of an army of FBI agents twisting and gasping on the forest floor, coughing up bloody foam as they died in agony. No, no, and no. She had to bring down the Beekeeper from within, and quickly.

"Don't, Ressler," Keen said. "We need to stay here."

"Are you crazy? We need to get the hell out of this nutbag house of horrors." Ressler held up a small object Keen couldn't see very well because of the shadows in Ressler's cell. "I managed to swipe this."

"What is it?" Keen asked tightly.

"A way out," Ressler said smugly. "Remember when I fell against that guard a while ago? That wasn't an accident. Now I have his keys."

"Ressler—" Keen began.

"You want to stay here?" Ressler interrupted.

Keen bit her lip. She didn't want to tell Ressler about the sarin gas in front of John and Stuart. The existence of a highly toxic, classified chemical weapon wasn't something you talked about in front of civilians, especially criminal civilians. She needed to delay Ressler until she could find a way to let him in on it. But how?

"Look, we need to talk about this," she hedged. "But later, okay?"

"When?" Ressler was already unlocking his handcuffs. They fell to his mattress with a soft thump. "We're never alone."

That last was true. She tried again.

"I need to talk with you about other stuff. Just… wait."

"Rules and regs, Keen." Ressler sorted through the keys until he found a likely one and reached awkwardly through the bars to test it. It failed. "It's our duty to escape as soon as possible. You know that."

"I'm with the young lady," Stuart said. "It's too risky. If you want to leave, just wait. Eventually *they* will find you."

They. The word wasn't lost on Keen.

"You won't rat us out?" Ressler tried another key and twisted. The lock clicked.

"Heaven forbid." Stuart leaned against the bars. "Tomorrow I'm working in the main room."

Ressler slipped out of his cell. Keen whisper-shouted at him, "How are you going to get past all the drones?"

"Easy," Ressler said. "I'll conk one out and take his mask. The others won't know who I am until it's too late." He moved toward Keen's cage, key outstretched. "Come on."

Keen snaked a hand through the bars and grabbed his wrist. "No."

Ressler's blue eyes widened in surprise. "Are you serious?"

"Don't unlock that door, Ressler."

"They've gotten to you, haven't they?" he said, shocked. "You believe it."

Keen wanted to protest that it wasn't true. Then she saw it was her chance, and she took it.

"We are the Hive, Ressler," she said. "There *is* nothing else."

"Jesus," he said. "I'll get you out of here, okay? We'll get some of the best psychologists to de-Hive you or whatever it's called."

"Just go," she whispered. "Before someone sees you."

"Take me with you." John clutched at his own bars. "Please!"

Keen retreated to the back of her cage. Stuart glanced at her and nodded in approval. She stared at him for a moment, then said, "You knew."

"Sorry?" said Stuart.

"You knew about the Beekeeper and the Hive and how he operates before we got here. Before Reddington got here. You knew all about it. It's why you came, isn't it?"

Stuart sank to his new mattress, looking incongruous in his green jumpsuit. Keen continued to expect him in a brown three-piece.

"I said I wanted to get away. The memories are too much. The Hive will take them away. I made all my arrangements, and now I'm here. We are the Hive, you know."

Keen touched her chest. "We are the Hive."

Ressler, meanwhile, unlocked John the Bodysnatcher's cage. He bolted out of it. Ressler stopped at Keen's cage.

"Think of Reddington. He wouldn't want you in here, and he's like a father to you. A twisted, bizarro-world father, but still. You coming?"

"Go." Keen turned her head away. "Don't get caught."

"Let's move," John urged.

The two of them ghosted up the tunnel and vanished.

"That's a pity," Stuart said.

"How do you mean?" Keen asked, trying not to worry about Ressler and failing.

"It's going to be difficult for you, working in that room all by yourself."

A commotion broke out down the hallway. Shouts. Screams. Thuds. The high-pitched *zip* of a taser. More shouts. Keen found she was holding the cage bars in both hands and pressing her face to the space between them, trying to hear and see. Her heart sang in her ears and her knuckles were white. What had—?

A set of drone guards appeared dragging a semi-conscious Ressler and John the Bodysnatcher back into the cage room. Ressler hung between two drones and was bleeding from a split lip. Keen trembled with outrage and impotence inside her cage. What had they done to him? Damn it, she should have gone with him. John was struggling with his own guards, but to no effect. Behind them strolled the Beekeeper himself. The drones opened cages and flung both men inside.

"I wish I could say I was shocked, Donald," Dr. Griffin said through the bars, "but... well, you can probably guess how I'd finish that sentence. Every time we get a fresh batch, someone tries to escape at right about this stage in the process. Did you think I don't know how this works? It's quite orderly. *You* are quite orderly. The little boy in you was told by his daddy to escape, and so he tried. I don't blame you for it, Donald. I admire you. But you must be corrected."

Ressler only groaned from his thin mattress. John glared sullenly. Keen bit her hands to keep quiet.

"Here's something else I know." The Beekeeper tapped Ressler's bars. "From here on out, it goes faster and easier. I suggest you sleep as best you can. Tomorrow we really start in. On all of you. We are the Hive."

Stuart tapped his chest. "We are the Hive."

Keen touched her own chest. "We are the Hive."

CHAPTER ELEVEN

Raymond Reddington never paced. He never cracked his knuckles. He never twisted his hands or bit his nails. Every one of those behaviors betrayed fear or agitation, and he had ruthlessly quashed them, even when no one was looking. Instead, he indulged in very expensive twenty-year-old Scotch poured over ice made with energy drained from a star ninety-three million miles away. A long sip burned all the way down.

"Don't sweat it," said Mr. Brimley from the loveseat opposite Reddington's chair. He was leafing through a three-year-old copy of *People*. "Really. It'll be fine."

"I'm not worried," Reddington said.

Mr. Brimley peered over the top of his glasses at Reddington. His cannula made a clear plastic line under his nose and down to his wheeled oxygen tank.

"You're the best in the business, Mr. Reddington, but you hire *me* to interrogate, and I can see you're worried."

"Certain things, Mr. Brimley, the employer keeps to himself."

"Sure, sure." Mr. Brimley waved an airy hand. "I was just making conversation. No one cares."

Reddington set down his glass. "What was that supposed to mean?"

"You don't know?" Brimley looked surprised.

"If I knew," Reddington said slowly, "I wouldn't ask. What was that remark supposed to mean?"

Mr. Brimley shrugged. He looked like someone's visiting grandfather, who had overindulged in smoking and other vices in his youth and now was paying for it. Reddington happened to know he carted the oxygen tank around for reasons completely unrelated to any youthful smoking habit, and Mr. Brimley was angry about the entire situation. Most people would have turned that anger into a general hatred toward the world that would have strained or ended his relationships with family and friends. Mr. Brimley, however, had channeled that anger into his interrogations. It made him the best information extractor Reddington knew, and Reddington knew many. A lot of people thought Mr. Brimley used torture, and on occasion he did, but torture rarely worked in interrogation, despite what the unwashed masses thought. Mr. Brimley's methods were far more devious, more subtle, more cutting—without involving actual cutting. Which was why Reddington had snuck him into the park, at great expense. It had involved a helicopter, a motorboat, and a small SUV. It was a good thing Dembe was a qualified pilot.

"You think you have this mystique about you." Mr. Brimley picked up a Sudoku puzzle book and flicked out a pen. "The mysterious Raymond Reddington. What are your mysterious motives, your devious diversions? But really, no one thinks about you much at all. Nobody cares. That's what I hear, anyway."

Reddington folded his arms. "That's the way I

need it to be. It's never a good idea for someone in my position to keep a high profile."

"Yeah, okay." Mr. Brimley filled in a pair of numbers. "Seven and two are still nine, right?"

"I keep to myself on purpose," Reddington said. "I have to."

"Oh. Yeah, sure. And four, and eight, and six. Yes! You never worry about anything, no matter what anyone says. I got it. You don't have to tell me."

"I worry," Reddington said. "I know in my head that Lizzie is safe. The Beekeeper won't harm her. Not physically. And she's strong enough to keep him out of her head, so there's no risk of psychological damage."

"Sure, sure. If you say so. Four and seven—no! Six."

Reddington leaned toward Brimley, who was still intent on his Sudoku. "Of course I'm worried. I want her out of there, and I want her out of there now."

"Eight here, and two, and I think this must be one." Mr. Brimley moved his cannula aside so he could scratch his upper lip. "You sound pretty angry."

"You're damned right I'm angry." Reddington knocked back another hit of Scotch. "She ran off and got herself captured by the Hive when I specifically told her not to do it, and now I have to get her out before something terrible happens to her."

"Well, yeah." Mr. Brimley tapped his cheek with the pen. "Why don't you just call in the cavalry? You've got resources. Hey, you got *me* in here. That was a hell of a trip. You could get an armed group of men and take down the Hive."

Reddington slumped back into his chair. That was the first thing he'd thought of, naturally. The house had a satellite phone. His Russian… friend didn't like being out of contact, after all. A single call could bring in a battalion of armed mercenaries—or the FBI. But that would be a mistake. According to Dembe— and Reddington's own experience—the Hive was at least as heavily armed as the FBI would be. Bringing in an army would only create a terrible standoff. Reddington frankly didn't care much about most of the FBI agents, though if pressed he might admit to a slight fondness for Donald Ressler and Aram Mojtabai. And certain events had brought him quite close with Samar Navabi. But the rest of them mattered not at all. If they were wounded or killed in a confrontation with the Beekeeper, they were only doing the job they so foolishly volunteered to perform.

Drones fighting drones.

Reddington, however, didn't want the Hive destroyed. Not yet. Partly because Stuart was in there. He had need of Stuart yet. Reddington remembered when he was a much younger man, cocky, rough around the edges, and sure he knew everything. A bad turn that killed half a dozen friends in Madrid had taught him that perhaps he didn't know quite everything, and he found himself in Hyde Park in London with ten pounds in his pocket, the clothes on his back, and a sense that he was lucky to be alive.

One of his now-dead friends had mentioned the names Stuart and Vivian Ivy and the fact that they operated in London. Reddington had called from a red booth pay phone—what a shame those were vanishing from England now—and asked for help. Half an hour later, a car pulled up beside him and a motherly-looking woman with curly brown hair rolled the window down to offer him a ride. The car smelled of cinnamon rolls—she had brought him one, bless her. It was Reddington's first meeting with Vivian Ivy. He devoured the roll and swore to Vivian that he would love her forever. She smiled quietly at his American forthrightness and drove him to a small row house, where her husband Stuart was waiting.

When Reddington first laid eyes on Stuart Ivy, who was then in his forties, Stuart was in his basement surrounded by crates of machine gun parts. He was in shirt sleeves and up to his elbows in gears. The room was filled with the sweet scent of gun oil.

"Pardon me not shaking hands," he said. "Have to inspect the merchandise before I can pass it on. So Rex is dead, is he?"

"Enough of that," Vivian said. "The boy needs a bath and bed. And a decent supper."

"One of your cinnamon rolls would feed him for a week, darling." Stuart wiped his hands on a rag.

"That barrel is off true," Vivian said, pointing.

Stuart picked up the object in question and squinted along it.

"So it is. I'll put it in the refund pile. You always did have an eye for that. Mr. Reddington, how much do you know about weapons?"

"I'm one day short of graduating from the US Naval Academy," Reddington said. "I can assemble one of those guns in under two minutes and have it combat ready in four."

"Wonderful!" Stuart said, pleased. "I could use your help with this little project, then. It pays in cinnamon rolls."

"But first, Mr. Reddington," Vivian said, "a bath."

Reddington had spent the night, and the week, and the month. He had thought his own contacts in the underworld were already extensive, but he was astounded at the number of people Stuart and Vivian knew. But what amazed Reddington most was the fact that Stuart and Vivian never actually *did* anything. They didn't steal paintings. They didn't fashion weapons. They didn't cook meth. All they did was buy and sell.

"Only a fool *makes* anything, dear," Vivian told him. "Do the trading. It's less work, and if you get caught, it's harder to prove you did anything wrong."

"Even better if you pay someone *else* to do the trading for you," Stuart pointed out. "That's best of all. You just sit back and let the money roll in."

"But how do you get other people to just *give* you money?" Reddington asked.

Vivian smiled. All her teeth were straight and capped.

"Know your people, Red. Know *all* your people. Know their parents' names. Know their children's names. Know their favorite foods. When you don't know, pretend you know. And they'll do anything you want."

"But," Stuart added, "never let feelings for someone else jeopardize your own safety. We deal with nasty people, after all, and your own safety is always the first concern."

"Sounds like a pretty good rule in your line of work," said Mr. Brimley. "And a seven here and—hey! I got it!" He held up the completed Sudoku. "I'm still surprised you haven't called in a nuclear blast to wipe out the Hive, though."

"Because Lizzie is in there." Reddington snapped the glass down on the coffee table. "Because if I call in anyone, we'll have an armed standoff that will make that little tiff in Waco look like a schoolyard scuffle. Because

I have to get Lizzie out before anything else happens."

Mr. Brimley set the pen down and went back to flipping pages. "Stuart can die, though, right?"

"No!" Reddington was surprised at his own vehemence. "Not yet anyway."

"So there's a reason you're keeping him alive. Even though he taught you that stuff."

"He didn't teach me—well, now!" Reddington leaned forward. "Well, well, well."

A moment passed. Mr. Brimley looked at Reddington blandly. "What?"

"You were interrogating me," Reddington accused.

"Me?"

"All too successfully. Don't deny it."

Mr. Brimley went back to the magazine and pretended to examine an ad for stool softener through the bottom half of his bifocals. "Just passing the time with a little conversation. Nothing wrong with that."

Just then, Dembe burst through the back door. He was half dragging, half carrying the groaning form of a man in a green jumpsuit. A protective mask covered the man's face, giving him an insect-like appearance.

A Hive drone.

Reddington rose. "Fine work, Dembe. Mr. Brimley, where would you like to set up?"

"The spare bedroom." Mr. Brimley got carefully to his feet, minding his hose and his tank. "Whoo. This humidity is murder on what's left of my lungs. You got a sponge on you?"

"I certainly hope not," Reddington said.

"Find one. Gonna need it for this guy."

CHAPTER TWELVE

"Order, now," said the Beekeeper. "In today's session, you'll learn about stings and honey."

"Honey!" Pug said happily.

Keen just stared at the Beekeeper. Her mind felt as numb as her body. Exhaustion pulled at every muscle and bone, and she wanted food. No, she wanted *meat*. Something she could sink her teeth into. A steak. Ribs. Lamb kebab. Bloody rare or well done—she didn't care. The hunger for protein clamored inside her.

"We are the Hive," said Dr. Griffin, the Beekeeper.

"We are the Hive," everyone said. "Everyone" included the guards, Keen, Ressler, Stuart, John the Bodysnatcher. All of them had lost weight, except Stuart. The Beekeeper had given Stuart extra food. Keen hated Stuart. She hoarded the thought. It would be an easy sin to confess later.

"Recite Rule Number Three," the Beekeeper said.

"Work keeps the hands busy and the soul happy."

"Rule Number Two."

"A drone always speaks with respect."

"Rule Number One."

"The needs of the Hive outweigh the needs of its members."

"We are the children," Dr. Griffin said. "We are the orderly Hive, working together toward our heavenly goals. Here, we are safe. Together. If we follow the rules, there is no fear, no hate. All our needs are met. But even now, our enemies are massing against us. They are envious and fearful. They want what we have—our love, our safety, our security. We will defend ourselves, with swarms and stings. Together, we will triumph, and cleanse the country of the deadly scourge of our enemies."

Here Keen came more alert. The sarin gas was never far from her thoughts. The Beekeeper was making the stuff in his labs—or the drones were making it for him—and she had assumed he intended to sell it. This sounded like he meant to use it. But on who?

"Now we sit in judgment," the Beekeeper intoned. "To expiate our sins and bring ourselves closer to the Hive."

Keen did not grimace. She did not sigh. She did not grind her teeth. Neither did anyone else. But a soundless shift went through the group. No one complained outright, but Keen had become adept at catching subtle signs of discomfort.

The Beekeeper held out his hand, and one of the drones put a small case into it.

"John, you first."

John slouched into the center chair, his hands still cuffed before him. Keen's own hands were still cuffed too, and her skin was raw and chafed under the metal. Dr. Griffin cracked the case open and reached inside.

"I told you earlier that in this session we go deeper, that it becomes easier after today," he said, rising to stand near John. "Let me show you."

In a swift move, the Beekeeper snatched a syringe

from the case and stabbed John in the neck with it. John yowled in pained surprise. Dr. Griffin depressed the plunger and pulled his hand back. John slapped his neck.

"What was that?" he panted.

"My own concoction," Dr. Griffin replied pleasantly. "The Hive makes many forms of honey. We sell methamphetamine to outsiders to keep ourselves in the green and fund our other experiments."

"Honey," giggled Pug.

"And I make these." The Beekeeper held up the hypodermic. "The army, that bastion of order, told me they wanted me to find ways to bring their soldiers to order, make them *follow* orders more quickly, shorten the time for basic training. My methods worked. They were a delight. Within a week, I had an entire battalion following my every command. But the army didn't like that. Too experimental. Too strange. Too *brilliant* for them. They saw chaos where I created perfect order."

John weaved on his chair. His pupils expanded. A chill ran down Keen's spine.

"Humans mistake free thought for free will," the Beekeeper said. "They don't understand that to have free will we need to stop thinking. Our thoughts, our desires, enslave us. Buddha knew this. It's why he worked to extinguish thought. The Hive extinguishes chaos. The Hive extinguishes desire."

John's mouth was open, and he was panting now. His head came up, and he glanced quickly around the room like a rabbit that had heard a noise. Keen couldn't imagine what was in that syringe, and her tired mind was too foggy to think analytically.

"John," said the Beekeeper gently. "Can you hear me?"

John didn't respond. He pulled his knees up to his chin on the chair, balancing precariously. His breath was still coming fast.

"Can you hear me?" the Beekeeper repeated.

"I hear everything," John whispered. "I hear the stones. I hear the crack of light coming over the horizon. I hear the tears of a man striking the smell of pure oxygen."

"Good, good." The Beekeeper leaned toward him. "John, what is your worst memory from childhood? Tell us about it."

"I… I don't…" John rocked against his knees.

"Please tell us, John." The Beekeeper's voice was gentle and relentless. Keen recognized the technique—a command disguised as a request. "Please do."

"I'm seven years old and I'm walking into my mother's bedroom," John said softly. "It smells like darkness. It tastes like dust and stale air."

"Good, good," the Beekeeper said. "What do you see?"

"My mother is lying on her bed. The sheets are supposed to be white like ghosts, but there's a stain. I can hear the green stain crawling across the sheet, seeping into the cloth. She threw up. But the vomit is cold. I'm scared. I want to run away and hide. I wonder if I should call work for her like I've done lots of other times. But now… now I don't think I should."

"What do you do next, John?"

"I reach out and touch her hand. It's cold, too. I can see how cold it is. The sheet doesn't move. She isn't breathing. But her eyes are open and dull, and all the bottles are open on her night table, too. They're open like mouths, and they want to swallow me. They're going to swallow me down. My mom is dead. My mom is dead, and I'm all alone in the house. I'm all alone!"

"But you're not alone," the Beekeeper said. "We're here with you. The Hive is here. We're helping you." He reached down to stroke John's cheek. John shuddered once, and the Beekeeper dribbled honey into his mouth from a small bottle. John sighed. His muscles relaxed. "We're here, John. The Hive is here to help. We are the Hive."

"We are the Hive," said the room.

"We are the Hive," said John. Tears ran down his cheeks and Keen recoiled. "I... am the Hive."

"The Hive is love, John," said Dr. Griffin. "We are love. Take your rightful place with us."

Sobbing quietly, John stumbled to his chair in the outer circle.

"John is much closer to joining us now," Dr. Griffin proclaimed from behind his round lenses. "Donald, now you."

"No. I won't." Ressler tried to scramble to his feet, but the drone guards were already on him, and he was weakened from the lack of food and water, and the handcuffs hindered his movements. Pug wrestled him into the chair and held him down.

"Order," Dr. Griffin admonished. "We will have order."

He removed another syringe from the case and moved toward Ressler. Ressler struggled again, his eyes frantic. Keen knew his fear—Ressler had barely conquered an addiction to painkillers not so long ago, and he feared the Beekeeper's cocktail would bring it roaring back. And no doubt he feared what it would make him say. She wanted to help him, but she had drones of her own behind her. A sick feeling roiled through her stomach. Stuart watched with a stony face.

"No!" Ressler snarled again, still struggling. "I'll kill you, you son of a bitch!"

"No swearing," Pug admonished.

"Maybe there's another way!" Keen tried in desperation. But the needle moved closer.

"Kill you!" Ressler howled.

The Beekeeper stabbed his neck with the syringe, and none too gently. Bile burned the back of Keen's throat and she had to swallow hard to keep from throwing up.

Dr. Griffin depressed the plunger. Ressler's body relaxed and his pupils expanded, just as John's had done.

Pug let go. "That's better," he crooned. "You enjoy this. It will be fun."

"Let it happen, Donald," soothed Dr. Griffin. "It'll go much easier if you follow the rules. You like the rules. The rules tell us how to behave, what to expect, who to be. Without the rules, we are nothing."

"I... I..." Ressler's head slumped forward, and the Beekeeper tilted it back again.

"Can you hear me, Donald?" he asked.

"I hear you," Ressler said. "I taste your words. I hear the honey slide down my throat. I see my breath rattle in my lungs."

Synesthesia, Keen thought suddenly. The drug mixed up the senses. It must be a variant of LSD, which explained the hallucinations.

"Very good, Donald." The Beekeeper's voice was soft and hypnotic. "What's your worst memory as an adult? Please tell us."

Like John, Ressler resisted. He tried to turn in the center chair, away from the Beekeeper, but the Beekeeper turned with him.

"You have to tell us, Donald," he said. "It's the rules."

"The rules," Ressler echoed. "I can smell them. They come in orderly rows, one after another, like cooked sugar and wine and vinegar."

"What is your worst memory?"

"Audrey," Ressler said. "I'm in the car with Audrey and the jeep hits us. She's hurt, but Mako Tanida is firing on the car. Bullets flick by, scoring black lines behind them. I'm outside the car, firing back with black bullets of my own. My fear sounds like thunder drums and my anger tastes like burned onions."

The awful sorrow tightened Keen's chest and she wanted to put her hands over her ears, but the heavy handcuffs kept her still. She didn't want to hear this, didn't want to see Ressler relive this. She knew what had happened, had seen the aftermath crush him. His injuries had started him on the painkillers, and sorrow and depression kept him on them long after the physical pain had passed. Keen had coaxed him through the addiction that followed, and she prayed he wasn't going to have to go through it again.

"Audrey is stumbling from the jeep," Ressler said. "She leaves rainbow trails in the air wherever she moves. I want her to get back inside, but she doesn't understand. She's there, and I love her and it tastes like lilacs in May."

"Stop it," Keen said. "Please stop."

The Beekeeper ignored her. "What happens next, Donald?"

"Tanida's bullets tear through her. Scarlet flowers bloom on her stomach and spill red seeds on the cement. Tanida runs away. I'm trying to help." His voice rose and his eyes filled with tears. "Her blood is on my hands. On *my* hands."

"And then?" Dr. Griffin urged. "What happens then, Donald?"

"She dies." Ressler slumped into the chair, his cheeks wet, hands defeated in his lap. "She's dead. Gone. Her blood is on my hands."

"On *our* hands, Donald," said the Beekeeper. "We are here with you, Donald. We share your pain and sorrow. The entire Hive carries it for you, and you feel nothing."

"Nothing," Ressler echoed.

"Pain shared is pain lessened," the Beekeeper murmured. He stroked Ressler's hair like a loving father and dropped honey into his mouth. Ressler sighed and relaxed. "The Hive is love and love is the Hive. We love you, Donald, like Audrey loved you. No one here will leave you behind. We are order. We are the Hive."

"We are the Hive," said everyone else, including Keen.

"We are the Hive," said Ressler.

"Return to your seat, Donald. You are closer to joining us now."

Ressler numbly obeyed, his pupils still dilated from the drug. The Beekeeper turned to Keen.

"Now you, Elizabeth."

Keen froze. She had been so intent on Ressler she had forgotten the Beekeeper would require her to take a turn in the center chair. Her nostrils widened and her breath came in short, fearful gasps. The drones—Mala was one of them—whipped her into the chair, and before she knew it, a thin pain pierced her neck. She met Stuart's calm eyes for a tiny moment, then turned away.

"It's okay," Pug said. Keen suppressed a cold shudder.

"Let it happen, Elizabeth," said the Beekeeper, and by the end of the sentence, his voice had fallen far away.

A wave of dizziness swept her. The room rocked and warped as if the stone walls were made of marshmallow.

"Can you hear me, Elizabeth?" said Dr. Griffin above her, and his voice fell on her ears with the smell of spring rain and cut grass.

"I hear you," she said, the words that spilled from her mouth tasting like sugar and lemon. "I hear the stones and the lawn and smell words like water."

"Tell us, Elizabeth," said the Beekeeper, and this time his voice smelled different. It was the voice of a winter cloak, the voice of floral perfume and butterscotch candy wrappers. It tasted like a woman's voice. "Tell us your worst memory."

The air rushed around her like black bees, ready to sting. She was no longer in a cavern under an Appalachian mountain. She was a child, barefoot, in a nightgown. Smoke filled the house with choking white cotton. Heat licked her skin with a cat's tongue. She was screaming. Her lungs were heavy and tasted of stale crackers. The light faded and she was aware of people speaking red words. Fear and pain engulfed her in a cloud that smelled like rotten fruit and pain scorched her hand.

"Tell us," the Beekeeper repeated.

The black fear was so old, so heavy, so terrible. Keen needed to be free of it, find a way to crawl out from under it. And the only way to do it was to speak, shove it away with words, lay her soul bare to the Beekeeper and the circle and let them absorb her very self. She could see them inhaling, sucking in pink and orange air, ready to take in her pain. They would suck down her spirit, and she was happy to let them. She opened her mouth, eager to release everything.

And then her fingers touched the Y-shaped scar

at her wrist. The shiny, raised skin tasted like spring strawberries and sweet vanilla under her fingertips. It was strength and it was power. Keen's fingers traced the contours of the Y—up the arm, down the valley, back out again, and down the other side. She was tracing her past, her home. Her *self*.

"Elizabeth?" the Beekeeper said, and a note of impatience entered his voice. "Tell us."

She traced the Y again, and the words changed on her tongue.

"The day I learned my father died," she said. "He was in the hospital, alone. Cancer ate him from the inside with rotten worms. I wanted to go and see him, but he told me that I didn't have to, and I didn't, and then I got the black phrases spilling out of the phone that my daddy was dead. He's *dead*! I don't know what to do. I'm all alone."

"But you aren't alone," the Beekeeper said. "We are here. The Hive is here. We share your pain." He droned on in a variation of the litany he had given earlier. His words washed over her, but her fingers traced the scar and wove a shield around her soul. When he dropped honey into her mouth, she was unprepared for the way the world snapped back into focus. It clanged into sharp existence, and the force of it stunned her. She slumped in her chair, concentrating on just her breathing.

"You are closer to being one of us," the Beekeeper said over her head, and she hated him with a loathing that went deep and black as road tar. "We are the Hive."

"We are the Hive!" she said firmly.

She smiled at him with fake relief, and made sure the gesture reached her eyes. Dr. Griffin met her gaze and nodded in approval. One psychologist to another. She would bring him down and destroy his little kingdom, and she would do it from the inside, by any means possible.

Mala, in her mask, helped Keen to her chair in the outer circle. She squeezed Keen's hand in her smaller, cooler one for a tiny moment. Keen resumed her chair. What had that meant? Support? Congratulations? She kept her face stoic.

The Beekeeper turned to Stuart. Keen bit her lip. Would Stuart be able to handle the Beekeeper's cocktail? Her mind searched for a way to stop this, but nothing seemed feasible.

In seconds, Stuart was whisked into the chair. But instead of struggling, he cocked his head, baring his neck. "I am ready, Beekeeper."

The Beekeeper injected him without a word. Stuart inhaled sharply, and Keen wondered what he was tasting, hearing, smelling. Dr. Griffin asked if Stuart could hear him, then commanded him to tell his worst memory.

Stuart needed no coaxing, though his voice quavered and he kept his eyes shut.

"The day my wife Vivian died. It was a Sunday that tasted of sunshine and gold. The buyers, big men with guns of sweet oil and slick metal, transferred the money, and we were ready to hand them the weapons. Chemical weapons made special for our buyers. Slithering green gases and purple poisons and smart launchers with little eyes that peered around corners. But then Reddington—"

"Raymond Reddington?" the Beekeeper interrupted sharply, echoing Keen's own startled thoughts.

"Raymond Reddington, so young and proud and sharp as a box of tacks. He checked the computer and found the transfer was fake. No money for us. Red and

I became angry. Vivian tried to calm us down, but I was scarlet and acid and bile. And then the shooting started. At first, our guards did well, but the buyers slid around us and they had men we didn't know about, and it didn't go so well then. Our men ran and scattered. We three ran, and it was only then that I realized Viv, my dear Viv, wasn't with us. She was still inside the awful warehouse with the snakes and purple poison."

Small tears slipped out from under Stuart's closed eyes. Keen's heart twisted for him.

"Red wanted to go back for her, but I… I told him not to." Stuart swallowed, and the tears began in earnest. "Oh, god—I told him not to. Because of the iron rule."

"What rule, Stuart?" asked Dr. Griffin in his gentle voice.

"Never let your feelings for someone else jeopardize your own safety," Stuart whispered. "Never."

Dr. Griffin said, "Not even for your wife?"

"Not even for her." Stuart was shaking now. "I told Red to run and that I would go back for Vivian. But I lied. I didn't save her. Reddington ran off and I heard Vivian, my summertime love, my orange sweetness, scream and babble and then stop. And then I ran away."

Stuart swiped at his closed eyes with the sleeves of his jumpsuit, and the handcuffs gleamed on his wrists.

"Red always looked at me with the smell of cold ice behind his eyes ever after that, and one day he was just gone. I lost both of them. I have no one. I'm alone."

Dr. Griffin started to speak, and Keen knew what he was going to say, but Stuart continued before Griffin could say anything.

"Except here I'm not alone. Here I'm part of a group,

a smooth, silky community, and my pain eases."

"That's right," Dr. Griffin said. "We are here. The Hive is with you, sharing your pain."

"I can feel it," Stuart said. "I can feel the humming. I can taste the song. I can hear the honey."

Dr. Griffin took advantage of this moment to drop honey into Stuart's mouth. His eyes came open, and he staggered to his chair in the outer circle. Keen tried not to stare.

"We are the Hive," he said, and everyone repeated it.

"Stuart," the Beekeeper said, "you are excused."

Stuart blinked. "I am?"

"You have demonstrated over and over your commitment to the Hive. I—we—have seen it in your daily work and your dedication. Already your fellow drones have emptied your beginner's cell and you are reassigned to the men's barrack. Eat a full meal in the kitchen and go to work in the main room."

"Oh!" Genuine gratitude beamed on Stuart's face and his brown eyes filled with tears. "Thank you, Beekeeper! Thank you so very much."

"You have earned it." At the Beekeeper's gesture, one of the drones unlocked Stuart's handcuffs. They clanked to the floor. "You are one of us. We are the Hive!"

"We are the Hive!" said everyone.

Stuart stood on unsteady legs and toddled toward the tunnel entrance. He was met by Mrs. Griffin, who wordlessly took his arm and led him away. How long had she been standing there in the shadows?

"The rest of you may return to your cells," the Beekeeper said. "You've done well. Your thoughts are becoming more orderly. Soon you'll join us, just like Stuart."

On the way back to the cell room, Keen tried without

success to catch Mala's eye. The same happened when she brought the tray with the usual bland, carb-heavy food. She was avoiding Keen. Hmm.

"There's meth in the honey," said John the Bodysnatcher from his cell. "The bastard used to pay me with it sometimes. He has his little drones cook it for him. It's how they raise cash, and the Beekeeper calls it *honey* because he thinks it's cute. It acts as his antidote to whatever he was giving us in those syringes."

"I don't care anymore." Ressler slumped in his cell. "I want to know why the hell no one's come for us."

"They don't know where we are." Keen licked crumbs from her fingers. "No GPS, no cell phone—"

"That makes no sense," Ressler said. "We passed a crapload of cell towers on our way into this hellhole, and GPS is satellite-based. Why is there—"

"Jammer," the Bodysnatcher said flatly. "Army-grade signal jammer. The Beekeeper bought it years ago. Stops cell phones, GPS, anything you want. Only way to communicate is if you know the frequency of the signal they let through. They use it on their own walkie-talkies. So we're screwed. No one can find us in here. The park is the size of a small country. It's why the Beekeeper hides here."

"Hell of a thing about Stuart and Reddington," Ressler said. "If he was telling the truth. Jesus."

"I think he was." Keen ran a hand through her hair. She wanted a shower in the worst way. And she wanted real food. And she wanted to see the sun. And damn it, she wanted to see Reddington. Why hadn't he done anything? Was he dead? The cell felt intolerably tiny. She needed to run and find out if he was all right. Carefully, she forced herself to take a breath. Reddington hadn't been captured or killed.

The Beekeeper was a narcissist, and if he had captured Reddington, he would have flaunted it. Griffin was the last person to keep silent about something like that. Therefore, Reddington was safe.

She hoped.

"That thing Stuart said, though," Ressler continued, "about the iron rule. Never let your feelings for someone else jeopardize your own safety. He said he taught that to Reddington."

"That's not like Reddington at all, though," Keen said. "He always takes care of his people, even when he'd be better off not. He's risked himself for…" *me*, she thought "…other people lots of times."

"And that's not something you usually see in people who… do what he does," Ressler said with a sideways glance at John, who still didn't know Keen and Ressler—and therefore Reddington—worked for the FBI. John still thought Keen and Ressler worked for Reddington. "Most people like Reddington drop you in half a heartbeat."

"And maybe Vivian is why Reddington doesn't," Keen observed.

"I can't wait to ask him," John drawled.

"So what do we do now?" Ressler said.

"I think," Keen said thoughtfully, "we wait for Mala."

CHAPTER THIRTEEN

Mr. Brimley poked his head into the living room, the plastic cannula trailing behind him. "He's talking. You might want to come in for this."

Reddington set down the drone's weapon belt. Say what you might about the Beekeeper—he knew how to arm his people. Two gas grenades, three flash-bang grenades, pepper spray, a full complement of reload clips for the Glock, a water bottle, and a few rations, all tucked into a cunningly designed utility belt that would make any comic book hero fall into orgiastic envy. He rose somberly, buttoned his jacket, and strode into the bedroom where Mr. Brimley had been working. The room smelled of coffee and urine, a strange combination. There were no signs anywhere of whatever it was Mr. Brimley had been up to with his subject. There never were. Mr. Brimley was always meticulous about tidying up.

Shackles clinked. The drone stared blearily up at Reddington with large blue eyes. He was a young man, barely out of his teens, head shaved into a military crew cut. With his stained green jumpsuit and empty weapons belt, he looked like a kid playing army in the woods. Dembe had chained him to the chair for Mr.

Brimley's ministrations, which had gone on for quite some time, and the boy looked exhausted. One of his eyes was puffy but not blackened. Hmm.

"He'll talk. Isn't that right, buddy?" Mr. Brimley picked up a coffee mug and waved it in the drone's direction. The boy flinched. Interesting.

"Just… don't do it again," he said.

Reddington spun a ladderback chair around and faced the boy over the back. "How long have you been a drone for the Hive?"

"Four years. Look, I love the Beekeeper. I love the Hive. They're my family. See?" He stretched his neck out of his collar, revealing the tattoo of a honeybee.

"Where did you live before this, friend?"

"The streets. Miami."

This surprised Reddington. "And before that?"

"Bunch of foster homes. I took off when my last foster dad got a little too free with his fists—and the zipper on his pants. Streets were better."

"How did you come to join the Hive, then?"

"Some dude grabbed me while I was sleeping in a church basement with a bunch of other guys. He brought me here." The boy's eyes took on a faraway look. "Changed my life."

"How?'

"I have a family now," the boy said earnestly. "The Hive is love. I don't have to worry or wonder or be scared. They changed me. Helped me. Protected me against *them*."

"And *them* would be?"

The boy seemed to realize he had gone too far. He folded his lips and looked away. Mr. Brimley held up the coffee cup and tapped it with one fingernail. The boy paled.

"I... you can't get mad."

Reddington nodded. "Ah. *Them* would be me. Or anyone else who isn't in the Hive."

The boy nodded, then flinched. What had the Beekeeper done to deserve such fear and such loyalty all at once? Reddington half despised, half admired it.

"All I want is information," Reddington said reasonably. "I'm not going to get angry at you. I'm not Dr. Griffin."

"He's the Beekeeper," said the boy. "He keeps us."

"Keeps you."

"Keeps us safe. Keeps us happy. Keeps us *us*."

"Be that as it may," Reddington said, "I want to know how *us* hides from outsiders so well. The park is big, but no one can hide an operation that size for years, or even months, without outside help. You have to get food and supplies in there, not to mention equipment, machinery, and weapons, and it's simply not possible without attracting attention."

The boy hesitated again, and again Mr. Brimley raised the coffee cup.

"We have a bunch of... advanced members," he said. "They make the supreme sacrifice."

"Sacrifice."

"They leave the Hive and work elsewhere," the boy clarified. "They only come back to visit sometimes. And taste the honey."

"The park rangers," Reddington said. "They're Hive."

"Not all of them. But a lot of them. And we have people in town, too."

"This honey," Reddington said. "What's in it?"

"I don't know," the boy said, and Mr. Brimley tapped the coffee mug. "No! I really don't know. Only the Beekeeper knows."

"Laces it with a touch of his own potion," said Reddington, "to ensure loyalty and keep you coming back. I've seen the method used before. It takes a careful hand."

"Amateur," scoffed Mr. Brimley. "I've never had to use drugs in my work."

"Thank you, Mr. Brimley. We're all proud." Reddington took from his jacket pocket the much-abused map of the park and pointed at a spot on it. "This is where we are now. Tell me, and quickly please, where the closest outpost of Hive park rangers might be."

"The Hive will have noticed by now that one of their own is missing," Dembe said. "It is dangerous for us to be out and about. You have the satellite phone from the house, you know."

"Actually, I don't." Reddington consulted the map again. His navy training allowed him to read it more easily than most people, but said training had been… a few years ago and he was decidedly rusty. He had changed into khakis and an absolutely dreadful green golf shirt he had found in one of the bedroom dressers—fortunately he and his Russian friend were of a size, though he had been forced to wear his own shoes. Luck of the textiles apparently only took one so far. Reddington had also scrounged up a straw bowler to protect his head. It wasn't Savile Row or even Fifth Avenue, but it would have to do. He did have to admit that the golf shirt was more practical out here than his suit. Descriptions of sun-dappled glades, shady glens, and majestic mountains always left out the heavy heat, oppressive humidity, and omnipresent insects.

"The satellite phone connects to a single Russian

satellite and only operates when that happy example of Soviet technology is above the horizon," Reddington continued, "which it is only between the hours of three and five-fifteen A.M. Sufficient for getting Mr. Brimley here, but not for what we need next."

Dembe knew better than to ask what *next* was, which was one of the many reasons Reddington liked having him around. They ghosted through the woods—or rather, Dembe ghosted and Reddington followed as best he could. Twice Dembe gestured Reddington to the ground, and Reddington dropped like an anvil. Both times, heavily armed drones jogged past them, the plastic eye shield on their masks glinting in the patches of sunlight that found their way through the heavy forest canopy.

"They are on alert," Dembe said softly when the second group went by. "They are looking for the missing boy."

"They won't find him," Reddington said. "Mr. Brimley is an experienced jailor."

"We need to ensure they don't find *us*," Dembe said. "Come."

They followed the contours of the map until they emerged from the woods onto a paved road. About a hundred yards ahead of them was a log cabin made of that fake dark-brown wood so often found in state and federal parks. A sign on the road pointed up and proclaimed PARK RANGER. Reddington appreciated the delightful irony of putting park rangers in patently fake log cabins. When tourists arrived in their air-conditioned cars towing air-conditioned camper trailers that would allow them to experience a real wilderness, they found fake outdoorsmen in fake cabins. How splendid! Reddington, at least, admitted that he had no intention of experiencing the wilderness if he could possibly avoid it. There was no control in the forest, nature was unpredictable. People were another matter entirely. People he could handle.

"I don't like this idea," Dembe said, shifting the jacket he had swiped from a closet back at the house. He was sweating in the heat.

"I have every faith in you, my friend," Reddington said. "Shall we?"

They ambled toward the cabin. Reddington held the map up, obscuring most of his and Dembe's faces, and they argued loudly as they approached. The cabin seemed to stare at them through blank glass windows, and shadows moved inside. Reddington could almost feel the target sketched on his chest, but he ignored it and continued walking. Dembe gesticulated, but was careful to keep his face down. Reddington pointed at the cabin, and the two of them stormed up to a side door, which had an OPEN sign on it. Reddington pushed inside, the map still in front of his face.

Cool air wafted over him. Of course. The interior was darker than outside, and it took a moment for his eyes to adjust. A counter split the large room in half, much like a police station. The obligatory display of pamphlets took up one wall, and a large map of the park took up another. Behind the counter were three male park rangers, all dressed in brown. Each had a desk, and Reddington's quick eye picked out a satellite phone in its charger on one of them.

"I'm telling you it's farther north," Reddington said. "We're completely off the route."

"No," Dembe said. "It's *here*." He stabbed a finger at a random place on the innocent map in Reddington's hands. "And we are *here*."

"Do you need help?" said one of the rangers pleasantly, and Reddington saw the head of a honeybee tattoo peeking out from the cuff of his left hand. The holstered semi-automatic at his belt also caught his eye, and how many park rangers went armed this way? None.

"Can you believe? We seem to be lost," Reddington chuckled.

"We are not," Dembe said, edging closer.

"Where are you trying to go?" asked the ranger. The two remaining rangers, one of whom had a bee tattoo on his neck, exchanged looks. One of them slid open a drawer.

Reddington kept the map up with one hand and slipped his hand into his pocket with the other.

"My friend here hasn't read a map in twenty years, but on our first hike, he insists on taking charge. Maybe this will set us on our way."

Dembe whipped the young drone's pistol from under his jacket. Reddington flipped a small object over the counter and dropped straight down. Dembe fired two bullets into the first ranger even as the other two snatched weapons of their own from the desks. Dembe flung himself flat. The stun grenade Reddington had taken from the captive drone exploded in a blinding flash and an ear-splitting bang that blew the papers off desks and tossed telephones from their cradles. The two remaining rangers both wrapped their arms around their heads, blinded and deafened. Dembe, who had been protected by the counter, popped up and fired shots into the Hive rangers. They went down in a cloud of cordite smoke.

Reddington came up from behind the counter. "Well done."

"It took too long to bring down the other two," Dembe said.

"Don't be so hard on yourself, my friend." Reddington patted his shoulder. "A basic cleanup should do for now. I saw a wheelbarrow out back."

Dembe nodded and the two of them set to work. Reddington stripped the rangers of their weapons and Dembe used the wheelbarrow to cart the bodies outside. Reddington didn't spare another thought for the dead drones. They—or their compatriots—had killed a dozen FBI agents, and weren't worth considering further. Instead, he tidied up the mussed papers and righted the phones. Through the window, he saw Dembe pushing the wheelbarrow with a lumpy bundle covered in a tarp into the woods. He would find a good spot to stash the bodies, cover them with logs and deadfalls, and return. It wasn't worth the time it would take to bury them—it didn't matter much if anyone, including the Hive, found out they had been killed, at least not for a few days, and Reddington suspected it would indeed be a few days before anyone thought to check this outpost. Reddington stepped outside, changed the OPEN sign to CLOSED, and went back in.

Reddington checked the desk's landline telephones. They worked, but they were restricted to dialing within the park only. The satellite phone, the object of their current quest, came to life with satisfying ease. While Dembe continued to haul bodies, he made a call.

"Good afternoon, Gareth," he said into the phone. "It's me. I'm fantastic. How are those beagle puppies? Wonderful! You know, when they're old enough, I know a prince in Dubai who will pay top dollar for two of them. I'll be happy to pass your name along if—

of course! Listen, I'm calling because I have to move forward on that delivery soon, and I need the materials by tomorrow. Yes, tomorrow." He paused. "Then you'll just have to rearrange your schedule. I'm sure King Busari will understand, especially since he's still in arrears with you. That's wonderful to hear! Looking forward to it, Gareth."

He made two more calls while Dembe found a mop and a utility sink and got to work on the blood spills. The job wouldn't fool a competent police investigation—for that, Reddington would need Mrs. Kaplan and her strict standards—but it would do for now. Reddington made one more call.

Aram Mojtabai jumped when his phone rang. He always jumped when his phone rang. His phone only rang when someone from the Post Office was in trouble—they needed a database hack right now, or a face recognition on a blurry photo immediately, or a way to stop a computer virus before it accidentally launched a nuclear weapon. It would be nice to get a problem he could take his time with, and maybe even fail to solve, without worrying the world would end.

More than once he had considered leaving the Post Office, getting his clearance revoked, and working IT for a nice, dull corporation. Or maybe even opening his own computer shop, where he could fix laptops for middle-schoolers who downloaded viruses with their video games and rescue grandmothers who forgot their passwords on Facebook.

On the other hand, if his day were filled with those kinds of problems, he would probably go quietly insane. He worked sixteen-hour days at the Post Office mostly because he had literally nothing to do at home except get on his own computer, which was too much like work anyway. He had no challenges at home. If he also had none at work, what would he be?

Aram knew the answer to that. He'd be yet another Arab-American bachelor with a mother who begged him to find a nice wife and get on with those grandchildren, and a father who took him aside at least once a year to seriously ask if living in Washington had turned him gay. No, thank you. At the Post Office, Aram was still an Arab-American whose mother wanted grandchildren and a father who worried his son might be gay, but he was also a secret agent, and that, at least, made him different and interesting, even if he was the only one who knew it.

So Aram slapped the button that activated his earpiece and braced himself for another world-shaking problem. "Agent Mojtabai."

"Good day, Aram."

The familiar baritone on the other end sent ice down Aram's back. He put a hand to his ear. "Mr. Reddington? You're alive! Let me call Mr. Cooper. We've been so—"

"No, no," Reddington interrupted. "I want this between you and me, Aram. Are you alone?"

Aram automatically glanced around. The bullpen was never completely empty, but no one was close to him, and he always talked through his earpiece, so it was unlikely anyone would overhear.

"I... mostly."

"Perfect. Listen carefully to me, Aram. Lizzie and Donald are in the hands of the Beekeeper and his Hive. I believe them to be uncomfortable in the short term and in danger in the long term."

"Where are you?" Aram said nervously. His palms were already sweating and he felt a trickle drip down his back. He hated that. Ressler could talk face-to-face with Reddington and not turn a hair, but something in the man's eyes chilled Aram's blood and made him think of cement boots and corpses wrapped in chicken wire. "We lost your GPS days ago. We have agents scouring the area, but so far, nothing."

"What about local and state police?" Reddington asked.

"We can't get them involved without telling them about the Post Office and the task force. Classified information takes precedence even over an agent's, or even several agents', lives."

"Good," Reddington said, to Aram's surprise. "Let's keep it that way."

"I don't understand." Aram glanced around again. "Look, we can have agents there in a couple hours. What are—"

"The Beekeeper is heavily armed," Reddington interrupted. "And by *heavily*, I mean, machine guns and grenade launchers. If you bring the FBI in here, it'll create an abattoir. I will not put Elizabeth in further danger or allow anyone else to do so. Do I make myself clear, Agent Mojtabai?"

More sweat popped out on Aram's forehead and he swallowed hard. "I understand. Look, I want her back, too. And Ressler."

"Wonderful. What I need from you is a key."

"A key?" Aram continued to click over his boards, but he was coming up empty. Someone or something was stopping a trace, and Aram was *good* at tracing. He could tell right off that the signal was a satellite, and there were only so many satellites above the horizon at a given moment. On a second screen he called up the list and orbit patterns. Two hundred and sixteen candidates. Okay, eighty-three of them were military, and forty-seven were television. These sixty-four were GPS—he highlighted those to explore later, in case they turned out to have useful tracking information anyway—which left twenty-two that could carry a satellite phone signal. Eight of them were Chinese. Unlikely. That left fourteen for Reddington.

"A computer key that will intercept and override a series of class four military helicopter drones," Reddington clarified. "I need it delivered to the eastern entrance of the Sumter National Forest within twenty-four hours."

This got Aram's full attention. "Wait—an override key for helicopter drones? What for?"

"That's unimportant. I don't care if you buy it, build it, or steal it, but you will bring it to the east entrance of the park exactly twenty-four hours from now."

"*I* will?" Aram squeaked.

"How else will you get it to me without telling anyone else of its existence?" Reddington said reasonably.

The entire world tilted sideways, draining away Aram's self-satisfaction like the last drop of tea from a cup. He said, "Right."

"And you won't finish that trace on this call," Reddington continued. "I doubt it would work anyway."

He clicked off, leaving Aram staring at his blinking screens. Then he slowly shut down the tracing program and began a software search:

helicopter drone override key

CHAPTER FOURTEEN

Footsteps sounded, bringing Keen instantly awake. The guard drones approached the cages. Keen blew out a breath. Her skin itched all over, and she could feel the dirt on her face and arms. She had lost all sense of time. "Morning" was now defined as "when the sleep cycle ends." Meals were so irregular, she had stopped calling them anything like "lunch" or "supper." They were just meals. She had endured two more sessions in the Beekeeper's circle, one with drugs and one without. The Beekeeper himself continued to keep his distance from Keen, despite her machinations. She even imitated Stuart's behavior to the best of her ability, but something seemed to tell him she wasn't entirely "ready" for the Hive.

Twice, however, she had managed to catch Mala alone, and both times Mala had talked about Iris.

"The Bodysnatcher killed Iris," she said once. "And he's in that cage right next to you. I can't... I don't know what to think of that."

"You don't have to think anything," Keen said, playing the therapist. "How does it make you feel, though?"

"I'm... angry," Mala said. "The Beekeeper is

supposed to protect us. The Hive is supposed to protect us. But he brought a killer to us."

"Doesn't the Hive kill?" Keen countered. "I've watched them do it. They killed my friends."

"That's... different," Mala said, but she didn't sound convinced.

"Have you ever killed anyone, Mala?" Keen said.

Mala hesitated. "Yes. The Beekeeper wanted me to. He told me it would be all right. But I didn't do it. I... missed. With the pistol. I failed him. But then he grabbed my hand and made me shoot again. That time it... I killed him."

"Sounds to me like the Beekeeper did it and blamed you," Keen said.

"I'll have to kill for us eventually. Outsiders are coming for us. They *are*."

"Of course they are." Keen nodded. "That's why we're here, where it's safe. Is that why you joined the Hive, Mala? Because it's safe?"

"My father," she said. "He's... not a good man. My whole life, he wasn't. After my mom died, he spiraled down to even darker places, and he dragged me with him. I got away, but he kept following me. He gave me money, he tried to trick me. He made that stupid Stingster app to shame me. I thought about going back, but Iris stopped me. Then I heard about the Hive, and how they always keep their people safe. They don't move you from school to school, and they don't use their connections to shut off your electricity, and they don't hound you on the Internet. They keep you safe, and they don't change. They keep you safe from *them*."

"Who is *them*?" Keen asked again.

Mala made a vague gesture. "*Them*. The government. The people who are coming for us. Who want the honey, who want to take us over and the rest of the country. We're going to stop them."

"We're going to kill them." Keen nodded so fiercely she felt like a bobble-head. "All of them. They're damned scary. I want to put a gun to each of their heads and pull the trigger."

"…yeah," Mala said, but this time she didn't sound so sure.

Keen pressed her point. "We have to kill them all. Like the Beekeeper wanted you to kill someone. Like the Bodysnatcher killed Iris. She's one of *them*, right? I mean, it stands to reason. If she isn't one of us, she must be one of them. That's why the Beekeeper told the Bodysnatcher to kill her."

"He did?" Mala's head came up. "How do you know he did that?"

"I don't, I guess," Keen said with a shrug. "But why else would the Bodysnatcher have to be so sure she didn't talk about you? Why else would he have killed her?"

"… yeah," Mala said again, and then it was time for Keen to be back in her cage.

Now, though, Mala was opening the cage and gesturing for Keen to come out of it. In her hand, she held a sandwich. Keen smelled the ham before she saw it. The sandwich was thick, rich, and meaty, and brown mustard oozed under the bread.

"What's going on?" Keen asked, her eyes on the sandwich.

Mala handed it to her, and Keen bit into it eagerly. The ham was both sweet and salty, and there was a lot of it. The protein called to her, and she devoured the sandwich in moments, savoring the tangy mustard and the soft bread. From their own cages, Ressler and John watched with undisguised envy. Mala then handed

Keen a pair of gloves that matched her green jumpsuit.

"Come on," she said. "You're working in the main room now. Like Stuart."

"I am?" Keen swallowed the last bit of sandwich in surprise. "Why? What happened?"

"I talked to the Beekeeper," she said. "I told him I thought you were ready to move ahead. He was already on the fence about you, and I guess I pushed him over."

Ressler gave her a look of disbelief. Keen turned her back on him. This had to work. If anyone would fall under the Beekeeper's spell, it would be Ressler, with his dedication to the rules. Once the Beekeeper persuaded Ressler to follow his rules instead of the FBI's, it would be over. A small thrill of victory buzzed through Keen. She'd been right—Mala was the key to getting to the Beekeeper. Follow the rules, and everything would be fine.

She paused. Where had *that* thought come from? Never mind.

"Let's go," Mala said, and led Keen away.

The first place Mala took her was a sort-of locker room. The air was steamy, and Keen smelled actual soap. Mala handed her a towel and pointed toward a tiled-in area.

"You can shower in there. Shampoo and soap are in the dispensers."

"A shower?" Keen found herself unreasonably breathless. "Really?"

"You've earned it," Mala said. "Quick!"

Keen didn't need to be told twice. The hot water that clattered against the chipped tile and the cheap soap from the wall dispenser felt better than anything she might find at the most luxurious spa. The dirt and grease sluiced from her skin and hair, leaving her pink and clean, and she couldn't describe how fantastic a full belly and a hot shower made her feel. Thank heaven the Beekeeper had seen fit to grant her both.

She grimaced. No. The Beekeeper hadn't granted her anything. She hadn't earned anything. She had tricked them from her kidnapper. What was *wrong* with her?

Mala gave her a freshly laundered green jumpsuit, an equipment belt—though without weapons—and a mask, which she hung on her belt. Keen also donned the gloves that Mala had given her earlier.

"The shift is nearly over," Mala said, "but you can still join in."

Keen followed Mala down a series of tunnels, and felt that she was beginning to understand the layout of the place now. She passed a barrack, where several women slept in triple-tiered bunk beds, and it occurred to her again that most leaders of underground groups like this one required sex from their followers. A chill came over her, blunting her earlier good mood.

"You said the men don't touch the women here," she said hesitantly, "but does the Beekeeper bring drones to his bed? Uh… I'll be glad to do whatever he needs, but I'm just wondering—"

"Of course not!" Mala interrupted. "He's married, silly, and he's faithful to Mrs. Griffin. Eventually, you'll be married, too."

"I will?" Keen said, trying with middling success to mask her surprise.

"Sure. The Beekeeper will match you with someone. For replacement."

They were walking farther down the tunnel, and Keen heard laughter, a strange sound in a place like this.

"Replacement?"

"Right here." Mala pointed into another room. It was carpeted, and the walls were brightly painted and lined with shelves filled with picture books and toys. More toys—a play kitchen, an easel, a sand table, a set of toy tanks, a pile of plastic guns—were scattered about the room. Among it all roved a passel of small children. Keen put a hand to her mouth to hold back a gasp. The children were laughing and playing. A boy and a girl pretended to shoot at each other with a set of rifles. Two other boys tossed toy grenades at the tanks. Pudgy hands rattled tiny pots and pans in the plastic kitchen. A trio of women moved among them, guiding or stopping or redirecting. Another woman finished diapering a baby on a changing table. She put it in a playpen with two other infants.

"Replacement," Mala said. "The Beekeeper will match you so you can have your children, too."

Keen stared. These children had been *born* here. They lived here. They knew no other life than the Hive. How long had this been going on? These children were being raised as little drones, would know no other way to think, no other way to live. Would they grow into people like Pug? Her stomach roiled. Mala noticed.

"It's all right," she said. "We need to keep up the Hive, after all, and the Beekeeper will find a good man for you. People have used arranged marriages for thousands of years, long before the choice marriages *they* use, with high divorce rates and single parents and fatherless babies."

"I see," Keen stammered.

"What's wrong?" Mala asked with concern. "It's okay. Really! All the women do it. We are the Hive."

"We are the Hive," Keen repeated automatically,

surprised at how easily it came.

Mala brought her to the main cave, the one just inside the entrance. It was, well, a beehive of activity. Drones worked on the walls and floors and even the ceiling. Their little hammers rose and fell with clinking, tinking noises. One group was extending the frozen ocean waves. Another was smoothing the perfectly round stone sun. A third picked out more detail on the great tree that dominated the room. Still others were laying out wood on the floor or carrying supplies and other materials in and out of the cave. The air was heavy with stone and wood dust, and Keen put on her mask. She was startled to see sunlight pouring in from the cave mouth. Her insides rearranged themselves as she worked out that it was late afternoon. It must be a sign of the Beekeeper's trust that she was allowed to know such things.

One of the drones working on the tree took off his mask a moment to wipe his face. It was Stuart. Keen, greatly daring, trotted over to him.

"Stuart!" she said, taking off her mask so he would recognize her.

He blinked at her, then smiled, the wrinkles on his face rearranging themselves into a grandfatherly benevolence that clashed with his insect-like mask and his green jumpsuit.

"Elizabeth! I'm glad to see you out here. We are the Hive!"

Keen and the workers in the immediate area all repeated the greeting. The drones went back to work.

"Mala put in a good word, and the Beekeeper thought I could join you all," Keen said. "What are we doing?"

"I'm expanding the tree," Stuart said proudly. "Isn't it grand? It was the only thing in the cave when the

Beekeeper found it years ago. It was much smaller then, and it spoke to him with the voice of the Hive. He knew right away this was a holy place. Now it's my honor to continue the work."

Keen did her best to examine his face without seeming to stare. He looked utterly sincere.

"How do you know what to do?"

"The Hive speaks to those who listen," he said fervently. "We just… *know.* You'll understand when you start working yourself. I'm so excited for you!" Impulsively, he leaned forward and kissed her twice, once on each cheek.

"Thank you," Keen said, resisting the impulse to wipe her face.

"Maybe you could work here with me," Stuart continued with a look at Mala, who shrugged. "This tree is thousands of years old, but it's been altered. See this here?" He pointed to the trunk and some of the leaves. "This part is rougher, done with stone tools. But this part over here—" He pointed to the river and the tree roots that twisted around the boulder with a small G on it. For Griffin, Keen supposed. "This part seems to be newer, perhaps two hundred years old. Some of the other drones found a hand-forged chisel, in fact. They left it as a memory to the place. Bees build around what exists, you see. Marvelous creatures." He pointed. On the wooden floor was a small glass-topped case with an old chisel inside.

Stuart handed Keen a chisel and a hammer. For a wild moment she considered whacking him on the head with it and making a break for freedom, but she quashed the idea equally quickly. She'd only get a few steps before someone brought her down, and anyway, she needed to find a way to get closer to that sarin gas before the Hive could sell it. Working with a chisel on a stone bonsai tree in the weird underground lair of a renegade beekeeper wouldn't do that. She thought lightning-fast, and an idea came to her. It seemed sound on a number of levels, except one—it made her stomach tighten and her chest hurt with dread. It would be so much easier just to pick up the chisel and go to work on the tree.

Instead, Special Agent Keen of the FBI turned to Mala and said, "I was wondering if maybe I could work in the nursery?"

"The nursery?" Mala said.

"I've already... had a child," Keen said with a fake smile that broke her own heart, "so I have experience with babies."

Liar, whispered an internal voice. She ignored it.

"And I'd like to... prepare for when I become a mother for the Hive."

"You want to have a child, Elizabeth?" The Beekeeper was standing behind her. Keen jumped a little. Mala made a little noise and looked down. The drones kept working on the wall.

"I do," Keen said.

"That seems a bit of a change for you." The Beekeeper adjusted his enormous coke-bottle glasses and looked her up and down. A pace away stood his wife in her gray dress.

Keen was careful not to contradict. Protesting sounded like lying. "It's something I've realized more and more since I got here," she murmured. "And I thought me working in the nursery might help the Hive. But only if you agree, of course. I'm honored to work wherever the Hive needs me."

The Beekeeper didn't look reassured. He shook his head.

"Mala only recently convinced me to let you out of the training pen, my dear. I don't think you're ready for—"

"Aren't they short-handed in the nursery this week?" Mrs. Griffin said. "Maybe I'm wrong."

The Beekeeper turned to look at her. Mrs. Griffin's plain face remained blank, and she looked down. Keen held her breath. After a long moment, the Beekeeper cleared his throat.

"It's true, the nursery is going short lately," he admitted. "One of the drones has gone missing, and we had to pull people off nursery duty to help the search parties."

"Missing?" The question popped out before Keen could stop herself. She hastily added, "That's awful! I hope he isn't hurt somewhere."

"That's our assumption," said Dr. Griffin, and now Keen knew he was lying. The drone had gone astray, and she knew deep in her gut that somehow Reddington was behind it. But what was he planning?

"The nursery, dear," said Mrs. Griffin.

"Very well," said the Beekeeper. "Get a fresh uniform first. You're already covered in dust."

Keen pressed her hands together. "Thank you, Beekeeper. We are the Hive!"

"We are the Hive," he said.

"Good for you," Stuart said. "Good for *us*."

"Lucky," Mala said as they strolled away. "I never thought to ask."

"Thank you for bringing me out of the pens," Keen said quickly. "I never knew how wonderful freedom could be. Out here. I'm glad I was chosen."

Mala gave her an abstracted nod.

"Sure. John—the Bodysnatcher—is still in there, right?"

"I assume." Keen spread her hands. "He's not ready."

"Definitely not," Mala said firmly.

A few minutes later, Keen arrived in the nursery. Several children were rushing about shouting. A baby was screaming in one of the playpens. One of the harried women was changing another baby while the other was peeling damp clothes from a small child who had wet herself.

"I'm here to help," Keen announced.

The woman at the changing table didn't argue. "See what's wrong with Luke. Then see if you can calm the screamers down."

Luke needed a fresh diaper, too. Keen, who had earned plenty of money babysitting when she was in middle school, zipped him to the other changing table and set to work, trying to ignore the indignant wails.

"Are you all right?" the woman at the next table asked.

"Just the smell," Keen said. "No matter how many you change, it always gets you."

"I was in the military in my old life," the woman said. "Sometimes I think I'd rather be gassed."

Keen thought about the sarin just a few yards down the tunnel. "You know it. I'm Elizabeth."

"Roberta," she said. "That's Sally."

Keen finished fastening the diaper. Luke quieted and cooed a little. Keen couldn't resist tickling his pink tummy, and he laughed. The sound twisted her heart again, and she stopped. Luke went back into his playpen. Then Keen snagged two shrieking little ones.

"Time for a story!" she announced. "Pick out a book by the time I count to seven, the lucky number. One... two..."

It was a trick she had learned babysitting. By the time she got to seven, one of the children had thrust a picture book into her hands. Keen examined it.

"*Busy Buzzy Bee*," she read.

"Thank heavens there's someone new to read that to them," Roberta said. "Sally and I have it memorized."

Keen sat with the children and opened the book. It was home-made and crudely done, with hand-drawn illustrations and a story printed with a magic marker. Keen read aloud.

"Buzzy Bee lived in the happy hive. He made honey with his happy, buzzy friends every day and slept in the cozy cave every night. But across the forest lived the wild, wicked wasps!"

"Wicked!" said one of the girls.

Keen read on. Buzzy and the other busy bees struggled against the machinations of the wicked wasps, and Keen figured the story was going to stress making friends out of enemies, with the usual sappy ending. But halfway through, the story took a different turn.

"When the wild, wicked wasps rushed at Buzzy Bee's beloved hive, Buzzy and the other honey bees loaded their guns and blasted the wasps. Their blood poured out in red rivers—" Here Keen faltered. *What the hell?* The illustration showed anthropomorphized wasps curled on the floor of a beehive, each in a scarlet pool.

"—and the wild, wicked wasps screamed and *died*," prompted one of the boys. "You have to read it!"

Keen did, forcing herself to add emphasis and relish. The children hung on every word.

"*They* will come," said a little girl. "We'll be ready! We are the Hive!"

"We are the Hive!" said the entire room.

"You didn't say it," a boy accused her.

"Sorry," said Keen. "I was thinking about the story. We are the Hive. Now it's time for a nap. No arguing, now! The Beekeeper is watching."

It was the last phrase that did it. The children reluctantly slunk off to a series of cots pushed against one wall, and the three women tucked each of them in.

"You're good with them," Roberta observed. "I'm glad the Hive sent you down. You'll make a wonderful mother, once you're matched."

That sent another pang through Keen, but she forced a tiny smile. "Thank you. I'll need to learn their names, and their—"

One of the babies began to fuss in his playpen.

"I'll get him," Keen said. "He sounds hungry. You sit down."

"Sit?" Roberta laughed. "When they're asleep, we clean. He's probably hungry about now. Formula bottles are in the little fridge over there."

The fussy baby was Luke. Keen picked him up, and her babysitter instincts told her he was indeed hungry. *Sorry, little one*, she said to herself.

She heated a bottle from the fridge while Luke got fussier and fussier and finally exploded into full-blown crying. When Roberta and Sally weren't looking, Keen snagged a small rubber ball from the toy collection, washed it in the sink with her back to them both while the bottle was heating, unscrewed the top of the bottle, and popped the ball inside the nipple. When she cradled Luke to feed him, he sucked greedily, but nothing came out of the bottle. After a few seconds, he spat the nipple out and cried again.

"Poor thing," Keen murmured. "Take your bottle now."

She gave it to him again, and again he couldn't drink, so he spat it out and cried some more. Keen jigged him up and down in her arms, but that only made him cry worse.

"I think he's just cranky," Keen said. "How about I just walk him around a little to settle him down?"

Before either woman could object, Keen strolled out the door with the screaming Luke in her arms. The moment she was out of sight, she removed the ball from the nipple and gave the bottle back to Luke. Instantly, his cries ended.

"You're a good baby," she cooed. "Yes, you are. Yes, you *are*. And you're going to help Auntie Elizabeth destroy the Hive."

CHAPTER FIFTEEN

Aram Mojtabai's eyes darted back and forth as he scanned the final few lines of code. TV always portrayed IT guys and gals as pulling off miracles, and often they did, but the shows never showed how much *work* it took, especially when it came to code. You couldn't just whip together something in ten minutes. It took hours, days, to create something new, but thanks to television and movies, people expected computer techs to pull off the impossible in a flash.

Fortunately, in this case, Aram got lucky. The basic software he needed already existed, and the override key Reddington wanted was fairly straightforward. All it needed was a frequency detector, a direct-action virus, and a control system upload. Meld them together, and you were good to go. It was the melding that was the trouble, and that was what Aram was checking now. He had no way to field-test this before he gave it to Reddington, so he was triple-checking his triple-checking.

And through it all, he worried. He worried about Keen and Ressler, held in captivity. He worried about the pressure from Reddington if he failed to get the job done. And he worried about—

"Got an update, Aram?"

Agent Navabi.

She was standing behind him with a reusable mug from a chain store. It filled the air with the fragrant smell of salted caramel latte. Aram's stomach rumbled, and he tried to remember when he'd last eaten.

"The agents down in South Carolina haven't found a thing and they're ready to shove it," he reported, fairly sure the code on his screen would mean nothing to her. "If it weren't for the fact that so many of our agents have disappeared, they'd probably have given up by now."

"Cooper's getting antsy." Navabi gestured up at the Director's office. "He's fielded two more phone calls from Pavel Rudenko. The guy keeps offering—or threatening—to send in a team of mercenaries called Green Alpha Something-or-Other to find Mala, even though he wouldn't have any idea where to look. Panabaker's having fits."

"Still looking." Aram changed the subject. "Anything on the Iris Henning murder?"

"Her hyoid bone was broken, and the ME found evidence of petechial hemorrhaging. The decay hid evidence of bruising on her neck, but it was strangulation, no question. The techs didn't find anything in the apartment. Not a hair, not a thread, nothing."

"And the bath water?" Aram shuddered.

"Just her... material," Navabi admitted. "Gruesome work. You couldn't pay me enough. What are you working on now?"

Damn it. He'd been hoping the change of subject would distract her.

"Something unrelated," he said.

"Really?" She took a sip of latte. "Keen and Ressler are missing, Cooper said there *are* no other priorities. Plus Rudenko keeps a lot of Pentagon people happy, and they're leaning on us. Everyone is working on this case and nothing else. So when you say *unrelated*…"

"Right, no, yeah," he said. "I mean, I'm not looking at the case, you know, *directly*. I'm debugging a search program that I hope will help. So it's not directly related, but it's close to being related." He was babbling, and he tried to make himself shut up, but his mouth ran away with him, like it always did. "So I'm working on the case indirectly. Like when a Sherpa hauls equipment up Mount Everest for the climber and gets to the top but doesn't get credit for it. I'm debugging code, nothing weird or strange. Just… debugging."

Jeez, his friggin' *hands* were sweating. She looked at him coolly, her eyes empty of any suspicion or doubt. For a moment, he had hope. But with yet another thoughtful sip, Navabi put on her investigator face. Hope died and Aram was dead with it.

"So this program you're debugging," she said slowly, "it's for tracking something."

"What makes you say that?" he said.

"I'm not a programmer, but I recognize a megahertz frequency when I see it," she said, pointing.

He licked his lips. When Aram was eight years old, a horse of a boy named Gus Backmeijer had pushed him off his bike and ridden away on it, laughing. When Aram arrived home with bruised knees and a scraped face, his mother had demanded to know what had happened. Aram, greatly ashamed at losing a fight to a bully, had stammered out a story that he had fallen off his bike and flattened the tire, so he'd walked home. His mother hadn't believed him for a second, and asked for details about the encounter, poking at the holes in Aram's story until he'd tearfully admitted that Gus had stolen his bike. When Aram's father had come home, Mother had told him about it, and Father had stormed out of the house. A few minutes later, Aram's newly scratched and battered bike was back in the garage and Aram received a spanking.

"Only a fool lies to his mother," Father scolded. "Learn from this!"

Now he was facing down Navabi's implacable brown eyes as they bored gently into him, just like his mother's, and he found that both revelatory and disturbing. He sighed and resigned himself.

"Look," he said, "a couple days ago, I got a call. It was Reddington."

"Reddington *called* you?" she all but yelped.

"Sh!" He looked furtively around, but no one seemed to have heard. "Don't shout it around."

She brought her head closer and lowered her voice like impending thunder.

"Why didn't you say something?"

"He made me keep quiet about it."

"You need to explain that—and be pointy."

"Pointy?"

"No nattering. And you're stalling." She gave him a grim smile. "Besides, you'll feel better once you talk."

He sighed and explained.

"So Reddington needs this key and he wants you— us—to keep quiet because if we go in there with guns blazing, he's afraid we'll have another Waco," she summed up.

"That's about it," he said. "Are you going to tell Cooper?"

There was a long, awful pause. Aram realized she

was going to say *yes*. His heart sank, but with that also came some relief. He wouldn't be responsible anymore. Someone else could make the decisions. The burden would lift, he could take whatever lumps the FBI dished out for withholding information, and he could go on as before. Thank heavens. His posture eased as tension slid out of him.

"No," Navabi said.

"No?" he echoed stupidly.

"I think Reddington's right," she said, implacable as a bulldozer. "We'll have a massacre on our hands if Cooper and Panabaker find out. Keep your mouth shut, do as Reddington asks, and we'll deal with the repercussions later."

The tension tightened. "But—"

"What's he want the key for?" she interrupted pointedly.

Aram pursed his lips. Fine. He had no choice anyway. "I have no idea. But I have to get it there in five hours."

"And how," she asked, "are you going to do that when the Sumter National Forest is at least eight hours away by car?"

A pang speared Aram's stomach, and he checked his watch, a useless but automatic gesture. "Oh my god. I've been so focused on just *making* the key."

Navabi made a grim face. "You'll probably have a solution in just a minute." She nodded at the staircase to the Director's office. Harold Cooper and Cyntha Panabaker were quick-stepping it down the steps toward them.

Aram's heart sped up. "Are you going to tell them?"

"I think the tougher question is if *you* are going to tell them," she said. "You just can't hold it in, can you?"

"It's miserable," he admitted.

"Just follow my lead," she said.

It belatedly occurred to Aram that Navabi wasn't planning to say anything, was even going to help him. His knees went weak. Automatically he saved the new sets of code and fumbled in his desk for a flash drive.

"News," Cooper said without preamble. "Three bodies have washed up on the shore of the Parr Shoals Reservoir."

That was south of the Sumter National Forest, where Reddington was. Aram's fingers automatically moved, calling up maps and information on the auxiliary screens.

"The Parr Shoals Reservoir was created by a dam on the Broad River, here." He highlighted a section of the river south of the reservoir, where the highway crossed the water. "Very dangerous section of water—full of old trees, snags, and even houses that were covered over when the dam went in. Fishing not recommended."

"May I?" Cooper gestured at the boards, and Aram obligingly backed away, though he kept a nervous eye on his new program. Cooper called up photos of bruised and bloated bodies. All male, all naked. "As it happens, it was a group of adventurous fishermen who pulled these three bodies out of the water. They called the police, and we caught wind of it."

Aram swallowed nausea. He had seen hundreds of crime scene photos, many of them worse than these, but they still made his stomach roil.

"Our guys?" Navabi asked.

"Probably," Panabaker said. "The police still don't know about the manhunt, and we're keeping it that way. We need to send a team down there to find out for sure and to search for more bodies."

"We'll go with them," Navabi said promptly.

"We will?" Aram asked in surprise.

Navabi stepped hard on his foot. "Didn't you tell me you had that new sonar device for checking underwater?"

"Oh! Yeah." Aram coughed. "Yeah, I could totally try that out and look for other bodies."

"Good," Cooper said. "Get on the plane with the others. When you arrive, grab a van and head down there. Make nice with the locals, but I want those bodies back here by sunset."

"We might have to stay longer," Navabi said casually. "If Aram's sonar device gives us anything. We'll tell them all about it when we get down there rather than call now. It'll save time."

"Sure, sure," Cooper said. "Just get a move on!"

Plane, Aram thought, making grateful eye contact with Navabi. *And a van.* That would let him get down there in a couple hours. Aram tapped his keyboard with chilly fingers, moving the key to his flash drive.

Three hours later, Aram was driving a van down relentlessly sunny back roads. Tarmac rushed under the van's wheels, and the open windows let the hot breeze blast through the passenger cabin. Green mountains looked down on lush valleys peppered with clumps of houses and fenced-in farms. Many—too many—of the houses sat on cement blocks, reached by bowed wooden steps. Several looked like they'd been stitched together from a dozen different houses, showing different styles of siding or windows. Aram was no stranger to poverty—Washington DC had more than its share—but this was a different kind of poverty, the kind that was stranded out in the middle of nowhere, unconnected to a chance for something bigger or better. There was no subway, no bus—no escape to a different part of town that at least had a library or the occasional job. This poverty lay hidden, where no one could reach it, and it could reach nothing. It made Aram sadder than anything in the east side tenements in DC.

On the floor beside the driver's seat was a duffel bag. In his pocket was the flash drive. The latter weighed heavily, as if it were made of lead. Navabi had stayed with the team investigating the bodies, a team that mysteriously didn't learn that Aram had a fictitious sonar device, or that he was even supposed to be there with Navabi. He had used his ID and Cooper's name to get a van from the lot at the South Carolina field office after the plane landed, and now he was trying to follow the directions on the cell phone in his lap without getting into a car accident. The van had GPS, but Aram didn't want to risk using it.

The east entrance to the park was a little more than an hour away. Aram spent the time whistling tunelessly through his teeth and listening to preachers on the radio. Some of them seemed to live in a scarier world than even Raymond Reddington, which said something. That it was a world of their own making was both frightening and cheerless. Aram wouldn't trade places with any one of them, even now.

Eventually he started seeing signs for the park, and they increased in frequency as he got closer. He also noticed that several times his phone lost the GPS signal and had to hunt for it again. Fortunately, he didn't need it anymore, not with the steady stream of signage pointing him the way. When he was a few minutes away, he took advantage of a time when he actually had a signal to send a text message to the satellite phone signal he had gotten from Reddington earlier:

Almost there.

He got no response, and had no way to know if the message had gotten hung up in the poor signaling or if Reddington was keeping quiet. Probably the latter, knowing Reddington. Aram blew out his cheeks. This was fireable offense time. This was probably prosecutorial offense time. He should pull over, call Cooper, and come clean.

And then he thought of Reddington's eyes, with the screaming inside them, and his blood ran cold in his veins. Never mind, then. Besides, he couldn't get a decent cell signal to call Cooper anyway. Must be the mountains.

He pulled up to the park entrance, paid the entry fee to the smiling ranger, and drove in. Trees closed in around the van, and he put the windows up to make himself feel more secure. A few minutes later he arrived at an intersection. He pulled over, confused. What now? He had no idea which way to go.

A knock came at his window.

Aram yelped in panic and fumbled for his pistol, though he couldn't remember the last time he had fired it, god, he was supposed to keep current on his training and now he was going to die in this forsaken—

The knock came again. It was Dembe.

Reddington's bodyguard made a rolling motion with his hand, though no car built in the last fifteen years had a handle for rolling down a window. Aram thumped his chest a couple of times to make sure his heart was still working and brought the window down.

"Move over," Dembe said. "I will drive."

About ten minutes later, Dembe was leading Aram toward a falling-down wreck of a house half-buried in the side of the hill. Aram thought Dembe had to be joking. The place looked as though it was going to collapse into itself like a black hole at any moment. Outside the decrepit building was parked a battered brown van that looked like it might puff into rusty dust if someone blew hard on it. As Aram looked, two men emerged from the house. Swiftly they pulled a camouflage tarp over the van and trotted away. In the distance, an engine came to life and tires crunched away.

"Who were those guys?" Aram asked.

"No one you need worry about," Dembe said.

Seconds after that, when Aram had stepped beyond the falling-down shell and was standing in the well-appointed, airy living room beyond, he resisted the impulse to rub his eyes. It was, he mused, some kind of metaphor, but he wasn't quite sure what kind.

"Aram!" Reddington emerged from what Aram assumed was a bedroom. "I was wondering how long it would take you. It would be awful if you got lost out here and no one ever found you again."

"No," Aram said, clutching the duffel bag to his chest. "I mean, yes. I mean—"

"Don't forget I charge by the hour," called a wheezy voice from inside the bedroom. "The world's most expensive babysitter, that's me."

"Understood," Reddington called back over his shoulder, then said to Aram, "Another associate of mine. Likes his Sudoku."

"I… see."

"I'd offer you a drink," Reddington continued, "we aren't barbarians here, but I know you don't touch alcohol, and in any case, we're in something of a hurry.

You did bring what I asked for?" He chuckled a little too loudly. "What am I saying? Of course you did! You wouldn't come all this way just to disappoint me."

"No," Aram said again. "I mean, yes! I mean—here!"

He shoved the duffel bag at Reddington. Dembe quickly intercepted it, put it on the coffee table, and unzipped it. It held a small laptop computer, a helicopter drone with four propellers, and a video game controller that seemed to have lost a fight with a portable DVD player.

"Excellent, Aram," Reddington beamed. "What am I looking at?"

Aram swallowed and forced himself to stay calm. Reddington needed him. Reddington wasn't going to do anything to him. It was all in Aram's head. But Reddington's hard eyes still held the screams, and Aram's mouth dried up.

"Maybe that drink?" he said. "Club soda."

"With a twist, Dembe," Reddington added. "As I said, we're not barbarians here. Now, what is this?"

Aram sipped the fizzy water. His hand shook slightly. "The helicopter drone is the same kind you see people fiddle with on the beach. They send them into the air and take videos of their kids—or of their neighbors undressing at home."

"I'm familiar with the concept," Reddington said. "The military loves them, though each one has an explosively short lifespan. What are these devices?"

"This one," Aram picked up the controller, "controls the drone. Watch." With the flick of a switch, he activated it. The drone whirred to life and buzzed unsteadily toward the high ceiling. The screen on the controller showed the three men looking up at it from a foreshortened perspective, the sort of view a hummingbird might have of human beings.

"I'm not that great at controlling these things," Aram admitted. "My nephew has one, and he can send it all over the place. You know that delivery companies are playing with using these. They see a sky filled with drones one day."

"I look forward to practicing my skeet shooting when that day arrives," Reddington said. "What's the other device for?"

Now on territory where he was the expert, Aram felt himself relaxing a little. "Dembe, can you take over this?"

Dembe sent the helicopter drone skimming about the ceiling while Aram booted up the laptop and plugged what looked like a small walkie-talkie into it.

"You brought the key, didn't you?" Reddington said.

"It's here." Aram pulled the flash drive from his pocket and plugged it into the laptop next to the other device. He then clicked with the touch pad. A green light flickered on the walkie-talkie device, and a new program came to life on the laptop screen.

"This got tricky," Aram said. "GPS doesn't work very well around the park because of the mountains, so—"

"Because the Beekeeper is jamming the signals," Reddington corrected.

"Jamming?" Aram repeated.

"The effect is the same, even if the cause is different," Reddington said. "Go on."

"Oh. Hold on, then." Keys chattered beneath Aram's fingers. "I wish you'd said something earlier. I assumed it was the mountains—this changes everything."

"Explain," Reddington said in a voice that tightened the tendons on Aram's hands.

"GPS signals don't work like people think," Aram said. "The satellites kind of… spray a radio signal all over the world, and it has a time code in it. A GPS device down here receives the signal and figures out where you are. Most people think the satellite tracks you, but it doesn't. See, most GPS satellites were put up there in the seventies and they use really old technology, but it doesn't matter because your *device* uses the signal, not the satellite. When your cell phone or car receives a GPS signal, it triangulates your position based on the signals it gets from the four GPS satellites above you at any time." He was falling into a rhythm now, unable to stop himself. "Your device then figures out your position on a map. However, most personal devices don't have the memory to carry a detailed street map of the USA inside them, so your phone accesses a map on a remote database so it can drop that little pin for you. *That* transmission is what we at the Post Office use to track people's phones—we get the same information your phone is sending to the map database. Your phone tells us where you are. The GPS satellites don't tell us anything."

"What, exactly, does this have to do with jamming the signal?" Reddington asked.

"There are two ways to screw up GPS tracking," Aram replied. "Someone can stop your device from accessing its database. This is tricky because you'd have to watch for every device in the area and shut it down individually. The second way is much easier."

"And that is?"

"To jam the incoming GPS signal," Aram said. "You can do that with parts from Radio Shack, if you know what you're doing and if Radio Shack hadn't gone out of business."

"So the Beekeeper is probably jamming incoming GPS signals," Reddington said.

"Yeah. And it'll jam up the key, too. I can't do anything with it unless I have an incoming GPS signal."

"Are you telling me," Reddington said, too slowly, too quietly, "that your key won't do what I need it to do?"

All the ground Aram had gained vanished beneath him like sand in an earthquake. "I… I'm not…"

"Because if I got you here after all that time and effort," Reddington continued with cocked head, "I would have a right to be upset, don't you think?"

All Aram's voice deserted him. He simply stared at Reddington.

A sound emerged from the bedroom. Reddington jerked his head toward it. Dembe set down the helicopter control, leaving the drone hovering near the ceiling, and went inside. Aram belatedly wondered what Reddington had been doing in that room—and to whom.

"You know, when I was a student at the Naval Academy," Reddington said, "I knew a boy named Russ Dickworthy. A very unfortunate name, and, as you can imagine, the other cadets made his life miserable. The shared showers were a nightmare for him. But he stuck through it with clenched teeth and a loud *Yes, sir!* whenever someone called for one."

"And… he graduated?" Aram said.

"He would have," Reddington said amiably, "except that during a hand-to-hand combat class, he broke the neck of one of the other boys who had been particularly difficult to him with the soap. The *crunch* sounded like stale crackers. Two of the cadets threw up their shepherd's pie. The incident was hushed up, and young Mr. Dickworthy was sent home. I believe he owns a chain of shoe stores these days. He signs his last name D-Worthy."

"I see," Aram lied.

The helicopter drone continued to hover over both of them. Reddington leaned forward, right into Aram's personal space. He could smell the Scotch on Reddington's breath.

"What's your stale-cracker moment, Aram? When are *you* going to snap?"

Aram froze, a squirrel staring at the oncoming car. He started to speak, and his words would be angry. They would be strong.

A grunt came from the bedroom, and a muffled thud. Reddington continued his hard stare. Aram licked dry lips, and the angry words died in his throat. He looked down instead.

"Not today, then?" Reddington said. "Good." He leveled a hard stare. "Fix. My. Key."

"I never said I couldn't," Aram told him. "It's just—"

"Yes?"

"GPS satellites broadcast their signals on 1575.42 megahertz," Aram said. "If the Beekeeper has a jammer, it must be attuned to that frequency."

"What does that mean?" Reddington said.

"It means no drone in this area is receiving GPS signals, which means the computer can't tell where they are," Aram said.

"If that's true," Reddington said, "the Beekeeper's helicopter drones wouldn't work, either."

"Right. I'm assuming they do work—otherwise he wouldn't have them. However, the GPS satellites also broadcast a backup signal at 1227.6 megahertz. Most people don't know that, but the Beekeeper likely does.

He's probably attuned his drones to 1227.6." Aram's fingers jumped around the keyboard. "If I change the key to operate at that frequency, we should be in business. And... so!"

Aram's laptop screen flickered, died, then burst into a glowing map of the park. More than a dozen red dots clumped over one spot, and a lone dot blinked at another. Aram let out a long sigh.

"There," he breathed. "It works. Watch."

He selected the lone dot, then tapped at the keyboard again. The hovering helicopter drone shuddered, then zipped into the kitchen. It crashed into a cupboard and fell to the floor.

"Oops." Aram hurried in to snatch it up. "You get the idea."

"That's wonderful, Aram! I'm impressed!" Like a switch had been flicked, Reddington's countenance changed completely and he clapped Aram on the back in a gesture that nearly stopped Aram's heart. "How many of these can you control with that key?"

Dembe emerged from the bedroom. He was wiping his hands on a handkerchief.

"Uh... all of them," Aram replied. "Plug this key into any computer or device that can broadcast a signal, and you're good to go."

"Really? You could barely handle the one drone a moment ago."

"Well, yeah, but if you want to control a group, you probably want them all to go to one place, right? You enter the coordinates into the program here—" he demonstrated "—and the computer will handle the flying. The key will override their controllers and force them to go wherever you want. One of them or a hundred."

"Show me how to do it."

"You mind me asking what this is for?" Aram said, greatly daring. "I mean, Keen and Ressler are in those caves—that's where the helicopter drones are. Why aren't we going in there to get them out? And extracting this Beekeeper guy?"

"I imagine Elizabeth is doing considerable damage to the Beekeeper as we speak," Reddington said grimly. "But rest assured, Aram, I'm doing everything in my power to ensure her safe return, and this key is essential to that process. Now, if you don't mind demonstrating? I'm not at my best with computer technology."

Aram did so, trying not to cringe away from Reddington—and whatever he had in that bedroom. Now he could hear... wheezing? The sound of stale crackers crunched through Aram's head. Despite his earlier protestations, Reddington proved a quick study, and although he didn't actually activate the Beekeeper's helicopter drones with the key, he proved adept at overriding and controlling the one Aram had brought with him. It seemed strange to see Reddington at a computer, and Aram realized he had never actually seen Reddington touch one before.

When Reddington was satisfied he could control the drones with decent skill, he asked Dembe to kindly bring him another Scotch while Aram elaborately stretched his back. He couldn't wait to be away from here, and back on familiar ground.

"Well," Aram said, "now that you have everything you need, I'll be on my way. The rest of the team will be wondering where I've got to. Can Dembe show me the way out of the park?"

"Out?" Reddington said archly. "Goodness, no, Aram. I need you here. I assume you saw my friends delivering that van outside. Dembe will shortly be busy with other things, and I'm going to need a driver. I was thinking… you."

Aram heard the sound of more stale crackers.

CHAPTER SIXTEEN

Elizabeth Keen wandered into the Beekeeper's underground laboratory with baby Luke in her arms. He sucked greedily at the bottle. Unlike before, when Keen had slipped in with Mala, the lab now hopped with activity, and Keen took in details she hadn't been able to see in the dim light with Mala. People bustled around from table to table, working with complex-looking machinery. A great many small canisters, each the size of a jar of apple juice, stood in open-top crates, all marked with the chemical danger symbol. In the corner stood an emergency shower. One table was taken up with rows of computers, and a wall was stacked with racks and racks of helicopter drones plugged into their chargers. Keen blinked, remembering the remote-control test she had seen outside the Hive with Dembe, just before she had allowed herself to be captured. Now she could see them up close, and they were muscular helicopter drones, built to power-lift serious payloads. Military grade. The Beekeeper had fingers—antennae—in many places. She still had no idea what they could be for.

Several Hive drones in jumpsuits tapped away at

computers, and while they didn't wear masks, they kept them close at hand on their belts. Keen glanced at the canisters and felt uneasy without her own. If one of those things sprung a leak, she would be dead in seconds—along with nearly everyone in the Hive who wasn't wearing a mask. Including Luke. His soft milk smell filled her nose, and a vision of his face turning blue as he coughed up blood and stared up at Keen, not understanding why he was in so much pain as his tiny life slipped away, crossed Keen's mind. She swallowed nausea.

"What are you doing?" One of the drones rushed over to her. "You shouldn't be in here."

"Sorry. It's the baby," she said, presenting him. Luke continued sucking at the bottle. "Isn't he sweet?"

"He's not supposed to be here," snapped the drone.

"I'm walking him to keep him quiet. When I stop, he cries." She gave the drone a vacant smile. If she had been chewing gum, she would have popped it. "He seems to like it in here."

"Take him out," the drone ordered. He was a tallish man with receding red hair that was pulled into a small ponytail. "Scoot, lady!"

"Yeah, sure." She turned to go and used the gesture to pull the bottle from Luke's mouth. Instantly he set up a wail. Everyone in the lab looked up. Keen turned back around and put the bottle in his mouth again. Luke quieted. "Wow. He *does* like it here."

"It's like that Snoopy special," the drone said. "No dogs allowed. Or birds. Or kids. Out!"

"Okay," Keen said. "Hey, like, what's your name, anyway?"

"Vernon," the drone replied. "Vernon Headly. I worked with Dr. Griffin—the Beekeeper—back in his army days and now I run the lab for him. Why?"

This guy had been in the army?

Keen shrugged. "The Beekeeper wants his son happy, like, all the time, you know? When Lukey here cries, the Beekeeper gets kinda pissed, and I don't wanna get in trouble, right? So when he asks why Lukey's crying, I hafta tell him who told me to take him away from the place that makes him happy. I mean, I can't lie to the Beekeeper."

Vernon paled beneath his ponytail. "That's the Beekeeper's son? How can the Beekeeper have a son? Mrs. Griffin would never let him shag some girl drone in the off hours, man."

"Oops." Keen's face fell. "I wasn't supposed to say anything. This isn't his *real* son, like by birth, right? Lukey is his chosen successor. We're feeding him special stuff to make him grow strong. I wasn't supposed to say anything. You won't tell, will you?" She looked anxious. "It's our secret. Promise?"

"Oh." Vernon thought a moment, and a number of emotions crossed his face. "Sure. Promise. Rad."

"Thanks," she said. "Like, we are the Hive!"

"We are the Hive," Vernon repeated faintly.

"Anyway, we don't wanna make trouble in the lab, Vernon, so I'll go, even if it makes Lukey unhappy." Keen raised Luke's fingers in a wave. "Say *bye*, Lukey! Don't cry, okay?"

"Hey, that's all right," Vernon said. "Look, I'm sure it won't be a problem for… him. Just stay out of the way."

She shook her head. "No, I should go. I wouldn't want to make trouble."

"Really!" Vernon insisted. "Stay! It's all pumpadelic!"

"You won't tell anyone what I said?" Keen said

anxiously. "About Lukey? Before the Beekeeper announces it?"

"Won't say a word." He raised his right hand. "Word!"

"You're great, Vernon." Keen leaned toward him. "The Beekeeper comes into the nursery all the time, you know, because of… well, you know why. I'll say some nice stuff about you."

"Really?" Vernon smoothed the front of his green jumpsuit. "Thanks."

Keen checked the bottle. Luke was nearly done with it. "Where are things with the sarin gas, anyway? The Beekeeper talks about it a lot. He wants to know if Lukey is gonna be safe."

"We're almost done," Vernon boasted. "Right on schedule. We're just waiting on the final shipment of tributylamine."

"Try what?" Keen cracked her imaginary gum again.

"Tributylamine." Vernon gestured at the lab with obvious pride. He was clearly dying to talk to someone about all this, and Keen was happy to let him. "Rad stuff. Sarin is a binary chemical weapon, see. When it's stored as a single gas, it's harmless. Just before you use it, you mix it with tributylamine, and that makes it a mega-weapon. People clawing their eyes out, coughing up blood, mucus, guts, whatever the hell you want, man. Once the final shipment arrives, we'll have enough to weaponize the rest of the sarin, and the plan will be a blast at last."

"Right." Keen jiggled Luke on her arm. "The plan." She took a shot in the dark. "The helicopter drones— have they all been tested so they'll work right when the time comes?"

"Well, yeah!" Vernon looked offended. "They're all

slaved to the main computer with a special key I gave to the big man himself, and we tested them with some smoke capsules. They spread the stuff like a hooker spreads syphilis." He gave a little giggle. "With the computer in control to guarantee maximum efficiency, we'll wipe out the entire countryside in no time, just as the Beekeeper planned."

Keen's knees weakened and her arms tightened around Luke. Dread made her arms go cold. The Beekeeper had said he was planning to use the sarin, but he had been vague about who the victims would be, and when he wanted to use it. She hadn't considered he was planning to use it so soon and so close. She glanced at the sarin canisters, standing like little missile silos near their crates. How many thousands of people would they kill? How many people were even now innocently having dinner at home or playing in the back yard or kissing their loved ones hello, not realizing that only a few miles away, their deaths awaited at the hand of a lunatic in coke-bottle glasses?

"So the key," she said, "lets him control all the drones at once and wipe out a whole town? That's... pretty awesome."

"Isn't it?" Vernon smiled, and lowered his voice. "That must be why the Beekeeper has chosen a successor."

"A successor?"

"His son," Vernon said, a little suspicion in his voice now.

Vernon's words had distracted her and she fumbled to recover. "Oh! Yeah. I'll bet that's it. All part of the plan." She paused. "The key must be pretty cool. Can I see it? No, of course I can't."

Vernon wasn't up for the denial game this time. "It's in the safe over there," he said pointing. "It's not much to look at anyway. Just a flash drive you plug into the computer."

"Wow," Keen said. "I can barely, like, figure out a cell phone."

He gave her a condescending smile. "Rad. Once everything's been cleansed, we can come out from underground. We can take all of Roebuck and the other towns for ourselves, and the man won't be able to touch us. Not with the drones and more gas to protect us."

Keen was a trained psychologist. From her first days of psych classes at UVA through her behavioral sciences training at Quantico, it had been pounded into her head that there was no such thing as *crazy* or *lunatic*. There was an explanation for every strange disorder of the human mind, whether it was schizophrenia, narcissism, or dissociative identity disorder. But here diagnostic words failed her. The guy was plain nuts. This plan had no hope of succeeding. None. Even if the sarin gas killed the maximum number of victims possible, "cleansing" the area of all non-Hive people, the Hive wouldn't be able to spread out and take over the area just because they had gas masks and a bunch of weapons. The National Guard would eat them alive within hours.

But that hardly mattered. What mattered was that Vernon, that the Beekeeper, *thought* it could work, that they intended to kill thousands of people by unleashing a cloud of deadly chemicals big enough to wipe out an entire city. Suddenly the stakes were far higher than Keen had imagined. It no longer mattered if the FBI and the Hive got into a standoff. What mattered was shutting them down in any way possible. Taking the Hive down from the inside would take too long. She had to find a way to contact the Post Office, even if it meant she herself got caught in the crossfire.

Luke finished the bottle and spat the nipple out. He looked up at her with his baby's brown eyes. Luke. Keen clutched him to her chest. The babies. The children. She hadn't really thought about them, about their future. They were in terrible danger. If a Post Office task force showed up, they would be in even more danger. What was she going to do?

"That's… great," Keen managed, and put Luke over her shoulder to burp him. "I'm glad the Beekeeper's great plan is going perfectly. We are the Hive."

"We are the Hive, baby," Vernon agreed.

Luke burped in her ear.

Donald Ressler stared into the darkness of his damp cell and thought of home. He thought of his apartment in Washington, where he had a comfortable bed—and the occasional warm partner to share it. He thought about his living room, with the big TV and the video game system he'd had since college and still dragged out to play sometimes. He thought about the kitchen drawer filled with takeout menus from restaurants all over DC, places that would deliver pizza oozing with melted cheese, spicy Thai noodles, crispy sweet-and-sour pork, or tongue-blistering curry with pillowy naan bread. Oh, yeah. It was the food he missed the most. Even curled on a thin, nasty mattress he had folded in half to get maximum insulation from the ground, even in this itchy, filthy jumpsuit, even in this dark, damp, dull cell, the thing he missed most was the damn food.

He concentrated on the food, used it as both sword and shield. When the Bastard—Ressler's private name for the Beekeeper—ran him through those treatments and he could feel his mind crumbling bit by bit, he concentrated on the food to keep himself sane. Girardi's deep dish sausage and mushroom pizza kept him from feeling vulnerable when the drones stung him with their damned tasers. Jade Dragon's crispy duck stopped him from feeling ashamed when he confessed his sins in the circle. And Moon House's tender pad thai kept him from feeling naked and alone when the Beekeeper drilled into his mind with those horrible injections. Sometimes it felt like tiny pieces of himself were falling away, slipping through his fingers like water, and clinging to memories of home was the only way to slow the damage.

Slow it. Not stop it.

He knew he was changing. He noticed the way he automatically responded "We are the Hive!" whenever someone said it to him first. He noticed the way he flinched whenever one of the drones waved a taser. He noticed the way he salivated every time the Beekeeper opened that cooler like it was the treasure chest of an Egyptian pharaoh.

He didn't want to give in, but more than once he found himself thinking how easy it would be. Just do what the Beekeeper wanted, and he could sleep in a real bed, and have a hot shower, and eat real food, and do something besides chip at cold stone for hours on end.

Ressler shifted on the mattress. It was just him and John-the-Bodysnatcher in the pens now. Stuart, the weakling, had turned into a happy Hiver, and Keen had manipulated her way out of the cell one sleep ago. He hoped that she was figuring out a way to contact Reddington, or Cooper, or anyone at all.

More than once he had tried to find a way out of

the cell. He had gone over every inch of the place with eyes and fingers, but everything hard was bolted down and everything else was too soft to be useful. Even the so-called food was served on styrofoam, with no cutlery. Nothing to fashion a tool or weapon from. And the drones were frighteningly good at security. Even if Ressler managed to overpower the half-dozen of them that showed up to haul him and John to circle time, it would be all but impossible to make it out of the tunnels without being noticed and caught. Not without help.

FBI regs said when you couldn't do anything, you sat tight and waited. Eventually, the situation would change. And Donald Ressler always followed the regs. The regs worked. They were tried and tested methods of solving problems. They removed worry from field work. No matter what the situation, the regs had you covered.

Except when they didn't.

The regs didn't cover what to do when Audrey died in his arms, and they didn't cover what to do when physical and emotional pain became so great that the only way to get through another day was to cloud it with little white pills. But they *did* cover what to do when the little white pills took over those cloudy days—you had to quit cold turkey, and the pain came roaring back so bad that all you could do was yell into your pillow until your voice was gone. And then you *hated* the regs—but then it was yourself you really hated, because you were *weak*.

That was it, wasn't it? He was weak.

He had been too weak to stop himself falling in love with Audrey, too weak to stop her murder, too weak to keep himself off the pills. And that was why, once Keen had gone rogue, he had gone after her with a zeal that made him squirm even now, in this dark, damp cell on this unforgiving mattress. Even when she had shown him she was innocent, he had cited the regs and gone after her even harder, just to show that he wasn't weak. The regs made him strong.

But in the end, the regs had broken him again. Keen had proven to everyone that she was innocent, and the FBI had taken her back, while Ressler—the fool who had followed the regs—had been forced to beg her forgiveness. She said she understood, but that made it even worse. Keen had already ferreted out his love affair with the little white pills. If she understood why he had pursued her so relentlessly, it meant that she also understood he was weak, and he hated that.

He chewed the inside of his mouth. That wasn't really true. He liked Keen and respected her. They got on fine now. They did. He was putting his own thoughts into her. Or was he? He clenched a fist at his temple. It was hard to tell in this place. He was hungry all the time, and exhausted and stressed, and sometimes he felt as though it would be so much easier to just hand himself over to the Hive. The regs were really easy here: just do as the Beekeeper said. He'd be great on their security teams. He had already seen areas of inefficiency in their operation, and if Ressler told the Beekeeper about them, maybe even volunteered to help clear them up, he could probably get some extra food, maybe even some meat or peanut butter. He was used to commanding a team, so he'd be an officer or something very shortly. Why not? No more thoughts of Audrey, no more thoughts of pills, no more—

He pinched himself hard, his own private sting.

What was he thinking? It was this place, the way the Beekeeper drilled into his memory with those damned drugs and confession sessions. He had to keep it together. He had to…

"Ressler!"

The whisper jerked him upright. Keen was standing at the bars of his cage, her features barely visible in the dim light. Ressler scrambled to his feet, then wobbled under the head rush and the lack of food.

"Keen!" he said. "Are you all right? Are you holding… a baby?"

"No time," she said. "You have to escape. Now. Tonight."

"How?" Ressler hissed. "Keys. Guards. Drones."

Keen dropped a shiny object into the pen. "I lifted it off one of the drones. I'll take care of the guards. Wait for the signal."

"Why now?" he whisper-shouted. "What's going on?"

"The Beekeeper is making sarin gas. He's going to use it on the towns around this place to carve out his own little kingdom. Probably tomorrow." She shifted the baby. "You have to get help now!"

The blood in Ressler's body iced over. "Jesus."

"I have to go."

Keen turned her back and vanished up the tunnel, baby clutched in her arms. It was the strangest damn thing Ressler had seen, and in the Hive, that was saying a lot.

"Don't leave me here," John the Bodysnatcher hissed from his own cell. Crap! Ressler had completely forgotten about him. "You have to take me. If you don't, I'll shout."

"Yeah, yeah."

Ressler was already reaching awkwardly through the bars, trying to maneuver the key into the lock. It was freaking hard. The key was small, it was dark, and he was working from the outside in. Why couldn't Keen have just opened the lock for him? The key poked at the lock, missed, poked once more, went partially in, then slipped back out. Ressler gritted his teeth and tried again. Metal scraped on metal, horribly loud in the quiet cave. Someone would come any second now, he was sure. They'd see him with his arm outside the cage. He poked at the lock again.

An alarm shrieked in his ear and whirling red lights slashed through the darkness. Ressler jumped, and the key fell from his fingers. It tinked and bounced on the floor. No! Where was it?

"What the hell happened?" John demanded.

"That must be Keen's doing," Ressler said. "Where's the key?"

"You *dropped* it?" John clutched at his own bars. "Oh my god! You're dumber than a bowl of oatmeal."

"Not helping," Ressler snapped. "Do you see it?"

John craned his neck, trying to see through the bars. The alarm continued its screech. "Nowhere. Damn it!"

A gleam of silver caught Ressler's eye. The key was on the ground outside the bars. He lunged for it. His fingertips touched it. He scrabbled at the tiny bit of metal, praying to anyone who was listening. The key wouldn't come. Sounds of commotion could be heard down the tunnel.

"Come on!" John was dancing inside his cell.

Ressler snatched his fingers back, spat on them, and reached for the key again. The saliva made his skin slightly sticky, and it was just enough to drag the key into grasping distance. Relieved, he snatched it up, then wrenched his arm around, feeling for the lock. For once, something went right, and he was able to jam the key into the lock. The door clicked open, and he was free.

"Don't forget me!" John yelled.

For a moment, Ressler considered leaving him. It would take precious seconds to unlock his cage and the Bodysnatcher was a kidnapper and a murderer. But he had promised to free him, and the regs said you kept your word. Ressler yanked the key out of his lock and opened John's cage door.

There was a moment, a tiny moment, when they made eye contact across the threshold. Each man knew the other was thinking the same thing: *I'm your opposite. I should club you down and run like hell.* The moment passed. John bolted from the cage, and they ran down the tunnel—

—straight into four masked drones.

The drones paused in surprise. Ressler plowed into them without hesitation. He slammed his shoulder into one and knocked him into a second. The second drone's head smacked the tunnel wall with a wet *crack*. The alarm continued its blare. Ressler wanted to punch the first drone, but hesitated—the mask. The drone took advantage of the moment to snatch his taser from his holster. The end snapped with a blue spark.

One of the other drones rushed at John, who twisted aside. The last drone hesitated, as though unsure of which target to choose. The drone with the taser fired the extendable electrodes at Ressler. Ressler flung himself to one side, and the electrodes went into the back of the fourth drone. He went down, twitching. Ressler snapped a roundhouse kick at the drone with the taser. The taser went flying. Scuffling noises came from behind him, but Ressler ignored them. The drone went for the pistol at his belt. Ressler grabbed the gas canister on his mask and yanked. The drone went off-balance, and Ressler brought the drone's face down on his knee. Pain lanced through his leg when the mask hit. The drone went limp and collapsed. Ressler grabbed at his holster.

"Freeze!"

Ressler spun, winded, pistol in his hand. The last drone held John with a gun to his head.

"Back to your cell. Move! Or he's dead."

The perp had a hostage. Regs said to set his weapon down and back away. Do whatever the perp said until a chance came to save the hostage.

"I said back to your cell!" the drone barked.

The hell with the regs.

Ressler raised his own pistol. "So shoot him."

That gave the drone pause. "What?"

"I don't care if he lives or dies. Shoot him." Ressler took aim, both hands, feet planted. "Then I can shoot you and get the hell out of here."

"Hey!" John said.

The drone clearly didn't know how to respond to this. He actually leaned a little ways away from John.

Ressler took the shot.

It was clean. Straight through the drone's mask and head. Blood sprayed out the back. The drone slumped, nearly dragging John down with him. John flung the drone's arm away.

"What the hell was that?" he demanded as Ressler snatched up one of the masks from the floor. "That was a stupid bluff."

"Bluff?" Ressler pulled on a mask. "You're a killer and a kidnapper. What the hell makes you think I care if you live or die?"

"Oh. That." John put on a mask as well and reached for a pistol. Ressler kicked his hand away.

"Not for you," he said. "Let's go. Keen set off that

alarm somehow. We probably don't have much time."

Although it had felt much longer, the escape and fight had only taken a couple of minutes. Masked drones were rushing through the hive tunnels, and Ressler and John joined them, anonymous in their own masks. Most of them seemed to be heading in the same direction, so they followed the crowd.

A stream of drones filed from a small tunnel that seemed to be leading outside. The ceiling came down lower and lower, until Ressler was forced to hands and knees to crawl. A pair of hands pulled him out, and for a moment he panicked, thinking he'd been caught, until he realized the drone was there to help.

Outside, the sun was beginning to set. Warm air, the first summer breeze he had felt in so long, coursed over him, though he couldn't smell anything through the mask. A crowd of drones milled about uncertainly on the hillside. Ressler looked for Keen and Stuart, but didn't see either of them. If they were wearing masks, he wouldn't recognize them anyway.

"Any idea what's going on?" he asked the drone who was helping the masked Bodysnatcher out of the narrow tunnel exist.

"You mean you don't know?" the drone said.

Uh oh. Ressler thought fast.

"I was asleep when the alarm went off. I just grabbed my mask and ran, like protocol said."

"Evacuation alarm from the chem lab," he said shortly. "Someone probably dropped a beaker."

A ways down the hill came the Beekeeper himself, with his white hair and heavy glasses. He was shouting something.

Ressler grabbed John. "Come on."

They sidled toward the edge of the crowd of drones.

Ressler had no idea the Beekeeper had this many people under his thumb. There had to be well over two hundred here. And children! Jesus, they had children. Ressler had seen the baby in Keen's arms and hadn't had time to think about it, but babies meant children, and children always became human shields. God damn it!

Run now, worry later, he told himself.

They made it to the thicker part of the woods at the edge of the crowd and almost stumbled over the collection of boxy beehives. John swore and backpedaled. Two bees landed on the plastic eyes of Ressler's mask, and he was suddenly glad for the full-body jumpsuit. They skirted the hives and dove toward the hill as a voice shouted for them to halt. A pair of shots rang out.

"Go!" Ressler snapped, and ran himself, ducking and weaving. More shots zinged by, and bark chipped off a tree near Ressler's arm. John was a little behind and to Ressler's left.

"I need a goddamned gun, you asshole," he said, breathing heavily.

"Shut up and run." Ressler's legs were shaky. He could feel the energy draining from him. Days of confinement, bad food, and stress had taken their toll. Running downhill on uneven ground and forcing their way through brush made it all the more difficult. Thin branches scored Ressler's hands and whipped at the eyes on his mask, making him flinch. John stumbled over a root, recovered his balance, and kept running.

Shouts and barked orders rang from the woods around them. Already the Hive was mustering a search party. Ressler swore. They were organized and quick. He ducked under another branch and tried to keep his breathing up. Should they try to find a place to hide instead? Ressler glanced about him, trying to figure out where they were, but he was completely turned around and the mask made it hard to see. He snatched it off and flung it away.

An armed drone came out of a grove to Ressler's right. Without thinking, Ressler shot twice at the drone, and he went down. But another drone was following, and a second, and a third. John swore. Ressler leaped over a fallen tree for cover. The tree was on the downward side of the foothill, however, and the opposite side was much lower than the closer side. He landed badly. Bark and rocks scratched his side and red pain sliced up his ankle and shin. But the downward slope and the tree gave him more cover than he had expected.

On the other side of the tree, John shouted, "I surrender! Don't shoot!"

There was a clacking of guns. Ressler scuttled deeper into the undergrowth farther downhill. Part of him said he should go back and help John, but the more sensible part of him said that he was outnumbered and out-armed by at least four to one, and it was smarter to get the hell out of here, find help, bring back the FBI.

"Where's your friend?" a distant voice demanded. But Ressler kept moving farther and farther away. Finally, he deemed it safe to break into a limping jog. What little strength he had left was flagging, and he was alone.

He came across a narrow game trail. Ressler thought a moment, then chose a random direction and ran, hoping it wasn't taking him back toward the Hive. It was safer to stay in the woods, but on the trail he could gain some ground for a few minutes, then hit the trees again. The sun had sunk a little lower in the sky and it was still only early evening, but he was afraid of getting more lost in the trees anyway.

The voices he had heard had faded entirely. He paused once to listen. Nothing but bird song and insects. Heat lay thick over everything. Sweat ran down Ressler's back, and he mopped his forehead with his sleeve, then ran off again.

The trail abruptly came out on a dirt road. It was little more than a pair of ruts under the canopy of trees. Ressler hung back. Another conundrum. The road would make it easier to run and easier to find help, but it might also make it easier for the Hive to find him.

Wheels crunched on gravel and rustled against grass. Ressler dodged back under cover. A brown van hove into view. Should he run out and ask for help? It might be Hive. Ressler had no way to—

The driver was Aram Mojtabai.

CHAPTER SEVENTEEN

Elizabeth Keen dashed down the tunnel back toward the nursery from the chem lab while the alarm blared in her ears and red emergency lights glowed on and off. Luke was still asleep in her arms. With the evacuation alarm screeching and sending everyone outside, she wouldn't have to explain her absence from the nursery. She could just say she'd been caught in the evacuation with Luke.

The baby changed everything.

Keen couldn't leave the Hive or let it be destroyed. Not when babies and children were here. At least Ressler had gotten away. Now she just had to find a way to—

"Hello, Elizabeth."

Keen came up short as she rounded a bend in the tunnel. The Beekeeper was standing directly in front of her with a small swarm of drones behind him. One of them was Pug. The red lights gave them an eerie cast. Pug snatched Luke from her before she could react.

"I'm just… the baby…" she stammered.

"We were mistaken to put our trust in you so soon," the Beekeeper said, reaching into his jacket pocket and pulling out a syringe. "We think you need a private session in the Circle. You seem attached to the babies. We can use that."

"A baby is supposed to be in the nursery," Pug said.

Two of the drones grabbed her. She fought them hard as the needle came.

Ressler blinked. For a long moment, he couldn't move. His mind couldn't process what he was seeing. Aram. It was Aram. Driving a rusty brown van. Through a national forest. Five hundred miles from Washington. Ressler would have been less surprised to see a penguin on the road.

With a shout, he raced from cover, waving his arms. The van jerked to a halt. Ressler dashed to the passenger side, jerked the door open, and leaped in. Aram gave him a nervous little wave.

"Thank god," Ressler panted. "I can't believe it, Aram. What are you—?"

"Good evening, Donald," said a familiar voice from the back seat. "I'm glad to see you're safe."

Ressler jerked around. Reddington was sitting in the back, hat on his head, insouciant smile on his face. A jolt went through Ressler.

"What's going on?" Ressler said. "What are you doing out here? How did you find me?"

"Is Lizzie all right?" Reddington returned with a note of urgency in his voice.

"Last I saw. She had a baby with her."

"A baby," Reddington said slowly.

"It wasn't hers," Ressler said, not quite believing this was the turn of the conversation. "Look, we need to get out of here, find a phone, call the task force—"

"All in good time, Donald," Reddington said in that maddeningly calm voice. "Please reach under your seat and pull out what you find there."

Mystified, Ressler obeyed. He came up with a paper bag and a pair of handcuffs. Inside the bag were two protein bars and a bottle filled with a sports drink.

"We brought those just in case," Reddington explained as Ressler tore into the bars and gulped down the drink. Normally he hated the nasty green stuff, but now it went down like nectar. He felt some of his strength return.

"Thanks," he said, then held up the handcuffs. "What are these for?"

"Contingencies," Reddington replied blandly. "Aram, would you continue on our way, please?"

Aram did. He had to switch on the headlights now. Outside the van, crickets were chirping. An owl hooted in the distance.

"So what's the plan?" Ressler tossed the handcuffs aside.

"I assume by now you know about the sarin gas the Beekeeper is mixing together in his hive."

"Yeah. Keen told me. She found the lab."

Reddington nodded. "But perhaps you're not aware that spreading sarin gas is a two-step process. By itself, sarin creates an annoyance on the level of a smoky campfire. It must be mixed with tributylamine to become deadly. A colleague of mine was engaged to sell the Beekeeper the final shipment of tributylamine, but I intercepted it." He jerked his head behind him. Ressler peered into the darkness in the rear of the van and made out a number of crates piled in the back. His stomach crawled around his insides.

"Isn't that a little dangerous?"

"Not in the least!" Reddington said. "Not until it mixes with sarin, anyway. That's the whole point, Donald."

"So you intercepted the tributylamine, and the Beekeeper can't spread the sarin gas," Ressler said with relief. "Reddington, that's perfect! Now we only need to—"

"I'm afraid you've misread the situation, Donald," Reddington interrupted.

"What do you mean?" Ressler picked up the protein bar wrapper and hunted around the inside for crumbs. "We drive until we get cell coverage, call Cooper, and—"

"No," Reddington interrupted again. "Donald, I want you to use those handcuffs. One cuff on your wrist, the other on the door handle. Do it so I can see they're tight."

Ressler turned in the seat to see if Reddington was making some kind of joke, and found himself looking down the barrel of a pistol. Behind it was Reddington's round face and fedora hat.

"Now, please," Reddington said. "I should hope the threat is implicit and need not be stated."

"No," Ressler said. "Not until you explain—"

Reddington fired the pistol.

The sound was deafening thunder inside the van. The bullet speared the windshield behind Ressler and created a spider-web of cracks around the hole. Aram yelled and the van swerved a little. Ressler's ears rang.

"The second bullet will end up somewhere less pleasant," Reddington said as if he were ordering a honeyed scone. "The handcuffs. Where I can see them. I won't tell you again."

Aram made a small sound, but kept his eyes on the road. Ressler slowly clipped the cuff to his wrist, holding it so Reddington could see, then attached the other cuff to the door handle. Reddington put the pistol away and leaned back—well out of reach, Ressler noticed sourly.

"Are you at least going to tell me what's going on?" Ressler growled.

"You haven't figured it out? Donald, I'm disappointed."

"He's delivering the tributylamine to the Beekeeper," Aram said from behind the wheel. "For lots of money."

Now Ressler did yank on the handcuffs. "You son of a bitch! You had this arranged from the beginning, didn't you? You wanted to learn where the Beekeeper was so you could pull off a weapons deal. You used us."

"You make it sound sordid." Reddington sighed. "Your presence will help matters, you know."

"I'm not helping you," Ressler snarled. "Aram, why aren't you—?" But then he saw the handcuff on Aram's wrist, the one clipping him to the steering wheel.

"Just insurance," Reddington said. "Ah—our greeters seem to have arrived."

The van had emerged at the bottom of the hill where the Hive had its headquarters, and the headlights swept over the cave's main entrance. A dull ache started in the pit of Ressler's stomach as armed drones poured out of the cave to surround the van.

CHAPTER EIGHTEEN

Ressler pulled harder at the handcuffs, then froze when the barrel of a rifle poked itself at his cheek through the open window. Aram kept his hands on the steering wheel, his eyes wide and unhappy.

"Good evening, gentlemen!" Reddington called from the back seat. "You may recognize me from the earlier unpleasantness after we entered the park. I'm here to clear things up. Please be so kind as to tell Dr. Griffin that Raymond Reddington is here."

"Reddington?" The Beekeeper pushed his way through the drones and settled his glasses more firmly on his nose. Mrs. Griffin stood a step behind him. "What on earth are you doing here?"

"A small misunderstanding, Benjamin," Reddington said. "Your people opened fire on mine."

"You were following the Bodysnatcher," Dr. Griffin pointed out. "We assumed you were law enforcement."

"Nothing of the sort!" Reddington chuckled. "Fortunately for you, I have a forgiving nature. Though I should probably tell you I have a sharpshooter named Dembe with an infra-red scope trained on the back of your head at this very moment.

I'm forgiving, but far from forgetful."

The Beekeeper touched the back of his head as if an insect had bitten him there, then brought his hand down. "What do you want, exactly?"

"I've brought your shipment of tributylamine," Reddington said. "I believe you had an order in."

"Not from you."

"A minor shift in the market. But I'm pleased to offer it to you for a mere twenty percent hike in the price you agreed upon with your original vendor. I have expenses of my own to meet. A new car, for example."

"What's to prevent me from simply taking the tributylamine right now?" Dr. Griffin asked narrowly, and Ressler felt his scrotum shrivel.

"My sharpshooter, of course," Reddington replied breezily. "And the fact that you want my good will."

"I do?"

"Naturally. You intend to cleanse this entire area of human life so you can take it for yourself. Commendable. Everyone should have goals. But having isn't the same as keeping, is it? Eventually, someone—your enemies— will try to take this away from you, and you'll need more weapons than you currently have to hold the fort. I can supply them. Within twenty-four hours, I can get you enough to free a small South American country. Within forty-eight hours, you'll have enough to rule the Middle East. Your enemies won't be able to touch a hair on your head."

"We can't allow our enemies to come close," Mrs. Griffin said. "They're frightening!"

The Beekeeper thought about this. "You make a good point, Reddington. Let's talk, then. And call off your sharpshooter."

"Done." Reddington made a sharp gesture to the

empty air. "I also have a gift for you. Call it a good faith gesture. It's in my delightfully broken-in vehicle here."

In short order, the drones, including Pug, emptied the van of crates. When Pug uncuffed Ressler, using the keys Reddington gave him, and hauled him out as well, the Beekeeper inhaled sharply.

"This is the gift? That's a strange way to treat one of your own men."

"A wise man once told me never to let my personal feelings interfere with my own safety," Reddington said. "Or with business. I would rather have your faith than his loyalty."

"Son of a bitch," Ressler said, struggling in Pug's overwhelming grip. "I'll kill you, Reddington."

"That's not nice!" Pug admonished.

"I can use that attitude in session," the Beekeeper said. "You'll be buzzing my praises in no time." He opened his jacket and showed the row of hypodermics.

"What are you doing with him?" Aram demanded. He was being held by drones as well. "What are you doing with *me*?"

"I haven't decided about you yet," the Beekeeper said. "Perhaps you'll join us. Once your conditioning is over, of course."

"That one is still mine, Benjamin," Reddington reminded him.

"But we have business, first," the Beekeeper continued as if Reddington hadn't spoken.

He spoke with one of the drones, who rushed away and returned moments later with a filing box, the kind used to store paper in an office. Someone threw a switch, and hidden lights illuminated the area, pushing back the gathering shadows. The Beekeeper removed the box lid and showed green bundles of money.

"I have to do everything in cash," he said, "since it's the devil's own work to get an Internet signal through to a bank out here. This is the money we'd intended to pay the original buyer, plus the extra you asked for."

"Excellent. Put it in the van, please," Reddington said.

"And the tributylamine?"

Reddington said, "Before we get to that, I wanted to inquire after two other operatives of mine. A young woman and an older man?"

"They're mine now, Reddington," the Beekeeper said. "Both of them are part of my Hive."

"Oh? I find that hard to believe, Benjamin. Even your methods have their limits," Reddington said.

"Stuart Ivy, come forth," the Beekeeper said, and one of the drones pulled off his mask, revealing Stuart's face. "Stuart, Mr. Reddington will be staying with us for a short time while we work out some business. I'll give you a choice I have never given any of my children. When he goes, you can leave with him, or stay with us. Which do you want?"

"I want to stay," Stuart said promptly.

"This isn't a trick, Stuart," the Beekeeper said kindly. "We *want* you to go. We'll give you a hundred thousand dollars if you do."

"Are you throwing me out of the Hive?" Stuart sounded desperate. He dropped to both knees in front of the Beekeeper and tears sprang to his eyes. "Please! Don't make me leave! We are the Hive!"

"*We are the Hive!*" said everyone else.

"There, there." The Beekeeper raised Stuart up and kissed him on both cheeks. "Of course we don't want you to go, Stuart. You're one of our best workers, and our wisest."

"Thank you, sir," Stuart sniffed. "Thank you."

"Yay!" said Pug.

"You see, Reddington?" the Beekeeper asked. "No one leaves. No one wants to."

"I'm fascinated," Reddington said without emotion. "Do you suppose I could have a word with Stuart some time later? I would take it as another favor—and offer a discount on a future shipment."

"Nothing would please us more," said the Beekeeper magnanimously, and his presence filled the area before the cavern until the trees themselves seemed to bend out of his way. "Stuart, put your mask back on and rejoin the others. When we're done here, meet Mr. Reddington in the main cavern. We are the Hive."

"We are the Hive!" Stuart said, pulling on his mask. *"We are the Hive!"*

"Now what about the young woman?" Reddington said.

"Elizabeth Keen! Come forward!"

Ressler gasped as another anonymous drone removed her mask, revealing Keen. Her dark hair was disheveled, and worry bags darkened her eyes, but her expression was resolute. Ressler tried to read Reddington's face, but the man's expression was a mask.

"We offer you the same choice, Elizabeth," the Beekeeper said. "Freely given. You may stay here with us in the Hive. Or you may go back to your employer Raymond Reddington. To that, we will add the same bonus we offered Stuart, and one more thing." He smiled benevolently. "We know something about your father. A secret Mr. Reddington has been keeping from you. If you leave, we will tell it to you."

Reddington's face remained stony. Ressler's bones were tight with tension. Keen looked at the Beekeeper, then at Reddington.

"The babies," she said at last, her voice barely audible. "I won't leave the babies. We are the Hive!"

"*We are the Hive!*"

"Oh god," Aram murmured.

"Yay!" said Pug.

Nausea roiled in Ressler's stomach. He tried to catch Keen's eye, but all he saw was a blank, empty stare. Jesus. He had gotten to her after all.

"You see?" the Beekeeper said. "The military was foolish to kick me to the curb. They'll pay for that, in fact. And speaking of paying, I believe I've paid you a large sum of money for some tributylamine?"

Face still a mask, Reddington strolled to the heavy plastic crates, each of which was topped with a keypad and fingerprint scanner. Reddington punched in a code and allowed the scanner to read his prints. There was a hiss, and the first crate popped open. Reddington pointedly stepped back until one of the drones, realizing he'd been cued, came forward and reached inside.

Right, Ressler thought sourly. *Reddington won't even stoop to labor as common as unpack a weapon for a multi-million dollar client.*

The drone came up with a single canister with a nozzle on the end.

"That's it?" Ressler said without thinking.

"It doesn't take much," the Beekeeper said, and gestured again. A drone brought forth a canister the size of a can of soup. Another brought a helicopter drone and a remote control device. "Masks!"

Most of the drones were already wearing masks, giving Ressler the impression he was standing in a swarm of human bees. Those who weren't wearing theirs quickly pulled them on. Someone handed one to Reddington. Nobody gave one to Ressler or Aram. Ressler's ribs tightened around his heart. What the hell were they up to?

Two more drones made their way through the crowd. They were dragging something. A moment later, Ressler saw it was John the Bodysnatcher. He had a black eye, and dried blood crusted his chin. He seemed only half awake.

Mrs. Griffin watched him closely. Her hair was pulled into its bun, and she blinked rapidly, as if she couldn't quite decide what she wanted to do. Her gaze lit on her husband, and she wandered closer to him. The drones hauling John, meanwhile, flung him to the ground at the Beekeeper's feet. Someone gave Mrs. Griffin a mask, and she pulled it on, becoming another anonymous drone, except for her gray dress. Ressler scanned the assemblage. Where was Keen? And Stuart, for that matter? He had lost track of them in the swarm. They had to be here somewhere, though they could be anyone in those damned masks. Everyone looked alike, everyone looked the same.

"One attempt at escape, the Hive can forgive," the Beekeeper said. He connected the two canisters and pressed a button. There was a hiss. The Beekeeper tossed the tributylamine canister aside, racked the sarin canister into the helicopter drone, and flicked the switches on the control. The drone whirred to life. It buzzed around the assembled crowd, then dove down toward John the Bodysnatcher. Ressler watched in horror.

"It is flying!" Pug crowed inside his mask. "Like a kite! Or a bee!"

"Two birds, one stone," the Beekeeper said. "We can set an example and test the efficacy of our formula."

"I would like to watch, dear," said Mrs. Griffin from behind her mask.

The Beekeeper smiled at her. "Of course, darling."

Ressler glanced at Aram, who looked sick. The drone rushed down at John, who reflexively looked up at the buzzing above his head. The Beekeeper flicked a switch. The drone sprayed a tiny spurt of sarin over his face then zipped away. Reddington, masked now, moved back a step.

Nothing happened. Ressler realized he was holding his breath. The light breeze was blowing away from him, thank god. Then John coughed. He put a hand to his throat. His eyes were streaming. Mucus dripped from his nose. Abruptly, he vomited over the grass. His trousers wet, and Ressler caught the sharp smell of urine.

"Help him!" Ressler cried, struggling against the drones who held him.

"We can't," Aram said in a strange, sad tone Ressler had never heard from him before. "There are treatments for sarin gas, if they're administered quickly, but for a dose that large, there's little we can do."

"How the hell do you know?" Ressler demanded.

"I have relatives in Syria," he said in that awful, flat voice.

Coughing wracked John's body, and he squirmed on the ground. Bloody foam bubbled from his lips. Then the convulsions began. They wracked John's body, twisted him into a shuddering mess that suddenly went still. He wasn't breathing. Ressler closed his eyes. John the Bodysnatcher lay dead.

"He did something awful," Pug said in a hushed voice.

"The Hive does not tolerate insubordination!" the Beekeeper boomed in his rich voice. "The Hive does not accept weakness! We are the Hive!"

"*We are the Hive!*" shouted the entire crowd.

"Donald Ressler," said the Beekeeper. "Come forward."

"No!" Ressler fought again, but it had been a long day of running and fighting after many days of bad food and little rest. His strength was nowhere near normal, and Pug easily forced him down next to John's cooling corpse. The helicopter drone hovered high overhead.

"Don't do this," Ressler panted. "You don't have to."

"You did something bad," Pug said. "You have to be punished. It will be okay, though. Don't worry."

"I didn't make this decision," the Beekeeper said. "You did, the moment you tried to leave us."

The drone dropped lower. Ressler clenched his teeth and held his breath, though he knew it wouldn't help.

"Benjamin," said Reddington from inside his mask, "Donald is one of my more talented operatives. I would take it as a great favor if you would keep him around."

The drone paused overhead.

"And why would I do that?" the Beekeeper asked. "He's proven a great liability."

"You know, I once made the acquaintance of a major in South America. Had the respect of his troops and, more importantly, his wife and family. Great taste for wine, could never say no to a Burgundy taken from the right bank of the Chanteaux River, and who can blame him for that?" Reddington took off his mask and fixed the Beekeeper with a hard look. "But he had one too many secrets, including the fact that he spent a great deal of time with the privates in his army, if you'll forgive a vulgar jest, and when it came time for him to make an important move, one of the many people who held his secrets threatened to reveal them.

His superiors had to step in and order him to make the right decision. I was forced to quick-step it out of the country at that point, but later I heard he'd been shot in the head. A banal ending, really."

"What is your point, Reddington?" the Beekeeper demanded.

"Only that everyone should listen to good advice, Benjamin."

There was a pause. The Beekeeper snorted.

"I'll take it under advisement."

The drone dipped lower again, deadly canister at the ready. Ressler screwed his eyes shut.

"Darling." Mrs. Griffin touched the Beekeeper's elbow and removed her own mask. "Maybe you could keep this one for later. In case he's useful, like Mr. Reddington says. He might be a good source of children one day."

Ressler's eyes opened.

Dr. Griffin blinked at his wife. "Oh. Well, dear, I'm not—"

"Please, darling?" she said. "I don't think I can watch a second one today."

Another moment passed. The Beekeeper nodded.

"Very well. The Hive can be merciful. We will allow him more time in the Circle tonight. We are the Hive!"

"*We are the Hive!*"

"Yay!" said Pug. "See, Donald? I told you it would be okay."

Ressler felt ready to collapse.

"And now that we have everything we need," the Beekeeper continued, "we can at last begin the cleansing. Our talented drones will work through the night to create the final stage of the sarin gas and load it into the flying drones. Come sunrise, this country will be ours!"

* * *

Raymond Reddington stared up at the stone tree chipped into the cave wall. The details were exquisite. The roots wrapped around the boulder with the crude G on it with an almost loving embrace, and in the dim light of the cave, the leaves seemed to flutter and the river seemed to be flowing. It was a remarkable illusion, and Reddington would have delighted in meeting the original artist. Unfortunately, that individual was moldering in a grave somewhere. At least the art would last.

"Lovely, isn't it?" Stuart said, coming up beside him.

"I'm glad to see the Beekeeper is keeping his word about our chat," Reddington said. "But this tree isn't half as lovely as Vivian."

A distant scream came down the tunnel from the Circle room.

"That was unkind, Red."

"The truth is rarely kind. Why is that, do you think?"

Stuart folded his arms and leaned against the wall. The great cavern was deserted at the moment. The Beekeeper was occupied with Donald Ressler, and everyone else had been sent to bed after the exhibition outside.

"The reality is that the universe is falling apart," Stuart said. "Entropy. Eventually everything will end, everything will die. That's always the central truth, and it's painful to hear. You know that as well as I do. Where is your friend?"

"Aram has been shown to the guest quarters. Who knew the Hive had a guest room?"

Reddington touched the tree. The stones were rough

and damp under his fingertips. "The Bodysnatcher was an artist, you know. He raised vanishing to an art form. He operated for nearly twenty years, and no one even knew he existed. Not even I knew his real name. Now that he's dead, his art will vanish. Except his art was a lie, wasn't it? No one knew about it, no one saw it, no one appreciated it. Is it real art if it's hidden from the world?"

"The Bodysnatcher's art wasn't hidden," Stuart objected. "He operated out in plain sight. It was just that no one knew what they were looking at. His art was in the hiding. A true artist."

"Whose art will die with him," Reddington said, "since no one knew it was there. This beautiful tree, on the other hand, has lasted generations. The artist is long gone, but the art and its message both remain. That's art."

"But no one saw this art," Stuart said. "Until the Beekeeper came, no one knew it was here. You yourself said it's not art if no one sees it to appreciate it."

"They could, if only they came to look." Reddington touched the tree again.

"I've missed this, Red," Stuart said. "You and me, talking about art and philosophy. You were a remarkable young man, and you've grown into something more than I could have ever imagined. Certainly more than I ever became."

"You're not alone in those feelings, my friend," Reddington said, shoving his hands into his pockets. "I've missed it. I've missed *you*."

"But you never come by," Stuart said. "You know where to find me. Or you did. I hear of your exploits, my boy. I know you use some of the tricks I taught you, and you keep up your extensive contacts. I introduced you to some of them. But you don't keep up with me."

"You know why," Reddington said flatly.

Stuart sighed. "I had hoped to get past that."

"Why are you really here?" Reddington asked abruptly. "I don't believe this idiocy about you joining the Hive. It's complete nonsense. We both know it."

"I lost everything, Red," said Stuart in a soft voice. "After Vivian… the work was never the same. I simply wasn't as good without her. I made mistakes, I lost contacts, I made enemies. The house in London is gone now, you know. Lost to a shopping center. In the old days, I could have saved it by leaning on this official or buying stock in that company, but now I'm a toothless dog with a hoarse bark. I don't even have your friendship. Nothing's left except what's up here." He tapped his head.

"So the Hive is your retirement plan?" Reddington said.

"Why not? It's an army like any other. The bed is comfortable—now—and there's a purpose. There's fresh air and something to do. No one cares about my past. It's a far cry from living on benches in Hyde Park."

"But do you believe in what the Beekeeper is doing?" Reddington pressed.

"What does that matter? I haven't believed in anything since Vivian died. The Beekeeper is as good as anything. We are the Hive, Red. We will prevail."

"No," Reddington said. "You won't. That's the problem, you know. This plan the Beekeeper has—to 'cleanse' the area of people so he can carve out a chunk of the country for himself—won't work, and while he's never seemed particularly stable, I've never seen him as quite that lunatic."

Stuart shrugged. "It's something to do."

"Something else I can't reconcile," Reddington said, "is the way Vivian died. What really happened that day?"

"Oh, god." Stuart rubbed his face. "Red, I've told you. It rakes up a great deal of pain just thinking about it."

"Tell me, Stuart. I need to know."

Stuart sighed. "After I told you to run, I went back to save Vivian, but it was already too late. She was dead. The arms dealer had killed her. They nearly caught me, too, and I barely got out of the warehouse with my life."

"Stuart, we're standing under a piece of true art, a place where lies go to die, like the Bodysnatcher's art died and like your previous life died." He fixed Stuart with a hard look. "Tell the truth, Stuart."

A wan smile crossed Stuart's face. "I don't know how else to convince you, Red. That's the way it happened, and it hurts a great deal to think that—"

In a swift move, Reddington pulled his hand from his pocket and darted it toward the exposed skin of Stuart's neck. In his hand was one of Dr. Griffin's syringes. He had lifted it moments ago during the little show outside. The Beekeeper had never noticed, and Reddington was gratified that his skills hadn't degraded over the years. Stuart gasped as the needle went in and Reddington sent the plunger home.

"Stung," Reddington observed, slipping the needle back into his pocket. "I only gave you a quarter dose. Even a half dose would kill you, I believe. How are you feeling, Stuart?"

Stuart slid to the wooden platform built over the cave floor. His eyes had gone wide, his pupils dilated.

"I feel… I feel…"

"Think about the day Vivian died," Reddington

said. "Think about the warehouse and the guns."

"The smoke sounds like sandpaper on my ears," Stuart said. "The gunshots explode on my tongue like mineral water. I'm frightened. Red is there. We're hiding outside, arguing with blue and purple words. He wants me to go and get Vivian."

"But?"

Stuart's eyes were lost in the distance. "I'm running back towards the warehouse. Gravel crunches beneath my feet with pops of flashbulb light. The guns are still going off, and green screams tear the air. I'm behind the warehouse now. Red can't see me. I can hear Vivian pleading for help. Her voice tears my head in half. I might be able to help her. The gun is heavy in my hand like the smell of stone, and the Uzi pulls on my back with the snuffling of an elephant. I could help. Maybe."

"But?" Reddington repeated.

"I don't." A soft tear ran down Stuart's face. "I hear the awful voice of the buyer buzzing against the walls, but I don't go in. I mustn't. Vivian speaks again, and then... one more shot, and the dead flower smell of silence."

Reddington leaned forward. He had to know. Everything had come down to this.

"Why didn't you go in, Stuart?"

"Never let your feelings for someone else outweigh your own safety," Stuart said. "I taught you that, Red. I taught you. And I let my Vivian die."

Reddington let go of a long, long breath.

"I know. I always knew, you son of a bitch. For more than twenty years, I've carried that with me, and I've been waiting to hear you say it."

"That's why you came here, isn't it?" Stuart asked in his drug-slurred voice. "All this? You intercepted the tribu—tributt—the other gas just to get yourself here so you could get this from me, is that it? Good god, Red. I taught you better than that."

"I learned many things from you," Reddington said stonily. "You taught me that you don't know everything—in fact invariably the right way to operate is the very *opposite* of what you tried to teach me."

Reddington walked away.

CHAPTER NINETEEN

The chem lab bustled. Everyone who wasn't asleep was here. Canisters clanked, helicopter drones hummed, computer keys clicked. Gas hissed. Teams of masked drones filled little canisters with the deadly mixture of sarin and tributylamine and attached them to the sleek black helicopter drones. The process was laborious and careful, but the drones remained focused behind their masks. Reddington scanned the crowd, mouth tight. Even with the masks on, he was certain he would recognize—

There.

The one tapping at a computer near a set of helicopter drones. Reddington strode up to her and tapped her shoulder.

"Lizzie."

Great relief swept over him when she turned to him and pulled her mask off. She seemed to be uninjured. He hadn't been able to tell before. It had taken all his willpower to keep from opening fire on the Beekeeper and his vile Hive out in front of the cave. The only thing that had stopped him was the sure knowledge that he was outgunned, even with Dembe hiding in the forest with a sniper rifle. Damn it, why hadn't he seen this coming? He should have known Elizabeth would hare off to follow her plan. He should never have allowed her to set foot outside the house. She had been so sure she could outwit Benjamin Griffin, and now…

"Lizzie," he said again. "Are you all right?"

"We're working here, Reddington," she said. "You're slowing us down. See here?" She pointed at the screen. "We have the coordinates set for the cleansing. We have to move fast now, before *they* find out."

Reddington glanced at the screen, then at Elizabeth. He started to take her shoulders, but held back. Her eyes were hard and glassy.

"Elizabeth," he said in a low voice, "thousands of people will die at sunrise if we let the Beekeeper go through with this."

"Like I nearly died?" she countered.

That stung. "Has Dr. Griffin hurt you? We can leave right now, if you—"

"No!" she said. "I won't leave. I *want* to be here."

He drew her aside and the other drones continued their work, though more than one glanced their way.

"Listen, Elizabeth. I have something important to give you, and something important to say. You have to listen. Can we talk in private?"

"I'm protecting the babies," she said. "I'm going to be here for them, no matter what."

"The babies," Reddington repeated.

"You have to leave, Reddington," she said in a flat voice that chilled his spine. "You'll wreck everything. You wrecked my wedding. You wrecked the birth of my baby. You wrecked my life. That's why I'm staying, Reddington."

The words pierced him with icy daggers. Every fear

he'd ever had about Elizabeth roared to life inside him, including the fear that she was right.

"Lizzie, I never meant for anything to happen to you. I did my best to keep you safe and help your career."

"Leave me alone!" She slapped him—or tried to. He caught her wrist and they struggled for a moment. Blood drained away from Reddington's face at the look of hatred she wore. He backed up a step, fighting to keep his expression clear. A pair of drones detached themselves from their work stations and moved toward them.

Reddington said harshly, "Lizzie, you're not yourself. You don't know what you're—"

"Dude," said another voice behind him. A man with receding red hair pulled into a ponytail loomed. "I think Elizabeth wants to be left alone. Maybe you could toddle off to bed like Dr. and Mrs. Griffin, man."

Reddington rounded on him, glad of the distraction, glad of a target for his own fears.

"And who might you be, *dude*?"

"I'm Vernon. Dr. G's second in command, man," he said. "We're busy here, Mr. R, and Dr. G is totally safe in bed with his wife after a rad session with that Donald guy. I don't know why he's giving you the run of the Hive, but I wouldn't abuse it, you know?"

"Indeed."

This was a bad place to be. Reddington straightened his hat and nodded to Keen.

"Good night, then. I'll leave you to your honey."

He left, feeling Vernon's eyes on his back.

Aram had never seen a guest room with bars instead of a door before. On the other hand, he'd never been the guest of a weirdo lunatic before, either. He paced back and forth, trying not to feel like a panda in a zoo. No—a lion. Or a cheetah. Cheetahs were cooler than lions.

"You need to calm yourself," said Dembe. At Reddington's silent order, he had come in from the woods and was now lying on one of the beds with his hands tucked behind his head.

Other than the bars, the room was actually well-appointed, with comfortable twin beds, thick rugs on the floor, bright lighting, and even a small bathroom with a shower. Aram wondered who in hell the Beekeeper brought in as guests.

"I can't help pacing," Aram said. "How do you sit still?"

"As boys in an army we learned very fast to take our rest where we found it. We can do nothing now, so we rest until we can."

"Excuse me, Aram," said Reddington at the bars.

Aram leaped backward with a yelp. Dembe opened his eyes and sat up, his face inscrutable.

"Don't say it," Aram told him.

"As you wish."

"We have pressing business," Reddington said, ignoring the exchange. "Just when I think things can't get worse... well, you know how the sentence ends."

Aram grabbed the bars. "Why? What's gotten worse? Have they killed Ressler?"

"No, no. Donald is fine, if a little agitated. More on him in a moment. Right now, we have to get a signal out to the FBI."

"I thought we didn't want the Post Office to know anything."

"We didn't. But I just came from Santa's workshop up the hall, where they're combining the recipe for sarin gas and putting it in those drones. I got a look at the coordinates the drones were programming into the computer. They aren't for a town, or a city, or even anywhere near this lovely little park."

Aram shook his head. "Then what is he doing?"

"He's attacking Fort Daymon," Reddington said. "The military base."

"What?" Aram said. "He can't possibly—oh. Oh!"

"What?" Reddington said.

"He can." Aram was pacing again. "He absolutely can. Those are military drones. They emit a hard-coded signal that says *friendly* to the defense systems around the base. The base will detect the drones, but everyone will assume they're just flying maneuvers or something. And just after dawn is when the majority of the base personnel are outside. The drones will spray a cloud of sarin gas over the entire base and kill everyone in it before anyone knows what's hit them. Worst of all, Griffin won't get caught. No way to track him down because it was the military's own technology. The Beekeeper will tell his Hive people that the gas failed or something, and life here will go on as before. He'll have to kill us because we know about it, but I doubt that would slow him down. It's a perfect plan."

"Why would he do this?" Dembe asked.

"The most rad of all motives, my friend," said a voice. "Revenge."

Everyone turned to look.

Vernon was standing at the cave entrance. Three masked drones accompanied him. They were armed with tasers. Aram's bowels tightened.

"Oh, god."

Reddington's hand moved for his jacket pocket, then he apparently remembered that here he was unarmed.

"Good to see you again, Vernon," he said pleasantly.

"I'd offer you tea and honey, but we seem to be fresh out of the former."

"I had a feeling something funky was going down," Vernon said. "You think we're stupid because we're hiding in the woods, don't you? Dude, I have a master's degree and two Ph.D.s. You thought I was some stupid drone." He snorted. "Looks like I caught you working for the man. The Beekeeper's gonna be one unhappy dude, Red-boy."

Reddington cocked his head.

"So the mighty Beekeeper is out for petty revenge on the military base that rejected him and his training ideas."

"Rejected *us*," Vernon said. "You think he was working alone? No man is an island, man."

"This revenge plan is the reason he set up beekeeping *here*," Reddington continued, "because the park is so close to the base. And it's why he stole all those military-grade drones. So he could slip past the base's defenses."

"He didn't steal them, man," Vernon said. "I did. The Beekeeper's good with the psychology, but he's not much for logistics. That's my department."

"And what are your logistics telling you now, Vernon?"

"That there's four of us and one of you," Vernon said. "And the one of you is going to take a little zap-nap until the Beekeeper decides what to do with you. I don't like your chances."

The three drones moved toward Reddington, their tasers snapping sparks. Dembe was at the bars, his face contorted with anger. Aram couldn't think. He had no weapon, and no way to use one if he did. Reddington's hand moved toward his jacket before he apparently remembered he had no pistol there.

Vernon giggled. "A great many people want Raymond Reddington dead, man," he said. "After we wipe out Fort Daymon, we can create a rad execution video that will make a lot of people happier than a dime bag in a tank of nitrous oxide—and the rewards that pour in will fund my chem lab for decades." He gestured at the drones. "Take him!"

One drone drove the taser into the side of another drone. The drone dropped twitching to the floor. The third drone started to whirl in surprise, but the first drone cracked him across the back of the head with the taser. He went down. Vernon blinked. His mouth opened and shut like a beached trout.

"What—?" he said.

The drone, whose own taser was still recharging, snatched up another from one of the fallen drones and jammed it into Vernon's stomach. Vernon shuddered and jittered. Spittle flew from his mouth, and a long groan of pain escaped him.

"Holy cow!" gasped Aram.

Vernon dropped to the floor, still shuddering. Then he went still.

Silence rang through the little cave.

Then the drone stepped over the unconscious bodies on the floor, brandishing the taser. The drone brought up a free hand and pulled the mask off.

It was Elizabeth Keen.

Aram stared. All the breath went out of him, though he didn't know whether he should go limp with relief or tight with tension.

"That taser's going to wear off in a few minutes," Keen said. "We need to move."

"Elizabeth?" Reddington said. "Lizzie?"

"You… we thought you were…" Aram stammered.

"I told you what my plan was back at the house," Keen said. "Why would you think I couldn't do it? I fooled the Beekeeper into thinking I was a willing drone. He even thought I was willing to have children for him. He claims he's creating an equal society, but he assigned no males to nursery duty. And, along with most men like him, he thinks that just because I'm a woman, I'll do anything for a baby. Any baby." She patted down Vernon's body, checking his pockets. "We'll save those children just like we'll save the rest of the adults who were kidnapped and brainwashed."

Keen came up with a set of keys, which she tossed to Reddington. One of the drones groaned. Keen zapped him again, and he went still.

"Can we come out now?" Aram said.

Reddington swiftly sifted through the clinking keys and unlocked the door. They dragged Vernon and the drones into the room. Keen and Dembe confiscated their tasers. Keen gave Vernon another jolt.

"Just to keep him quiet for a while yet," she explained blandly.

"What now?" Aram asked.

"We need to get Ressler out of that pen, then get a message to the Post Office and tell them where we are," Keen said. "And we need to find the Beekeeper's computer key."

"What computer key?" Aram asked.

"Vernon said that the Beekeeper has a program on a flash drive that lets him control all the helicopter drones at once," Keen explained. "The flash drive is in a safe in the lab. We need to get that key so the Beekeeper can't release the sarin gas."

"A key for the helicopter drones?" Aram said. "We have—"

A sharp pain creased his arm. Reddington had pinched him—hard. Aram fell silent.

"Have what?" Keen said.

"Uh… we have very little time," Aram said. "What else?"

"We also need to get a message to the Post Office, either by shutting down the jammer or by using the Beekeeper's own equipment," Keen said.

"Weren't we worried about a Waco standoff?" Aram said.

"That was before we knew the Beekeeper had the power to annihilate an entire military base at a distance," Keen said. "The only problem is, I don't know where the Beekeeper's jammer is, though it's probably in the lab. Aram, would you recognize it?"

"Maybe," he said doubtfully. "It's not like they make beep-beep noises and have a sticky note on the side that says *jammer*. And even if we found it, I'd have to figure out how to disable it without drawing attention to myself or the—"

"Would this help?" Reddington drew an object from his jacket pocket and handed it to Aram. He looked at it.

"A satellite phone?" he gasped. "Where did you get this?"

"From some park rangers," Reddington said. "Extremely helpful lads. Did I ever tell you about the time my plane was forced down in—"

"No," Keen said. "Will this thing work?"

"It's not dependent on regular cell phone signals or GPS," Aram said. "The Beekeeper's jammer shouldn't affect it much this close to the Hive."

"I managed an iffy phone call at best," Reddington admitted. "For a large part of the business I arranged,

I was forced to use a thing I believe the young people call *texting*."

"Yeah, texts should go through fine," Aram said. "But we'll have to be outside. Even a sat phone can't penetrate ten feet of solid rock."

"Okay, new plan," Keen said. "Split into teams. We sneak outside and get a message to the Post Office, then we get Ressler out. We also steal the key from the lab so the Beekeeper can't launch in the morning."

"And all before Vernon and his friends wake up and start shouting," Aram said. "That'll be a trick."

"Dembe," Reddington said, "perhaps you could keep a door key and a taser and stay with our guests so that they remain... comfortable. Put one on the bed under a blanket to be Aram and put the others under the bed. You stay in the cell in case anyone comes to check."

"I would rather stay at your side," Dembe protested gently, the only way he ever protested.

"You have duties here, my friend." Reddington gave a small smile. Dembe nodded. "Besides, the Beekeeper still thinks I'm an ally."

Keen didn't wait for further argument. "Aram, keep that taser, grab a mask and come with me to the lab. Reddington, you should go grab Stuart."

"Stuart?" Reddington said.

"Do you want him here when everything goes up?" Keen asked.

Reddington crossed his arms. "I find I don't care one way or the other."

"I'm not into whatever game you're playing, Reddington." Keen sighed and took the ring of keys back. "Save him or not. He's your friend, not mine. Come on, Aram."

They ran down the hall.

* * *

Samar Navabi dropped onto the cheap motel bed with a deep sigh. In a moment she would take a shower, swallow a handful of ibuprofen to stave off body aches, and climb under the covers, but for now she just lay on the thin mattress, thanking heaven she wasn't in a swamp. Her clothes and hair stank of muck after a long day of staring at the mangled bodies of the dead agents who had washed up in the river with no ID or any other possessions to tell who they were. Their fingertips had been cut off and their faces slashed with knives or machetes to stop fingerprinting and fool facial recognition software.

It was nearly a sure thing these men were among the missing FBI agents—it was estimated that they had been killed some time after the team had vanished. The definitive identifiers would have to be DNA and dental records. Thank god she didn't know any of them personally, and she didn't envy whoever was handed the job of alerting the families. Navabi had spent the day taking photos of teeth and scouring the area for clues and fending off Harold Cooper. In fact, she was due to update him right about—

Her cell phone buzzed. Sighing, she checked the screen. Cooper. She took the call.

"I'm on speaker with Cynthia Panabaker," Cooper said. "Any good news? Like a lead?"

"The dead bodies are our people, that's obvious," Navabi said, "but the medical examiner will want to cross the i's and dot the t's. They were killed in a gunfight and mangled afterward. No clues about where they went into the river. Tomorrow we'll be sending a team of boats upriver to have a look."

"What about Aram's sonar device?" Cooper pressed. "Did it work?"

"Nothing," Navabi said.

"Maybe we should talk to him," Panabaker said.

"Let me get him," she said, always surprised at how easily the lie slipped from her lips. Navabi had always been good at lying, even as a child. She moved the phone away from her ear. *"Hey, Aram! Cooper wants to—oh."* She brought the phone back. "He's just jumped into the shower."

"Are you two in the same motel room?" he said.

"Sure." She put a shrug into her voice. "I don't mind—it's like sharing a room with my brother."

"Tell him to report in when he gets out," Panabaker said.

"No problem, but I think he was planning to go straight to bed. We're both pretty wiped. Maybe we could do a full report in the morning? Really, there isn't much to tell."

Cooper sighed. "All right. Both of you get some sleep."

"Thank you, sir. I'll call you when—"

Her phone buzzed with another text. Automatically she checked it. A gasp snapped from her chest and she nearly dropped the phone.

"What is it?" Cooper said. "What's going on?"

"I just got a text," Navabi said. "It's Agent Keen. She's in the Hive."

Cooper's voice snapped to attention. "Keen? The Hive? What's the Hive?"

"It's a long text. Hold on… hold on…" She scrolled through the message with shaking fingers. "It says someone named Benjamin Griffin—the Beekeeper— is planning to spray sarin gas over Fort Daymon at dawn. He has military-grade drones with clearance codes that'll let them slip right under the fort's radar."

"Jesus," said Panabaker. "I'm getting the Pentagon on the line."

"Where *is* she?" Cooper demanded.

"Getting that now," Navabi said. "The Beekeeper and his people are hidden in caves in Sumter National Park. She, Ressler, and Aram are there now."

"Aram?" Cooper sounded startled.

Oops.

"Yeah. Uh… we'll need to have a conversation about that. Probably later, sir," Navabi said. "Reddington got involved, and—"

"You're right," Cooper said tersely. "We'll have a conversation later. Right now, we have to deal with this situation. Tell me. All of it."

In the background, Panabaker was talking urgently in a low tone, presumably on her own phone.

"Reddington wanted Aram to create a program that controlled the Beekeeper's helicopter drones," Navabi said, getting the words out rip-the-Band-Aid-off quickly. "Then he had Aram deliver it to him in the park. We think Reddington intended to sabotage the Beekeeper's plan from the inside with Keen."

"Keen's phone last put her near Fort Daymon," Cooper pointed out. "We sent people to look for her there, even though Aram said we'd been spoofed. We found nothing."

"Right. The Beekeeper spoofs GPS and jams cell phones to keep himself hidden. Visitors to the park think it's the mountains interfering with the signal. The Beekeeper's people grabbed Keen and Ressler and killed the others, I think. Reddington escaped to a safe house and was coordinating their escape. That was where Aram came in."

"And you didn't tell us about this," Cooper said.

"The Beekeeper is heavily armed, sir," Navabi said. "Military-level armed. Reddington was afraid you—we—would storm the place and turn it into a siege."

"Putting Keen in even more danger," Cooper finished. "Unfortunately, I'm starting to understand how Reddington thinks. Her life is more important to him than the entire task force. But why is she contacting us now?"

"The attack on the military base," Navabi said. "There's more to the text message."

"Go."

"Ressler and Reddington are still inside the Beekeeper's caves. Keen sent coordinates."

"Cynthia, can you get us a team of helicopters?" Cooper said.

"Already on it," she said. "But it's going to take a few hours, and we won't be able to do much until sunrise."

"Sir, Keen and Aram are going back into the caves to get Ressler, Reddington, and Dembe out. And—oh god."

"What?"

"The Beekeeper has children on the premises," Navabi said. "Babies."

A moment of silence followed that.

"Jesus," Cooper breathed.

In the background, Panabaker was on her phone again. Another long pause followed, punctuated only by Panabaker's terse conversation. Navabi was suddenly very, very glad she wasn't in charge.

"What do we do, sir?" Navabi said.

"There's no choice. We have to go in," Cooper replied.

"Yes, sir," Navabi said.

"How fast can you get over there?" he asked. "This

is turning into a military operation all too fast."

"I thought it was illegal for the military to act against fellow Americans," Navabi said.

Panabaker came back, apparently in time to hear the last remark. "Sarin gas is a terrorist's weapon, and the Beekeeper is planning to use it against civilians and our military. I'm classifying him as a terrorist. He's no longer a fellow American."

"Understood," Navabi said.

"I want my eyes at that operation," Cooper said. "Go!"

Navabi fled the motel room, leaving sleep and guilt behind.

CHAPTER TWENTY

Summer crickets chirped, and warm, muggy air wrapped itself around Keen like a damp blanket. The satellite phone screen's glow was already attracting bugs—and maybe other attention. She snapped it off.

"I think I got through," she said. "It shouldn't take the Post Office more than a couple-three hours to get down here."

"I'm in trouble," Aram moaned. "Cooper's gonna be pissed that I went AWOL like that."

Keen arched an eyebrow, though she doubted Aram could see it in the dark.

"Really? We're in the middle of a trackless wilderness near a madman armed with enough sarin gas to take out a small town, and you're worried about how the boss will react?"

"It's no fun when Cooper yells," Aram muttered.

"We have to get back in there," Keen said, straightening and flicking leaves off her jumpsuit.

"In *there*?" Aram gestured at the cave entrance several yards away. "Why would we go back in there?"

"We have to get Ressler out of that cage. And we have to get the Beekeeper's drone key out of the chem lab."

"Why?" Aram repeated. "Cooper will alert Fort Daymon so they can take proper precautions. All we need to do is wait out here for Cooper to show up with a nice, big army. Once the Hive is outnumbered, we can—"

"Aram," Keen said, "if the Beekeeper knows his attack on the fort will fail and then the FBI arrives on his doorstep, who do you think he'll use the sarin gas on?"

Aram opened his mouth, then closed it. "Oh."

"Yeah. Dead FBI everywhere, while the Beekeeper and the Hive hide in their gas masks. Or the Beekeeper will send the drones to hose Roebuck, just for spite. Or any number of other things. We need to get that key, and fast."

"Yep." He took up his gas mask, the one he had taken from the drone who had come to the guest room with Vernon. "Let's go."

As Keen pulled on her own mask, she mused that Aram might come off as fearful on the surface, but if you looked closer, you realized that he only looked that way when things were uncertain, when he didn't understand what was going on. When he knew what was coming or what he had to do, he was as straightforward and brave as any agent she knew.

They slipped back toward the main entrance. There were no guards on duty tonight. Everyone was either asleep or working in the chem lab. Under many circumstances, Keen would have found this lucky, but since it meant the Hive was working busily to kill all the soldiers at Fort Daymon, she found it more chilling than fortunate. Still, they kept their masks on. Keen wondered where Stuart was. She hadn't seen him in several hours. Sleeping, she supposed. He definitely wasn't working in the lab.

The cave floor crunched quietly beneath their feet and Keen's breath rattled inside the mask. She had mixed feelings about Stuart. On the one hand, he was quite the fascinating old gentleman who had both a tragic past and some entertaining stories about Reddington when he was young—and Keen had to admit those were fun to hear. On the other hand, he had dived into the Hive awfully quickly, and anyone with his kind of criminal past wasn't in the least bit trustworthy. There was also the backstory about his wife Vivian. She could see the way it complicated his and Reddington's relationship. Reddington probably thought he was hiding it, but Keen could see how deeply he was hurt.

She pursed her lips inside the mask. It was so tangled up! Why couldn't anything be simple?

"Is this a good time to say," Aram said, "that there's a second key out there?"

Keen wrenched her head around so fast, she almost dislocated a pair of vertebrae.

"What do you mean?"

The main cavern, with its beautiful carvings, was empty, so Aram was safe in talking.

"I mean I created a key for Reddington. That's why he wanted me to come. I was supposed to deliver it to him."

"And did you?"

Aram nodded. "He has it. He didn't want me to tell you."

Keen's head swam with the possibilities. Why would Reddington want to control the helicopter drones? He didn't have his own plan of mass destruction, did he? No. That wasn't his style. To Reddington, killing was a deeply personal act, something done up close and for good reason. It wasn't the mass slaughter of people he didn't know. So what was he up to? Why would he go to great lengths to bring in Aram with a drone key?

"Would your key be able to override the Beekeeper's?" she asked. "Could you take control of his drones away from him with it?"

"I doubt it," Aram said regretfully. "Mine isn't very sophisticated. I had to make it fast, and I copied half the codes from—"

"Okay, okay," Keen interrupted. "Don't tell Reddington you told me."

"I'm not very good at secrets, you know," Aram muttered.

The tunnels were dimmed at night to save power, which made Keen feel safer—they were cloaked in partial darkness, though she had to admit there really wasn't anyplace to hide. If someone challenged them, their only options were to try and talk their way out of it, or attack. Not for the first time, Keen marveled at the amount of work that had gone into enlarging the caverns. It was incredible what a group of people could do when they cooperated—and a horror that it was all done for a murderer.

They were almost to the room with the pens in it when Mala caught up with them. Keen swore under her breath.

"Elizabeth!" Mala said. "I've been looking everywhere for you."

Wondering how Mala recognized her with the mask on, Keen removed it, turned, and forced a smile. "We had some work to catch up on," she said.

"I wanted to warn you," Mala told her in a hoarse whisper.

Keen shot Aram a look. "Warn me? About what?"

Mala licked her lips and glanced down the dim-lit tunnel. "I've been thinking about what you said. About the Bodysnatcher killing Iris. And how the Beekeeper made me shoot someone on my first day here."

"What have you been thinking?" Keen asked quietly.

"I'm… confused," Mala said in a small voice. "The Beekeeper made me pull the trigger. I told myself it was wrong, but then I told myself it was okay because the Beekeeper said it was okay, but the more I thought about it, the more confused I got. I wanted to be here, Elizabeth, really I did, but I think I changed my mind and I got scared and please don't tell the Beekeeper, because I'm scared of what he'll do."

"I won't tell him," Keen promised. "Neither of us will, right?" She poked Aram, who vehemently shook his head.

Mala seemed to notice him for the first time. "That's not Donald, is it? I thought it was."

"I think Donald is still in the cage room," Keen said. "This is someone else. But he's a friend. I promise. We won't tell the Beekeeper. But Mala—what aren't we supposed to tell him?"

"I was in the lab earlier this evening," Mala said shakily. "And… I snuck some time on the computer when Vernon wasn't looking and sent a message to my father."

"Your father is Pavel Rudenko," Keen said. "Stingster and weapons."

"Yeah. How did you know that?"

Damn. "I read—used to read—the *Wall Street Journal* a lot. Why did you contact him, Mala? You said you hated him."

"I don't. I mean, I do, but not really." She wiped her nose with her sleeve. "I just want a dad, you know? A real dad. One who doesn't shout or hit or kill your dog? Sometimes I get away, but he always seems to pull me right back. I thought I got away for good this time, but now… I'm so confused. I told Dad where we are. He has a whole band of guys he keeps around to 'test the weapons,' he says. Hired mercenaries is what they really are. Team Green Alpha. They'll probably be here any—"

An explosion rocked the tunnel. Keen lost her balance. Aram hugged the tunnel wall for support. Dust sifted down from the ceiling.

"They're here," Mala said. "Oh god, I'm sorry!"

"Ressler!" Keen said. "Come on!"

Alarms blared, and the hall lights turned red. Keen rushed down the tunnel to the cage room, not bothering to see if Aram and Mala were following. She found Ressler curled up in a ball on his mattress.

"Ressler!" she said, shaking the bars. "Ressler! Time to leave!"

Another explosion shook the floor.

Ressler didn't move.

Keen fumbled with the ring of keys. Her hands were shaking. Shouts and cries and two gunshots echoed from down the hall. So far no one seemed interested in the cages, but that could change, especially since the Beekeeper had to be awake by now.

"What are they doing up there?" Aram demanded.

"Getting the Hive's attention," Mala said. "The commander's name is Steele. Ryan Steele."

"Are you kidding me?" Aram said. "Does he drink his martinis shaken and not stirred, too?"

"I think he changed his name."

Keen finally got the door open. She hurried to Ressler and shook his shoulder. "Wake up! We have to get out of here!"

"The room smells orange," Ressler muttered.

"Oh, god." Keen hoisted Ressler upright. "Come on. We don't have time for this."

Aram came to help. Together, they got Ressler on his feet and half dragged him out of the cage. The alarms continued to blare.

"Attention!" said the Beekeeper's voice, and Keen jumped. She hadn't known the Hive had a PA system. "We are under attack! *They* have found us! All drones to battle stations!"

Mala squeaked. Four drones charged into the room, pistols drawn. Keen and Aram both froze.

"What the hell are you doing?" one of them barked.

Keen didn't even think. "We have to move the prisoner. There's an escape tunnel in the back of his cell, and someone is trying to break through. Hurry!"

Three of the drones rushed into the cell. Keen kicked the door. It slammed shut and locked.

"Hey!" the fourth drone said. He whipped his pistol around. "What are—?"

But Aram got him with the taser. He went down, twitching.

"Stung," Aram said.

But the drones in the cell still had their weapons. Already they were spinning around, pistols coming up.

"Run!" Keen barked.

The drones fired through the bars. The four of them dove for the exit, slowed by the half-conscious Ressler. Fortunately, the drones weren't taking much time to aim and were further hampered by having to aim through the bars of the cage. Bullets ricocheted off stone like angry wasps. Keen ducked and hauled Ressler with her down the hall. The hail mercifully ended.

"I can walk," Ressler panted. He shook his head.

"Moving makes it better. God, this is awful. I feel like I'm in a blender. That alarm sounds purple."

A third explosion.

Keen nearly went to her knees. The air was filled with throat-choking dust now, and she pulled on her mask. The others followed suit. Immediately it became easier to breathe.

"What now?" Aram said.

"The kids," Keen said. "We're getting them out."

"We also have to get that key from the lab," Aram said.

Keen tried to think. That stupid alarm kept up its buzz and blare. Okay, Ressler was still woozy. Aram was the best choice to handle the computers, but he barely knew the Hive complex. There was no way Keen was letting anyone else handle the children. Aram needed a partner. The solution was obvious.

"Mala, can you take Aram to the lab? He'll take care of the key. See if you can shut down that stupid jammer, too. Ressler and I will get the kids out."

Aram said, "But—"

"No time! Go!"

She and Ressler took one tunnel, Aram and Mala another.

CHAPTER TWENTY-ONE

The nursery was in dire straits. All five little children were crying and the three babies, including Luke, were wailing. Roberta and Sally were rushing about, trying to be eight people and calm everyone down.

"It's *them*," screeched a little girl. Tears made wide tracks of terror down her face, and Keen wanted to choke the life from the man who had instilled such fear in a child. "*They're* going to kill us!"

"We're evacuating!" Keen had to shout in Roberta's ear over the children's cries and the siren's blare. "No time to take anything. Grab the children and follow me!"

Roberta and Sally didn't question the order. People in emergencies rarely questioned anyone who seemed to be in charge. Keen snatched up Luke while Roberta and Sally took a baby each and a diaper bag. Keen pressed the hand of the crying girl into Ressler's hand. Thank god the kids were used to the gas masks and weren't scared of them.

"The Beekeeper said we have to go to a safe place," Keen announced firmly. "We're all going to be brave and safe together. Everyone hold hands with our friend Mr. D. March together, now! We're going to be as quiet as baby bees."

Her firm, even tone calmed some of the children down. Sally handed around bottles of formula to give to the infants in hopes of stopping their crying, and two of them quieted immediately. Luke continued to fuss in Keen's arms. Ressler stared down at the little girl's hand. Keen hoped he wouldn't say her fingers felt like a sunset or something.

"Off we go, now!" she called. "March, two, three, four! March, two, three, four!"

They marched.

The tunnels were filled with drones now, rushing about like angry yellowjackets. They bristled with weapons. Most of them ignored the little procession. Twice someone approached, and both times Keen barked, "Child evacuation! Make a hole!" and they backed away. Keen tried not to pant with fear. Blood sang in her ears, and the children kept whimpering. Luke squirmed in her arms.

They were nearly at one of the rear exits when a fourth explosion hit, sending everyone to their knees. The children screamed and the babies howled. Jesus! How would they survive outside? How would they—?

A hand plucked at Keen's elbow, nearly sending her through the stone roof. She spun, her taser at the ready. Roberta gasped.

Mrs. Griffin.

"Where are you going, dear?" she asked. Her gray eyes blinked rapidly. Incongruously, she carried a large handbag. "Did my husband order the children to be taken out?"

Keen cast about. "It's the safest thing to do," she said.

"Why, dear?" Mrs. Griffin asked. "With all those

weapons going off outside."

"Grandma Griffin!" said one of the children.

"Er…" Keen tried to think, but the children and the sirens and the pressure made it impossible to get her brain moving.

Ressler spoke up from inside his mask. "They won't shoot children, and we don't want them in the caves if they…" He glanced at the children and decided to spell out his final word. "C-o-l-l-a-p-s-e."

"What are we doing?" said Sally in the near darkness. "I'm confused. Did the Beekeeper order us to evacuate or not?"

Another group of drones rushed down the hall. Keen didn't know what to do or say. Where the hell was Reddington when she really needed him?

Then Mrs. Griffin said, "You stay here, my dear. I'll take the children outside. They won't shoot at me. Go back to your duties."

"But—"

"Keen," Ressler said. "Other people need your help. I'll get the kids out."

"We'll be fine, dear. We have to protect the children at all costs."

Ressler gave Keen a hard look and a sharp nod. She could see he was on his last reserves. He had to get out. Meanwhile, she still had to deal with Reddington and that drone key. Ressler would take care of it. For the second time in her life, she gave a baby over to a man.

"If you let anyone hurt him, I'll slice your ear off," she warned. "And it won't feel like blue."

"Come along, children," said the Beekeeper's wife. "Grandma Griffin will show you the way."

* * *

Ressler followed Mrs. Griffin up the narrow cavern tunnel. He had a baby in one arm, and his free hand held the small, sweaty fingers of a child. His mask was hot and uncomfortable. The two child-care women, whose names he didn't know, brought up the rear with babies of their own. Ressler had no idea whose children these were or how they got into the Hive. All he knew was that he had to get them out. God only knew what they'd been through already, and they couldn't be allowed to suffer further. Unfortunately, he had the feeling they were going to see a great deal more tonight than any child—or adult—should see in a lifetime.

His knees were shaky and his muscles were still flaccid from the Beekeeper's latest treatment, hours of being dragged through his own drug-induced nightmares of losing Audrey while the Beekeeper's relentlessly gentle voice told him the Hive was there for him, the Hive would share his pain, the Hive... the Hive... the Hive.

The helplessness turned to rage, rage turned to impotence, impotence turned to apathy. In the end, he had just lain there and let the Beekeeper do as he pleased. He wasn't Donald Ressler, FBI agent. He wasn't Donald Ressler, American. He wasn't even Donald Ressler, human being. He was a sack of meat for the Beekeeper to pull apart and dump in a cage like a dog. He had, in fact, been on the verge of letting his entire self fall into darkness when Keen had shown up. She had pulled him, physically and metaphorically, out of the black and into harsh red light. And he was grateful to her for it.

Now he was leading a pack of screaming children down a tunnel behind a little old lady while hired mercenaries tossed explosives at them.

Okay, Donald, he told himself. *One step at a time. Solve one problem at a time.*

At the mouth of the tunnel, Mrs. Griffin shifted her handbag and gestured at everyone to halt. She edged out into the open with her arms up. Ressler hoped whoever was out there could see her—it was still night, though he could see a full moon.

"Don't shoot!" she quavered. "We give up! We have children! Don't shoot! We have children!"

The baby in Ressler's arms chose this moment to start crying again, underscoring the truth of Mrs. Griffin's words.

"Can we all come out?" she said. "You don't want to hurt children, do you? Or an old lady?"

A pause followed, then a voice on a megaphone said, *"Come out, hands raised. We won't shoot unless you make a stupid move."*

Ressler went next, doing his best to shield the baby with his body, though he didn't know how much good that would do against a high-powered rifle. His mouth was dry and his arms shook. He could feel the sights trained on him. The woods around the caverns were well-lit with silver moonlight that turned the leaves to paper. A breeze trembled the trees. The baby quieted.

"I have a baby," he shouted. "Don't shoot!"

"Come out of the cave!" came the bullhorn. *"We'll take you to shelter. We don't hurt kids."*

Mrs. Griffin gestured at the cave mouth, and the rest of the children, along with the other two women, emerged like frightened rabbits from a warren. They didn't fully understand what was going on, or the danger they were in—Ressler hoped—and were only scared because of the explosions and the shouting.

From the trees several paces away came five men with helmets, Kevlar, and assault rifles. They were dressed in pixilated desert camouflage, which said *outdated* to Ressler.

"Who are you?" Ressler said. "You want to point those rifles somewhere else? We got kids here."

"How about you remove that mask, buddy."

Oh.

Ressler flicked a glance at Mrs. Griffin and slowly pulled his mask off. Mrs. Griffin didn't even blink.

"Harris, search him," said one of the men.

"Sir!" Harris did a quick pat-down of Ressler, then of the women and Mrs. Griffin. He shone a light into Mrs. Griffin's handbag and checked her cell phone. Ressler briefly wondered why she had one—they didn't work out here.

"There's no point in searching me for a pistol, dear," Mrs. Griffin said. "They're too heavy for me these days."

"Are you going to search the babies, too?" Ressler said. "From the smell of it, this one might have a cannon in his diaper."

"Over here," Harris said, pointing the way with his rifle barrel.

The men led the group of crying, gasping children to a small encampment. An additional dozen men milled about the area. Outdoor lights had been set up and a grenade launcher stood on a tripod. Not far away was parked a large truck.

"I'm Lieutenant Ryan Steele," said another man with a blond crew cut. Ressler checked the insignia on his sleeve. It said *Team Green Alpha*, and didn't match any military Ressler was familiar with. "Where's Mala Rudenko?"

"This isn't the best way to find her," Ressler said.

"You're bringing the roof down."

"Just warning shots," Steele said. "Gets your attention."

"You've scared these children half to death, dear," said Mrs. Griffin. "How could you do such a thing?"

"We have our orders, ma'am," Steele said. "Bring us Mala Rudenko and we'll be on our way."

Mrs. Griffin sighed, set her handbag down, and sat on a stump near the grenade launcher. It made for a strange picture.

"Now listen, boy. You aren't going to get what you want by smashing your way in. You can't—"

"Look, lady," Steele said, "this Hive thing is some kind of weirdo cult. Fine. You do what you want. I don't give a flying goose's ass what you bee people do to each other in the woods. But the boss wants his daughter back, and we're here for her. Bring her, or we'll bring the roof down piece by piece. *Capisce*?"

"You do that, and Mala dies," Ressler pointed out. "Is that what her dad wants?"

"Looks that way." Steele shrugged. "If he can't have her back, the Hive doesn't live to enjoy her, or whatever it is they're doing with her. Mr. Rudenko doesn't take rejection well, and I think the last few months with her missing have been really hard on him."

"Jesus," Ressler breathed.

"What should we do with the kids, Lieutenant?" asked Harris.

"Put 'em in the truck, give 'em something to eat. Sit with 'em, Harris."

"Me? Aw, come on! You can't—"

"Go, Harris."

Grumbling, Harris took the baby from Ressler and led the whimpering children to the truck, along with the two child-care women. Ressler started to follow, but Steele grabbed his arm.

"Nuh-uh. You and the old lady are going back inside to deliver our message."

"What message, dear?" Mrs. Griffin asked.

"Mala Rudenko emerges from that cave in exactly twenty minutes, or we bring it down." Steele showed his phone. It had a countdown timer on it that showed 19:59.57. "Hobble fast, lady."

Ressler glanced at the truck. Harris was helping the women get into the back with the babies. They were as safe as could be for the moment. Keen would be satisfied. A part of him wanted to run for it, try to get far enough away to call the Post Office for help, but it was night, and he had already made one unsuccessful bolt for help. If it hadn't been for Reddington, the FBI might already be here.

Reddington.

Jesus, just when Ressler thought he had the old bastard figured out, he pulled something like this.

One step at a time, Donald, he reminded himself. *One at a time.*

"Let's go," he said to Mrs. Griffin, and let her take his arm. Her hand was light and feathery.

"Nineteen minutes, thirty seconds," Steele called after them.

Just outside the mouth of the escape tunnel, Mrs. Griffin halted. "You know, I forgot my handbag. And none of those boys said a word about it."

"Oh," Ressler said, a little confused. "I don't think we can go back for it."

"I wasn't suggesting, dear. I was observing that they aren't very observant. They didn't notice the false bottom, either." From her pocket she produced her cell phone and pressed a button.

The explosion lit up the trees. Screams and shouts from the encampment immediately followed. Ressler reflexively dropped to the ground. Mrs. Griffin stood upright and watched, a prim smile on her face.

"That should teach them not to mess with the Hive," she said as drones swarmed out of the tunnel. "Shall we go back inside, dear? And why are you out of your cage?"

CHAPTER TWENTY-TWO

The Beekeeper's thunderous voice echoed off the walls of the chem production lab.

"We will keep working!" he boomed. "*They* will not stop us! *They* will only spur us to great flight! Hurry, my children! We will spread our pollen far and wide."

Under his orders, masked drones continued their work. They mingled sarin and tributylamine in canisters and locked the canisters into the carrying clips of the helicopter drones. Ten of them, a dozen, a hundred. They lined up at the exit in deadly rows. Every one had the power to kill hundreds of people.

Other drones moved quickly about the lab, operating machinery and computers or clearing debris away. The explosions had brought down a lot of dust, and several drones wielded brooms. Aram grabbed one, and Mala followed his example. They pretended to sweep, but edged their way toward the corner, where the safe and the helicopter drone key lay.

Aram leaned close to Mala and touched their masks together. "What's the combination?" he asked quietly. The masks conducted his words.

"I don't know it," Mala replied in the same way.

"Can't you hack it or something?"

"With what?" Aram said. "I don't have any equipment to hack a computer lock."

"It also takes a keycard," Mala said hopefully. "The Beekeeper has it on his belt."

"Okay, okay." Aram thought. "There's one other way. Social engineering. Get closer to him."

"What are you going to do?"

"I don't know yet."

Aram abandoned the sweeping pretext and moved closer to the Beekeeper, who was engaged in earnest conversation with another drone.

"I don't care," he was saying. "Find Vernon! I need him in this lab! And where's my wife?"

Aram edged closer. Okay. Yeah. He could pretend to trip, fall into the Beekeeper, and grab the card when they tangled together. It could work. As long as he wasn't caught. As long as the Beekeeper didn't notice his card was missing. As long as Aram didn't screw it up. He licked his lips inside the mask, wishing his heart would stop pounding. Blood sang in his ears.

The drone stared at the floor. "I don't know, sir. We're very confused right now."

"Just find them!" the Beekeeper snarled. The drone fled.

Aram stepped forward just as the Beekeeper also turned. There was a moment, a tiny moment, in which everything came together. Aram saw it. The Beekeeper was a little off-balance. Aram was right there. A half step to the left, and he could slam hard into the Beekeeper perfectly. A single half step was all it would take. He took a breath—

His courage failed him. He turned aside. The Beekeeper moved past him without noticing.

Aram cursed himself for an idiot. It had been the perfect—the only—chance. Now he'd have to figure another way to—

Another explosion, a worse one, rocked the cavern.

Canisters fell over with metallic clunks. Drones flailed about. More dust sifted from above. Aram took the shot. He shoved himself backward and fell straight into the Beekeeper. They both went down in a tangle of limbs. The Beekeeper's fleshy body was soft under Aram's. The Beekeeper swore and pushed about. In the confusion, Aram's mask popped loose and came over his head. Aram had to choose between refastening it and going for the keycard. Split-second decision.

He went for the keycard.

Aram deliberately tangled himself further, as if in a panic, all the while feeling about for the card. His fingers encountered plastic, and he snapped it up.

At last the Beekeeper managed to shove Aram away. Mala hurried over to help the Beekeeper up.

"Are you all right, sir?" she asked. "Are you hurt?"

"I'm fine," the Beekeeper said shortly.

"Sorry," Aram said, staying on the floor as if terrified. He fumbled with his mask, keeping his face away from the Beekeeper. "Sir, I didn't mean to—"

"I don't think I know you," said the Beekeeper, looking down at him just as Aram managed to shove his mask back into place. "When did you join, boy?"

Aram's heart leaped into his throat. "Sir, I—"

"Beekeeper!" Another drone rushed up. "We need you to finalize the dispersion pattern at terminal five. The explosions are making everyone nervous, and the technicians still can't locate Vernon."

"Yes, yes. I'm coming." The Beekeeper raised his voice again. "No fear! Keep working! I want these drones ready to go by sunrise! We are the Hive!"

"We are the Hive!" barked everyone in the room. Aram only just remembered to join in.

The Beekeeper strode away. Aram let out a long, heavy breath. Mala hurried over, though she didn't say anything. Aram scrambled upright and showed her a corner of the keycard he had lifted. She squeezed his hand in acknowledgment. They slipped closer to the safe. It was the size of a shoebox and mounted waist-high in the cave wall with a keypad and a card reader set into the door.

Aram glanced around. Lots of people in the lab. Someone would notice them.

Mala set to work with her broom. Clumsily. In seconds, she raised a cloud of dust. Before he could lose his nerve again, Aram swiped the card.

ENTER CODE, said the screen.

Aram swore. The safe required both a swipe card and a PIN. He entered 1234, the most common PIN.

ERROR, said the screen. ENTER CODE.

Aram's stomach churned. He entered 1111, another common code.

ERROR, said the screen. ENTER CODE.

"Hurry up," Mala said. "I think the Beekeeper's coming back."

Aram's breath echoed inside the mask. The code was probably a birthday or a phone number or some other important number to the Beekeeper. The trouble was, Aram had no idea what that number might be and no way to find out in the next few seconds.

"He's going to see us," Mala said. "Do it now!"

He turned the card over nervously in his hands. And then he saw it. Written on the back in black marker. 0156. Aram almost laughed. He punched in the numbers.

The safe beeped once and the door clicked open. Aram reached inside and found a pile of cash, two gold bars, and a flash drive. He snatched up the drive, slammed the door shut, and strolled away. As he went, he dropped the card in front of Mala's broom.

"We are the Hive," Aram said as the Beekeeper passed by him.

"We are the Hive," he replied tersely. "Did you see a—?"

"Sir, did you drop this?" Mala said, holding out the dusty card. "I just found it on the floor where you fell."

He accepted it with obvious relief. "That's what I was looking for. Thank you, child." The Beekeeper clipped the card to his belt and hurried away.

The rush of relief was so great, Aram wove unsteadily for a moment.

"He wrote his PIN on the back? " Mala said incredulously.

"You'd be surprised how many people do that. It's why banks still have to tell customers not to." The helicopter drones were nearly all set up now. Aram glanced at a computer screen. Sunrise was coming quickly.

Mala poked Aram with her broom. "Shouldn't we destroy that drive?"

"When we're alone."

"So what now?"

"We find Reddington and get out of here."

Keen dashed back to the guest room, ready to fling herself to the floor at the next explosion. She had no idea where anyone was—Reddington, Stuart, Aram, Mala, Ressler. Only Dembe had to be where she had left him. The children were safe. Aram would steal the drone key. She had to trust in that. Part of working for the FBI was being a team player, having faith that everyone would do their bit. Oh, but it was hard! Deep down, she didn't quite trust Ressler to see to the children, and she certainly didn't trust Mrs. Griffin. Aram was a fantastic IT guy, but he wasn't a field agent.

You can't be everywhere at once, she told herself firmly. *Do your job and let them do theirs.*

Reddington was in the guest room with Dembe when Keen arrived. Two bundles lay under the blankets atop the beds. The other men were nowhere in sight. Dembe was just shutting the barred interior door. Someone had shut off the damn alarms, thank god, but the lights in the corridors still glowed red.

"What happened?" Keen demanded.

Then she knew.

"You killed them."

"There was no point in upsetting everyone over an unpleasant necessity," Reddington said. "Aram is especially sensitive about these matters."

Keen knew she should be upset, or at least pissed off, but she didn't have it in her right then. Vernon, in particular, had set her teeth sideways. He'd tittered as he filled little silver canisters with flying death, and she couldn't think of any reason to mourn his passing or condemn those who had brought it about.

"We aren't done, Reddington," she said. "I know you have a key like the Beekeeper's."

He folded his arms. "Do you?"

"What do you want, Reddington?" she said. "Why do you have that key?"

"To ensure the Beekeeper couldn't release his deadly swarm," he replied easily. "The key will let me take over his drones once they're in the air and redirect them harmlessly away."

"Then you won't mind giving it to me." She held out her hand.

"Do you know how to use it?"

"I'm sure Aram can figure it out, since he built it."

Reddington sighed. "You know, one day I'll have to have a chat with Aram about secrets between gentlemen."

"Hand it over, Reddington," Keen said.

"You know, I think I'll keep it," Reddington said. "If Aram gets hold of the other key, the Beekeeper will commit murder to get hold of mine, and an older man of my acquaintance once taught me never to give up a bargaining chip."

"Reddington—"

Aram and Mala burst into the room.

"They got Ressler again!" Aram said.

Keen whirled. "What?"

"He's back in the cage room," Mala said. "We overheard one of the other drones. Mrs. Griffin caught him after the children got out."

A strange mixture of relief and tension pulled Keen in two directions. The children were safe. Ressler was in danger.

"What about the Beekeeper's key?" she said.

"We got it!" Aram held it up. "And now we have to run. Fast."

Keen tensed again. "Now what?"

"Dr. Griffin saw Aram's face in the lab, but didn't quite recognize him," Mala explained. "When he opens the safe and sees the key is gone, he'll know it was us. We have to run!"

"The key." Keen held out her hand again.

Aram dropped a flash drive onto her palm. "It's plug and play."

Keen started to snap the drive in half, then paused. No.

She dropped the key into her pocket. "An older gentleman of my acquaintance once told me never to give up a bargaining chip. Let's get out of here. Come on, Reddington."

"Me?" Reddington looked genuinely surprised. "Good gracious, no! I'm not going anywhere."

"What are you talking about?" Aram said. "We've got maybe ten minutes before the Beekeeper opens that safe and raises the alarm."

"The good Dr. Griffin still sees me as an ally," Reddington said. "That gives me an edge. Besides, I still have to track down Stuart."

"Stuart?" Keen repeated. "I thought you didn't care about him."

"We have unfinished business." Reddington waved them toward the door. "And someone has to fish poor Donald out of those cages. Do you still have my satellite phone?"

Keen touched her pocket. "I do."

"You have a satellite phone?" Mala said in surprise.

"I assume you've gotten hold of Harold, then," Reddington said, ignoring her. "Keep it, so you can talk to him further. He'll need your help far more than I will."

"What is your game, Reddington?" Keen growled. "You're the one who got us into this in the first place. You brought the tributylamine to the Beekeeper and started this mess. Why would you do that?"

"Elizabeth," Mala said, "we need to leave. Now. The Beekeeper will—"

"I only intercepted a shipment that was already on its way," Reddington protested. "If I had done nothing, the chemical in question would still have arrived and I'd be the Beekeeper's enemy. This way, I'm inside and the Beekeeper thinks he's my friend. What could be better?"

"Elizabeth," Mala said, "come *on*!"

Keen glared at Reddington, not sure if she should be worried, exasperated, furious, or all three. Then she pulled the stupid mask back on and hurried from the room with Aram and Mala close behind.

They were almost outside when the Beekeeper's voice thundered behind them, "Grab them! They took the key!"

They bolted for the mouth of the tunnel. Shots cracked behind them, but Keen was already outside the cave and in the fresh air beyond. She dove right, yanking Mala with her. Behind her, Aram yelped, but he kept running. The sky was lightening and a few birds were calling among the trees. Keen yanked off the mask so she could see better and ran for the cover of the thicker wood. Unfortunately, Hive drones were pouring out of the cavern in an angry hornet swarm. Adrenaline thrilled through Keen's veins and plucked at her nerves. Mala had ripped off her own mask, and her face was tight and white-lipped. Bullets snapped and pinged off the trees as the two women flung themselves into the undergrowth. Aram came with them, his own expression drawn. Automatic gunfire rattled, then voices shouted.

"Come out! We just want the key!"

"They went that way!"

"Don't stand there—grab them!"

"Come on!" Mala hissed. "This way!"

Keen followed her, keeping low. Aram did as well, though he was limping.

"What's wrong?" Keen asked.

"Leg was grazed," he grunted. "It's not bad, but it hurts like hell, and it's going to slow me down."

"Damn it. Let me see."

They stopped for a moment and she sank to her knees to check Aram's leg. His upper thigh was bleeding. Keen bit her lip. Not only was Aram wounded, he was leaving a trail.

"We should get you to Reddington's safe house," Keen said.

"Safe house?" Mala said. "What kind of safe house?"

Aram poked his head around a tree.

"They're fanning out," he reported. "They'll find us soon if we don't move. I don't think we have time for the safe house."

"Why not?" Keen said.

"Very soon the Beekeeper will find those bodies in the guest room and realize that Reddington isn't a friend. When he does, he'll search Reddington and find the duplicate key. Once that happens, he'll launch the helicopter drones and all those people will die. We have to stop him. Now."

"Yeah," Keen said. "Puts us in a bind. Let's find a better spot to hide so we can—"

"Here they are!" A rifle muzzle poked into Keen's shoulder from behind. "Don't move, bitch. You've been stung."

"You did not just say that," Keen said.

"Get up." There were three drones behind them. Masked, of course. Keen was getting truly tired of masks. "The only reason you aren't dead right now is that the Beekeeper is afraid you've hidden his key somewhere."

Keen got to her feet and made a fist. "You want the key? It's right here." She made a throwing motion and opened her hand. "Go get it, bee boy."

As she expected, the drone turned his head to watch where she had "thrown" the key. Keen moved. She shoved the rifle barrel upward, moved in and under the weapon, and elbowed the drone in the solar plexus. He collapsed with an outrush of air. Keen wrenched the rifle away from him.

Aram wasn't still either. He turned halfway around, wrenching the second drone's gun barrel so it was pointing away from him. He grabbed the gun stock and the scope and *yanked.* The rifle barrel whipped around and cracked the drone across the side of the head. The man went down to one knee, dazed.

The third drone swung his rifle away from aiming at Mala and aimed at Aram. Keen snapped her new weapon up.

"Freeze, asshole!" she barked.

"Paul," Mala said. "You don't want to do this."

"You know him?" Keen said.

"Of course I know him," Mala snapped. "We're all Hive. Paul, come on! The Beekeeper wants to kill all those people."

"That's the whole point," Paul said inside his mask. "The others are *them.*"

Keen licked dry lips. Shouts and calls came from the woods around them. Other drones were getting closer.

"Paul, I wanted to be here, too," Mala said. "I wanted to join, just like you. I got the Bodysnatcher to bring me here and wipe all traces of me. I thought I could hide here forever, but my dad found me. You can't hide here forever, Paul. They find you. Them, not *them.* There is no *them.*" She held out her hand. "Paul, please. Put down the rifle and help us. All those people don't deserve to die."

Paul hesitated. His breath sounded harsh from inside his mask. Keen held her breath.

"Your friend is dead," Paul snarled. His finger tightened on the trigger.

Keen shot him. A bloody flower blossomed on his chest. He stood there a moment, as if uncertain about what had just happened. Then he dropped. Mala gave a low cry.

"No!" she moaned. "Paul!"

"I'm sorry, Mala," Keen said, meaning it. "He didn't give me a choice."

"He came in with me," Mala said. "The Bodysnatcher helped him disappear, too. I—"

"Over here!" bellowed a voice, disturbingly close.

"The shot gave away our location," Aram whispered. "We have to run!"

Mala gave Paul's body one last look, and they ran. Keen felt a heavy weight of guilt settle over her. At least now they had rifles.

Twigs and leaves whipped past Keen's face as they shoved through the woods. She prayed the drones weren't talented trackers. Her chest burned. Days of enforced inactivity had sapped her fitness. Aram was also short of breath. The rough terrain and the slope of the hill made running much harder. The shouts of the drones were behind and to their left now, and Keen tried to figure out where they were.

Just keep running, she told herself. *Run until you can't run another step, then run some more.*

They burst into a clearing. The sweet smell of burning, charred flesh reached Keen's nose, and she jerked to a halt, her breathing hard. Blood slicked the grass and sprayed the damaged trees. Bloody camping equipment was scattered everywhere. A tall truck stood to one side, spattered with blood and dirt. And interspersed were the bodies. Chopped and charred and shredded bodies.

Coming to a halt beside her, Aram and Mala both gasped. Mala retched.

"What in holy hell happened here?" Aram said.

"I'd guess a bomb with shrapnel in it," Keen said. "One of the explosions we heard underground. But who are these guys?"

"They work for my father." Mala's hand was over her mouth. "Team Green Alpha."

"Wow," Aram breathed. "The Hive ate them alive."

The truck door banged open. Keen snapped her rifle up. Aram took a second longer. Roberta clambered down.

"Elizabeth?" she called. "Oh my god! Is it you?"

It took Keen a second to recognize her from the nursery, and she was surprised at how relieved she felt to see the other woman.

"Are you all right?" she called. "Where's Sally?"

In answer, Sally cautiously emerged from the back of the truck. "The children fell asleep. They're exhausted. What happened?"

Keen trotted closer. "I was going to ask you the same question. The last I saw you, Mrs. Griffin and… the other guy were evacuating you."

Roberta caught Keen up in a hug. "I was so worried! And scared! We've been in that truck for hours! After those… men put us in there, everything just went up. The children were terrified, but at least they weren't hurt. We didn't dare bring them outside, and now we don't know what to do."

Keen thought fast. "Can you drive the truck?"

"No keys."

The distant shouts and yells seemed to grow closer

again. Keen turned to Aram. "Can you hotwire this thing?"

"I'm computers, not cars," Aram protested. "I don't know a thing about engines."

"Let me." Mala pushed them both aside and vanished underneath the truck's dashboard with the knife from her belt.

More shouts, more yells. Brush cracked.

"What's happening?" Sally demanded. "Is there an attack going on?"

"There will be soon," Keen said. "That's why we have to get the kids to safety. Do you understand? Even though it means taking them out of the park."

"Away from the Hive?" Roberta protested.

"The Beekeeper's orders." Keen brandished the satellite phone, as if the Beekeeper had just called. "Their safety above all. When *they* attack again, he doesn't want the children caught in the crossfire."

"The patrols are coming," Aram said casually.

"Almost done, Mala?" Keen asked through clenched teeth.

"Nearly… got it…" Mala said. "Ha!"

The truck cranked to life. Sharp-smelling exhaust fumes puffed from the tailpipe. Keen could make out individual voices among the patrollers now.

"Get the kids out of the park," she ordered with steel in her voice. "Drive! Before *they* get here. We are the Hive!"

"We are the Hive!" Roberta said, and jumped into the driver's seat while Sally got into the back with the kids. Aram closed the rear door. The truck lumbered away, down the rutted road.

"Why didn't we go with them?" Aram said.

"Ressler, Reddington, and Dembe are still in the Hive," Keen replied tersely. "So is Stuart. Come on!"

They fled back into the woods. The sky was fully light now, and Keen had her bearings, but that also meant the patrollers would have an easier time spotting them. Howls of surprise came from behind them as someone found the gory scene. Maybe it would slow them down.

"Where are we going?" Aram said.

"Elizabeth Keen!" crackled the Beekeeper's voice over a distant bullhorn. *"I know you can hear me. You have my key. I have your friend Donald. Come to the main entrance within ten minutes or I will shoot him in the head."*

Shit.

Keen wanted to throw up. Hadn't they been through enough? Why was the Beekeeper always a step ahead, no matter what?

The Beekeeper repeated his announcement.

"Have I said lately how much I hate that voice?" Keen asked.

"What do we do?" Mala asked in hushed tones. "The Beekeeper wants us to come back, and if we don't, he'll be angry."

"He's already pretty pissed off," Aram pointed out. They were still following Keen through the woods and trying to watch in all directions at once. "It would take a couple pounds of Valium to calm him down now."

"There's a vantage point up here," Keen said. "We'll go up there to get a look at the situation. I just hope Ressler's okay. And what the hell is Reddington doing?"

It was the same rocky outcropping Keen and Dembe had used to spy on the Hive. The trio hid themselves under some bushes, and Keen used the scope on her rifle to sweep the area. The first thing she saw was the set of boxy beehives under the trees near one of the side exits not far from the main entrance. With those to orient herself, she quickly found the front of the cave, which was perhaps thirty yards below them, down the slight incline of the hill. The Beekeeper and, oddly, Mrs. Griffin were standing near the cave entrance with a couple of drones—and Reddington. Ressler was on his knees in front of them, looking defiant, and the Beekeeper was pointing a gun at his head from behind. Two drones brandished machetes. Pug held a bullhorn for Dr. Griffin.

"I have to call Cooper," Keen said, drawing out the satellite phone again. "This is the first chance we've had since we got out of the caves."

Aram checked his watch. "We don't have long before the ten minutes is up."

As if in response to this, Pug held the bullhorn in front of the Beekeeper's mouth.

"Elizabeth Keen, you have two minutes to bring me the key, or Donald Ressler dies."

Keen called up the satellite phone's screen with chilly fingers. One of the contacts caught her eye.

"This phone contains a listing for Dr. Griffin," she said. "What the hell?" She made a disgusted noise. "Reddington!"

"Just call Cooper!" Aram hissed. He had torn part of his shirt away and Mala was helping him use it to bandage his bleeding thigh.

Keen punched in the number from memory, praying the signal would get through. She held the phone so the others could hear, but didn't activate the speaker in case it carried downhill.

Cooper answered on the first ring.

"It's me," she said.

"Elizabeth!" Cooper's husky voice sagged with relief. "Are you all right? Where are you?"

"I don't have much time," Keen said. "The Beekeeper is going to execute Ressler if I don't give him the key to launching a chemical attack on—"

"I know all about it," Cooper interrupted crisply. "We're almost there. The helicopters should be on site in less than an hour."

"We need help now," she said. "The Beekeeper wants the drone key, or Ressler's dead."

Cooper hesitated a fraction.

"He can't have that key, Elizabeth. No matter what, he can't have that key. Do you get me?"

She did. If it came to a choice between a thousand people and one FBI agent who had sworn to protect them, there was no choice.

"Understood," she said hoarsely.

"The team is coming. Hold tight."

The line went dead.

CHAPTER TWENTY-THREE

"I don't usually pray," Aram said. "But maybe now would be the time to start."

"Can't you shoot him?" Mala asked.

"I'm a profiler, not a sharpshooter," Keen said. "And Ressler's right there. Miss and I might hit him."

"Why isn't Reddington doing anything?" Aram moaned.

"Your time is up, Elizabeth Keen!" boomed the Beekeeper. *"Watch as your friend pays the price. I'll count three. One... two..."*

A ringing sound came from the Beekeeper's pocket. It sounded tinny at this distance. Surprised, the Beekeeper looked down. He holstered his pistol and pulled a satellite phone from his pocket.

"Elizabeth?" he asked, and his voice came from the phone in Keen's hand.

"Dr. Griffin," she replied, digging into her memory for her hostage negotiation training and forcing a note of respect into her voice. "Let Ressler go, and we'll talk about arrangements."

"Where are you, Elizabeth?" His voice was calm and flat, like the psych patients she had observed during her residency, the ones who set fire to puppies and tried to bite the fingers off their nurses. "I'd rather talk about this in person. Where I can see you."

"I'm too far away for that," Keen said. He had put the phone on speaker, and she double-heard the faint echo of her voice in the distance. "I'm almost out of the park."

"That's a lie," the Beekeeper said. "You fooled me once, and it was spectacular. You used your memory of your baby to make me think you had converted to my cause. I have to admit you did a fine job. Lots of my captive drones have tried to fool me into thinking they were coming along for the buzz, but their attempts were obvious, and every one of them shared the fate of drones from my beehives every autumn. Do you know what happens to the drones in a hive of bees when autumn comes, Elizabeth?"

Aram and Mala exchanged nervous glances.

Keep him talking, Keen thought. "I don't know."

"The female workers drag them to the entrance of the hive and slice their heads off."

One of the masked drones, a tall woman, waved her machete, and Mrs. Griffin nodded. Ressler glanced behind himself. Keen knew he was calculating his chances of grabbing either the machete or the Beekeeper's pistol, but both Beekeeper and drone had wisely put themselves out of arm's reach.

"Decapitation might be more fitting than shooting, don't you think?" the Beekeeper said.

"Ohhh, I don't like that," moaned Pug. "Please come down, Elizabeth!"

"Pug, you don't have to do what he says," Keen said. "You can do whatever you want. If you don't like a head getting chopped off, you can stop it."

Pug wavered for a tiny second, then said, "No! The Beekeeper knows what is right."

"Don't do that again, Elizabeth," the Beekeeper warned.

"Let me talk to Reddington," Keen said, switching tactics.

"Oh, no, no, no." The Beekeeper shook a finger. "You are not in charge here. Mr. Reddington is not in charge here. He is, in fact, hostage number two."

"Reddington's a hostage?" Keen repeated around the growing pit in her stomach. "Does he know that?"

The Beekeeper shook his head. "You need to think, Elizabeth, and try to remember some of the things you babbled in the Circle. I know you very well, and I'm sure you were about to say that if Ressler dies, I lose my leverage. But I don't. I have Mr. Reddington. And his cabana boy Mr. Dembe awaits just inside the mouth of this cave. Hostage number three. I know you're watching me, Elizabeth. The only question is, from where? And how fast will my drones find you?"

Reddington stood stock still to one side. He had to have heard the Beekeeper. How could he not? But he wasn't reacting in the slightest. Mrs. Griffin watched them both primly. Keen stared at her for a moment and chewed the inside of one cheek. A bomb had destroyed Rudenko's hired mercenaries. Who had set it off? She hadn't had time to think about that. Roberta and Sally hadn't done it—they wouldn't have spent hours cowering in the truck with the children if they had, and in any case, where would they have gotten explosives? The mercenaries might have set off a bomb by accident, but that didn't seem likely. The timing on the explosion had been too convenient. That left Ressler and Mrs. Griffin. Ressler certainly didn't have access to any explosives. That left Mrs. Griffin. And her big handbag. Now that Keen thought about it, who carried a handbag in the middle of a forest? Another chill slipped through her blood.

"You're running out of time, Elizabeth," the Beekeeper said. "Where's my key? You have thirty seconds, and then Donald is dead."

"What are we going to do?" Mala hissed.

Keen swept the area, looking for a solution. There was always a way out. Always. God, where was Cooper? *Keep him talking.*

"Hey, I'm willing to discuss this," she said, and played a standard tactic by adding, "but you have to give a little, too. How about you release one of your hostages as a sign of good faith, and—"

"What is that, page seven from the negotiator's handbook?" the Beekeeper said. "Don't insult me. Get down here with that key."

He jerked his head at the woman, who raised the machete.

And something snapped inside Elizabeth Keen. The Beekeeper was bullying, pushing, pulling, manipulating every step of the way.

Enough. It was over.

"No," she said into the phone.

"Sorry?" said the Beekeeper. "No, what?"

"If you're looking for me to say, *No, sir*, you can stuff your honeycomb up your ass. I mean, no, I'm not negotiating with you. My name is Elizabeth Keen, and I'm working with the FBI. I've already alerted the Bureau to your location, and they'll be here any minute."

"FBI!" Mala gasped.

"Shush," Aram said.

"The FBI," the Beekeeper said slowly, and a ripple

went through the assembled drones. "You're bluffing."

"No," Keen said. "I'm *them*."

This time the ripple was more pronounced. Keen gave a grim smile as the Beekeeper turned to stare at his drones.

"Not *them*!" cried Pug. "Elizabeth wouldn't be one of *them*!"

"It's all right, dears," said Mrs. Griffin. "She's a damned liar."

"Indeed!" Dr. Griffin added quickly. "She's telling tales to save herself."

That seemed to settle the drones a bit, so Keen spoke again. "The FBI doesn't negotiate with terrorists," she said. "You can give yourself up and just spend some time in jail. But if you kill Ressler, there's nothing to stop us from opening fire on you and your people. In fact, Ressler is the only thing stopping me from killing you right now."

"So you *can* see me," the Beekeeper said, scanning the hills around him. "Where are you, Elizabeth? Can I stand here, behind my Ressler shield, long enough for my people to find you? Or maybe I'm threatening the wrong hostage. During your Circle babbling, you mentioned a great attachment to—"

"Surely we can resolve our differences in a more sophisticated manner than this," Reddington said abruptly, stepping forward. "Listen to yourselves! Squabbling like children! It's gotten to the point where you don't even know why you're fighting! This puts me in mind of the two families in *Romeo and Juliet*. I saw a delightful production of the play in Paraguay, though it was in Spanish and lost something in translation. Still, the story rivets audiences the world over."

"What are you babbling about?" the Beekeeper snapped.

"I was going to say the same thing," Aram murmured, but Keen waved him to silence.

"The Capulets and Montagues remain at war with each other, which forces their children to hide their love affair and eventually commit suicide with knives and poison," Reddington said. "And what was behind it all? Money! The real evil in the world. Repercussions that lead inevitably to death." He chuckled. "What is it Romeo says when he hands over gold for the apothecary's little flask? *I sell thee poison. Thou hast sold me none.* Wisdom from a dying man. Don't you agree, Stuart?"

One of the drones pulled off his mask, revealing Stuart Ivy.

"I don't know what you're talking about," Stuart said, his voice just barely carrying into the phone.

"Of course you do, Stuart," Reddington said. "*I sell thee poison.* Don't you recall a handful of years ago, just as now, a chemical weapons deal that went down in a place much like this one? The repercussions of that deal led to the deaths of thousands of innocent people in the Middle East. Money. Poison. Honey."

A jolt went through Keen.

"Oh my god."

The Beekeeper seemed to sense he was losing control of the situation. "Look, Reddington, you're a hostage here. One word to my people, and—"

"Oh, Benjamin, is your memory going, too?" Reddington interrupted. He strolled closer to the Beekeeper, a friendly smile on his face. "You had black hair back then and you didn't wear the glasses, but weren't you involved in that other chemical weapons deal? The one that went wrong?" His jovial tone hardened. "And didn't it end in the death of a woman named Vivian Ivy?"

"Jesus!" Keen said, forgetting that the phone transmitted her words to the Beekeeper.

"Who's Vivian Ivy?" Aram said.

Stuart's face, until now a picture of composure, twisted into a rictus of agony. "You killed my Vivian, you goddamned son of a bitch!"

"No swearing!" Pug admonished.

"Such language from a pensioner," Reddington said. "Benjamin, I believe you're looking for this, is that right?"

Keen gasped. Reddington was holding up his flash drive.

The abrupt change in subject seemed to confuse the Beekeeper for a moment, and for a split second he looked like a tired old man blinking behind coke-bottle glasses like a half-blind insect. Then he recovered himself and the confident mask returned.

"Give it to me, Reddington," he said.

"What the hell is he doing?" Keen breathed.

"It's yours, Benjamin," Reddington replied, holding it out. "A gift."

Griffin stepped over to Reddington and reached out to pluck the flash drive from his hand. At the last second, Reddington moved. He flicked his free hand into his coat pocket, snatched out a hypodermic, and stabbed it into the Beekeeper's neck.

"For Vivian, you bastard," he snapped. "A little overdose."

The Beekeeper slapped a hand to the wound. "What—?"

The drones and Mrs. Griffin looked on in startled shock as the Beekeeper dropped to the ground. He writhed and squirmed in obvious agony.

"Sweet," he groaned. "Oh, god. The sky tastes… sweet."

Then he shuddered hard and went still.

"I have sold you poison," Reddington said. "Or perhaps you sold it to yourself."

"No!" cried Mrs. Griffin.

Pug dropped the bullhorn and put his hands over his face with a low moaning sound.

Several drones drew on Reddington. Dembe emerged from the cave mouth and tackled one of the drones from behind.

Ressler shot to his feet. With a quick movement, he wrested the machete from the female drone and clocked her with the handle. She went down. Ressler threw the machete at one of the drones, hitting its arm.

Dembe wrestled his drone's pistol away.

The other drones swung their own weapons around toward Ressler and Dembe. They hesitated a tiny moment, uncertain about firing toward their own people, but Keen knew they wouldn't hesitate for long.

She scanned the area, desperate for something, anything, that might help. Then she saw it. Without another thought, Keen sucked in her breath and aimed the rifle.

"What are you doing?" Mala asked tensely. "They'll kill everyone!"

Keen fired three rounds. All three went straight into the boxy beehives.

Bees poured from the hives.

They boiled out in an angry cloud that attacked everyone and everything that moved. The drones' masks protected their faces, but not their hands or necks. The bees crawled up their sleeves and stung. The bees crawled down their shirts and stung. The bees crawled up their trouser legs and stung. The drones, including Stuart, yelped and howled and slapped at themselves. Most dropped their weapons. Nearly all of them fled toward the trees. Pug completely ignored them, groaning into his hands like a tree in a windstorm. Only a few drones remained behind.

"Yes!" Aram whooped. "Keen, that was brilliant!"

In the confusion, Dembe went for Reddington. He hauled his boss away from the center of the group of drones. Ressler followed, wincing as all three of them got stung as well. Ressler pointed a little ways away from the cave mouth at the stockpile of weapons Keen had noted earlier, when she and Dembe had first arrived at this vantage point. Most of the drones had by now vanished into the woods.

The trio ran past Mrs. Griffin. She scrambled to her feet and, ignoring the bees, plowed into Reddington with surprising strength. The move caught him and Dembe completely off guard. Mrs. Griffin snatched the flash drive from Reddington's hand, then staggered away shouting. Keen couldn't hear what she said—the Beekeeper was lying on the satellite phone.

"Come on!" Keen yanked Aram to his feet. "We have to help!"

"Why doesn't Dembe get the flash drive from Mrs. Griffin?" Aram panted.

"He only cares about Reddington," Keen replied grimly. "Go!"

They ran down the slope toward the cave with Mala close behind. Aram's teeth were tight against the pain of his injury. Dembe and Reddington had reached the weapons dump and were yanking the camouflage netting away from the crates with Ressler's help. Where had Stuart gone? Mrs. Griffin stood in the mouth of the cave, and now Keen could hear her.

"Jakes and Billford! Hurley and Wells!" she snapped. "Stop Reddington. I want him dead! Lawford, Hill, and Pug, you're with me. Back to the chem lab!"

Keen stared. Mrs. Griffin? What was going on here? She was always so quiet, so mousy, so—

No. She wasn't.

In a split second, Keen's mind flicked back over the times she had seen Mrs. Griffin. Heard her suggest. Listened to her hint. Watched her gesture. And every time she asked for something, Dr. Griffin gave it to her.

"The Beekeeper is still alive," she whispered.

"What?" Aram said, startled.

"The Beekeeper isn't Dr. Griffin," Keen said. "It never was. It's always been Mrs. Griffin. A Hive is always run—"

"—by a queen," Mala finished.

Mrs. Griffin, Pug, and the two other drones bolted back into the cave. Keen's heart tightened beneath her ribs. Mrs. Griffin—the real Beekeeper—had the key, and had power to launch the helicopter drones. She pelted toward the cave entrance.

The trio reached the thinning cloud of bees. A red-hot needle pierced the back of Keen's neck, and another stung the back of her hand. She ignored them and kept running. The rifle banged against her back.

"Lizzie!" Reddington shouted.

"Hold them off!" she ordered over her shoulder. "I'm going after Mrs. Griffin!"

The four drones to whom Mrs. Griffin had snapped orders managed to get weapons up and were firing at the weapons dump, ignoring Keen. Red welts were already rising on their skins. Bullets chattered and pinged off the crates while Reddington, Ressler, and

Dembe crouched behind. Two of the drones were moving around, trying to flank the dump while the other two continued firing from the front. Dembe's hand showed momentarily over the top of the dump, and a small object arced toward the flanking drones.

"Jump!" Keen barked.

Mala and Aram leaped for the cave mouth just as the grenade went off. The explosion crashed against Keen's ears and bones. She landed hard and stomach-surfed a yard or two onto the wood floor of the main cavern. Aram and Mala came to earth beside her with pained grunts. Shouts, screams, and more shooting came from outside the cavern. Keen thought of Reddington, Dembe, and Ressler out there. They could take care of themselves. The helicopter drones had highest priority.

The main cavern was empty. The carvings, including the Great Tree and its boulder, crawled eerily over the walls, their beauty a sharp contrast to the sounds of combat leaking in from outside the cave. The stings on Keen's hand and neck burned.

"Where is everyone?" Aram said.

"The chem lab," Mala said. "This way!"

They scrambled toward one of the side tunnels. Belatedly it occurred to Keen that it would have made more sense to circle around and come into the lab from its own outdoor entrance, where the helicopter drones were lined up and ready to go. Now it was too late and too dangerous to take that option.

Many of the lights in the tunnels were out. Someone had cut power, at least partly, maybe to slow them down. Was it Mrs. Griffin? God, the woman was a general. Keen made her way through the gloomy cave. Damp, chilly air pressed in on her from all directions.

Aram's breath wheezed behind her. Mrs. Griffin as the queen of the Hive. It made sense now, and in retrospect it seemed foolish of her to have missed it. The way the Beekeeper didn't use any of the drones for sex should have been the biggest clue—all cult leaders used sexual dominance to hold their position. The Beekeeper didn't because he wasn't really in charge.

They rounded the bend in the tunnel. The chem lab was just ahead. Keen heard the noises of the lab, including shouted orders from Mrs. Griffin. All traces of the gentle old lady were gone.

"We can stop her," Aram said. "We can—"

Pug loomed in the tunnel ahead of them. His head nearly brushed the ceiling. His face was as hard as the cavern walls. They jerked to a halt. Mala gave a squeak.

"You want to hurt Mrs. Griffin, and I will not let you," Pug said.

Keen slumped. Not this. None of this was Pug's fault. Dr. Griffin and Mrs. Griffin had done this to him.

"I don't want to fight you, Pug," she said, bringing up her rifle. "And I definitely don't want to shoot you. Let us pass."

"You made Mrs. Griffin very angry," he said. His massive form all but filled the cavern. "And the Beekeeper is dead. A very bad man killed the Beekeeper. I am sad. And I am angry. I will not let you pass me."

"A lot more people are going to die," Aram said. "Mrs. Griffin is going to kill them."

"Too many words. You must be punished now."

Pug rushed toward them. Keen fired.

Or tried to.

All she got was an empty click. The rifle was out of ammo. Keen had just enough time to register this before Pug slammed into her. She flew backward and hit the tunnel wall. Pain thundered up her back.

Aram, not a fighter under the best of circumstances, snapped a punch at Pug. It connected with Pug's mid-section with a *thud*. Pug looked down as if a butterfly had landed on his stomach. He plucked Aram's wrist away with a meaty fist, and Aram screamed with pain. Pug gave a casual twist and tossed Aram aside like an old sock. He slammed to the floor. Keen heard a terrible, wet snap.

Mala backed up a step. "Pug," she said. "Listen to me. I know you loved the Beekeeper. But he wasn't as nice as we thought. He and Mrs. Griffin are trying to kill thousands of people."

"Mrs. Griffin said to kill you," Pug snarled. "You will die now."

Keen struggled to hands and knees. With every muscle aching, she crawled toward the two of them. Pug's back was to her, and around his bulky body, she could just see the terror in Mala's eyes.

"What would your mama think, Pug?" Mala said.

Pug halted. "My mama?"

"Didn't you tell me she came to every one of your football games? How proud of you she was?"

"I liked football," Pug said. "Mama always watched."

"You loved her," Mala told him. "What would she say if she knew you helped kill all those people?"

"Kill them?" Pug said. "The Beekeeper said it's okay to cull people if he said so."

"Would your mama say it's okay?" Mala said, backing up another step. Keen crawled another couple of steps forward. She was right behind Pug now, but had no idea what to do. She looked around him and up at Mala, who glanced in her direction.

Pug shook his head. "You're confusing me! Mrs.

Griffin said you have to die! You have to be punished or I will be in trouble! I—"

Mala bolted toward him. The move caught Pug off-guard, and she slammed into his chest. He outweighed her nearly three pounds to one, but he tipped back just a little bit. Straight back into Keen's hands-and-knees prone body. It was the oldest trick in an elementary schoolboy's book, but it worked. Pug tripped over Keen and his legs went out from under him. His arms pinwheeled in frantic circles. More pain slammed across Keen's back, and she forced herself to roll free of Pug's kicking feet. One of them caught her on the shoulder, but she got clear. Pug went down with a tree trunk crash. He gave a soft groan and lay still—out cold on the stone floor.

"Poor guy," Keen said, and meant it.

Aram tried to get to his feet, grunted, and fell back to the floor. "Oh, man. Oh my god."

"Are you all right?" Keen asked.

"No." Aram tried again, winced, and sat back down. "I think something's broken. I can't stand up. God, it feels like knives. It's already swelling up."

Keen ran her hands gently over Aram's leg. He sucked in his breath, and it didn't take an expert to tell his lower leg was indeed broken. That in addition to the gunshot wound on his other thigh.

"You'll have to leave me here," he said. "I'll be fine. You have to stop Mrs. Griffin."

Keen nodded reluctantly.

Mala, meanwhile, did a fast search of Pug's belt. "He has a pistol, but no rifle ammo."

"Give it," Keen said, and checked the action. She left the rifle on the tunnel floor. "Let's go. You'll be fine, Aram?"

"I'll have to be. Cooper should be here any second, but not fast enough to stop her. Go!"

Keen and Mala tried to dash down the tunnel but Keen found she could only manage a fast limp. Her back was on fire, and she clenched her teeth to keep back little yips of pain. The tunnel opened into the enormous, echoing chem lab. Keen caught a glimpse of the helicopter drones on the far side of the room with Mrs. Griffin hunched over a computer nearby. A shot rang out, and a bullet glanced off the stone wall. Keen whipped back into the tunnel, and her back screamed at her.

"She's got more guards—"

"Lawford and Hill," Mala supplied.

"And she's getting ready to launch," Keen finished. "Where are the rest of the drones?"

"I think they scattered after the Beekeeper died and the shooting started," Mala said. "They'll come back, and soon. We'll have to hurry."

"I'll give cover. You get in there and grab her. Go!"

Without waiting for a response, Keen poked her head around the corner and fired three times. Underneath her arm, Mala scuttled into the room, diving for cover under a work table. Lawford and Hill, standing a ways from Mrs. Griffin, saw Mala and fired, but Keen shot again in their general direction, forcing them to drop low and turn their attention to her.

Mrs. Griffin typed frantically at the computer. Reddington's flash drive was stuck into one of the ports. Some of the drones hummed to life.

Lawford and Hill fired back at Keen. She ducked away for a moment and closed her eyes, trying to remember. The two drones were holed up near a shelf of chemicals. She thought for half a moment longer, then whipped around the corner again. Taking aim for a split second, she fired again, this time at the jars above the drones' heads.

Glass shattered. Liquids sprayed in all directions. Lawford screamed and went down, clawing at his eyes. Hill bolted away. He escaped the cascade, but smoke of some kind gushed up from the floor and table where the chemicals mixed. It created an eerie, foul-smelling fog that seeped quickly through the lab, making it difficult to see more than a few feet. Keen prayed it wasn't poisonous.

The soft sound of humming helicopter drones drifted through the large cavern.

"A hive can only have one queen, dear," Mrs. Griffin's voice called through the mist. "The first always kills the second. Run!"

"I thought the younger one killed the older one."

"Not in my hive, dear. Old age and treachery beat youth and beauty."

Keen crouched low, ignoring the screaming pain in her back, and crawled into the room.

"You don't need to do this, Mrs. Griffin. Those people out there are innocent. Babies. Children. They didn't do anything to you."

"Didn't they?" The sound of more typing. "I pushed my husband into using the right methods for training people. I gave him the formulas for the drugs and the chemicals. But when the army learned it all came from a mere woman, they revoked his clearance and threw us off the base. They called us lunatics. They called us thieves. Thieves!"

"The army didn't like the methods. They didn't care about the source." Keen crept through the room. Hill was in here somewhere, but she couldn't see. The mist clogged her throat, tickled it and made her want to cough. She held it in. And where the hell was Mala?

"You have nothing more to say, dear," Mrs. Griffin said. "You have only a few moments to—" She gave a screech. Glass shattered. "Get away from me, you little c—"

A shot.

Mala screamed. Her voice came from the direction of Mrs. Griffin's computer.

Abandoning caution, Keen rushed toward the spot. The buzzing of the helicopter drones grew louder. The mist was thinning now. Mrs. Griffin was standing over Mala a few paces away with a pistol in her hand. Blood spattered Mala's jumpsuit. Sorrow and rage thundered over Keen in equal parts. Her hands shook with both.

"You bitch!" Keen snarled, and snapped her pistol up.

A pair of arms wrapped around her from behind. It was Hill. Her pistol went flying. "Gotcha!"

Keen didn't hesitate. She stomped Hill's instep and simultaneously elbowed behind herself, catching him in the gut. The air whooshed out of him and he doubled over. Keen shoved hard, and they both went over backward with Keen on top. Adrenaline zipped across Keen's nerves. Hill was bigger, but the wind had been knocked out of him.

Keen felt around and found Hill's taser in his belt. She yanked it out, rolled over, and socked him across the bridge of the nose with it. He yelped and went limp. Keen scrambled to her feet—

—and found herself facing Mrs. Griffin's pistol.

"I told you there can only be one queen, dear," she said.

Keen thumbed the trigger on the taser. Nothing happened. She must have broken it when she hit Hill with it. Mrs. Griffin snorted and tightened her finger on the trigger. Then she convulsed, dropped the pistol, and fell twitching to the floor. Two little barbed darts were stuck in the back of her dress, trailing silver wires across the floor to Stuart Ivy, who held a taser in his hand.

"Horrible woman," he said. "Reddington got Benjamin, but I got her, at least."

"Stuart?" Keen tossed the broken taser aside. "What are you doing here?"

The mist had entirely cleared by now, and all the drones were hovering three feet above the cavern floor. Stuart gave a small smile.

"Sorry I didn't arrive earlier. I was delayed. I'm actually a bit disappointed." He reeled in the darts.

"I don't understand," Keen said.

"That you actually thought I had betrayed you all and joined the Hive," he clarified. "Really! It takes a con man to con a con man, I suppose, but I never expected it would fool the likes of *you*. FBI indeed!"

"Uh… sorry."

"I was waiting for the right time to strike. I knew from the beginning he was the weapons dealer who had murdered my Vivian. I can't tell you how difficult it was to sit next to him in that damned Circle. But I had no idea that Reddington also knew." He grimaced and pointed to Mrs. Griffin's unconscious form. "At least I got *her*."

"Congratulations, Stuart," Reddington said from the tunnel mouth. "You won the consolation prize."

"Red." Stuart looked like he would have tipped his hat, if he'd been wearing one. "I can't describe how it feels to see you right now."

"This isn't the time, boys," Keen said.

The helicopter drones were still hovering at the

cavern's exit, waiting for a final command, and no doubt the scattered Hive drones would return soon—two situations that needed immediate attention. But Mala was bleeding on the floor. Keen knelt next to her. She was still breathing, and the wound in her arm looked superficial. Keen found a first aid kit—the lab was well supplied—and tore open a bandage.

"Is Ressler all right?" she asked while she worked.

"We dispatched the drones who came at us and now he and Dembe are standing guard at the nicely provisioned weapons dump," Reddington said. "And I all but stumbled over Aram and that very large man in the hallway on my way in here. No sign of Mr. Cooper so far. I have to say I'm disappointed with his timing."

"Stuart, can you shut down the drones?" Keen pressed the bandage into Mala's shoulder. Mala's eyes fluttered open. The pain had stirred her.

"I'm not dead," she said in surprise.

"You're a hero," Keen told her with a smile. "We have to get you out of here."

"I'm an orangutan when it comes to computers," Stuart said at the terminal. "I don't even understand what I'm looking at here."

"Unfortunately for all of us," Reddington continued as if no one else had spoken, "I believe the human drones who scattered at your inspired example of apiarian marksmanship will return soon, a number of them through that very doorway." He gestured at the great opening beyond the hovering drones. "We should evacuate."

Stuart left the computer and strode toward Reddington. "You knew. All this time, you knew."

"So did you," Reddington accused. "Vivian's death was mine to avenge, not yours, Stuart. You were the one who let her die."

"Perhaps we should be angry at the Griffins," Stuart said. "Always put the blame where it belongs."

"Another of your aphorisms?" Reddington scoffed.

Stuart crossed his arms. "Without me, you'd be a very different man, Red."

"You let Vivian die!" Reddington almost shouted.

"You don't think I know that?" Stuart cried. "Every night, I sleep in a bed of guilt, Red. Every morning I wake up under Viv's gravestone. Every day, I wish Griffin had shot me instead of her. Your judgment pales at the lashes I give myself."

Mala screamed and pointed. Keen whirled.

Mrs. Griffin was awake. She hauled herself up to the keyboard and slapped a key. An alarm sounded, and the helicopter drones whirled in unison. They fled out the cavern exit and buzzed away.

CHAPTER TWENTY-FOUR

Reddington watched the drones buzz away with enough payload to wipe out a city. He schooled his features into a bland, calm expression despite the tension that torqued his gut.

"What have you done?" Lizzie gasped.

"They'll deliver the payload, dear." And the horrible woman slapped another computer key.

An alarm rang through the cavern.

A red anger descended over Reddington. His fingers twitched. If her neck had been between them, the old bat would have been dead, and not just for her role in Vivian's death. She was responsible for causing Lizzie pain. That was something Reddington could not forgive anyone for—not Benjamin Griffin, not his wife.

Not himself.

"More sarin will flood this room in five minutes," Mrs. Griffin finished. Then she snatched the flash drive from the computer and snapped it in two.

"Why?" The horror was writ plain on Lizzie's face. No matter how many terrible things she faced as an FBI agent, no matter how many awful things Reddington brought into her life, she still managed to be shocked at the dreadful deeds of other people. It was one of the things he loved most about her. He put his hand into his breast pocket.

"My husband is dead," Mrs. Griffin said. "I have nothing more to lose."

Three shots rang through the chem lab. Mrs. Griffin jerked under three red wounds that opened up across her chest. She dropped without another word.

"You had more to lose than you knew," Reddington said across his pistol.

The computer screen flickered into countdown mode.

4:40.45.

Keen leaped for the computer, ignoring Mrs. Griffin's body under her feet. Desperately she clacked at the keys. She could get other programs to respond, but not the one controlling the drone or the countdown. A small dialog window popped up.

PLEASE INSERT KEY.

"We can't do anything without the key," Keen called to Reddington and Stuart. "But Mrs. Griffin destroyed it."

4:01.54.

Shouts came outside the cavern. Foolish Hive drones returning to the caves, likely covered with bee stings and extremely unhappy. Reddington was fairly certain they also wouldn't take kindly to finding Mrs. Griffin dead.

"You have yours, don't you?" Reddington said. "Give it to me."

Her hand shot to her pocket. "No. I'll use it."

"Do you know how?" Reddington asked reasonably. "Aram showed me but he's hardly in a position to show you."

Lizzie glared at him, then handed over her key. "Hurry up, damn it!"

"First, you run, Lizzie," Reddington said gently. "Get the others out of here. Get yourself to safety."

"But—"

Reddington kept his face implacable. Always play for the win. "You know I'm right. I won't plug this in until you leave."

3:50.36.

Lizzie blew out a heavy sigh.

"All right. But…" And here her voice choked a little, which gladdened Reddington's heart. "Don't you get yourself killed."

"I shall stay to guard Reddington." Stuart grabbed Hill's pistol.

Reddington set his jaw. The mistrust ate at him like a crocodile chewing his liver. Even after all this time, he couldn't bring himself to trust Stuart. Vivian had been so kind to him. Her memory was a daffodil blooming in desert sand. Stuart had poisoned it, revealed himself as selfish, just like the people he worked with.

And that was the heart of the matter, wasn't it? Stuart had proved himself just as selfish as everyone else. Every person in the world was motivated by self-interest. Everyone cared about themselves first. That was the real lesson Stuart had taught Reddington that black day. It wasn't until Lizzie came along that Reddington had thought otherwise, that some people might truly be unselfish. It had been a long set of years in between.

"Go with Lizzie, Stuart," Reddington said. "Make sure the others get out. Including you. That's what you want, after all. I can talk my way past these poor, foolish Hive drones, and I do have a pistol for when words fail."

"They outnumber you, Red," Stuart said. "You'll die. I'm staying to—"

"Betray me? You go, or I don't plug this key in," Reddington said. Play to win. "Leave, Stuart. Now."

Stuart worked his jaw back and forth. The shouts outside grew louder. Reddington could discern individual voices. His heart was racing now.

Lizzie snatched up Mrs. Griffin's pistol, and helped Mala to her feet.

"Hurry!" she said.

3:12.82.

At last, Stuart nodded. He helped Lizzie with Mala. They hobbled toward the main caverns. Reddington waited until they were at the mouth of the tunnel before he plugged the Beekeeper's flash drive into the computer.

2:40.75.

The countdown shrank to a smaller window to one side. Reddington saw an icon labeled JAMMER. He clicked on it, and to his relief found a toggle for shutting it off. Suddenly, the helicopter drone program popped up, showing dozens of little dots moving across a map. They were closing in on the town of Roebuck. The old bat must have decided to attack civilians after all. A last stab from the grave. One drone, however, was showing at Reddington's location. It must be hidden somewhere in the lab. That must be how the sarin was going to be released into the caverns. Reddington slid the mouse toward the program to shut off the sarin.

2:02.96.

"Hey! You at the computer!" A Hive drone at the outside entrance leveled a pistol at Reddington across the lab. Five other drones were with him. "Hands up!"

Reddington slowly put his hands up.

"Gentlemen," he said, "I'm sure we can find

common ground for an arrangement."

The shooting began.

1:57.66.

Keen and Stuart staggered down the tunnel with Mala. They rounded the curve and came across Aram sitting on the floor with the still-unconscious Pug.

"We have to get out of here," Keen panted. "The whole area will be flooded with sarin gas in about two minutes."

"There should be gas masks all over the place," Aram said.

"Pug has one," Mala reported. "I have another. Everyone's wearing the rest. Where are yours?"

"We dropped them," Keen said tersely.

"How will we get your friend here out?" Stuart asked. "His left leg appears to be broken and his right has a bandage on it."

Pug groaned and sat up. "Mrs. Griffin?"

Mala drew away. Aram tried to, and sucked his teeth when his broken leg shifted.

Inspiration struck Keen. "Pug, listen to me." She put every bit of authority she could muster into her voice. She spoke like a strict mother, like a severe teacher, like a knowing doctor. "I've just spoken with Mrs. Griffin. She had to go away. I'm in charge now. You must do as I say."

"You," Pug said.

"A hive only has one queen," Keen said. "First it was your mother. Then it was Mrs. Griffin. Now it's me. Are you ready for your first orders from the new queen, Pug?"

Pug stared at her for a long moment. Aram started

to speak, but Keen shushed him with a small gesture and kept her face regal.

"Okay," Pug said. "What do I do?"

"Carry Aram here out of the main cave. Take Mala with you. Don't let anyone hurt them." She glanced over her shoulder toward the chem lab. God, what was happening to Reddington?

Pug nodded once, firmly.

"Okay." He picked up Aram, who yelped when the motion jostled his leg. "Follow me, Mala. I will not let anyone hurt you."

"What about you?" Mala said to Keen.

"I'm going back to help Reddington," she said.

"What about me?" Stuart said.

Keen looked at him. "What *about* you?" She kept her queen's severity. "What are you going to do? You have Vivian's memory to keep you company."

Stuart looked stricken, lost. "I…"

Shots rang from the chem lab. Keen bolted toward them without another word, leaving Stuart behind.

When she arrived at the entrance to the lab, she saw Reddington hunkered down behind a fallen stone table while nearly half a dozen drones fired on him from the main entrance. Two of them moved closer in, running a few steps forward to kneel and fire again. Reddington could only pop up and fire back without aiming, so his shots went wide. Glass jars shattered all around the lab. The cracks and pops of pistol fire echoed harsh and loud against the unyielding rock.

"Reddington!" Keen shouted, and fired into the room. One of the five drones went down. The others turned their attention on her and fired back. Keen ducked around the corner as bullets pinged and pocked. She whipped into the room and fired again, three times, then yanked herself back out.

"There's a lot more of us out here!" she barked around the corner. "Give it up!"

"Liar!" someone shouted back, and shot twice more toward her.

"We have forty-five seconds, Elizabeth!" Reddington shouted. "I've been trying to tell our friends about the gas, but—"

More gunfire erupted.

Keen checked her pistol and grimaced. Only a few bullets left. If she didn't do something, and quickly, an entire town was going to die—starting with everyone in these caverns. She might have to make a run for it and hope. This wasn't the way she'd figured on dying. On the other hand, she'd never figured on dying at all. She traced the scar on her wrist one more time—up the Y, down into the valley, back out of it, and down the other side—made three quick puffs of air, then rolled into the room toward Reddington, firing as she went.

Don't stop moving. Keep firing.

Her pulse thundered in her ears. A drone cried out and went down, but she couldn't tell if he was dead or not.

No time to check, keep moving.

Her pistol clicked. Empty. She threw it aside and dove toward Reddington. Two drones took careful aim at her. Reddington fired one more time, and his own pistol clicked. Keen's adrenaline-hyped senses watched their pistol barrels track her as she flew through the air toward the cover of his table. Her muscles tensed in anticipation of the coming bullets.

Four shots.

Keen flinched, expecting the painful tear of muscle and the hot spurts of blood. None came. She landed hard near Reddington and scrambled to her feet.

Four more shots rang through the cave.

"Are you all right, Lizzie?" he asked.

"What happened?" she snapped.

They both peered over the table. The drones were all lying on the floor. Behind them, in the main entryway, stood Stuart with his smoking pistol. Beside him were Dembe and Ressler, also armed. All three were out of breath.

"I got them here!" Stuart said. "I couldn't leave you behind, Red."

"The sarin!" Keen said.

0:10.86.

Reddington lunged for the computer. "The drone that will release the gas is somewhere in this cave," he said tightly. Keys clacked. "I think I can send it out of here."

0:06.79.

There was a buzzing in the cave, and a helicopter drone rose from the shadows in a corner. Beneath it, as if hanging from a set of claws, hung the deadly little canister of sarin gas. Keen cast about for a mask. The closest ones were on the dead drones, too far away to do any good in the next few seconds.

Reddington tapped keys. The drone zipped toward the main exit, brushed the side of the cave mouth, righted itself, and flew outside.

0:03.24.

"I'm sending it straight up," Reddington said. "That should be high enough so the gas won't—"

The computer screen flashed red.

0:00.00.

Everyone in the room froze. Keen could hear her own heart beat. With her mouth dry, she waited for the scent of chemicals, some tell-tale sign of terror. Nothing.

"We did it!" Ressler said.

"Not quite," Reddington reported from the terminal. "There are still another three dozen drones heading toward Roebuck."

Keen peered over his shoulder. The red dots were indeed converging on Roebuck like piranha on a bloody cow. "Can you catch them?"

"I believe so," Reddington said. "Aram was an excellent teacher." He took a piece of paper from his pocket, squinted at it, then tapped more keys.

ACCEPT NEW COURSE? the dialog box asked. Reddington clicked the mouse. Almost immediately the red dots turned aside. Reddington let out a deep breath.

"There!" he sighed, and yanked the flash drive out of the port. "They'll be in safe custody any moment now. Thank you for coming to my aid, Lizzie."

She gave him a small smile. "If anyone kills you, Reddington, it's going to be me."

He laughed expansively and turned to Stuart Ivy. "And you." Reddington shook his head. "After all that, you came back."

"Of course I came back." Stuart produced a handkerchief—where the hell had he gotten a handkerchief? Keen wondered—and mopped his forehead. "I couldn't leave you, Red. Even after everything you said."

"I'm still a bit surprised, to be frank."

Keen shifted, uncomfortable at witnessing this moment between the two friends.

"I never told you the full story," Stuart said sadly. "I should have, but you were so angry."

"About how you abandoned Vivian for—"

"No." Stuart held up a hand. "I did that, yes. And I

live with the pain of it every day. But the reason I did it… that's what I never said."

Reddington cocked his head in a gesture Keen knew so well, a gesture that seemed strange here in a buried chemical lab.

"What reason is that, Stuart?"

"I was protecting *you*," Stuart replied, tenderness and pain suffusing his words. "You were the son I never had, Red. I knew if I went in there, I would probably have died along with Vivian, and you would have come charging in after me because that's who you were… who you *are*. And you would have died, too." His voice trembled. "I let Vivian go so you could live, but in the end you left anyway, leaving a black trail behind you." Stuart swiped at his eyes with the handkerchief. "So you see, my little aphorism about never letting personal feelings get in the way of personal safety proved right. I did let my personal feelings get in the way. If I hadn't, Vivian might be alive, and you might be dead."

A long, heavy moment dragged through the room. Keen didn't know how to respond or what to do, so she did nothing. The others also stood quietly.

"I think I knew that," Reddington said at last. "From the moment it happened, I knew. I was angry that you chose me over Vivian. She was the best of all of us, and I hated to think I was alive when she was dead. I'm sorry, old friend."

And he reached out to embrace Stuart. Keen let out a breath she didn't realize she was holding. Tears ran openly down Stuart's face while Reddington's showed its usual round stoicism, but Keen could see how moved he was, and she found herself strangely glad to know he could feel this way.

"The remaining Hive drones will be coming back soon," Dembe finally said. "We should not remain in this place."

And then, only then, did they hear the blessed sound of FBI helicopters in the distance.

CHAPTER TWENTY-FIVE

"Where are those helicopter drones, Reddington?" Navabi demanded.

Reddington cocked his head. "That seems to be the question of the day."

They were all standing in a large tent hastily erected by the FBI task force that had arrived with the three helicopters sent by Cooper from the South Carolina field office. FBI agents in Kevlar vests and hard helmets were swarming over the Hive's caverns, gathering bodies, storing evidence, and rounding up the last of the drones. With the Griffins dead, none of the drones seemed particularly interested in fighting, and they appeared resigned to giving themselves up to *them*.

Aram sat in a corner of the tent with one leg in a new bandage and the other in a Velcro brace, his face slack with painkillers. Ressler was at a camp table, shoveling down field rations like they were free pizza in a frat house. Mala sat in another corner, a blanket around her shoulders. Any time someone had tried to take her too far from Keen, she went into hysterics, and it had been easier just to let her stay. She was consulting with Aram and tapping furiously on a borrowed cell phone.

Now that Reddington had shut off the Beekeeper's damned jammer, everything was working fine.

Pug was outside in handcuffs, but Keen had exacted heavy promises from the agents that he was not to be mistreated. She would talk to Cooper about his case later. A lot of the Hive drones would, in fact, have to be evaluated for psychological coercion, especially the ones taken by the Bodysnatcher. Dembe had conducted a pair of agents to the safe house, where they had found a young drone, sedated and zip-tied to a heavy chair, with no one else in evidence, though one of the agents reported finding what looked like strange little cart tracks on several rugs and a stack of completed Sudoku puzzle books in the trash. The truck with the children in it had already been intercepted, and that would be a project and a half for an entire team of child psychologists. While Stuart...

Stuart had been allowed to quietly slip away. Keen hadn't been too happy with the idea, but Reddington had insisted. "What good would it do to hold and interrogate him?" he pointed out. "He helped us, for heaven's sake. He's harmless and he has no money. He's not going to hurt anyone."

And Keen had reluctantly agreed.

Navabi gestured at the laptop on the table. "You were the last one to control them, Reddington, and now we can't find them anywhere."

"Well, you wouldn't, would you?" Reddington said mildly. "They're designed to fly under normal radar, and military detection systems register them as friendly. It's fiendishly difficult to follow them overland. No one expects you to find them."

Something inside Keen's head clicked. "That was your plan from the start, wasn't it?"

"My plan?" Reddington folded his arms.

"Oh!" Ressler looked up, still chewing. "The sarin gas! It's worth millions on the black weapons market. Once Aram made you that key, you needed to get yourself into the Hive so you could get your hands on it. That's why you bought that shipment of tributylamine and then turned me over to the Beekeeper—it was your way inside. You didn't really care about the Beekeeper at all!"

"You're selling chemical weapons?" Navabi spat. "My god. That's... I can't even think how awful that is."

"No," Aram spoke up from his corner. "He's not selling the sarin."

Everyone turned to look at him.

"How do you know that?" Keen asked.

"Once you've combined sarin with tributylamine, it becomes unstable," Aram said. "After a few hours, it breaks down into harmless compounds. The sarin will be worthless by sundown."

All heads turned toward Reddington, who returned their gazes coolly. "Sorry to disappoint, Agent Navabi."

"Aram is right," Keen said slowly. "He's not selling the sarin. But that doesn't mean he's not selling."

"Can someone just please explain?" Navabi complained.

"Have I ever told you about my cousin Greta?" Keen said in a tone similar to Reddington's. "Lovely girl. Adored tequila. Looked great in a two-piece. Every six months, she took a trip down to Mexico in a delightful Corvette convertible—cherry-red, her favorite color. She said she was visiting her ailing mother who lived in Guadalajara, but the border guards figured she was up to something, so every time she crossed, they searched her convertible for contraband. They even got out the drug-sniffing dogs, if you can believe it! But they never found anything. She crossed the border this way for years before one enterprising detective figured out what she was doing."

"And what was that?" Ressler asked.

"She was smuggling cherry-red Corvette convertibles," Keen said.

Silence fell across the tent. Navabi pursed her lips. "The drones."

"Dozens of them." Keen nodded. "All equipped to fly under radar and evade US military detection. Hundreds of millions on the black market. And we let Reddington fly them to an undisclosed location."

"I took the liberty of using a taser on the key not long after your colleagues arrived," Reddington said. "We wouldn't want those drones to accidentally fly into a school or a hospital."

"Or leave a record of where those drones went," Ressler said sourly.

"I do have expenses, you know," Reddington said. "Including a new car."

"Where is she?" A tall, thin man with dark hair and an equally thin nose burst into the tent. "Where's my daughter?"

"Pavel Rudenko," Keen said, and Ressler got to his feet with a stony look. "Your hired mercenaries were less than useful. Discharging and firing military-grade weapons on federal land—that's a double fistful of felonies."

Rudenko straightened an off-the-rack suit. "What are you talking about? I never hired nobody! They must have snuck in here to conduct maneuvers or somethin'. And since they all kicked it, you can't prove otherwise. I want my daughter."

He tried to peer around Ressler at Mala, who kept her face down and continued tapping at the phone.

"Actually, Mr. Rudenko," Ressler said, arms crossed, "we found one of your men still alive. He spent the night bloody and half-conscious, but alive. He's already given us a bunch of details about your hiring process."

"So?" Rudenko shot back. "His word against mine, and anything *you* say won't be worth a dog's fart in a hurricane by the time my lawyers get done. You get that through your head, boy."

"Look," Ressler growled, "I'm not in a mood to deal with your—"

"Let me see my daughter!"

"Here, Dad." Mala rose and let the blanket fall from her shoulders like a queen's cloak.

Pavel Rudenko rushed toward her, his arms open for an embrace, but Mala held up a hand. "No, Dad. I'm done. You're done."

"What are you talking about, angel? You're coming home. You *need* to come home. You're just a girl. If you don't—"

"You'll what, Dad? Cut off my electricity again? Bad-mouth me to my landlord so I have to move again?" Her face was cold. "No. I'll tell you what you're going to do, Dad. You're going to leave me alone. Forever."

"Yeah? Why would I do that?" he asked in a soft, dangerous voice that made Keen's skin crawl. Ressler reached for a non-existent pistol.

"Because you won't have the resources to come after me anymore." Mala held up the phone. A wasp buzzed across the screen and popped a smiley-face, which deflated. YOU'VE BEEN STUNG! the screen announced.

"Stingster, Dad." She handed him the phone. "I

told Agent Mojtabai over there what cloud service you used for your business files, and he made a few… suggestions. I just now grabbed some of the better documents and uploaded them to your own app. They're all over the Internet now. Business deals, client lists, delivery schedules, receipts. Stung!"

The blood drained from Rudenko's face.

Ressler casually glanced over his shoulder. "Huh. How many of those clients live in countries the United States has forbidden its citizens to deal with? Besides trailer parks?"

"You can't use this," Rudenko whispered. "You didn't get it with a warrant."

"We don't need a warrant," Ressler reminded him. "This information was released by an anonymous source on the Internet and will spark a nice, long investigation. Maybe you and I can go talk. I think there's a trailer outside. I'll feel more comfortable in there." He hauled the protesting Rudenko out of the tent.

"Wow," said Navabi.

Mala sank back into the chair. "I did it. I can't believe I did it."

"You did, Mala." Keen squeezed her hand and looked at Reddington. "You definitely did."

"What's the real reason you went in there, Reddington?" Keen demanded.

They were outside now, well away from the beehive of activity the FBI had created. Birds sang, insects buzzed, and clouds rolled away from a boiling sun. Reddington wore his hat.

"Why must there be a single reason, Lizzie?" he

countered. "People are complicated, and they rarely do anything for one single reason."

"Keen!" A helmeted agent trotted up with a clipboard. "We need you to sign this."

She glanced at the form and signed. The agent bustled away.

"That's absolutely not true," Keen said. "Brass tacks, people are simple. They have a need to fulfill and they try to fill it. What need were you filling here? Money? Revenge?"

Reddington sighed. "Whatever my motivations, they didn't include you going into the Hive, my dear. That was all you, and you nearly derailed everything."

"I'm not some drone you can order around," she shot back. "What was the secret the Beekeeper said he knew about my father?"

"Don't you know?"

Keen blew out a breath. "He didn't know anything. It was a lie, just like everything else in the Hive."

"You're a wise young woman, Lizzie."

Another agent strode up. "Keen, the team that's processing the guest room is short-handed. They won't be finished in time."

"I think Rogers and Barry are about done packing up the chem lab computers," Keen replied. "Tell them to go help."

"Gotcha." She left.

"New queen bee?" Reddington asked archly.

"Don't even. And you deflected my question about your motivations."

"I will always want you to be safe, Lizzie," Reddington said. "If you're looking for a simple motivation, there it is. You can accept that or not. It's the truth."

Keen searched his face and several moments went by. At last, she nodded. It wasn't everything she wanted, but it would do for now. She turned her attention back to the new hive below.

EPILOGUE

Night drifted up out of the valley. It started at the bottom, where the shadows always turned purple before they climbed the sides of the hills and finally the mountains. Crickets chirped shyly, then more confidently, and the gathering darkness chased the day's heat away. A river flowed like liquid silver at the bottom of the valley, churning over rocks and rushing around boulders and filling the air with water smells.

Stuart Ivy strolled along the high riverbank with a flashlight in one hand and a shovel in the other. The river flowed by several yards below. As the shadows deepened, he followed the bank until he came to a great oak tree with its roots wrapped around a boulder the size of an easy chair. Stuart set the shovel down, knelt with a groaning of old joints, and crawled around the boulder with the flashlight until he came to a small carving near the bottom. The flashlight beam picked out a crude letter G.

Humming to himself, Stuart took up the shovel and started digging. Time passed and the sky was turning purple when the shovel blade hit wood. Stuart dug more carefully now, and from the hole pulled a box perhaps a foot across. It was heavy, and something inside it clanked.

"My beauty," he breathed. "Oh, yes."

The latch was stiff, but he got it open and shined the light inside. An impressive pile of badly tarnished silver forks and spoons and knives looked back at him. Mixed in with the silver were dozens and dozens of gold coins that gleamed like little suns in the flashlight. A small bag of rotting leather was tucked into a corner. Stuart flicked the bag open with one hand. Emerald rings and brooches, green as new grass, spilled into his palm. Smiling, he put them back in the bag, then gave a little laugh and held one of the spoons up to the light. The handle was engraved with an elaborate G. He laughed again. "Fantastic! Oh, my. Fantastic!"

A small cough came from behind him. Stuart jumped, dropped the spoon, and spun. Raymond Reddington was sitting on a fallen log a short distance away, his brown suit and fedora looking out of place in the wilderness. Elizabeth Keen stood near him.

"Good evening, Stuart," said Reddington. "Always a pleasure to run into an old friend."

Stuart snatched up the spoon, dropped it in with the others, and slammed the box shut. "Red. Honestly! What are you doing out here?"

"You're holding the answer in your hand, Stuart. Though at your age, holding much of anything in your hand is quite an accomplishment."

"I didn't see you offering to help with the digging." Stuart picked the box up and clutched it to his chest. Gritty dirt lined his fingernails. "Leave it, Red. We've resolved our differences. This one is mine."

"Walk with me back to my new car," Reddington said. "I'll give you a ride."

A few minutes later, the two men were sitting in

silence on either side of the back seat of the new sedan while Dembe guided the car out of the park. Keen sat up front, but turned to look in the back.

"Now I know how dear Elizabeth feels," Reddington said. "The way I see it, that box of silver—"

"—and gold," Keen interrupted.

"—is the real reason you brought me the information about the Bodysnatcher taking people to the Hive in the first place," Reddington finished.

"You wanted to insinuate yourself so you could look for it," Keen said.

"It's the Gorey family treasure," Stuart said. "Vivian is descended from them. Part of the family story was that Robert and Jacob Gorey left a carving in a cave somewhere to remind themselves of where the treasure was buried."

"The Great Tree," Reddington said. "We were standing underneath it."

"You even worked on it," Keen added. "A stone-age carving from Native Americans that the Goreys expanded to use as a map."

"Griffin must have known most of that tree wasn't much more than three hundred years old," Stuart said. "I think he decided to make it a centerpiece, a sacred spot to inspire awe in his followers, and they elaborated on it. They even found the chisel Robert and Jacob used to carve it. What a find that was! I could scarcely hide my excitement."

"Why now?" Reddington said. "Why not ten years ago? Or twenty?"

"I didn't know where to look. Only some time after the Internet was invented did it occur to me to research caves close to the Gorey family farm, and by the time I had narrowed things down, the Beekeeper had already taken them over. So I turned to you." He looked down at the box with a faraway stare. "Vivian loved that story, of Robert and Jacob slipping into the woods and hiding the family treasure and leaving a secret carving. How she laughed! I would give anything to hear that laugh again, Red. Memories are all I have left of her, and I won't apologize for taking this."

"I wouldn't dream of asking you to apologize for anything, my friend," Reddington said with genuine affection. "And I do mean *friend*."

Stuart relaxed a little. "Her ghost can rest now that I've found this last piece of her family history."

"Of course," Reddington continued, "you aren't really a descendant of the Goreys. You only married into the family, as it were."

"What are you talking about?" Stuart's guard was up again.

Dembe pulled the car into a driveway. The house was tall and white, with spindly pillars holding up the front porch. A generous flower garden made up a large part of the front lawn. The place had clearly been added to over the years, but needed work, including paint and new windows. A green historical marker out front proclaimed that it was the Gorey House.

"I believe a Mrs. Rowena Kelvin, born Rowena Gorey, lives here now with her husband and four children," Reddington said. "Your second or third cousins, are they not?"

"Oh, no." Stuart clutched the box tighter. "No. Red. You can't mean this."

"It's only fair," Keen said.

Moments later, a startled Rowena Kelvin, née Gorey, was accepting a box of clattering silverware and gold coins from a young woman and two odd men, the second of whom thanked her for her time, and tipped his fedora.

"At least drop me off at my own car," Stuart complained as they drove off.

"I wouldn't dream of leaving you stranded." Reddington took a case from his jacket pocket. "Cigar?"

"No, thank you," Keen said.

"May as well." Stuart clipped the proffered Cuban and accepted Reddington's light. "I'm broke, you know."

"You'll survive, Stuart," Reddington said. "You're one of the smartest men I know."

They arrived at Stuart's car, which he had left near the ranger station at the edge of the national park. Dembe opened the door for Reddington, and he and Stuart shared a final embrace.

"Keep in touch," Reddington said.

"Don't be a stranger," Stuart said.

"Another aphorism?" Keen asked archly.

"More of a white lie," Stuart said, and both men grinned.

Keen got into the car with Reddington and Dembe drove off. She watched Stuart through the back window until he faded from sight.

"I feel bad for him," Keen said. "Even after everything he put us through, I feel bad for him."

"I wouldn't." Reddington puffed on his cigar and blew smoke out the open window. "Stuart will land on his feet. He always does. By the way, have I ever mentioned a Blacklister to you, one by the name of the Gamester?"

And Keen closed her eyes.

Once Reddington's sedan had disappeared into the night, Stuart got into his own car, leaned back against the headrest, and sighed.

"Thank you, Viv," he murmured.

Then he reached into his pocket and pulled out a rotting leather bag. From it spilled a family fortune in emeralds.

"Thank you, indeed," said Stuart Ivy.

ABOUT THE AUTHOR

Steven Harper Piziks was born with a name that no one can reliably spell or pronounce, so he often writes under the pen name Steven Harper. He lives in Michigan with his family. When not at the keyboard, he plays the folk harp, fiddles with video games, and pretends he doesn't talk to the household cats. In the past, he's held jobs as a reporter, theater producer, secretary, and substitute teacher. He maintains that the most interesting thing about him is that he writes books.

Steven is the creator of The Silent Empire series, the Clockwork Empire steampunk series, and the Books of Blood and Iron series for Roc Books. He's also written novels for *Star Trek*, *Battlestar Galactica*, and the *Ghost Whisperer*.

The Blacklist: The Dead Ring No.166

Jon McGoran

A massive fire on a bridge in West Texas: a tanker truck released its load and incinerated twenty-three cars and seventy-two people. A tragic accident, or something more sinister? Raymond Reddington reveals to Elizabeth Keen that this and many other horrific incidents in past years—seventy people killed in a warehouse fire in Turkey, a mine collapse in South Africa, 120 dead in a capsized ferry in Indonesia—were not the terrible accidents they seemed to be but were in fact collateral damage in a highly lucrative and deadly game known as The Dead Ring…

An all-new original *The Blacklist* novel.

March 2017

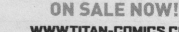